Untold the Evil

Ellen Larson

And is this all?
Then, O you blessed ministers above,
Keep me in patience, and with ripen'd time
Unfold the evil which is here wrapt up.

Shakespeare, Measure for Measure

Savvy Press
info@www.savvypress.com

Unfold the Evil

Published by:
Savvy Press
PO Box 84
West Rupert, VT 05776

http/www.savvypress.com/evil

Visit out website for a behind-the-scenes look at the making of
a mystery, and to find out about other titles in this series.

Website design by:
Starving Artists Workshop – Cinema of the Mind

ISBN: 0-9669877-1-3
LCCN: 00-104185

Printed in the United States of America

5 4 3 2 1

*The first message is not true (Nat will be at the Crime Bureau meeting Tuesday
morning). Therefore the second message is true. The wise woman said there
was only one true message, so the third message must be untrue. So if it's not
true that she won't meet him at the gazebo....*

To

The Friends

Who have Supported and Guided

(in order of appearance)

Vicki Wyan, Deloris Harrison Netzband, T.L. McKeighan Wesley,
Ruth McClellan, Anne Theodorovic Young,
Wanda Laurie Putnam Almosnino, Val Almosnino,
Keith Montgomery, Mike Sissons, Barbara Comar,
Tara Luguri, Charlie McBride, Barbara Fudge,
Marja Pheasant, Bedraya Mohamed Abdel Maksoud,
Patrice Lord, Ray Blanch, Frances Hill Delgado, Tess Mackenzie

This Book is Dedicated with Love and Gratitude

Characters (in order of appearance)

Daniel Joday, brother to Natalie
Gayanne, daughter to Daniel
Natalie Joday, staff reporter for the *Star*
Ginny Chau, Crime Bureau reporter for the *Star*
Rudy, mailroom clerk at the *Star*
Louise Hunt, advice columnist for the *Star*
Rebecca Elias, a psychologist, girlfriend to Daniel
Tyler Hanson, head of the Crime Bureau at the *Star*
Myra Vandergelden, CEO and Editor-in-chief of the *Star*
Lance Wenger, attorney for the *Star*, Myra's close friend
Peter Kovaks, candidate for New Jersey State Senate, ex-*Star* board member, Myra's close friend
Maurizio Marconi, a dead liberal thinker
Marcia Alexander, secretary to Byron
Byron Shapiro, Assistant Managing Editor of the *Star*, Natalie's boss
Linda Kovaks, a behind-the-scenes player, wife to Peter
Angela Marconi, widow to the late Mr. Marconi
Davis Skemp, a computer geek, librarian at the *Star*
Sgt. Geoffrey Allan, a felony-homicide detective
Lt. Camilla Perry, a felony-homicide detective
Laticia, secretary to Myra
Armand Vitek, an elusive informant
Mr. & Mrs. Weller, a quiet couple from Cresskill whose dogwood tree was decked with toys one night
Max Bludwort, a reporter for the *Bugle*
Glen Matsuma, entertainment editor at the *Star*
Mike Morrisey, owner of *Michelangelo's*, a bar
Dottie Marconi, first wife to Maury
Francesca, a typesetter at the *Star*
Sportswriters, financial editors, movie critics, interns, and stringers at the *Star*
Detectives, patrol officers, forensics specialists, desk sergeants, medical examiners, and assistant district attorneys from Bergen and Rockland Counties

Prologue

Airports gave Daniel Joday a headache. They were such confusing, dehumanizing places, where the air might be either too hot and stuffy or too cold and drafty, but always smelled of industrial detergent. The color-coded signs, jumbo arrows, and unreadable TV monitors were manifestations of the sort of impersonal authoritarianism he dreaded. Still ten minutes away from Exit 14, he started to sweat just thinking about trying to interpret the Flight Information on the Big Board. Even following the trail from short-term parking to Domestic Arrivals would require constant attention to keep from straying in the wrong direction and ending up at International Departures, or worse.

At least, on a day dulled by heavy rain, he had the luxury of driving to Newark. This thanks to his sister Natalie's offer to let him borrow her Volvo.

Actually, "You're taking my car," was the way she had phrased it.

"Thanks!" He really had appreciated it, not having wanted to take the bus. But…. "Aren't you coming?"

"Nope."

"But I thought…. Don't you want to come?"

"I want many things," she had said mysteriously. "Sometimes two things I want conflict, and I have to choose…."

Daniel had given in—a little hurt, a little relieved—without really understanding what she meant. But he knew better than to waste his time trying to get her to open up when she had that cross-the-gypsy's-palm-with-silver look on her face. So he was driving southbound on the New Jersey Turnpike through the rain alone, struggling to overcome his fear. The squeaking windshield wipers seemed to say, "You can't do this thing yourself," "yes you can," "no you can't," "yes I can."

♥ ♥ ♥

He deposited the Volvo in short-term parking. He followed the brown arrows to Domestic Arrivals. He cruised the Big Board and studied the relationship between On Schedule, Landed Such-and-such a Time, and In the Baggage Claim Area. Noting that Flight 422, arriving at Gate 12, was still at the On Schedule stage, he made a foray to the food court and paid double for a Cherry Coke to calm his churning stomach.

♥   ♥   ♥

He staked out a vantage point in the lounge from which he could see both the walkway leading from Gate 12 and a flight information monitor. There were no chairs, of course. Someone might, like, sit down, and be comfortable. He leaned against a carpet-covered pillar with his arms crossed over his breast. He stood for twenty minutes—his eyes flicking back and forth between the monitor and his watch—until he was good and stiff. The plane was late. By three minutes. Five. Was it the weather? He glanced at a window and watched the raindrops smack against the glass. The wind had started to gust. Good God, why did it have to be such a miserable day! What if something happened? Fear slammed into him and his heart throbbed with the pain of the blow. He looked at his watch. The numbers blurred. Damn! He rubbed his knuckles in his eyes. Seven minutes. He looked at the monitor.

Landed On Schedule.

His heart rate soared. Taking a deep breath, he fixed his eyes on the walkway. The minutes ticked by. His eyes began ache, and he forced himself to close them. Idiot. It took time to get the bags unloaded in the rain, and the gate wasn't going anywhere. Probably he still had half an hour to wait. Very well. He was good at waiting.

A flight attendant appeared on the walkway, pushing a luggage cart. Beside her walked a young girl. She wore sneakers, chartreuse board shorts, and a Sierra Club T-shirt. Her travel-mussed hair was frizzy and red. Her face had the transparent, unselfconscious look of a very young child. Yet she was quite tall and rather gawky—maybe twelve. Too old, he told himself. Wait.

But he couldn't take his eyes off her.

He watched as she looked expectantly around the hall. He saw the hint of apprehension cross her pointed face, and the yearning intake of breath.

Daniel straightened, uncrossing his arms and letting them fall to his sides.

Then she saw him.

Her little mouth opened in a brief O of surprise, and her face lit up like Christmas. She waved to him with both hands.

6

His hand raised—seemingly of its own accord—to wave back. He could not otherwise move. He watched her turn to the flight attendant, who smiled and nodded.

She headed toward him, trying not to run. But surplus excitement animated every step, until she was hopping up and down instead of walking— all arms and legs. Then she was before him, swaddled in ecstasy, her hands held out in front of her, twisting her fingers into knots.

"Hi!" she said. "They brought me off first, 'cause I'm a minor traveling by myself. Did I surprise you? I didn't recognize you for a minute— your hair is so short. Did you recognize me? I've grown two and a half inches since New Year's."

He could find no words, but he reached to take her hands in his. She clutched at his fingers eagerly, and looked up into his face with blue eyes full of unspoilt love. His throat tightened and his eyes swam with tears. Gently he knelt down before her and opened his arms to her, and all at once she began to cry, her face twisting with quick emotion, tears flooding from beneath her eyelashes. He pulled her to him, filling his arms with her, and she froze onto him, wrapped her arms around his neck and digging her fists into his back.

"Oh, Daddy!" she sobbed, "Daddy!"

He rocked her in his arms for a little eternity, whispering, "I'm right here, sweetheart, I'm right here. I'm right here, and I'll never go away again."

Level I

A fool must now and then be right by chance
(Section quotes from William Cowper, 1731–1800)

Chapter One

N atalie Joday balanced herself with both hands on the arms of the chair and raised her feet off the floor. Ignoring the wobble, she crossed her legs and sat Indian-style on the swivel chair. Satisfied with the result, which had the effect of realigning wrists and keyboard at an angle better suited to her long-term physical well-being, she pulled herself, castors moving unwillingly over the newsroom linoleum, snug against the desk. Thus primed for action, she addressed the computer:

Police Puzzled by Dollhouse Dilemma

A Hackensack family awoke yesterday morning to find 22 tiny dolls and pieces of dollhouse furniture dangling from the branches of the crabapple tree in their front yard, sources at the Bergen County Sheriff's Department say. Stumped law enforcement investigators are toying with the idea that it's just a prank undertaken by local youths. But, according to investigators, the absence of any signs of trespass indicates that care was taken to hide the identities of the perpetrators. "It's the second time since January we've seen this scenario played out," says County Superintendent Sandrine Louden. "We have a lot of serious questions. For example, why was the plastic poodle in the little refrigerator?"

"Joday!"
Natalie turned to the newsroom doors and beheld Ginny Chau, ace Crime Bureau reporter, dressed uncharacteristically down in a strapless red dress, sandals, and large-frame sunglasses.

Ginny made her way through the maze of desks and flopped onto a nearby vinyl chair. "Dja miss me?"

"Ceaselessly," said Natalie. "But you're not due back till after Labor Day."

"This is just a pit stop." Ginny crossed her legs, flashing her golden toenails. "I'm off to Montreal tomorrow."

Natalie hit save and leaned back. "Did you have a nice vacation?"

"Working holiday." Ginny chucked her handbag into Natalie's in-box. "Which didn't stop me from having a fine time. To think I never knew Virginia had a beach!"

"How was the conference?"

"Oh, the usual." Ginny hooked her arms over the back of the chair. "Jaded Washington insiders being cynical about politics. Seminars by one or two of the giants—guys who've covered crime since Cain v Abel. Made some contacts with a few TV producers, talked shop…. Y'know."

Natalie shook her head. "Same ol' same ol'…."

Ginny cast a lazy look around the newsroom. "Nothing much different, here, either…. Although I saw in yesterday's paper that *Star* stock dropped four points while I was gone. Not that I'm implying a connection…. What about you?" She flipped the sunglasses onto the top of her head, wrecking havoc with her black bangs. "How did you enjoy your stint in the Crime Bureau? You sure look at home at my desk…."

"It's my desk till next Tuesday at nine AM, so keep your mitts off it." Natalie straightened the keyboard. "My computer at home became obsolete when that graphical Internet browser came out."

"Poor baby. And how did you get along with—" She glanced toward the cubicles at the far end of the newsroom. "Tyler…?"

"Fine." Natalie removed a twist from the mouse cord. "No problems. Not one."

"Sure." Ginny stuck her tongue in her cheek.

"I'm serious!" protested Natalie. "He never said a word out of line. Of course…." She laid a finger against her cheek. "Now that I think of it, he never actually spoke to me at all…."

"I knew it!" Ginny sat up and uncrossed her legs. "His nose is out of joint because I suggested you to cover for me. Tch. He's been running the Crime Bureau with his antiquated ways so long he thinks every story is an exclusive with his name on it."

"He's only 46…."

"Like I said! Antique! His approach is twenty years out of date!" She

9

fished in Natalie's candy dish. "His idea of covering a crime is to report whatever his police contacts tell him. He thinks of a trip to the Courthouse as being in the field. These days there's plenty to go around for two reporters—I mean, three. The competition for readership is too fierce for a paper to cover just the murders and the hold-ups and let the rest go! There are scads of good juicy felonies going unreported!" She unwrapped the candy.

"There didn't used to be so much crime in Bergen County," sighed Natalie. "In my day, my brother and father were the only crooks I knew."

Ginny grinned as she popped the butterscotch into her mouth.

"Oh Miss Hunt!"

Both women's heads turned. A scrawny young man in an orange coverall leaned against the counter that separated the mailroom from the newsroom. He held up an envelope and wagged it back and forth. Natalie and Ginny turned to follow his gaze.

An elderly woman was standing stock-still by the double doors to the hall. She wore a high-waisted polka-dot dress that accented the hips of her plump figure. As the young man called out again, she swung her head from side to side, then turned and looked.

The young man flipped the letter up and down with his forefinger. "One more for you, Miss Hunt." His little round eyes were open wide, expressive of an innocent desire to help.

The woman clutched her book bag to her bosom and walked toward him with the air normally associated with martyrs on their way to the lions.

Ginny spoke out of the side of her mouth. "And here's another example of what happens when you hire fossils instead of journalists."

Natalie nodded in reluctant agreement. Thanks to her nephew, who sat on the Board of Directors, Louise Hunt had been taken on as the *Star*'s advice columnist (Ill at Ease? Ask Louise!) the previous fall. It was an open secret (thanks to the indiscretions of Rudy, the mailroom clerk) that for the first three months of her sojourn (and despite the regular appearance of her 500 word column in the *Sunday Star,* Life Styles section), she had not received a single letter. Further, it was widely assumed (particularly by the writing staffers, wizened past-masters at judging these delicate matters of "style") that such letters as had arrived shortly after Rudy let the cat out of the bag had one and all flowed from the same lugubrious pen.

Rudy showed his teeth as Louise approached. "You get so many letters these days I just can't keep track of 'em." His tenor voice was audible from end to end of the suddenly hushed newsroom. He looked at the envelope before he gave it to her. "River Vale," he said helpfully. It was a standing

10

joke that Louise spent all her spare time crisscrossing Bergen County to ensure that the letters she sent herself carried different postmarks.

Louise, cheeks scarlet but head held high, took the letter and mumbled her thanks. When her back was turned, Rudy clutched his sides and mimed helpless laughter, then disappeared into his den.

Natalie watched the double doors swinging in Louise's wake. "What a vile young man." She turned to Ginny. "What's his problem, anyway?"

"Congenital viciousness." Ginny held her butterscotch between her front teeth. "That said...Louise shouldn't have gotten into this situation in the first place. Or rather, she shouldn't have been allowed to get into it. The poor woman can't even type—and yet she's hired to work for a paper with a circulation of 100,000? This Dickensian management style is ridiculous!"

"Oh, I know what you mean, but—there are places for all kinds of journalism, Ginny. Even the frivolous." Natalie glanced around the busy newsroom. "Just because you or I don't want to write advice to the love-lorn doesn't mean there's no place for it. We'd all shrivel up and die on a steady diet of serious news."

"There's a difference between frivolous and ridiculous. No—don't go all philosophical on me! Tell me you don't blush whenever you read that applesauce Louise writes."

Natalie gave a grudging nod.

"Of course you do." Ginny pointed a finger. "You want substance as much as I do. And if not substance, at least some drama, or something with a little shock value. Which reminds me—what have I missed? I'm counting on you to help me catch up on all the latest suburban villainy. Anything really big hit while I was gone? What are you working on?"

She got up and moved around to Natalie's side of the desk. Leaning both hands on the ink blotter, she straightened her bronzed arms and peered at the monitor. She read for a minute, crunching her candy.

She shifted her gaze. "Where do you get these stories?"

Natalie, anchored to the desk with one hand, rocked the chair back and forth. "Odd-ball, isn't it? There's something about it that struck me. Somebody went to the extent of drilling little holes in all the dolls so they could be hung by those little Christmas ornament hooks. I think the story has legs...."

"You do. Unh hunh. I see." Ginny glanced downward. "Do you have your feet on my chair?"

♥   ♥   ♥

An hour later, Natalie fired the dollhouse piece off to the summer editor, who changed the title (to "Police Perplexed by...."), cut an adjective, cut a line about the history of dollhouses, and approved it (Local News, page 3).

Natalie glanced at her watch as she waited for confirmation that typeset had received the approved version: 1:15 PM. An hour before deadline. She might just pay a quick visit to the mega-toystore down the street and check out their dollhouse furnishings. Get a feel for what was available.... The "Thank You for Filing" icon flashed on her monitor, and she logged off the Network with fingers accustomed to the task. She shoved her notebook into her briefcase, switched off the computer, and headed for the exit.

Her mind preoccupied with visions of miniature kitchen appliances, she barreled through the double doors and straight into Louise, who staggered back, waving her arms.

Natalie moved quickly forward to lend a steadying hand. "Jeez! Louise! I'm sorry!"

"Oh no...it's my own silly fault." Louise slid out from under Natalie's grip. "Stupid of me to be standing so near a door...."

"Are you okay? Did I hit you...?"

"I'm fine...." She touched a wrinkled hand to her hair.

"I'm so sorry!" Natalie looked Louise over anxiously. "Are you on your way out? Can I give you a lift?"

Louise looked down the hallway. "No...I'm not on my way out."

"Of course...." Natalie smiled foolishly. It had been an hour since she had seen Louise leave. "Did you come back for something?"

Louise glanced up the stairs. "No, no, I wasn't coming back...."

Natalie's smile grew fatuous. Louise's problem expressing herself was not limited to print media. "Well, I guess I'd better be going and let you go do...whatever you're doing."

Louise's eyes wandered to Natalie's face. They were large, brown eyes, filled with trepidation. "May I speak with you a moment, Natalie?"

Natalie shifted her briefcase from one hand to the other. She really wanted get to that toystore.... "Well...gee, what about?"

The doors burst open and a summer intern appeared carrying a bundle of files. She glanced at them, then clattered up the stairs.

"I know we don't really know each other...." Louise lowered her eyes. "But—you are so intelligent, and so tactful, too. I admired the way you handled yourself in the Dow murder investigation last spring. So sensitive.... I promise not to take up too much of your time. I've been waiting here hoping—"

"Here? In the hall? Louise!" Natalie looked around in dismay: there wasn't even a place to sit. "Why didn't you just call me on the interoffice line?"

"I didn't think of that." Louise's round bosom rose and fell. "That's just it—I'm not good at analyzing a problem and coming up with a plan of action. I just do the first thing that comes into my head." She looked at Natalie timidly. "Are you angry...?"

"Of course I'm not angry! I'm just...." Natalie groped for an adequate descriptor. "Confused.... What do you want to talk about?"

Louise's soft brown eyes widened to the maximum and then blinked. "Something odd has happened, and, although it may be embarrassing for me—professionally—I know I can't handle it on my own anymore."

Curiosity kindled in Natalie's heart and burst into flame. She took a step closer to Louise, and lowered her voice. "What is it?"

Louise moved closer, too, and placed her fingers on Natalie's arm. "Someone's been writing me letters!"

Chapter Two

They have?" Natalie heard herself saying. She winced. "I mean, of course they have!"

Louise's face flushed rosy pink, and she lowered her eyes.

"Well that's great!" said Natalie heartily. But her congratulations seemed only to etch the lines of worry more deeply into Louise's pink face. "Isn't it?"

Louise shook her head, then opened her mouth to speak.

There were footsteps on the stairs below, and a member of the maintenance crew appeared, toting a toolbox.

Natalie made up her mind. Dollhouse research, however intriguing, would have to wait. "Let's go someplace we can talk."

Relief flooded Louise's eyes. "Oh, thank you!" She hefted her book bag and followed Natalie down the stairs.

From the front door of the *Star* Building it was only a step or two across the pedestrian terrace to Charlie's Diner, preferred hangout for *Star* employees since the paper had moved to Hackensack in the 1960s. Natalie led the way beneath a venerable oak tree and up the cast iron stairs of the diner. They secured a back booth, and—since it was Wednesday—ordered hazelnut coffee. Charlie only made the hazelnut on Wednesdays.

As the waitress left, Natalie turned to Louise. "So something odd has happened?"

"Yes." Louise fingered the silverware. "I've been so foolish. I should have told someone sooner, but...when the letters first appeared, they seemed harmless. Just nonsense, you know. I didn't think it would go on and on like this...."

Natalie held up a hand. "When did the first one arrive?"

"Last May. I was so excited!" When she smiled, her eyes crinkled up and a pair of dimples appeared. "I've had some difficulty building up my clientele, you see, and...the mail had been...slow."

"That happens sometimes—it's seasonal." Natalie winced again, but Louise nodded as if receiving one of Life's Great Lessons.

"But the letter was very strange," continued Louise, "disjointed and hard to make sense of. He said he knew a terrible secret about someone he called the Villain, who had once destroyed the life of someone he called the Victim. He thought it wasn't fair that such a hypocrite should get away with the terrible thing he had done, but he worried that if he exposed the Villain, he would be doing exactly what he had condemned him for. But if he remained silent, the Villain would remain unpunished. He wanted me to tell him what to do. He signed it, 'Enigma.'"

The waitress arrived with their coffees, along with a complimentary plate of vanilla wafers. Natalie picked up a cookie and ran a mental check of Louise's recent columns, which she read as the fan of a losing team glances at the box scores. She couldn't recall this scenario. "How did you answer it?"

"I didn't." Louise stirred sugar into her coffee. "I thought it must be someone playing a joke on me. Someone mean-spirited, or perhaps deranged."

"You didn't answer it." Natalie eyed Louise over the rim of her cup. "Your biggest worry is…building up your clientele…but you don't answer a letter when you get it?"

Louise blushed. "It…didn't seem to fit the scope of the column."

Natalie let it go. It was no use talking to Louise as if she were a fellow journalist; she just didn't get it. "So what happened next?"

Louise put her spoon down. "I threw the letter away. I thought that would be the end of it. But it wasn't. He sent another one. He sent one every week. As time passed, he became…annoyed with me. Because I was ignoring him, you see. He tried to give me more information, so I would understand what it was all about and be able to help. But I never really understood him. Then today…." She reached into her book bag and pulled out a letter.

Natalie examined the envelope. Postmarked Valley Ridge on Monday. She pulled out the letter.

Dear Louise,

What to do, what to do, whack a do? I open the paper on Sunday morning, my little hands trembling with expectation as I flip to Life Styles, my little heart going thumpa thumpa. But nada. You dash my hopes, you really do do do.

It is the injustice that brings on the nightmares. In the evening they come, though I do not call, and in the day they disappear, though no one takes them away. I wake up screaming—the Villain is getting away with murder and I am doing nothing! You aren't doing much either, are you sweetie. It's killing me. Why do you ignore me like this? Do you think the Victim deserved what he got? Because he was uncouth and made mistakes? I say no! Even a boy from the sticks has his weak spots, no matter how hard a mother tries to prepare her son to face the cruel world. That was no excuse for the Villain to expose this sorry chronicle, and to snuff out the light in his eyes.

And who knows what that Gang of cutthroats is up to?

I wear a man's clothes, but I've never had a wife.
I have a job, but I've never had a life.
Many fear me, but I've never hurt a fly.
I worship the sun, but I've never seen the sky.

I do not know what to do. I grow desperate. If I elect to tell the world what I know, am I just as evil as the Villain? But if I am silent, a grave injustice will be done—and at what cost? Another life down the drain? It's such a puzzler. I am so torn. And you continue to be deaf to my clarion calls for help. Am I beating a dead horse or what? Maybe I should write to your bosses and let them handle it. Is that what you want? Hey—I'm easy. It's your funeral.

Enigma

PS What's black and white and red all over?

Natalie raised her eyes and looked across the table.
"Oh," said Louise. "Didn't I mention the riddles?"

♥   ♥   ♥

Natalie took a sip of coffee. "So what exactly is the problem?"
Louise stirred her cup. "He seems angry, doesn't he? And he…he mentions writing a letter to my boss. If he does, I'm afraid it will get me into trouble with Mr. Shapiro." Byron Shapiro was Assistant Managing Editor at the *Star*.
"Why?" Natalie frowned. "You haven't done anything wrong."
"Mr. Shapiro might be mad because I didn't answer the letter right away. And he might not like it if he knew I got nonsense mail like that. My nephew says the Board brought in an outside consultant to analyze the

16

readership and streamline the focus, and my column isn't highly rated." She laid her spoon on the saucer. "He says they're looking for people to...let go. I didn't want Mr. Shapiro to examine my mail more closely.... I didn't want to give him any reasons to...to...." Her eyes pleaded with Natalie to understand.

Which Natalie did. Thanks to Rudy, the whole newsroom knew Louise never got any letters. But did the editors in the front office know? Fond as she was of Byron Shapiro, she knew he had a preference for waiting until problems solved themselves. If he had been looking for a way to get rid of Louise, this would play right into his hands. "I see what you mean."

"I've never been good at...confrontation. But I have to stop this, one way or the other." Louise clutched her napkin in both hands. "I've been so worried.... Some of the letters contained references to crimes being committed, and to a thirst for vengeance. Some of them called me names."

Natalie saw the look of pain cross Louise's face, and felt a wave of anger rise against Enigma. What a rotten shame if Louise was canned because of some coward who wouldn't sign his name to a letter. But.... "I have to tell you, you really should have told Byron early on. It's against the law for this guy to be sending you that kind of stuff. It's also *Star* policy to report nuisance mail. Not everybody does, but still...."

Louise looked up. Her eyes were lovely, in a dreamy, old-fashioned way. They shimmered in her soft face like amber glass. "Then you think I should tell Mr. Shapiro, and take whatever comes?"

"I didn't say that...." Natalie frowned at her empty cup. "There may be another way." She looked around and caught the waitress's eye. "When's your deadline?"

"Friday noon."

"What if we take a shot at answering Enigma's letter? We may be able to shut him up if we put our minds to it."

The waitress swooped down on them, coffeepot poised. As her cup was being replenished, Natalie glanced across the table. "You didn't drink your coffee!"

"I'm sorry...." whispered Louise.

The waitress cocked an eyebrow. "Tea drinker, hunh?" Louise nodded, blushing. The waitress grinned cheerfully. "I'll bring you a cup, hun. On the house." She picked up Louise's saucer and sped away.

"Why didn't you...?" Natalie stopped in mid sentence. What was the point? If Louise couldn't even stick up for herself enough to order tea instead of coffee...! No wonder Rudy walked all over her—she was prob-

17

ably the only person on the planet more ineffectual than himself. "Anyway, not answering Enigma hasn't worked, maybe answering him will. Shall we give it a try before we go to Byron?"

Louise looked around. "But I don't know what to write."

Natalie smothered a smile at Louise's misunderstanding of her polite use of the "editorial we." What was this woman doing writing for a newspaper? "I'm willing to have a go at it. It's just a question of coming up with the right language."

"Oh, if you could! But—are you sure it's the right thing? I wouldn't want Mr. Shapiro to be angry with you if he found out."

"I'm not worried." And why should she be? Her position at the *Star* was secure. "This sort of quirky problem is right up my alley." Besides, thought Natalie, somebody ought to stand up for Louise. "I have a psychologist friend I want to talk to about this. Only that won't be till Friday night, so we'll miss this week's column. Fortunately Byron is on vacation till next week, anyway, so we couldn't tell him if we wanted to."

"I can hold on for a week, as long as I know something is being done. I'm so grateful…." She put a hand on the menu as the waitress set her tea in front of her. "Can I treat you to something?"

"Actually, I've got to get going soon." Natalie glanced at her watch. "Got to pick up my niece from school over in Bergenfield."

Louise blinked. "School doesn't start till next Thursday."

"Summer school, or 'Summer Adventure' as they call it now."

"She's your brother's daughter, isn't she? Came in from California last month? Is she settling in all right?"

It amused Natalie that the tendrils of the newsroom gossip octopus had touched even Louise, who came in but rarely and hardly ever stayed to visit. "'Settling in' isn't the term I'd choose. I'd go with 'struggling along.' But my brother has 'settled in'—with a vengeance. He wore a suit and tie when he took her to meet her teachers. I didn't think he owned a tie. I never saw him wear one."

Louise smiled wistfully. "Oh, but she's his child. I imagine he'd do anything if he thought it might help her. Anything at all."

18

Chapter Three

Natalie paused before pouring the coffee beans into the grinder and regarded the tall, dark-haired woman standing at the sink. "You're a clinical psychologist...."

"Uh oh." Rebecca applied a sponge to a soapy bowl. "Whenever anyone starts by reminding you of your profession, it means they're gonna ask you a question they think they should've been able to answer themselves. A sad attempt to ward of feelings of inadequacy."

"I rest my case." She put a hand on the grinder and turned it on.

They were in the kitchen of Daniel's apartment, which occupied the third floor of a gray clapboard house on Pleasant Lane in Haworth. Originally, it had been a sprawling, five-bedroom home on a ferociously manicured acre—a combination deemed to represent the bare essentials of suburban existence in the 1940s. In the 1980s, propelled by an unexpected slump in the economy and the traditionally high property taxes, the house had been converted into four inconvenient apartments. The third-floor apartment (originally the attic), was the most inconvenient of the lot, its impressive square yardage rendered meaningless by its slanting roof, which made standing upright anywhere but in the central "gallery" impossible.

When the grinding ceased, Rebecca spoke. "So what's up?"

Natalie placed a filter in the coffee maker. "A friend of mine at the paper has been receiving some rather odd letters...." She went on to explain about Louise, Enigma, and Louise's inability to defend herself. "In the end, I offered to write a reply. Something that would encourage this creep to leave Louise alone."

Rebecca dried her hands on a towel. "I suppose giving the letter to the police and letting them handle it is out of the question."

"Heretic." Natalie unhooked a couple of mugs from the cup tree. "You know it's against my religion to fraternize with the cops."

"Oh really?" Rebecca folded the towel. "Didn't you tell me last May, in the strictest confidence, that there was a certain Sergeant with excellent clothes sense who'd made a believer of you?"

"Fortunately I came to my senses before I was baptized into the faith. And he does felony-homicide, not mail fraud." She reached into her back pocket. "Anyway, the cops would give this a cursory glance and throw it away. Take a look." She handed the letter to Rebecca, who unfolded it and began to read.

Natalie leaned against the counter. A noise from the dining room at the other end of the central gallery made her look up. Through the door she beheld her brother, seated with his back to her, and her niece, heads bent studiously over a couple of notebooks. Gayanne giggled again, then put a hand to her mouth and tried to look serious. But every few seconds she glanced with bird-like swiftness at Daniel's face. When she moved, the yellow light from the chandelier made her red hair glint with gold.

"Humph," said Rebecca. "This reads like high comedy. Or maybe camp."

Natalie rubbed the heel of her shoe against her shin. "Does style matter? The question is, how do we get him to stop before he extends his campaign and everybody finds out what's been going on?"

"Normally I try to open people up, not shut them up. Not that I haven't wanted to tell a client or two to muzzle it…."

"Now's your chance to say all those nasty things you've always wanted to. Go on…let all that stifled hostility out."

"I have a better idea." She returned the letter to Natalie. "Tell him he's one sick cookie and recommend that he seek professional help at once. That usually scares people away by the bus load."

Natalie returned the letter to her pocket. "Won't he know we're bluffing?"

"Tell him you've talked to a mental-health-care professional who's willing to meet with him—trust me, he'll head for the hills."

Natalie turned to the coffee maker. "Are we sure he's a he?"

Rebecca shrugged. "I don't get a feeling one way or the other. 'Enigma' has a feminine ending, but that doesn't mean much."

"What if he really wants help?" Natalie picked up the coffeepot.

"No problem. It won't kill me to take on another *pro bono* client. But chances are you won't hear from him. Whatever is going on, it has nothing to do with someone seeking help on a moral issue. Be sure you avoid playing his game—don't argue an obvious point he's only pretending not to understand. That always annoys me."

Natalie poured a cup of coffee and slid it toward Rebecca. "I never realized how much psychologists and advice columnists had in common."

Rebecca picked up the cup. "Neither did I."

They wandered over to the "living room," an awkward area under the western eaves. Natalie sat in an armchair with sawed-off legs, while Rebecca fashioned a beanbag chair into a shape that accommodated her long legs. Although it had acquired character by the addition of a bubble skylight and an array of unusual furniture, the apartment was not designed to arouse the passions of the average Bergen County resident. In fact, prior to Daniel's occupation, it had been used exclusively by visiting performing artists, the entire building being owned by Martin Montgomery, Artistic Director of the New Globe Theater—Daniel's employer.

"But I did it right!"

Natalie and Rebecca looked around. Gayanne knelt on the seat of her chair, leaning across the table on her forearms. She bumped her head down on the wooden table.

"You did it right, but you went too fast." Daniel's quiet voice dispelled the echo of his daughter's shrill cry. "Try it again." Gayanne's shoulders sagged in sullen resignation.

Natalie turned to Rebecca. "I appreciate your help. We don't approve of people who make anonymous threats in my profession."

"Or in mine. But…honestly, this letter is pretty tame. More full of riddles and puzzles than threats, isn't it?"

"That's what interests me—more's the pity, as Ginny Chau would say…." Natalie grinned.

"Yes, but why the need for secrecy?"

"I don't want this to work out badly for Louise."

"Why would it? She hasn't done anything wrong."

"No, but…. Have you ever read her column?"

Rebecca shook her head.

"Louise has been an office joke since the day she arrived." Natalie sipped her coffee. "She doesn't get much of a response to her column…. Doesn't get…any…response. She's a nice, motherly soul, so of course she doesn't have a clue how to stand up for herself. She's afraid if this gets out it'll be used to close her down."

"I see. You know…." Rebecca crossed her legs. "If she's not doing her job well, you won't be able to protect her—no matter how much you'd like to."

Natalie hooked a little stool shaped like a turtle (last seen in the Globe production of *Dracula*) out from beneath the coffee table. She placed her feet on it and regarded her toes.

"I say that," continued Rebecca, "because you have a slight tendency to be overprotective of people you see as defenseless."

"'Slight?'"

"I was being tactful. I'll use 'titanic' if you insist on accuracy. Now, in appropriate circumstances, this is your most admirable trait. If you had not stuck by your brother I would not be sitting here admiring the span of his shoulders. But like everything else in life, context counts."

"I'm not trying to protect Louise! All I'm doing is giving her a little professional help. If it—"

A wail of misery rose from the dining room. "But I don't get it!"

Gayanne, still kneeling on her chair, slumped backward onto her heels, her chin against her breast and her arms dangling at her sides. Her fingers twitched then went limp, allowing her purple-and orange-striped pencil with the kitty-cat eraser to drop to the floor.

Daniel, his chin cupped in his hand, eyed his daughter thoughtfully. "Five minute break?" he suggested at length.

Gayanne wobbled her head back and forth in a sluggish gesture of agreement.

"Well pick up your pencil so I don't step on it, and we'll go see what's for dessert." He arose from his chair and headed for the kitchen, stretching his arms over his head as he went. Gayanne slid sideways off her chair and landed hands first on the floor. She captured her pencil, and bounded after him on all fours.

"If it doesn't work," continued Natalie, "I'll inform Byron." She crossed her feet on the turtle stool. "Unless I can come up with a viable plan B...."

"I rest my case." Rebecca smiled smugly.

"Okay, so I don't want to see a nice lady who never hurt a fly get trampled on. What's wrong with that?"

"Not a thing—if you can draw the boundary there. Helping Louise cope with a nuisance letter writer is one thing. Helping her keep her job is another. I'm only suggesting you'll be more effective if you're clear as to your motivations."

"Which you are now going to outline for me."

"Nope." Rebecca reached for her coffee cup.

Natalie smirked. "Jeez, you're good at this. Did you ever think of doing it for a living?"

"No. I want to be an Indian scout when I grow up."

"Ah! That explains your interest in mountain adventures." In response to Rebecca's puzzled look, she continued: "Daniel told me about the cabin in the Catskills for Labor Day weekend." She glanced toward the kitchen and lowered her voice. "For the record, I told him he ought to go."

"It worked out for the best, I think." Rebecca sipped her coffee. "Nice idea, bad timing."

"I could have taken Gayanne. I know stability is important for her right now, but she would have been fine...."

"But would Daniel have been fine? That's the question. Actually, I was proud of him for deciding not to go—although I admit I wanted him to. He's learning to say no and be tough."

"Learning?" Natalie leaned over the arm of her chair. "I'd say he's graduated. What's with cracking the books on a Friday night? On a Friday night six days before school starts?"

Rebecca's lips twitched. "They agreed to finish the workbook before the weekend—you know how far behind her grade she is. It's just four problems a day. And Daniel wants her to get used to doing homework."

"This from someone who never did his homework once in eleven and a third years of school, as far as I can recall...."

Rebecca lowered her voice as the kitchen door opened. "Then I'd say he ought to know."

Gayanne passed them carrying a plate on which sat a pinwheel of apple and orange slices, with a sprig of purple grapes at the hub. Daniel followed with a pitcher of lemonade.

"Yeah, well," continued Natalie when the scholars were back at the table. "I say he could've used the break. He does all the shopping, cooking, and cleaning, works all day, and spends his evenings doing homework with Gayanne. I don't see him enough...." She spoke out of the side of her mouth. "And I bet you don't, either."

"Only on weekends for now. But we talk every day, so wipe that look off your face." Rebecca flipped her ponytail over her shoulder. "Gee whiz. Louise, Daniel, me.... Don't you have anything of your own to worry about?"

"I have everything I want. Except a new computer. Guess I'll have to wait for prices to drop, though...."

"I thought you were contemplating a new job at the *Star*. Wouldn't that pay more?"

"I'd make more as a senior reporter attached to one of the bureaus, yeah. And I'd work on bigger stories."

"Sounds great. What's the hold-up?"

"There are a lot of factors to consider. For one thing, I'm not sure I want a heavier workload right now. Gayanne is going to come to my house every afternoon. I've got to keep a flexible schedule. And for another thing, one reason Ginny wants me in the Crime Bureau is so she can get Tyler Hanson kicked out on his ass. I don't care much for that sort of office politics and I never have. I'm not sure I'm ready to give up my autonomy."

Rebecca picked up a small red sneaker from behind the beanbag. Its laces were knotted. "You and Daniel have reversed roles. He's the one looking for structure and you're the free spirit."

There was a shriek from the dining room. "I get it!"

Gayanne was leaning over the table again, laboriously manipulating the striped pencil across her workbook. Daniel, head resting on his knuckles, watched her intently.

"That's so easy!" scoffed Gayanne. "Lemme do another one."

Natalie and Rebecca looked at one another.

"Where were we?" asked Rebecca.

"I have no idea," said Natalie.

Rebecca looked at the sneaker. "What's Plan B?"

"What?"

"If the letter you're going to write doesn't work and he writes again. You said you had a Plan B."

"I was just speculating...."

"No you weren't. I could see the wheels turning. Let me say that if the first letter doesn't work, I would advise against another. You'll just be encouraging this guy to continue."

"No, not another letter." Natalie pursed her lips. "I was thinking of threatening to expose him."

"You'd have to identify him first. That won't be easy."

"Maybe not. Maybe yes." Natalie removed her feet from the stool. "Don't you think there might be some clues to Enigma's identity in the letter?"

"You mean the riddles?" Rebecca worked at the knotted shoelace. "I didn't get them. Except the black and white and red all over. That one's pretty lowest common denominator."

"Hey!" Gayanne was before them, her hands on her hips and a look of surprise on her face. "Are you guys doing fractions too?"

"No, we're solving riddles." Natalie pulled the letter out of her pocket. "Come help us."

Daniel put the fruit down. "I'm no good at riddles." He lowered himself onto the futon, and Gayanne nestled in the bow of his arm.

"What's black and white and red all over?" asked Natalie.

"That's too easy," said Gayanne. "A newspaper."

Rebecca picked up a slice of apple. "Or an embarrassed zebra."

"I know one!" Gayanne looked into Daniel's face. "What has four eyes but can't see?"

"Don't tell me." Daniel closed his eyes to concentrate. Gayanne laid her head against his chest and fiddled with the cuffs of his shirt.

Natalie looked at the letter. "'I wear a man's clothes, but I've never had a wife. I have a job, but I've never had a life.' Does that mean someone who is unfulfilled, or somehow imprisoned, possibly in a one-sided relationship?"

Rebecca took the letter. "'Many fear me, but I've never hurt a fly. I've never seen the sky....' If it's someone wrongly convicted of a crime, they might long for the sun but not see it from their cell."

"'Many fear me but I've never hurt a fly' suggests Quasimodo to me—a gentle giant...."

Rebecca shook her head. "Even if you get the answer, I don't see how it will help you identify Enigma. Prisoner, unfulfilled, giant—they are too general."

"Yeah, but there's more here than just the riddles. Don't you find the language...suggestive?"

"I'd say peculiar." Rebecca eyed the letter. "Worship the sun. Could that be someone who is blind? Four eyes.... Mississippi.... I got it!" Rebecca turned to Gayanne—and made a noise.

Daniel and Gayanne were sound asleep on the futon.

Natalie contemplated the scene: the worry lines had smoothed from her brother's face, and he looked much younger than his 27 years. Gayanne's face was invisible beneath his arms except for a glimpse of her turned-up nose, and the curve of her closed eyelids.

Natalie shook her head. "This is so maudlin."

"They're bonding," said Rebecca. Then she sighed.

"Gee." Natalie regarded her watch. "Friday night; eight thirty. Getting late." She shook her head. "Guess I'm going home."

Rebecca put down the sneaker and looked again at the tableau on the futon. "I guess I am, too."

Chapter Four

Arriving at the newsroom early on Tuesday morning following the holiday weekend, Natalie removed all evidence of her three-week occupation from Ginny's desk. It was perfect timing, really. Working at home, she could mind Gayanne from 3:15 until her brother got home from work at 5:00, an arrangement that allowed her to spend time with her niece, and allowed her brother to stay at his job. Those were the important things right now; furthering her career could wait. It was so convenient that she lived across the street from the Haworth Elementary school. And that the *Star* was an afternoon newspaper, with a deadline of 2:15 PM. Of course, the marketing people had been trying to change that for years. But: "*Star*s come out in the evening—not the morning," had been the decree of Myra Vandergelden, *Star* CEO and Editor-in-chief.

Having emptied the contents of her in- and out-boxes into her brief-case, she switched said boxes from the left side of the monitor to the right. She moved the paper holder from the right side to the left. From the desk drawer she retrieved her pens and pencils and her personal supply of plastic-covered paper clips. These important tasks accomplished, she turned on the computer. The *Star* had its own brand new Network, and, in the absence of a designated computer, her permanent files usually remained password protected on the Server. But while at the Crime Bureau (to avoid the hassle of accessing each file through the slower Server), she had pulled all of her working files onto Ginny's hard drive. Now she moved the contents of these files back to her folder on the Server. Finally, she checked to see if she'd left any stray files floating around.

There were not many. In an effort to wrap things up before Ginny's return, she had filed three pieces the previous week. The dollhouse dilemma was her only active story. With Byron out of town, it was going to be a slow week—which was just fine with her. She had an idea she was going to be busy with school issues....

She deleted or copied the half dozen personal files she had left on the desktop. She smiled as she saw what she had written—short notes to self about appointments, potential contacts, and tricky bridge hands. It hadn't taken her long to fall into all the old habits and make things just like home. Just exactly like home.

Her fingers hovering over the keyboard, waiting for instructions to either delete or save last week's shopping list. From nowhere came the realization—in complete contradiction to her reverie about how nice it was to be going home—that it had been very satisfying to have her own desk in the newsroom, exciting to have the focus working for the Crime Bureau had provided. The thought of returning to the old routine of general interest stories, and, when in the newsroom, of being forced to use whatever communal workstation was free, held little appeal. She frowned at the enormous brass reproduction of the *Star* masthead that decorated the south wall.

She did a double take: *Bergen Evening Star.* Stars come out in the evening, Myra Vandergelden had said…and disappear in the day, though no one takes them away!

"Well, well, well," she said softly.

"That sounds like a deep thought." It was a man's voice, close behind her. The lock-jawed Connecticut drawl and whiff of pipe tobacco made identification a snap.

Natalie deleted the shopping list with a flick of her fingers. "Cliché: minus five style points."

K. Tyler Hanson the Third, head of the Crime Bureau, moved into her field of vision and looked down with tolerant amusement. "I'm afraid you've lost me. Was that supposed to be funny?" He was of the tall, loose-jointed variety; a man who habitually dressed in a comfortable sport-jacket, heavy-rimmed glasses, and very nice shoes. You couldn't imagine Tyler in jeans.

"What are you doing here at this hour?" challenged Natalie. "Everyone knows you have breakfast at Charlie's and never arrive in the newsroom before nine."

"There's an emergency Board meeting this morning, and Myra need's my help. But she's in the front office with a couple of editors, so I have a few minutes to kill." He put a hand on the back of the chair Ginny had so charmingly occupied the previous Wednesday. "May I sit down?"

"If you tell me what the emergency is about…."

"And how long do you think I'd last in this job if I couldn't keep a confidence? You'll have to wait like everybody else."

"Just as long as we're not going tabloid…. Speaking of which, did you see the *Bugle's* lead story yesterday? Pregnant Girl Found Living in Sewer: Father Says He's Good Provider."

27

He opened his mouth as if to laugh, but no sound came out. Natalie knew Ginny considered this habit a black mark against him.

"So what can I do for you?" she asked.

"You've been on my mind…." He smiled as if he'd done her a favor. "I'd been hoping to catch you before you ended your stint with the Crime Bureau."

This from a man who had studiously avoided her for three weeks, thought Natalie.

"I enjoyed your piece last Friday," he continued. "The one on illegal trafficking in imitation baseball bats."

"Thank you."

"Quite an important issue—if not exactly headline material. But the safety implications of defective bats splintering at the rate your research indicates are very disturbing."

"I thought so. Most people think of black-market knock-offs in terms of CDs and designer jeans, but it's a much broader problem."

"And thanks to you we can all be on the alert for the bogus bat." His words rippled with humor—a humor of ambiguous origins, leaving it open as to whether he was laughing with her or at her.

Natalie, reaching to the back of the desk drawer, found her bag of candy, and fished it out while framing a retort.

But Tyler's attention had wandered. "Rudy! My man!"

Natalie turned her head and beheld the mailroom clerk, looking like a scarecrow in tight jeans and tighter T-shirt, just entering the newsroom. His sullen face brightened when he saw Tyler, and he hurried over to shake hands.

"Hi, Mr. Hanson." He turned to Natalie with the deferential grin he reserved for the full-time writing staff. "Hi, Ms. Joday."

"Hi, Rudy."

"Rudy!" continued Tyler in hearty accents. "Were you able get those limited edition classic car stamps?"

"You bet, Mr. Hanson!" Rudy's anemic chest swelled. "They're in the mailroom. I can get 'em for you now if you like."

"All right!" Tyler raised his hand above his head and Rudy obligingly slapped it with a delighted giggle.

Natalie, finding this public display of locker-room antics misplaced, turned back to the computer until they had gotten it out of their systems.

Tyler shook his head as Rudy disappeared into the mailroom. "Not a bad egg—surprisingly ambitious. Of course he doesn't have much in the way of natural resources…." Tyler tapped his head. "I've taken him under my wing, lately."

"You stamp collectors always stick together, don't you."

Tyler laughed noiselessly again, then cleared his throat. "So…. I hear you're leaving us."

"I am?" Natalie experienced a slight adrenaline buzz. "That's funny. No one's mentioned it to me."

"I mean leaving the Crime Bureau." He laughed silently again. Natalie was beginning to appreciate Ginny's point. "I've been meaning to talk to Byron."

Natalie frowned. "About what?"

"Your potential as a crime reporter, of course. Don't tell me you haven't considered it. Or are you one of these modern youngsters who thinks that careers happen accidentally?"

"I've thought about it. About doing investigative journalism, anyway. There are options besides crime: environment, social science, political beat. Look, what is this?" She leaned back and crossed her arms. "It hasn't been a year since you wrote that infamous memo saying one full-time person was plenty in the Bureau."

Tyler brushed her off with a wave of his hands. "I made my recommendation at a particular time and context. The *status quo* has changed, therefore what I said a year ago is irrelevant."

"So now you think there are enough stories for three?"

"Well…." Tyler raised a hand to his glasses. "Maybe not three…. My point is it's just as well to think ahead, Natalie—let people know your intentions. Believe me, people don't fall into the plum positions: they stake them out, then fight to protect their territory."

She eyed him warily. "Why this sudden interest in my career?"

"It can get ruthless out there, and it never hurts to have friends in high places." He winked at her. "I've been in this game a long time. Nobody knows the importance of good connections better than me. And frankly…. I've gotten to a point in life where I'm ready to share what I know. I wouldn't mind having a protégé."

"Like Rudy," said Natalie, indicating her irony with her tone and raised eyebrow.

"Now don't underestimate yourself," he cautioned.

Natalie leaned forward and switched the computer off. Her irritation was nearing the red zone, not least because it was unclear whether Tyler was being intentionally offensive, or merely exhibiting the interpersonal skills of a wasp.

The glass doors to the front office swung open and Myra Vandergelden appeared: a tiny figure in a tailored suit of apple green, her red hair fluffed out like an aura around her head. In her wake came, as usual, Lance Wenger, the *Star*'s corporate lawyer, his ponderous frame encased in a light tan suit, his large hands sticking out at his sides like flippers. Behind them walked a tall, clean-featured man in a charcoal-gray suit, moving with an easy elegance that bespoke his familiarity with power and position.

"Look!" Excitement made Tyler's voice jump. "There's Peter Kovaks! It's his first visit since he resigned from the Board last May to run for State Senator. Good to see him back! Probably going to thank the Board for the *Star's* endorsement. The announcement will be in today's paper, you know." He looked at Natalie and winked again. "Come on over. I'll introduce you."

"No thanks," said Natalie.

He left her without further comment. The urgency with which he hurried across the newsroom, and the forward stretch of his chin, mirrored the obsequiousness she had seen in young Rudy's face, and aroused a similar reaction in her egalitarian breast. Although she could not hear his words as he joined the group that had formed around Myra, she could see his ingratiating expression. It thus gave her satisfaction to see Peter Kovaks walk past him without a glance as he ushered Myra across the newsroom and through the double doors to the corporate offices upstairs.

♥   ♥   ♥

Late the following morning, Natalie and Louise met in the corner booth at Charlie's. The waitress steamrolled by, saying over her shoulder, "One tea and one hazelnut, right?"

Louise, looking like a double carnation in a white ruffled blouse, handed her a letter. "More of the same from Enigma."

Natalie looked at the postmark. Dumont. Enigma knew how to play the game.... She skimmed through the letter, then put it back in the envelope. "Can I keep it for a while?"

"I wish you would. I don't like having it in my house."

Natalie put the letter in her briefcase and pulled out something else. "Here's our reply to Enigma." She handed a sheet of paper to Louise. "I don't mind admitting I rather enjoyed that."

"Are you sure it didn't take too much of your time?"

"It's always slow the week after Labor Day." Her pallet tingled as the waitress approached with the coffeepot. "Go ahead, read it."

Louise took a pair of glasses from her handbag.

Natalie thanked the waitress, and was lifting her cup to her lips when something caught her eye.... Charlie had acquired new place mats.... She moved the saucer to one side. *How much dirt is in a hole 6.5 ft deep and 1.25 ft in diameter?* She sipped her coffee....

Several minutes later Louise looked up. "It's so—forceful." She handed the paper back to Natalie.

"Thanks." Natalie put down her cup and skimmed her masterpiece with modest pride:

Dear Enigma,

Since you have been writing to me for a long time I feel I owe you the courtesy of one response. But understand something: this will be the only one. Your question answers itself. By any standard of morality, there is no excuse for vengeful or destructive behavior. You don't need me to tell you that.

It is clear that your real problem is something else entirely. You are seeking attention in unacceptable ways for reasons that may not be clear even to you. I recommend strongly that you seek professional help, and if you will send me your contact information I will put you in touch with the right people. That is the only advice you will get from me.

Louise

"Of course we have to conform to the format of the column." Natalie handed Louise a second sheet of paper. "But you don't want to quote his whole letter—that'd make him feel too important—so I've suggested an excerpt that will give your readers some background: 'Dear Louise, I have learned a secret about someone, and I am torn as to whether to tell what I know or not,' etc."

Louise glanced at the paper, then at her teacup. "How did you learn to write like that, Natalie? So...direct."

"It's just a matter of intention, Louise. Words come in different groups, associated with different intentions. We want to shut this guy up, so we pick words from the forceful group. If I wanted to show my sympathy for him, I'd pick from another bag."

"And can you shift anytime you want to?"

"Sure."

"It sounds so...calculating. I thought writing was an art form...creative."

31

"Fiction and poetry, maybe. And some lucky people don't have to think when they write—it just flows. Not me. Newspaper writing is pretty formulaic." Natalie reached for her coffee and settled back. Then she saw Louise's expression. "Is something wrong?"

"I'm just...not sure...." A pink blush crept over her face.

Natalie pursed her lips. "You don't have to use it if you don't want to, Louise. Or you can use it as a sample, and write something in your own words."

"It's not that. But I fear.... I know I'm not very experienced in these matters, but won't it be obvious that—I didn't write it?"

"I didn't think of that." Natalie stirred uneasily. "Let me see what else you've got this week."

Louise pulled a green notebook from her bag and slipped out a sheet of loose-leaf paper. "I'm sorry it's handwritten. Ms. Alexander always types it up for me...."

Natalie took the blue-lined paper and read:

Dear Louise,

Things are very slow at work this summer, and I'm afraid my boss is thinking of laying me off. I keep as busy as I can, and always volunteer for the jobs nobody else wants, but without seniority, what can I do?

Willing to Work

Dear Willing,

Try to remember your boss has his job to do, too. If you are as conscientious as you say, your boss knows it, and will do everything he can to help you stay on the job. If worse comes to worst, tell him you understand, and are willing to come back to work when he needs you. You'll have that seniority before you know it.

Louise

Natalie cringed as she skimmed down the page. Her letter to Enigma stuck out like a nettle in a bed of posies. "You're right. You'd better try to put what I wrote into your style."

"Oh, but—wouldn't that weaken the impact? I truly do want him to stop, and besides...." She pointed to Natalie's opus. "I like this.".

Natalie gestured helplessly. "I don't know what to do, then!"

"Couldn't you make a few amendments in my replies?" Louise's eyes pleaded with her. "So that the difference isn't as evident?"

Natalie hesitated. Concocting stern warnings to nuisance-letter writers was one thing. But engaging in advice writing!?

"I'm sure you could do it." Louise voice was all encouragement. "With all your experience and knowledge, you can write anything!"

"Well...." Natalie ran a hand through her hair and looked sidelong at the loose-leaf paper. "I suppose you could say something like.... 'Dear Willing, If you volunteer for the unpleasant jobs, you may insure your longevity, but you risk being taken for granted....'" Natalie tapped a forefinger on the paper. "'And if you're seriously worried about losing your job, the time has come to consider looking around for something else. Don't be afraid of change—if you know you are good at what you do, you don't want to work for someone who doesn't appreciate you, do you?'" She raised her eyes to Louise's startled face. "Whatcha think?"

Louise's eyes widened. "Oh!"

♥   ♥   ♥

Back at the newsroom, teetering on a chair with legs of four different lengths, Natalie perused the second Enigma letter.

Dear Louise,

The world forgets the truth, but I remember. Between my tears, I sing a dirge to the past. I am the guardian of our times, a lone sentinel waiting to feel the light of the truth on my face. I am also a candidate for the loony bin, because you...drive...me...crazy!!!

I am still undecided. Will I condemn myself to eternal damnation if I speak? And if I don't? I'm living a lie by keeping silent. Once I knew a liar. Every day he told twice as many lies as he had the day before. After 73 days, he was lying all the time. Do you know on what day he was lying exactly half the time?

If they knew, they would come and get me. They are a traitorous Gang, and the night winds whisper of an Evil Deed they once did—

My pride won't let me tell my name,
But if you guess it I'll be tame:
    Begin with twenty-six,
    Take twelve steps forward,
    Subtract three,

Add six,
Then take one step backward.

Don't think that this was the Villain's only crime. And now he asks us to trust him? It's all more hypocrisy! He is the one who should face the tribune. I really can't bear it. I want to tell every-thing I know! I want to convince you that my campaign for the truth is worthy of your attention. I want to tell you all. But I'm afraid he'll come for me in the dark.

Enigma

PS What did the Norwegian call the electroplated detective?

Natalie's brow furrowed. "What...?" she bent closer over the letter, and read it again.

♥   ♥   ♥

She took photocopies of the letters, then went to her desk and stared at them. Here and there she underlined a word or phrase. The newsroom hub-bub faded from her consciousness. She made a list of words, then a list of numbers. Once she went to Byron's empty office and consulted his Dictionary of Greek Mythology.

After an hour, and with her notebook propped up before her, she turned on the computer and logged onto the Network. She called up the Virtual News Archive. This was the brainchild of Davis Skemp, the *Star*'s resident computer guru. Using VirNA, she could search the newspaper's database, a vast cyber-warehouse containing a text and graphic record of every issue of the *Star* since 1962 (Sunday edition included from 1974).

When the familiar pink screen appeared, she clicked on the search engine, typed "Enigma" into the text field, and clicked GO. A message appeared in a green box. "This search may take up to ten minutes. If you narrow the parameters, or add a cross reference, it will go quicker." Natalie's lips twitched, but she clicked GO again.

In the ensuing hour, Natalie learned two things. First, there was nothing to be found in the database regarding any person known as Enigma, and second, the search would have been a lot faster if she had made it case sensitive (capital E), the first time.

Having exhausted all variations on Enigma, she returned to the search utility and typed in "Achilles." The ancient computer chugged, and, after a five-minute wait, informed her that there were 97 references for Achilles between 1962 and 1993.

The entries were sorted in chronological order. Consulting her notebook, she scrolled down the list to 1972. There were six entries for Achilles that year. She clicked on the first one.

The screen went white, and the text from May 15, Section D, page 3 appeared. She scrolled down until she saw the word Achilles highlighted in red.

It was a short paragraph, one of several under the header, "Party Leaders Announce State Slate."

Four-term Ridgewood Selectman Maurizio Marconi was tapped to run for the State Senate seat being vacated by Al Dorazel. Marconi, owner of Achilles Shoes in Ridgewood, is the lone liberal in a district known for its conservative leanings. Newcomer Andrea Parks is one of three women candidates....

Natalie went back to the search results and checked the next two references, both of which concerned the Marconi candidacy. One outlined his position on the issues and one gave the details of a fundraiser at a local high school. The fourth reference, for October 7, was longer.

Disgraced Candidate Calls it Quits

—Staff

A box of campaign buttons in a garbage can outside a quiet home in Ridgewood was the only reminder of the failed campaign of Maurizio Marconi, former candidate for NJ State Senate from District 2 in Bergen County. It was a sad token of a campaign that stirred passions and inflamed animosities alike with its liberal platform. Marconi, four-term Ridgewood selectman and owner of Achilles Shoes, withdrew abruptly from the race yesterday after being read the text of a story the *Star* was preparing to run (*Bergen Evening Star*, Oct. 6, 1972). This story exposed an affair Marconi had with another man earlier in the year. This brings to an end one of the most controversial State races seen in the past two decades.

Marconi's downfall began last week during a heated exchange with media at a press conference in Ridgewood. Reporters questioned Marconi about recreational drug use prior to his election as a Ridgewood selectman, which Marconi had acknowledged earlier in the campaign, claiming that "the occasional joint is no different from the occasional drink." Questions then turned to Marconi's relationship with his wife. Both Marconis are on record as supporting what they term "sexual liberation." The candidate grew angry at the nature of the questions, accusing the press of yellow journalism and "pandering to the worst instincts of its readers." Marconi, who has taken a liberal stance on issues ranging from ERA passage to gun control, stated: "All you need to know is that Dottie is the only woman in my life, and has been since the day we were married." He then abruptly ended the press conference.

Announcing Marconi's withdrawal from the race, campaign spokesperson Becky Schmegal issued the following statement: "Maury and his wife are deeply saddened by this attack on their private lives in the name of the people's right to know. This is gutter journalism at its worst. Maury's withdrawal from the campaign is not to be construed either as a signal that the report is correct or as a statement that same-sex relationships in any way preclude a man or woman from seeking public office. His withdrawal is a choice he and his wife made together, based on the impossibility of operating a campaign in an atmosphere of persecution created by the news media in general and the *Star* in particular. To his friends and supporters he offers the following: 'Your support and generosity have made this campaign something I will always be proud to remember. Don't ever stop striving for your goals. Forgive me for leaving you before we have reached them.'"

—Click here for photo—

Natalie clicked. The hard drive chugged, and a black and white photograph of Maurizio and Dottie Marconi drew itself on the screen. His was a round face, with cheerful eyes that crinkled up at the corners, and receding curly hair. He looked like the type of guy who would be fun at parties—not at all like a politician. Dottie was taller and leaner, her expression more reserved. She had long blond hair, parted in the middle, and large intelligent eyes. They both wore buttons that read: Can Do in '72.

Twenty-one years ago. She'd been eight at the time—too young to understand or care about a local political scandal. And what a nasty little story it was. What on Earth had the *Star* been doing, digging up stories about a person's sex life—just like a tabloid…just like the *Bugle*! She was glad

.

things had changed since then.

She pulled up the October 6 issue. The front page contained a verbose account of the *Star*'s first year as a corporate entity following the departure of its former owners, the Mill family. In Section D she found the following:

Marconi Tells Half-truths to Press

—Staff

Evidence that Maurizio Marconi, candidate for State Senate from District 2 in Bergen County, engaged in an extramarital affair earlier this year has been received by the *Bergen Evening Star*. An investigation by the *Star* followed Marconi's declaration last week that his wife Dottie was "the only woman in my life, and has been since the day we were married" (*Bergen Evening Star,* Sept. 29). Over the weekend, the *Star* interviewed the man with whom the Ridgewood shoe-store owner and political hopeful had the alleged affair. The man told the *Star* he was speaking out because of the hypocrisy of Marconi's statement, which made it appear that he had been faithful to his wife, when he had not been. The man provided the *Star* with convincing proofs of his story, which involved several encounters at the Marconi home last July when Dottie Marconi was visiting family in Connecticut.

Marconi's campaign has been one of controversy ever since the 46-year-old shoe-store owner declared his candidacy in June. Allegations of marijuana smoking and a long-time association with a Hindu faith healer made even local liberals keep their distance from the fiery son of an Italian immigrant. Marconi is a well-known supporter of gay rights and other liberal causes. According to political analysts, this could spell the end of Marconi's campaign.

Natalie exited VirNA, and went to the *Star*'s Who's Who. She typed in Marconi's name. After the inevitable delay, a list of articles was displayed on the screen. Beneath the list was his bio:

Born St. Patrick's Hospital, Brooklyn NY 18 April 1926; graduated Newark College 1948 with B.Sc. in sociology; married Dorothy Piedmont Gayle 1965; owner Achilles Shoes, Inc., Ridgewood, NJ; one son Richard b. 1967; Ridgewood town counsel 1966–1972; unsuccessful bid for NJ State Senate 1972; divorced 1973; declared bankruptcy 1974; unsuccessful suit against Mayor of NYC for damages after car crash left him blind in one eye 1975; second marriage Angela Belt 1979; died Dec. 23, 1992 from injuries resulting from a fall on an icy staircase.

—Click Here For Obit—

Natalie chewed her lip. What a depressing tale—a long slow fall from liberal activist to bankrupt to buffoon to pointless death. Maury, if ever there was one, was a capital-V victim. But who was the Villain of the piece? One obvious choice, she thought, was whoever had conducted the "*Star* investigation," and, presumably, written the article that had exposed Maury. But all the stories she had found on the subject were written by "Staff."

She went back to the VirNA main page, and spotted a link for *Star* staff. Sure enough, it was organized by year, and divided up among editors, printshop, artists, and writers. The writers were further subdivided by bureau. The list of writers in the Political Bureau in 1972 seemed unusually long—fourteen. She didn't recognize any of the names—except one: K. Tyler Hanson the Third.

♥　　　♥　　　♥

"Louise? Hi. I've been thinking about this Enigma business. Could you jot down as much as you remember from the earlier letters? No…I just want to be prepared—in case he writes again…."

Chapter Five

On Thursday, Natalie wrote a routine story about the amount of paperwork necessary to extradite a prisoner from New York State to New Jersey, a topic that had caught her attention during her Crime Bureau stint and appealed to her contempt of the prison system. She left after filing at noon, and spent the afternoon working at home, making regular trips to her front door to gaze across the street at the Haworth Elementary School to check for signs of smoke issuing from beneath the green roof of that red brick edifice. Much to her relief, none appeared.

♥   ♥   ♥

Early Friday morning she took a call from one of the assistant editors, who asked her if she would, as a personal favor to the short-staffed Political Bureau, lower herself to do a function piece for a political fundraiser Peter Kovaks was holding that night. The function piece was considered a distant and socially unacceptable cousin to newspaper journalism (as the spider monkey to the human being). Date, times, directions, and a quote or two from over-enthusiastic organizers about expected attendance figures were all that were required. Natalie, who (as the ingratiating assistant editor noted) was well past this sort of work, and who, furthermore, had always avoided stories with a political flavor, surprised herself (and the overjoyed editor) by accepting. She made only one snide remark about the *Star* giving free publicity to its favorite son, State Senate candidate Peter Kovaks, and then meekly took down the contact info the editor rattled off.

♥   ♥   ♥

"I'd like to thank you for coming all the way out here." The trim, middle-aged woman in the tight red peddle-pushers and the bright red lipstick smiled sympathetically. "Normally we would just send in a press release—but this all came together at the last minute and…well. We're used to being spoiled by the *Star*, I guess. Hi!" She thrust forward her hand. "I'm Linda Kovaks."

"Pleased to meet you." Natalie took her hand—she was a firm and speedy shaker. "Natalie Joday."

"I don't think we've met, have we, Natalie?" Linda wore her straight dark hair very short, with a few bangs pulled over her forehead. It was a young style for a woman in her fifties, but she did not look foolish. "Of course I don't get to the newsroom as much as I did in the old days, when I used to bring Peter his lunch."

"No, we haven't met."

They were in the Mahwah Town Hall, site of the impending rally. Around them, busy men and women were preparing for the event—young people setting up chairs and decorating the walls, carpenters putting up a temporary platform. Linda led Natalie to a card table littered with Styrofoam cups and surrounded by half a dozen chairs. "Are you new?"

"I've been with the *Star* about four years."

"Four years!" She pulled her lips back in an expression of guilt. "Now I really feel bad! Why didn't Paula send an intern?"

Natalie plastered on a reassuring smile. "I was happy to oblige. I've been thinking lately about getting some experience in the political arena." Well, since she had read about Maurizio Marconi's story, anyway. "I'll use this to get my feet wet—and add you to my contact list. I even thought I might get to meet the candidate." She looked around hopefully.

"That's the spirit!" Linda's green eyes sparkled. "Peter is traveling today, but next time I'll get you an interview with him. It's an exciting area to get into. Let me know if there's ever anything I can do to help."

They pulled a couple of chairs up to the table and sat. The noise from the carpenters was distracting, but Linda rattled off the details of the upcoming fundraiser like a machine-gun spits out bullets.

"...And you'd better mention that we're having door prizes—an autographed campaign poster, and one simply gorgeous signed photograph of me and Peter in a maple frame. After the speeches we'll have a mingle, where everybody can meet the candidates. It's the first of what we hope will be a series of such events, culminating in an extravaganza right before the election. Our local bakery is supporting us by supplying cookies with red, white, and blue stripes on them. Low-fat—can you work that in?"

"I'll try. But as you know it's up to Paula." Who, Natalie well knew, would rather die than mention the caloric content of cookies in a political function piece.

"We get so much support from the community." Linda glanced around the room, catching the eye of one of the chair-setter-uppers and nodding. "The band, for example. You'd better mention that it's a live band—a local group from Clifton called the Rumbles. Don't forget to say we're hoping to attract the young crowd."

"Got it."

"We'll wrap up at ten thirty sharp." She raised a hand to one of her blue-star earrings. "We try not to kill ourselves and our loyal volunteers with late hours. The campaign trail is known for being rocky and all uphill. We think we do a good job of keeping everybody cheerful—and getting enough sleep is half the battle. Now what questions do you want to ask, Natalie Joday?"

Natalie turned a page in her notebook and crossed her legs. "I think you've about covered it. Uh, will there be Q and A?"

Linda tipped her head back, displaying the clean lines of her neck and chin. "Not this time. But I'm hoping to line up a series of debates." She smiled disarmingly at Natalie. "Between you and me and the polling booth, the opposition is not too keen on the idea. They know how good a forum the debate is for Peter."

Natalie pictured Peter Kovaks' rangý frame. "I believe you."

"Five years ago, Peter confronted an eleven-member oversight panel on the brink of ending an investigation on advertising ethics at a certain company. He spoke for an hour on behalf of what appeared to be a losing cause, but because he knew his facts—it turned out that the ad exec was taking kickbacks—he eventually swayed everyone on that panel over to his side. That's the kind of man he is…the kind of State Senator he'll be."

"I wish you good luck in the campaign."

"Why thank you, Natalie." She sounded as touched as if Natalie's politeness had been a benediction. "I'm glad we've met. You have a real head on your shoulders. Let me know if you want to do a feature on the campaign, okay? I mean it. I can tell Paula…."

"Thanks. I might just do that." Natalie hesitated. "I, uh, stumbled across something recently that caught my attention—I'd like to write something about how hard it is for politicians to live up to the expectations of their constituents. About how imperfect candidates cope in a world that expects perfection."

Linda listened intently, then nodded. "Can I speak frankly? That's been done. What I'd like to see is a piece on how the political campaign affects the candidate's family. Because politics is a team sport, and requires a team effort. It's not only the candidates who are expected to be perfect, it's the family, too. That's your original angle."

"Behind every great man is a great woman?" Natalie smiled. "I think

41

that's been done, too."

"Certainly." Linda's carefully groomed expression of attentiveness never wavered. "But that's only a one-line platitude. What I'd like to see is some in-depth reporting on the changes that occur in the family—some planned, some not—because of the campaign. It's an opportunity for great growth, but it's a testing time, too."

"I believe you," said Natalie cordially. "And I'll think seriously about it." She got up, said her thanks, and left. She would file this baby in ten minutes, and head home.

♥   ♥   ♥

"Can you squeeze me in, Marcia?" Natalie balanced on one foot outside the glass doors the following Monday morning.

"Possibly…since it's you, girl. He's full of meetings, but they're scattered." Byron's secretary pulled out a daily planner and twiddled her pencil against its pages. "How much do you want?"

"Five…ten minutes?"

"If only some people I could name were so sensible…." Marcia closed the planner and pointed at her telephone. The button for line one was lit. "Wait till he gets off the phone and go in—he'll only be a minute."

Natalie sat next to Marcia's desk. This instant access pleased her. Since her first day at the *Star*, four years previously, she and Byron Shapiro, Assistant Managing Editor, had maintained what Natalie considered an ideal working relationship. Ninety percent of their communication consisted of marginalia on pieces she was writing. Short interoffice e-mails listing possible story ideas and instructions to cover such and such an event made up another nine percent. Once every couple of months would they discuss business face to face—as if their relationship were a well-cared-for car being brought in for a 5,000-mile check. In one way, they knew one another very well; each aware of the other's journalistic expectations and prejudices; trusting each other to do their job. But beyond the confines of their job descriptions, they knew each other not at all. Which, thought Natalie, suited her just fine.

♥   ♥   ♥

"Hello, Natalie!" Byron rose and reached out from behind his desk to shake hands. He was a man of average height and slender build, with straight sandy-colored hair that he wore in a side part. Wherever he had been on his vacation, it had not been in the sun. "I thought you'd be stopping by." He motioned her to the red leather chair that sat at the corner of his desk. "I thought I'd better touch base before I got back to the old routine." Natalie sat and opened her organizer.

"Well, good!" His midwestern accent, remnant of the days before he had left home to work on a big east-coast paper—and had ended up at the *Star*—suited his low-key approach and polite, slightly self-conscious manners. "What's on your plate?"

Natalie flipped through the organizer. "My guess is the Fair Lawn arson story is dead for the foreseeable future...there's still a detective assigned to the case, but you know what that means. We could milk it for another paragraph or two if you're short of filler, but I honestly don't see the point."

"I agree. The wrap-up you did last week is enough."

"Then there's this peculiar dollhouse story. Do you want me to keep on with that or hand my notes over to Ginny?"

"Oh, unh-hunh?" Byron shoved his glasses up the bridge of his nose. "Which do you think is best?"

"I don't think Ginny would thank me for giving it to her." She grinned cheerfully. "Plastic figurines hanging from trees are not her style. But I think there's something in it—in fact I think it'll happen again—so I'd just as soon stay on it. Also I'm lining up an interview with the family that experienced the first incident last May."

"All righty," said Byron. "What else?"

"Well that's it, actually."

Byron's eyes narrowed, though his mouth still smiled. "Aren't you doing leg work on the pizza demo scam for Tyler?"

"No. I was on the arson story, so he said he could handle it."

"Oh, unh hunh? I thought that mall story was right up your alley—some interesting characters...no? Well then, never mind. I could have sworn Tyler said he was going to use you on it, though...." He looked at her, still smiling. "So now what?"

Natalie scratched her chin. "I haven't run across much that has piqued my interest." Except the Enigma letters, she thought, but did not say. "I admit I haven't really started looking yet. I thought I'd see what you've got for me at your end, first."

"Well, let's see." Byron turned to his computer and pecked at the keyboard. Squinting at the screen, he worked the mouse with that hesitant motion peculiar to those lacking a native talent for the digital experience. "Hmm. There doesn't seem to be much going on that seems right for you."

Natalie resettled herself in the chair. "Oh."

He turned back to her, his smile intact below his squinting eyes. "Why don't you just carry on as you're doing. Take a look around and see what interests you. Keep me posted as usual." He picked up his fountain pen—his signal that the meeting had come to an end.

"Okay." Natalie put her hands on the arms of the chair, but did not rise. What was this? It felt like a brush off.... She had built her reputation on being a dependable workhorse. Wasn't that good enough any more? "I'll come up with something this afternoon."

"Take your time. You know how it is in summer."

Indeed. Last year she had survived by writing a series on the dying traditions of Summer Camp, acquiring an assortment of camp songs along the way which ought some day to be made into a collection. But never before in four years had Byron failed to gratefully hand over to her a mountain of half-completed stories and tedious but unavoidable assignments whenever he had the chance.

"What about the borough news?" That chore had always belonged to her....

"Our interns are working out well for once. They've got it covered." He turned back to his computer. "You've been around too long for that entry level stuff, don't you think? Why don't you just follow your instincts for a while. See where they lead you."

"And what if I end up on a wild-goose chase?"

"As long as it's a goose with a story to tell...." He thrust his chin toward his monitor and wrinkled his upper lip.

Natalie rose slowly. She felt strangely abandoned. She liked running on a loose rein, but she felt as if Byron had taken off saddle and bridle, booted her out of the corral, and closed the gate behind her—and she was too young to be set out to pasture!

♥   ♥   ♥

Back in the newsroom, she found an empty desk and sat in a solitary study of a murky hue. Had she done something to upset Byron? Or...was it possible there were problems at the *Star*? Not that that would have anything to do with her, but it might explain why Byron had been so lackadaisical. Or—she looked toward Tyler's glassed-in cubicle and frowned—had she become entangled in a Crime Bureau power play? What was that about the pizza demo story? Well, never mind. She had nothing to fear! She was not without resources. She knew how to do her job!

Revived by this thought, she switched on the computer and glanced around as she waited for the ancient machine to boot. The newsroom was never busier than at nine o'clock on a Monday morning. Less than six hours till deadline. "You judge a daily by its Monday edition," Myra Vandergelden had said at last year's general meeting. "The Monday *Star* must be a showcase." Six hours to brush away the weekend cobwebs, pick up the threads left hanging from Friday, incorporate last minute changes, write, get your editor to sign off, and file. No wonder people raced around as if it were fourth and long with no timeouts remaining.

In the early days, Natalie had been overwhelmed by the confusion and surprised by the lack of organization in the jumble of desks, computers, and chairs oriented every which way. She had wondered how anyone could work, given the noise and lack of privacy. But her perspective had changed. She had learned that the noise became a racket only in that final pre-deadline hour, when everyone's concentration was so highly focused anyway that no one noticed it. And she had come to have an affection for the mayhem, finding in it a refreshing lack of authoritarianism and a fitting backdrop for the interoffice battles that raged between amiable combatants: surreptitious battles over hard-earned desk, phone, and computer privileges; noisy battles over journalistic content and style; and unspoken battles over who got the more important—or more interesting—assignments.

Interesting assignments.... She had always gloried in her reputation for liking oddball stories. True, she sometimes took a secret amusement in them, but she always treated them seriously. Like Enigma—what a very odd thing, that such letters should be sent to an advice columnist.... She logged onto the Network, typed in her password, accessed her files, and opened her Ideas Folder. Throw her in the deep end to see if she would sink or swim, would he.... No worries.... She had begun collecting notes on possible stories when she was sixteen....

An hour later she was still looking at the monitor, but with far less confidence. Her resources had turned out to be for the most part yesterday's news, the files she remembered as killer ideas grown somehow tepid. What had happened? Had the stories changed, or had she? Oh, there were one or two nuggets she knew she could make something of—she had always wanted to do that piece on reptiles in the sewer system—but nothing that called to her, or challenged her half as much as, say...the Enigma letters, and the story of Maurizio Marconi.

What was that anyway, about having a job but no life?

♥   ♥   ♥

Natalie left early, and spent the rest of the day working at home. She made a few phone calls and put together a few outlines. It was uninspiring work, and she missed the atmosphere of the newsroom, so conducive to productivity. The highlight of the afternoon was Gayanne's arrival at 3:17, exhausted from the trials of the day and in desperate need of reassurance. Visions of alligator-infested sewers faded into the background.

Hoping the atmosphere would revive her spirits, Natalie returned to the newsroom at 9:30 the following morning. She selected a story from her ideas files about the railroad bridges in Bergen County. Bridges, which had both history and distinguishing characteristics, were always good for a little nostalgia writing. But alas, her words did not flow any better in the newsroom than they had in her living room.

She set the bridges story aside to air and turned on the computer. She would check the Police Ticker for fresh news on the dollhouse dilemma. The hard drive chugged, and, after a time lag suitable to a three-year-old computer relegated to communal chores following the acquisition of new and faster models the previous month, displayed the familiar bullet text of the ticker. Nothing untoward had been found hanging from the tree branches of Bergen County, but there was big news about a robbery in Upper Saddle River. A major electronics outlet had been hit in the early hours of the morning. The perpetrator had entered the building via an inaccessible rooftop air vent and walked off with enough computer parts to start a retail store. Estimates of losses were not yet available.

Natalie's fingers tapped the keys. That was a juicy one. She had hoped to get something like that during Ginny's absence. But the only real teaser had been the Bergen Mall pizza demo scam.... She wondered if Ginny and Tyler knew about this one. She glanced toward the front office. The two of them were in with Byron now—the usual Tuesday morning meeting of the Crime Bureau.

Her monitor froze, and she rebooted with a vicious swipe at the computer's on/off switch. She would have to send another note to Marcia about the uselessness of the computers....

Steeling herself, Natalie returned to the bridges piece. The tricky part was to get around the fact that the old wooden bridges she remembered from her youth had long since been replaced with less romantic steel structures. She rearranged her notes uneasily. Was that going to be a fatal flaw? Her attention wandered. Somebody had left a copy of the Bergen County phone book on the desk next to her. That reminded her...she had wanted to check and see if there were any Marconis still living in the area. She retrieved the phone book and flipped through it. There it was: M. & A. Marconi, 141 Hill Crest Road, Ridgewood. She wondered if Angela Belt Marconi knew about the old political scandal. She could take a run out there and poke around a little…see if anything turned up that gave her a lead on Enigma. The idea attracted her, but…. Shaking herself, she turned back to the bridges piece. What was she doing wasting her time over this pointless little puzzle? She had a job to do!

She had a couple of paragraphs roughed out when she looked up to see Ginny exiting the front office, moving with purpose.

Ginny veered toward her in response to her wave. "I've got about—" she raised an arm and looked at her watch, "three minutes to get to the Courthouse for the DA's press conference."

"What's up?"

"Robbery in Upper Saddle River last night. I got it."

"I was wondering if you'd heard about that. Congratulations."

"I thought the whole newsroom would hear Tyler's yowl." She grinned from ear to ear and trotted off without further ado.

Right on cue, Tyler appeared, also moving fast. His eyes scanned the newsroom, spotted her, and he headed in her direction.

"Natalie!" He rummaged in his pocket. "I'm in a rush. Got to find my photographer and get to Upper Saddle River for a piece on the crime scene."

"Oh yeah? Great."

"I need some help."

"Shoot."

"I've left my car in the underground car park. They never have change and I have no time today." He pulled a ten from his wallet. "Got two fives?"

"Sure…." Natalie stuck her hand in her pocket.

"Thanks!" He hurried away.

The newsroom was humming. Less than five hours to deadline. Rudy emerged from his den and started his rounds with the mail trolley. A trio of morose graphic artists emerged from the office of the Art Director and headed downstairs. The paper was chugging along as usual. She turned back to the railroad bridges.

It was a stupid piece. It wouldn't enlighten or inform, it would hardly even entertain. She was wasting her time—trying to make a silk purse out of a sow's ear while everybody else was out chasing down the hot stories on the front line of the journalistic battle.

"What the hell!" Byron had said to follow her instincts…. She threw her papers in her briefcase and headed out the door.

Chapter Six

Natalie pulled the Volvo away from the curb (only senior staffers could afford the car park) and headed north on Grand Avenue. It should have been a quick trip, but she had a hard time finding Hill Crest—a little side street tucked away in the northern extension of Ridgewood. Number 141 was a salmon-pink split-level with white ginger-bread trim. It sat on a sloping front lawn yellow with late summer dandelions. She parked the Volvo on the side of the road and climbed out.

It was hot in the mid-morning sun, and she pulled at her white linen slacks as she went up the inevitable colored slate walkway to the front stoop. There was no answer to her first ring. Or the second. She listened for telltale noises from within, but was distracted by sounds from the far side of the house.

Now, in a place such as Bergen County, where the houses are never more than a few hundred feet apart, and lawn and garden care is as much a prerequisite as high taxes, one learns to distinguish among the many yard-care sounds that fill the summer air. The sounds of electric shrub shears, hand clippers, weed-whackers, and lawn tractors are as distinctive to the indigenous population as the calls of birds to the ornothographer. Thus Natalie knew, without having to think about it, that on the other side of the salmon-pink house with the white gingerbread trim, someone was trying to start a gas-operated rotary lawn mower, pulling again and again at the starter cord with no hint of success.

Natalie cut across the grass to the driveway and followed it around back. There she beheld, in the middle of a sunny yard, a woman, dressed in cut-offs and a bikini top, standing with one sneaker on the ground and the other on an elderly push lawnmower. The woman pulled the starter cord for all she was worth. Thrrrrrrrrrrump…poop. She reached for the handle again.

"Hello…." Natalie raised a hand and craned her neck.

The woman straightened up and turned to Natalie with an open mouth. "Oh!" She pushed a few wisps of very blond hair out of her eyes, then checked to make sure her bikini was doing its job.

"I'm sorry to intrude." Natalie gripped her briefcase handle with both hands. "I rang the bell...then I heard you trying to start the mower."

"Darn thing stalled out on me and now it won't start." She kicked at one of the grass-encrusted wheels, lost her balance, and grabbed at the handle. "Shoot."

She was considerably older than the average bikini-wearer—and considerably heavier around the hips and waist. Her face, heavily made up around the eyes, was wrinkled and her chin sagged. But her legs, long, smooth, and golden brown, were Betty Grable.

"Maybe it's out of gas," suggested Natalie, wondering with a thin person's innocence how excess poundage could gather like that at one part of the body and leave another unscathed.

The woman shook her head. "I filled 'er up. And it started okay before."

Natalie looked at the crooked alley that ran through a jungle of ryegrass and dandelions from just opposite the garage to the woman's feet. She eyed the rest of the lawn. It did not appear to have been cut for a month. "Maybe it's flooded."

The woman's dark eyebrows came together. "They send you over from the garden center? What—they got a clairvoyant mechanic now?"

"Sorry." Natalie grinned sheepishly. "My name is Natalie Joday. I'm a reporter with the *Bergen Evening Star*."

"Oh yeah?" The woman put her hands on her hips and squinted. "Home and Garden section, right?"

"No, I—"

"Don't tell me! You're doin' a piece on unsightly yards!" She looked around in dismay. "I knew I'd have the zoning committee on my tail any day now.... Well I'm sorry!" The hands flew off her hips in a plaintive gesture. "I didn't know the grass would grow that fast! My husband was the gardener, and you should a seen how nice he kept it—all flowers, and the fig tree...." Her gaze fell on a weedy bed of perennials and grew sad. "Aw, he'd be so disappointed if he could see this place now."

"I bet you can start it." Natalie stepped off the driveway and approached. "It's probably just flooded—or the spark plug is old."

"Oh yeah?" The woman lifted her head. Her blue eyes searched Natalie's face with open calculation. "So what do I do about it?"

"Well, we can clean the spark plug—if you have a monkey wrench so we can get it off."

"Monkey wrench. Sounds like a wrestling hold. Is that somethin' that'd be in an old guy's workshop?"

"Yeah."

"Then we got one. Maury had everything." The woman turned and headed toward the garage. Natalie had to trot to keep up with those long legs. They passed a steep wooden staircase that ran alongside the wall of the garage up to the screened-in porch above.

Inside the garage there was a workbench beneath a pegboard. A dazzling array of house and garden tools met Natalie's gaze. "This'll do," she said, lifting an adjustable wrench from its hooks. "And we need a rag...."

"How 'bout this?" The woman pulled a square of red plaid from a bucket.

"Perfect."

"I bought him this shirt...." She sighed and fingered the threadbare material.

Back at the lawnmower, Natalie adjusted the wrench and removed the spark plug. She worked gingerly, not inclined to get any oil on those white linen pants.

"Will ya look at that," said the woman when the spark plug came out. "You're some smart, aren't ya."

"Unfortunately, you have now seen the extent of my knowledge about two-cycle engines." Natalie straightened up and took a step back from the mower. "If it doesn't work, we're putting it in the trunk of your car and taking it to the shop."

"Like I said—smart."

Natalie, drying the plug, smiled and shook her head.

The woman offered a hand. "I'm Angela Marconi."

Natalie nodded. "Pleased to meet you." She held up her hands. "Oily fingers."

"So you're a reporter. I always thought that was a ritzy job." She watched as Natalie scratched at the head of the plug with a fingernail. "Now I know."

Natalie grinned. "Now you know. This plug is too old. See the corrosion here? You need a new one. But maybe we can get this to work for today. I just need a knife, or some sandpaper."

Angela put a hand to her back pocket. "Will this do?"

"Why not?" Natalie applied the emery board to the spark plug.

Angela craned her neck to see. "Hey, it's nice and shiny on that little arm thingy, now."

"That's the idea. Now we have to adjust the gap. Well...I'll just have to guess...." Natalie pushed the spark plug against the top of the mower, then reseated it. "Give it a try."

Angela once again braced a foot against the chassis. She pulled the cord and the mower roared to life.

"Hallelujah!" Grinning happily, Angela set off across the yard, her long legs driving like pistons.

The engine chugged as she hit the tall grass. Natalie, hurrying in her wake, adjusted the throttle, and the engine changed key in appreciation.

"You gotta go slow," she bellowed above the sound of the engine. "Or give it more juice when the grass is thick." She lowered the throttle until the engine began to strain, then raised it again. "You can tell by the sound. Get it?"

Angela turned her blue eyes on Natalie. "Got it, Sparks."

Natalie returned the wrench and the rag to the garage, then stood in the shade of a red maple. Angela made a couple of passes around the yard, turned off the engine, and joined Natalie on the driveway.

"Okay, so you earned whatever it is you want from me." She dabbed with a tissue at the sweat that glistened on her freckled bosom. "But you gotta promise to make it start again before you go. If I don't get this lawn mowed today I just know my neighbor's gonna file a complaint."

"I promise, Mrs. Marconi."

"Call me Angela. Gee. I always wondered how you reporters get people to tell you things that are none a your business. Now I know. You want some iced tea?"

♥   ♥   ♥

It was the real thing—light amber in color, thirst-quenching, and neither too sweet nor too bitter. Natalie drank deeply, then leaned back in her chair and crossed her legs.

"So what's the story?" asked Angela.

"I'm working on a piece about political life in Bergen County. How political campaigns affect people's lives...the difficult changes they cause as well as the rewards."

"Aw, you caught me." Angela refilled Natalie's glass from a pink plastic pitcher. "I'm not even registered to vote."

They were on the porch above the garage, sitting on white wicker chairs at a round glass table. They had a nice view of the partially mown backyard—although that view was somewhat marred by the four pots of long-dead impatiens that hung from the ceiling. In fact, the porch was cluttered with boxes, brown paper bags, and flowerpots full of dirt and no flowers. Stacks of old newspapers surrounded them like the walls of a bunker.

Natalie clasped her knee (having washed her hands) and settled more comfortably in the chair. "I'm focusing on the candidates. What life in the public eye is like; how the family is affected. I was hoping you would be able to give some insights on the late Mr. Marconi's experiences."

"Why Maury?" Angela raised her shoulders. "He gave up that stuff twenty years ago."

"I know. But what happened to him—the way he left the race for State Senate—was unique in Bergen County politics. It must have had far-reaching effects on his life."

"Yah...." She reached for the gold cigarette case she had brought with her. "Some people would say it killed him."

Natalie looked up. "I understood he died as the result of a fall."

"That's right. I go out Christmas shoppin' and he guzzles down all the eggnog I made—four quarts—then goes out onto the porch to take a leak, and takes a header down the staircase, instead. All that frozen eggnog down his shirt...."

Natalie's confusion deepened. "But what does the campaign—?"

"I'm sayin', maybe if all that hadn't a happened back then, maybe he never would a become a drunk." Angela played with the clasp of the cigarette case. "Maury always enjoyed a glass of wine—hey, he was Italian—but after 1972 he became a full-fledged alchy. A real binger. I'm not saying it came on all at once, but that was the big factor, wasn't it? What with everything that happened and the campaign debts, and then his first wife left, he got hooked and went down the toilet. I thought he'd got it licked, but I guess I thought wrong, cause it killed him in the end."

Natalie watched Angela's fingers toy with the gold clasp; they were on the short side, plump, with magenta nails. "It's a tragic story. It's also exactly what I'm looking for in my feature. From what I understand, Mr. Marconi was a champion of liberal causes. He—" She stopped.

Angela was shaking her head. "Look, I gotta tell you, I don't like the idea of what happened back then being smeared all over the papers for a cheap thrill again. He's dead, yah, so he can't defend himself." She straightened her arms, raising her shoulders.

Natalie nodded. "I'm not looking to titillate, Angela. And I'll give you editorial control over what I say about Mr. Marconi and how I say it. If there's a characterization you don't like, we can change it—as long as the facts are presently fairly. Anyway, I don't want to discuss the details—

that's the point." Having jumped blind down this journalistic rabbit hole in pursuit of her instincts, Natalie was beginning to see its potential. "I want to discuss the aftereffects of what happens when the focus has been on the personal life, rather than on the politics. I want to show the effect of the time period; that what might have been socially unacceptable in one decade is acceptable in the next."

"Ya think so, do ya?" Angela opened the cigarette case. "How old are you, anyway—twenty-eight?"

"Twenty-nine."

"Then you won't know, would ya?"

"I know what I've read. It's pretty well documented that society is becoming more tolerant."

A smile curled around Angela's face. "You believe everything you read?"

"Not everything." Natalie smiled, too. "And I'm open to hearing evidence to the contrary. That's what happens when you research a story— sometimes your initial assumptions are proven false. It doesn't matter. My job is to record what I see and hear."

"Yah, but that doesn't mean people won't read it for the sexy parts and ignore your goody-two-shoes message." She fished in the case with a finger. "What d'ya have to say about that?"

"It's not clear-cut, I know. What do you think Mr. Marconi would have chosen to do?" It was a shot in the dark, but worth a try.

Angela's hands grew still, and she stared through the window at the half-mown lawn below. Then she shrugged and sighed. "Okay you got me. I'll talk. Maury was a pushover for anything that looked like a good cause— and he didn't give a hoot about his reputation. Which is I suppose why he got into politics."

Natalie concealed her exhilaration behind a look of polite interest. "Did you know him then?"

"Nunh unh." She pulled out a cigarette—it was narrow and brown— and raised her lighter. She grinned at Natalie's look of surprise. "It's clove. Never seen one of these?"

"Nope."

"Wanna try one?"

"No thanks."

"Why not? Aw! You modern girls. You may be smart but I'm not convinced you have as much fun as we did in my day." She lit the cigarette, squinting at Natalie's left hand. "You got a boyfriend?"

"Nobody in particular."

"Whew." Angela took a deep drag. "When I was your age, I'd rather a died than admit I didn't have a boyfriend. People on TV say it's different now. They make it sound like she's doing somethin' smart if a girl's on her own. And they say you gotta watch out for AIDS." She took another drag, and the cigarette crackled faintly. "Not that I'm one to be talkin'—sittin' here on my lonesome trying to keep this ol' house from going to the dogs. Hunh. I just realized this is the first time since I was fifteen I didn't have a boyfriend for nine whole months. I ought a start think' about that." She inhaled and looked out the window. "Either that or gettin' a job." She turned her blue eyes back on Natalie. "You think I could do reportage?" She rolled the R and batted her eyes.

"Why not, if you wanted to? You might have to take some college courses, first."

A grin spread over Angela's face and the tip of her tongue appeared. "You got all the cheery answers. Prob'ly if I said I wanted to be an astronaut you'd tell me to go to NASA space camp and give it a whirl. Anyway, I'm just pullin' your leg. I'm too old and lazy to start a career, let alone one where you gotta be able to use computers and all that. But what about you—you like your job?"

"Very much," said Natalie. "I've got security and a very flexible schedule."

"I always said the *Star* was a classy paper. But say, what's this rumor about its being bought out by the *Bugle*?"

Natalie's head snapped as if someone had clipped her on the jaw. "Where did you hear that?"

"Where? Uh, lemme think…. I take all the papers, y'know—mostly for the funnies but I read 'em, too—especially since Maury died. Must've been in the *Bugle* a couple a weeks ago."

"The *Bugle*? Then it's definitely not true. They'd say anything if it was the right length for a headline."

"That so? You ever write for them?"

"I'd rather eat crushed glass." Natalie opened her briefcase and pulled out a notebook. "And now I think we'd better get started."

"Okay." Angela's tongue was in her cheek as she tugged at the underside of her bikini.

"Here's my press ID, by the way." Natalie laid it on the table.

Angela picked it up. "Very photogenic…." She dragged at the cigarette. "You'd be a knockout with a touch of makeup."

Natalie scribbled a little at the top of a page. "Ya think?"

"Oh, yah. People with long noses like you gotta do something to get some width or you look kind a cross-eyed. If your eyebrows were a little longer…and something to accent the eyes."

"I'll keep that in mind." Natalie licked her lips self-consciously. "Now about Mr. Marconi…. Do you know what his original motivation for getting into politics was?"

"Sure. He wanted to burn his leaves in the street."

Natalie raised pen from paper. "Sorry?"

"Y'know, he wanted to have a leaf burning day in the fall, and have the fire brigade on call. The town selectmen were dead against it. Maury started a petition. Got twelve hundred signatures—or so he said. He had a tendency to exaggerate. Then he picketed the selectmen's meeting, and they came to terms and he got his leaves burned. People told him he ought a be a selectman himself, 'cause he could get things done. So at the last minute, he ran and won." Angela inhaled, waited, then exhaled. "The rest is history."

"I see. And when he ran for State Senate?"

"Don't know exactly, but…. I think he must a got a big head—he was real popular in his little corner of the community, y'see. He got a lot a town ordinances from the Stone Age canned, and he started to think it was his mission in life to get the world to wise up. Dottie was just as bad. Him and her were involved with all the civil rights causes. They were in Martin Luther King's march on Washington—can you believe that? I thought they only let you march if you were Black. And a course he was a big leader in the anti-war protests."

"Which war?"

Blue smoke spouted from Angela's nostrils. She flicked ashes into a pink-hued seashell. "Vietnam."

"Oh, of course." Natalie raised a hand to her hair and nudged it back from her forehead. She had found out her father was dealing in her sophomore year of high school, and had missed a lot. "Was his sense of civic duty genuine, or was it all swelled head?"

"I don't know. Don't they go hand in hand?"

"I'm not sure." Natalie put down her pen and took a sip of iced tea. "Isn't it common to say a person's motives are either genuine or warped by a desire for personal gain? One or the other?"

"Not in my experience." Angela took a final drag and leaned forward to put out the cigarette. "And honey, I've had some experiences. Off the record, I, uh, ran with a fast crowd in my youth. Some a the nicest people I ever met were very serious about personal gain. But they still always thought about others first. Take Maury. He was the kind a guy who'd hear somebody broke their leg, and he wouldn't just send flowers or a card, he'd buy a bunch a stuff from the deli, go over, and fix up a banquet. And he'd clean up the kitchen after. A course, by the time I met him, his head was pretty deflated. Not to mention soggy."

"So you think his motives for entering politics were good ones?"

"Yah, sure. I'm just also sayin' he thought he was hot stuff. See, he thought he was gonna be the first honest politician." A fly buzzed by and she swatted at it with her hand. "He thought he could talk about anything; break all the taboos."

"Why did he want to break them?"

"Because he thought they kept people from thinkin' about the real issues. So he talked about religion, and sex, and drugs—and made jokes to try and show people how unimportant they were. He wanted everybody to admit they weren't perfect—sort a get it out a their systems—so they could forgive other people for not being perfect, even though they were different. Then he figured he could talk about the real stuff like funding education, ending racism, and universal health care."

Natalie was impressed. "That sounds reasonable."

"Nah, it was dumb." Angela reached for the cigarette case. "He thought he could talk to the press about anything he wanted. Boy, if I'd a been there I'd a put the kibosh on that one."

"Why?"

"Because there was stuff he didn't want to talk about. He thought everybody would lose interest if politicians would just talk honest. But that's not what happened—it only made the press work harder to find out what juicy details they were missing. And they had the percentages on their side, 'cause honey, everybody's got something to hide."

"But if that's true, then nobody should run for office, because whatever they've done will be found out."

"You missed the point. He didn't get into trouble 'cause he let too much booze land him in bed with a guy. It was 'cause he lied about it. He just begged the reporters to go after him, the dumb shit, and they did." She fidgeted with the gold clasp again.

Having arrived at the point she had been angling for, Natalie reminded herself to keep it casual. "Do you know if it was any one particular reporter that went after him?"

Dottie shrugged. "Not that I ever heard. It annoys reporters when you lie to 'em, y'know."

"He didn't exactly lie…."

"Yah, he did."

"But it was a personal matter; none of the public's business…."

"Baloney! He wanted to have it both ways. He wanted to be able to say, 'Sex is a biological act and it's no big deal if you have a lot of partners—or want to have.' Then he wanted to say, 'But of course I don't do that.' The way I see it, he lied and he got caught, that's all. A course, the nature of the story didn't help…."

Natalie's eyebrows arched a little higher. "So it was true?"

"I wasn't there, but given the tailspin he went into after I'd say it was a sure bet. What, are you wonderin' why a guy who was swept off his feet by another guy had so many wives?"

"No. I was wondering if he was set up."

"By one a you high-minded newspaper reporters?" Angela shrugged. "I doubt it, although I admit I'm speculatin'. He didn't like to talk about the bad old days."

"It must have been a tough time."

"You ain't just whistling Dixie. He was in a hell of a financial mess from the campaign—they'd spent money they didn't have, because he was drawing such great crowds, and was gettin' so much press coverage. But after, the Party people dropped him like a hot potato, and he had a face a string a lawsuits. And it couldn't a been much better at home—he started drinkin' heavy then. Dottie took it for a year, then ditched him—took the kid and split. Then he lost the store. Within three years he was one wet mess. That was what attracted me to him. I was always a sucker for a hard luck story—and you gotta admit, his was a doozy. Yah." She pulled a cigarette out of the case. "I never met anybody so totally alone."

"It's amazing to me that he could be so generous to others, as you described, if he was always in such bad shape himself."

"Did I say always? He wasn't. He starting going to AA about when we met, and got his life back on track."

"Was it a hard transition?"

"What do you want? Details on how many times he puked his guts out on the TV room floor? How many times in fifteen years he fell off the wagon? That's personal, and I already told you I'm not into that." She put the cigarette between her lips.

"Yeah." Natalie nodded. "Sorry. I'd better stick to what happened right after the campaign fell apart."

"Ainh." She removed the cigarette from her mouth. "I don't know too much about that. The one you really should talk to is Dottie—Maury's first wife. By the time I met Maury he was through the worst of it, ready to crawl back up out a the sewer. But Dottie took it on the chin."

"I'll do that. Do you know where she is?"

"Yeah. We had to sort out the financials when Maury died. For the boy, mostly. Dottie had her own money. She's somewhere up around Poughkeepsie." She fluffed her pale blond hair. "I'll give you the address before you go."

"Thanks." Natalie studied her notebook. She had registered Angela's hint, and knew the interview must end soon. There was the mower to start, and it was getting on toward noon. "I wonder if there's anyone else I should talk to…anyone who thought Mr. Marconi had been victimized, or treated particularly unfairly…?"

"Beats me. It was all a long time ago."

Natalie closed her notebook. "I appreciate your talking to me. I hope Mr. Marconi would approve."

Angela placed the cigarette between her lips and fingered her lighter. "He'd think it was poetic justice. It was the press that ruined him, and now it's the press that's gonna tell everybody what a cryin' shame it all was. Well…. I guess that's hypocrisy for ya." She flicked the lighter and touched the flame to the end of the cigarette.

Chapter Seven

As an afterthought, Natalie concocted a proposal for a feature on the effects of the campaign trail on the private lives of the candidate and family. This was a prudent rear-guard action. She was required to keep a record (submitted monthly) of her work-related trips, to allow Management to monitor her productivity, and, more importantly, to claim recompense for her gas mileage. Besides, it was her duty to keep Byron posted and she intended to do so—short of revealing Louise's Enigma problem. She sent him the proposal Wednesday morning, noting with complete honesty that she had gotten the idea from Linda Kovaks. Byron duly gave his electronic approval for "Campaign Close-up: Life in the Political Limelight," adding that if she mentioned the Kovaks candidacy (thus demonstrating the *Star's* continued support for its old friend), she'd have to include his opponent, too (thus demonstrating the *Star's* commitment to fair and impartial election reporting).

She then went to carry out her hard-won interview with the Borgani family, who had awakened one morning the previous May to find three dozen pieces of dollhouse furniture and figurines hanging from the overgrown rhododendron in their front yard....

♥   ♥   ♥

Louise called in the afternoon to report that, for the first Wednesday in four months, there had been no Enigma letter.

"You knew just what to do," she said, her voice full of gratitude. "I can't thank you enough"

"No problem," said Natalie. "I just wish...." She stopped herself. No point in bothering Louise with the details.... "I wish you hadn't been put through all that."

♥   ♥   ♥

At home that evening preparing to shower and change, Natalie was in a thoughtful mood. The news that her letter had done the trick ought by rights to have inflated her ego and provided a fitting ending to the Enigma affair. For it had occurred to her to ask, if the story of the Victim was indeed the story of Maurizio Marconi, what possible effect could her offensive little letter have had on Enigma's anger? If she had been a betting person, she would not have put money on her success.

She turned on the shower. What she needed was to talk it all over with someone she could trust....

The phone rang.

"Joday!"

"Chau! Old partner. Just the person I wanted to talk to!"

"Me first. What's this about you doing half-assed political stories? Haven't you talked to Byron about the Crime Bureau yet?"

"Not yet...."

"I can raise the subject, if you're shy."

Natalie pulled a fresh towel from the closet. "Ginny...!"

"Then talk to him yourself! You earned it with your work on the Dow case, and I'm telling you, the only reason he hasn't suggested it himself is because he doesn't want to ruffle the scales of the dragon lady upstairs."

"Then he probably knows best."

"More likely he's waiting to see if the situation will resolve itself without having to take any action. Tch. I wish I knew how such a namby-pamby got to be Assistant Managing Editor. All right! I know you're a fan of Byron's, but I'm telling you he knows the Vandergelden witch hates to be reminded that her band of flying monkeys doesn't have what it takes anymore. Which, of course, includes K. Tyler Hanson. Now listen up...I heard management isn't hiring right now, so it's the perfect time for you to move over."

Natalie sat on the edge of the bathtub. "Is something going on with the paper? You're the third person I've heard dropping hints."

"I'm not union, so how would I know. Look, I'm just telling you, Myra Vandergelden is afraid she'll lose her stranglehold on the company if she makes too many changes. Getting her to hire new blood is like getting the Pope to hire women priests."

Natalie kicked off her shoes. "She hired you."

"Peter Kovaks hired me," corrected Ginny. "He's famous for making gambles pay off—he was the one who pushed the Polaski Group to acquire Bench Press—two days before the release of Shape Up or Flip Out, which is still on the *Times* Best Sellers list. He has a nose for success. And so do I. Well?"

"I'm sorry, Ginny, I'm just not sure. With all that's going on with my family right now, I think I should just keep my head down and go with the *status quo* for a while."

"Nonsense. You're wasting your talents on these stories about dollhouses and baseball bats. I mean it. Okay, okay, I can take a hint. Now, what did you want to ask me about?

Natalie fumbled for the top button of her blouse. "You've already answered me, thanks. I'll catch you in the newsroom."

♥   ♥   ♥

As the water hit her head and ran down her back, Natalie experienced a flash of insight: Ginny preferred cases with a clear moral attached. It was the excitement of being in the middle of the action that attracted her, of being in on the know, not the delight of pinning down an elusive fact or putting together the pieces of a puzzle. No point trying to engage Ginny's interest in Enigma.

She leaned back and let the water hit her forehead and run down her face. What she really needed was someone who would not think less of the puzzle because it appeared unimportant; someone who would take an intellectual approach; someone trained in the investigation of human aberration.

Later, she twisted the handle of the faucet and stepped out of the shower. A sheath of water coalesced into a drop at the rim of the shower nozzle, quivered, and fell into the tub with a splat.

♥   ♥   ♥

"Rebecca Elias speaking…."

"Hi, me. I promise not to keep you long…."

"I'm not going anywhere…. What's that noise?"

"Hair dryer—I'm on my way out the door…almost. But I have a problem. Remember Enigma?"

"Of course. Was there another letter?"

"Nope. That's the problem."

"Excuse me?"

"Louise got another letter last week that was even more suggestive than the one you saw. I've been looking into it, and think I'm on to something."

"Such as?"

"It's a long story. But the bottom line is: I want to find Enigma. And I need professional assistance to do it. So I'm looking to hire a consultant. Someone to whom I can tell everything while maintaining a veil of ignorance in public; someone who'll work in the background to help identify Enigma; someone who'll discover why he or she is sending letters riddled with riddles."

"And you thought of me? I am bursting with pride! But…we're not trying to find Enigma just to protect Louise, are we?"

"No. It's gone beyond Louise. She's off the hook now that the letters have stopped. But I'm coming to think that there's a story hidden behind all those riddles. We're motivated solely by intellectual curiosity—the thrill of the hunt, Chingachgook."

"Good enough reason for me. I'm in."

"I should warn you that the pay is minimal. Nil, in fact."

"For work undertaken in pursuit of such high-minded motives, what need of recompense?"

Natalie switched off the hair dryer. "And the hours may be long."

"Fortunately my free time is in abundance. In fact, I should pay you for providing me with a nice harmless occupation that will keep me off the streets and provide healthy exercise."

"It's a deal, then. I've got quite a file for you to review. Are you free tomorrow evening?"

"If it's Thursday I'm free. Why don't you come over for dinner? Oh, this is perfect. I've worked with the police a few times, and I feel they lack objectivity. I want to see how a reporter matches up…and I want to see if I can keep up with you."

"I thought you psychologist types knew better than to turn everything into a contest." Natalie fumbled with the phone as she pulled a sheer black blouse over her head.

"That's kindergarten psych. We're talking one professional to another, here, right? You're going to eat my dust!"

"That's the spirit! Hey. I gotta go—I'm now officially late, and this guy I'm meeting is the nervous type—thinks that if the paper says the movie starts at 7:40, it really starts at 7:40. Tch."

"Sounds like he's made for you. Someone special?"

"Oh, no." Natalie angled her face into the mirror. "But fun."

♥   ♥   ♥

Rebecca put the folder on the teak coffee table and ran a hand along her ponytail. The light from the standing lamp behind her cast deep shadows across her angular face.

"It is intriguing." She reached for her wineglass. "Only I don't have a clue why you think Enigma is connected to Marconi."

"Doesn't it fit?"

"Yes, it fits! Psychologically speaking, it fits like a glove. Victim; unfair exposure of private affairs; ruined life." She reached toward the bowl of popcorn. "But how did you know?"

"The reference to Achilles." Natalie sipped her wine.

Rebecca raised her eyebrows. "What reference to Achilles?"

"You didn't get that?" Natalie opened the folder. "In the first letter, Enigma says, 'even a boy from the sticks has his weak spots, no matter how hard a mother tries to prepare her son.' Achilles' mother dunked him in the River Styx to protect him from harm—but the magic water didn't touch him where she held him by the heel. Sticks…Styx; weak spot…heel. Get it?"

Rebecca put her wine down and took the letter from Natalie. "It's so obscure…. You went to see Mrs. Marconi based on this?"

"There's more. Look at the political language. Elect, official, campaign, candidate…. That fits, too. And when I found out that the Marconi scandal happened in 1972, I was certain I was on the right track." She handed Rebecca the second letter. "The answer to the riddle about the liar is 72. Get it? The number of lies doubles every day. If the liar told twice as many lies on day 73 as he did on day 72, then on day 72, he told half the number of lies as on day 73."

"Incredible." Rebecca held the letters up in front of her. "Okay. I'm convinced. Enigma is writing about Marconi. But I still have a problem. What were the odds against finding what you were looking for in the *Star* database?"

"Not bad." Natalie reached for popcorn. "It's clear as day the newspaper business in involved. What's black and white and red all over? A newspaper. Again, look at the language: clarion, times, observer, sentinel…. All names of newspapers. And what comes in the evening and disappears in the day? A star…the *Star*."

"You're saying…." Rebecca looked quickly back and forth between the letters. "Every word of these letters could be a potential clue to the mystery—not just the riddles!"

"Exactly. Which is the sort of thing you'd expect from someone who signs their letters 'Enigma.' You were right when you said Enigma wasn't seeking advice. So tell me, what *does* he want?"

"He…or she…wants the Villain to be punished. And the Villain would be…." She looked at Natalie. "The *Star*? No. Enigma can tell the difference between a singular and plural noun. The guy he had the affair with? Or the reporter who went after Marconi?"

"One or the other, I guess. Unfortunately, I don't know the guy's name, and the articles were written under a staff byline. Angela didn't know who wrote them. I've tried to call Dottie Marconi—Maury's first wife. She hasn't returned my calls. Myra Vandergelden would know, but I can't just walk into her office and ask. She'd pin me down in two seconds and I'd have to tell her about the letters, which I can't do because of Louise."

"Local political groups?"

"I tried every one I could find. Only one person remembered the story, and she had no idea who broke it."

"Other newspapers?"

Natalie shook her head. "All the other newspapers that were in print at the time have folded."

"Oh? Wasn't the *Bugle* around then?"

"I said newspapers, not muckraking scandal sheets."

"Yes, but this story is right up their alley. Shouldn't you ask—?"

"No! If I can't find out the answer to a simple question without resorting to the aid of that sleaze rag I'll turn in my press ID. Don't worry, I'll figure it out. Someone must remember…."

"Enigma is right. The world forgets…." She made a face at Natalie. "You've made a good start. What do I do to catch up?"

"Okay. I'll work on the Villain angle, and you take a look at the Enigma angle. Here's a copy of the notes Louise wrote about the lost letters. Go through them and see if anything strikes you. Louise didn't remember any of the early riddles—or much else. But something may jump out at you."

Rebecca nodded. "Okay."

"Any feeling yet if Enigma is male or female?"

"No. If you apply traditional stereotypes, the free flow of emotions and the desire to remain unknown point to a woman. But the complexity of the riddles and these very mechanical hints point to a man. But I wouldn't guess."

"I thought you psychologists could tell that in a snap."

"Sorry—some cases are obvious, but not this one. Look who's talking! I thought you writers could tell male or female in a snap!"

"Not this time. What about psychological characteristics?"

"We can say that he—meaning he or she—is highly intelligent."

Natalie munched her popcorn. "Agreed."

"But not highly educated."

"You're judging from the non-standard grammar?"

"Yes. Don't you agree?"

"No. Every writer knows that trying to mislead your readers about your education only works in one direction: if you're educated, you can fake uneducated, but not the other way around."

"Okay." Rebecca leaned back and hooked one leg over the knee of the other. "There is one thing. Enigma loved the Victim dearly...dearly enough to want to take on part of his persona now that he is dead."

"So we're talking husband, wife, or lover? That helps a lot!"

"I said 'loved,' not 'was in love with.' No one relationship holds a monopoly on deep love—just as the fact that two people have a sexual relationship is no guarantee of depth of feeling. Enigma could be a son trying to avenge his dead father, a mother breathing life into her dead child, a brother, sister, or even a life-long friend."

"I get you." Natalie fished in her popcorn bowl. "And I'm sure you're right. Whenever I've been nearest to going off the deep end and sending crossword puzzles to the sports editor, it hasn't been on account of someone I was sleeping with."

Rebecca smiled. "Ah, but you've never been in love...."

"I beg your pardon!" Natalie twisted in her chair. "I'll have you know as a freshman in college I was in love four times in one semester—and I have the rotten grades to prove it! And no doubt you've heard I made a fool of myself over that miserable lawyer...."

"Forgive me! I have overstepped the bounds of friendship!" Rebecca laid a hand against her breast. "Believe me, I was speaking not to contradict but to clarify. Please accept my apology."

"There's no need for that." Natalie settled back. "It's just—I'm more used to being told I should be in love less often—not more."

"I would never dream of telling you either of those things." Rebecca's voice verged on reproachful—and then changed. "Any more than you would tell me not to fall in love with an ex-con."

"Right...." Natalie looked up. Rebecca's almond-shaped eyes were hard to see in the shadows. "So...what exactly did you mean?"

"About Enigma?" Rebecca nibbled her popcorn. "Only that although it isn't any *more* likely that Enigma is a husband, wife, or lover, it isn't any *less* likely, either. About being in love? Only that emotions become more complex over time."

Natalie's eyebrows flicked. "Well, then you're right about me. I've never been much on complexity in relationships. Or time."

"At any rate, if the Victim is Marconi, then Enigma is probably one of a relatively small circle of people."

Natalie regarded her notes. "Wife, child, parent, lover, friend."

"Yes."

"Maury had two wives, at least one lover, and one son. All good candidates for Enigma. This is encouraging. Any one of these might think Maury was unjustly treated during the 1972 campaign."

"Natalie...." Rebecca was scanning the letters again. "Are you sure the injustice committed against the Victim refers to 1972?"

"Sure. Didn't we agree it fits?"

"Yes, but...now that my eyes are open.... Look at this." She pointed to the first letter. "'The Villain is getting away with murder.' Do you think...?"

Natalie shook her head. "That's just a figure of speech."

"So is 'boy from the sticks.' And look.... You've got all these words...dirge, grave...funeral...."

"Jeez.... You're right." Natalie skimmed the letters. "I missed that. But Marconi died in an accident. He went off the wagon, got sozzled, and fell."

"People can be drugged; people can be pushed."

"He had eggnog frozen on his shirtfront! The staircase was icy!"

"Even so...if it were me, I'd want to see the autopsy report. I'd want to see his blood alcohol level. I'd also want to make sure there weren't any barbiturates in his system."

"Jeez...." Natalie stared at Rebecca. "Do you really think...?"

"I don't 'think' anything." Rebecca reached for the bottle of wine. "But you said you wanted a professional consultation. If you were the police, that's what I'd tell you."

"Okay. Then we follow up." Natalie settled her notebook on her knee. "I don't have any contacts in the coroner's office. Tyler does, but I don't see how I can ask him."

"I can find out. I know one of the assistant MEs"

Natalie made a note. "Better say you're checking for a *Star* reporter, if they need an explanation. Jeez...do you really think...?"

"I told you, I don't know. Thinking's your job."

"It can't be true." Natalie tapped her pen on her open notebook. "What about all that campaign language? The 1972 scandal has to be involved. Besides, if it was as straightforward as a murder, Enigma would just go to the police. It can't be true."

Chapter Eight

Charlie's Diner had built its reputation on supplying good coffee, the latest editions of all the best papers in the Greater Metropolitan Area, and a suitably non-intrusive environment for the enjoyment of both. It was a real newspaper diner, where customers could buy both local and national papers off the rack and be left alone to read them. Charlie's catered to the *Star*, literally and figuratively. He supplied coffee and bagels to the resident staff and packed lunches for busy reporters on the go. He kept newspaper hours—early to rise and early to bed. Likewise, the first stop the *Star* delivery van made was at Charlie's: 3:05 every day. His standing order was fifty copies.

At seven AM on Friday morning, Natalie stepped through the glass doors of the diner and turned left at the newspaper racks. The smell of fresh-ground, mingling with the aroma of fresh-baked, was more all-pervasive at that hour than later in the day.

She reached the corner booth and observed her quarry for a moment without speaking.

He sat alone, a half-eaten breakfast special—two eggs, toast, hash browns, OJ, and coffee—before him. He was reading the *Times*, neatly folded so as not to interfere with his repast. A copy of the *Philadelphia Inquirer* lay at his elbow. He turned a page, showing no signs of having noticed her hovering.

"Morning, Tyler."

He looked up with a bit of a "Who dares to disturb my solitude?" expression, but spoke with cordiality. "Natalie Joday. You're early on the prowl.... Chasing a hot story?"

"No, just hot coffee. I saw you sitting here and thought I'd come bother you.... I've been thinking over what you said the other day about my career." She rested a hand on the back of the empty seat.

"By all means." He gestured for her to sit.

"Thanks." She righted the waiting coffee cup and looked around for a waitress. "I need some advice from someone who's got a little practical experience."

"Did you talk to Byron?"

"Yeah, but not about the Crime Bureau. In fact, he didn't talk about the future. I wondered if there's a problem at the paper."

Tyler put his elbows on the table and laced his fingers in front of his chin. "Byron gives you short shrift and you conclude that the paper has a problem? I see your ego is in good shape."

She lowered her voice. "I've been hearing a few things that've made me wonder, that's all."

"Like what?"

"Like an outside firm studied the circulation demographics, and like the results were not encouraging."

Tyler's dark eyebrows rose above his glasses. "You heard that?"

"Yeah. Someone else mentioned a freeze on hiring. And...did you know the *Bugle* ran a piece about a takeover of the *Star*?"

Tyler reached for his last piece of toast. "Please don't mention that birdcage liner. I have a delicate stomach." He took a bite and chewed. "I should think that you—a loyal *Star* reporter—would have better things to do with your time than read the *Bugle*."

"I don't read it!" cried Natalie. "I've never read it! I'd rather be boiled in oil than have anything to do with a tabloid. They are the antithesis of everything I believe in about journalism. I told you I'd heard some things...somebody else mentioned it, that's all...."

"Well good." He touched his napkin to his lips. "I would have thought less of you."

Natalie was annoyed with herself for rising to the bait like that. The waitress's arrival, with a steaming coffeepot, helped her regain her focus. She admitted to herself, as she ordered a cinnamon bagel, that she was not used to working at this early hour.

"I didn't say I'd heard anything definitive," she continued when the waitress had left. "I'm just telling you why it's got me thinking about the future. I've been reviewing my options."

"And?"

Natalie shrugged. "I've never thought much about career advancement. But like you said the other day, I can trot along and do whatever comes my way—or think about specializing. Maybe this is the right time." She sipped her coffee. "Or maybe it isn't."

Tyler smoothed his newspaper. "I've already told you I think you should advertise your desire to stay in the Crime Bureau. Do you need me to pump up your self-esteem with overblown praise?"

She smiled sweetly. "It's kind of you to offer, but no thanks. My ego's in good shape." That was better. The coffee helped. "Look. Here's my problem. Ginny is a friend of mine—she's the one who pushed for me to take over for her when she was out of town." She looked into Tyler's brown eyes. "You two fight like cat and dog from dawn to dusk. I'm not interested in taking sides—but if I'm forced to, well...."

He met her defiance with a curl of his lip. "If you're that sensitive, you have a lot to learn about career advancement."

"I don't doubt it." Natalie fingered her coffee cup. "But there are other reasons why the Crime Bureau isn't a good choice. I'm not sure I want to spend my life hanging around cops and courthouses. So I was thinking...investigative reporting doesn't have to be about crime, does it?"

"I can't wait to hear where this is leading...."

The waitress arrived with her bagel, piping hot, and a generous wedge of cream cheese. "As a matter of fact, I'm trying my hand at political writing."

"You're kidding." Tyler's eyebrows twisted in amusement. "Has Byron got you playing revolving bureaus? No wonder you're worried about your job."

"It was my idea and I'm not worried about my job."

"I'm relieved to hear it. But—are you under the misguided impression that in the Political Bureau you will be free from any risk of stepping on the toes of colleagues jostling for limited resources and elusive fame? Really, Natalie...I'm blushing for you. This is just too naive."

Natalie felt herself blushing, too. "I'm not...I told you, I've never thought about this before."

"Fair enough—and don't worry, your secrets are safe with me. You were right to want to discuss this." He folded his paper and put it to one side. "My dear Natalie, let me start by saying that compared to the Political Bureau, our little imbroglio in the Crime Bureau is a church picnic. Those people have a public bloodletting twice a month, and use new recruits as gophers and typists. You would be hamburger within minutes. Politics is an amoral field, and you can't cover it without being scarred for life."

Natalie shrugged. "I've heard that said about a dozen other fields by people who didn't know the ins and outs. My observation has been that you get out of something what you put into it. In other words, if you're already a jerk, you'll—"

"I got it the first time. Natalie, I'm not talking as a rank outsider. I started out at the *Star* in the Political Bureau."

"You did?" Natalie widened her eyes. "When?"

"Fresh out of college. 1970."

"Really?"

"Yes, really. Myra Vandergelden was kind enough to bring me in as a junior reporter for local politics—which meant reporting the minutes of town board meetings and covering the campaign for Fire Chief. But I had ambition! I once wrote a feature taking a position against a bill to fund a daycare center here in Hackensack. My editor tore it up in front of my eyes and assigned me to cover the NOW chapter meetings for punishment." Tyler grinned, and a pair of dimples popped out. "I was a cub reporter, all right."

"It sounds quite innocent." Natalie dabbed her finger at a bit of cinnamon. "What about the cut-throat tactics you promised?"

"They were there. The venom flowed so thick the bureau head changed three times in a year. I got the donkeywork—call up Congressman So-and-so and get a quote about the Ervin Committee hearings. That was the year of Watergate.... Everything around me was mayhem. Four reporters quit in a month and one was fired."

"Ethical problems?"

"That and more. It was understood that the politicians would say anything to get elected, but the reporters would say anything to get a story. Anything unpleasant was fair game—the juicier the better."

"I touch on that in the piece I'm writing: how to draw the line between a politician's job and his personal life."

"It's a trite question." Tyler picked up his knife and fork. "I'd think twice about using it, if I were you. Some people say there is no line, some say there is. There's no answer."

"I'm not necessarily looking for an answer. But I do think some of these issues are clearer from a distance."

"In the heat of the campaign, there is no perspective."

"That's my point. Maybe the public should get some. Maybe the press should, too." The waitress cruised by and topped off her cup. "Were you around during the Marconi candidacy in 1972? There's a case in point."

Tyler drew his eyebrows together. "I remember that one. Not pretty." He looked at her suspiciously. "How'd you hear about it?"

"I dug it up in VirNA the other day, researching my story. I was surprised to see that the *Star* broke the story. Did you cover his campaign? I hear he was something."

"I never saw him in action. I was out of the Bureau by then."

"Do you remember who worked the story?"

Tyler shook his head. "No idea."

"But it must have been the talk of the newsroom...."

"If so, I didn't pay any attention. That's the sort of political reporting that made me switch to nice clean crime."

"But can you blame the reporters? It's the editors who decide whether or not to run a piece."

"I'm not saying the Political Bureau is wrong to do what it does. News is news." He mopped up a bit of egg with the last of his toast. "I'm just saying it's not my cup of tea. And it's not yours, either."

"How can you be so sure?"

He smirked, and popped the toast into his mouth. "I know your type, Natalie—rigidly moral, superficially independent but secretly longing for acceptance, with basic if not brilliant writing skills...."

"Thanks...."

"And you believe in the fantasy that people are basically good...oh, don't be insulted! I believe it, too. I'm saying, the people who make it in political reporting don't believe it. They don't believe in anything; they lack heart. And they don't care what they have to do to get their story. Even if you don't crack under the strain of watching your colleagues demonizing the people they cover, you'll never be able to keep up if you don't use their tactics."

"You make it sound like the paper's ethical guidelines don't apply to the political gang."

He fussed with his napkin, cleaning the handle of his fork. "Welcome to the real world."

"I'm not convinced. Things are different now. Maybe what happened to the Marconis of that world wouldn't happen today."

"I wouldn't bet on it. Sex still sells papers."

"Sex? I thought it was his lie that made the story newsworthy."

"Maybe. Or maybe they used the lie as a warrant to search his private life from cellar to attic. Or maybe they knew about his private life and were waiting for him to lie. Do you think it matters?"

"Yes."

"Then stay out of the Political Bureau, where these moral dilemmas grow like mold on bread, and think again about the Crime Bureau, where you can tell the cops from the robbers."

"I get it." She drained her cup. "Okay. I'll think it over again."

"Good." He picked up the *Inquirer.*

Natalie stirred. "My cue to go. I'm glad I ran into you."

Tyler pinched his lips together. "You're quite welcome—but I think we both know you didn't exactly 'run into' me."

Natalie allowed a puzzled caste to color her expression. "What do you call it then, kismet?"

He reached for the cream pitcher. "No. You sought me out."

"I did?"

"Of course! You know very well that I come here at 7:45 every morning, five mornings a week. You, on the other hand, never come here this early. At least, I've never seen you, and since I'm always here, I'd say I'm in a position to judge. Yet here you are! It is obvious that you came to pump me for information on something."

Natalie's pulse raced. "It is?"

"Of course. I don't blame you. If I were you—young, inexperienced— I'd be wondering what was going on, too. You know I have a long-standing relationship with the top brass at the *Star.* Oh, I saw the look in your eye the other day in the newsroom! Naturally you concluded I knew something about the paper's long-term future."

"Looks like you got me." She smiled weakly.

"Unfortunately, I'm not about to break the trust these people are generous enough to have in me by talking out of turn." Tyler snapped open the *Inquirer.* "Don't take it personally."

"I won't." Natalie slid out of the booth and got to her feet.

"If you're going to try to get into the Crime Bureau, you're going to have to learn to be a little more subtle." He raised the paper and buried himself in its estimable depths.

Chapter Nine

Natalie spent the morning trying to identify the name of the *Star* reporter who had written the stories on Marconi by a process of elimination—who was working in the Political Bureau in October 1972, what they were working on, and what they did next. She devoted six pages of a notebook to the task.

She made no progress. No fewer than 21 writers had contributed to the political section that year—seven more than were on the official Political Bureau list—all of whom, except Tyler, had since left the paper. No one person appeared to have been assigned to the state elections—no doubt due to the turmoil Tyler had described. In the face of this evidence, Natalie had to consider that the articles may have been written by committee after all. Maybe nobody had wanted the job.

♥   ♥   ♥

In the afternoon, Tyler emerged from his cubicle, threw his jacket over his arm, and headed in her direction.

"Hard on the trail of suburban pathos?" he asked.

"The scent is so strong I'm salivating," she replied.

He opened his briefcase and pulled out a piece of paper. "Have you seen this? Some of your dollies were found up in Rockland County this morning...." He tossed the paper onto the desk. "Damaged."

Natalie snatched at the paper. "Hey, thanks."

He pulled a little case out of his inside jacket pocket, and took out a pair of sunglasses. "If you're working on a criminal case, it pays to check your sources every couple of hours." He put his regular glasses into the case, tucked it into his inside pocket, and headed for the double doors.

Natalie skimmed through the coding at the top of the page—proof, if she had needed it, that Tyler had pulled the material from the Police Ticker—and down to the story.

09:15 ALLENDALE/PDCR-BCPF/COOP_REPORT

Only the cops hadn't figured out that using all caps was a hindrance to comprehension. Not to mention the abbreviations....

• AT 08:02 ON 09/17/93 ROCKLAND PATROL OFFICERS DIS-
COVERED A CACHE OF DOLLS AND TOY FURNITURE IN
A ROADSIDE DITCH IN THE BOROUGH OF ORANGEBURG.
THE ITEMS WERE CONCEALED IN A BROWN PAPER GRO-
CERY BAG. SOME OF THE DOLLS HAD THEIR HEADS CUT
OFF AND A TOY CAR APPEARED TO HAVE BEEN BURNT.
THE ITEMS MAY BE RELATED TO THE RECENT APPEAR-
ANCE OF TOYS HANGING FROM THE TREES OF TWO
HOMES IN BERGEN COUNTY, NJ. POLICE ARE ASKING
ANYONE WHO WAS AT THE INTERSECTION OF RTE. 7 AND
THE NEW YORK THRUWAY (EXIT 1) AND WHO SAW ANY-
ONE ACTING IN A SUSPICIOUS MANNER TO GET IN
TOUCH WITH THEM AT 201-555-4987. REF 080793-27B.

Natalie read it through twice. She wondered if the toy furniture was of the same manufacture as the previous two incidents. Must be, since the police were interested. She pulled the desk phone closer and dialed the number of the Bergen County Courthouse.

She asked the switchboard operator to put her through to Lt. Veissman. After several minutes on hold, a female voice asked: "Who are you on hold for?"

"Lieutenant Veissman, please."

Another minute on hold, and a male voice came on the line and said, with palpable insincerity: "Sorry to keep you waiting.... Who was it you wanted to speak with?"

"Lieutenant Veissman, please."

"About what did you want to speak to him in reference?"

She loved that pretzel-shaped sentence—anything to avoid ending a sentence with the dreaded preposition. "The dollhouse case."

"Just one moment, Ma'am."

She could feel her blood pressure rising in counterpoise to her plummeting patience. There would be unappreciated plusses in doing an advice column.... She'd never have to talk to the cops again.

The clock in the upper right-hand corner of the monitor blinked cheerfully. One minute.... Authority—faceless authority, this time, but still that's what it was. Two minutes….

"May I help you?" came a fourth voice (male) in her ear.

"Lieutenant Veissman?"

"He isn't avail—"

"Great," said Natalie acidly. "Any possibility of letting me speak to someone who knows something about the dollhouse case? Y'know—today?"

"I know a little about the case." His tone was like a cool breeze on her hot temper.

But she was not interested in being soothed. "How much—"

"Ms. Joday?"

Her mind did a pirouette. "Sergeant," she heard herself saying. "I…didn't recognize your voice."

"Really. I was told recently that I'm starting to sound like any old policeman. I refused to believe it but…maybe it's true after all…. Happily I had no trouble recognizing your distinctive style."

Natalie leaned her elbows on the desk. "Sorry. I've been on hold for a decade. And I never could handle being…."

"…Being kept waiting. I know."

Silence.

"How are you?" he asked.

"Fine…."

"And your brother? I trust his daughter arrived safely?"

Natalie felt a stab of guilt. Had it been that long? She should at least have informed him of Gayanne's arrival…a cordial note, perhaps. After all, he had helped, in his own way, to make it possible. "Yes, they're both fine." She licked her lips. "So how are you?"

"The same."

"Unh-hunh."

More silence.

"I've seen your byline in the crime section lately."

"Just filling in for someone who's been on vacation." She spoke quickly, the better to drown out the memory of his voice saying, *Why aren't you doing investigative reporting?* "Nothing permanent. I'm back on my usual beat now. Except for this dollhouse story. So what are you doing working on that case? Don't tell me you've been demoted…."

"Not yet…. I'm not on the case, although I'm familiar with it. I heard about it at a staff meeting and thought it was…."

"Interesting…."

75

"Yes."

"...That there has to be something more to it."

"Yes."

"...Because it's a professional job...."

"But professionals don't play with dolls."

"Nor do they rip off their heads."

"You heard about that already?"

"Sure. Police Ticker is on the Internet."

"I see the *Star* keeps up with the times. Excuse me—"

The phone went dead in her ear for half a minute. Enough time for her heart to stop pounding.

He was back. "I've got to go—shall I tell Veissman you called?"

"Yes. Thanks."

"Is there...anything else I can do for you?"

Natalie tried not to bridle at his forced politeness. "Not a thing."

She hung up the phone and stared at it. That hadn't been so bad. As well as could be expected. It was a wonder she hadn't run into him before. Hearing his voice had unsettled her at first—she could admit that. But it had always been her style to remain on good terms with ex-boyfriends. Of course—he wasn't an ex-anything, having never reached boyfriend status. She drew a deep breath. In which case, maintaining a cordial professional relationship on those rare occasions when their paths crossed would be easy.

♥   ♥   ♥

Saturday morning found Natalie going through her weekend routine without the pleasure such simple tasks as checking her e-mail, making coffee, and feeding the cat usually afforded. In fact, her server was down, she had run out of her favorite coffee, and Trick would not eat his breakfast at all.

"Forget it," she told him as she carried her breakfast dishes to the sink. "You do not need to eat the most expensive cat food on the planet. Happy Cat is good enough for you. It's time things started shaping up around here. Look at me—do you see me complaining because I am not drinking Spiffio's best French blend?"

Trick sat in the middle of the floor and stared at her.

Natalie turned on the hot water tap. For once there was nothing pressing on her schedule. She would indulge in a nice lazy day: lounge around the house, wash the car, get lost in a book.... She'd do some thinking about the Enigma case…. What was that about taking twelve steps forward and three back? One of those math puzzles…she was no good at those…. But those others…she was sure she could solve them given enough time…. But what good would that do if she could not put a name to the Villain? How irritating that she, a newspaper reporter, could not find out who had written those stories! She had tried every trick she knew, exhausted every avenue of investigation. Well, almost every avenue….

"This is silly." She thrust her hands into her pockets and slouched against the counter. Trick sat and stared at her. Natalie scowled at his reproachful yellow eyes—what did he understand of her feeble excuses and petty prejudices?

"All right!" She threw up her hands. "I'll do it! But if anybody finds out about this…." Her eyes moved from left to right as she lowered her arms. "What I need…is a disguise…."

♥　　　♥　　　♥

From a box that lived on the shelf in her closet she pulled a pair of pink and yellow culottes—a Christmas gift from an old boyfriend she had obviously been justified in dumping. They needed ironing, but the moths had left them alone…assuming moths ate rayon. She tossed them onto the bed. From her dresser drawer she pulled a yellow cotton shirt. It was sleeveless and scoop-necked—quite nice really, but in combination with the culottes made quite a fashion statement. The shirt landed beside the culottes. In the back of her sock drawer she found a six-pack of socklets—the kind with little pompoms attacked to the heel to keep them from hiding in your sneakers. She pulled the pink pair out. As an afterthought, she went to the closet next to the bathroom and rummaged in a large cardboard box full of tennis balls and old sneakers. Near the bottom, she found a golf hat with the emblem of a local club emblazoned on the front in green and gold.

"Perfect," she told Trick, who had watched this exercise in self-mockery without comment. "If I can storm the gates of the enemy in this getup, surely you can swallow your pride and eat the Happy Cat." With which, she threw back her shoulders and set out to invade the unholy bastion of the *Bugle*.

♥　　　♥　　　♥

The drive to Hackensack was swift on a Saturday morning, and she had no trouble finding a parking place. It was a simple task before her; she wouldn't need to explain what she was looking for or why she wanted it.

Yet as she neared the fortress of the enemy, Natalie, despite having pinned her hair into unaccustomed 1920s flatness and concealed her ever-questioning eyes beneath a pair of Raybans, felt the creeping tendrils of self-doubt fasten themselves upon her determination. Surely the klatch of newsies lounging down the front steps of the office block that housed the *Bugle* would sense instinctively that she was a member of their own species (*Journalistica vulgarus* subspecies *Star*). She drew the golf cap down until it touched the top of the Raybans. And what if this rotund security guard with the pretty eyes went through her bag!? She should have left her press ID at home…. What if they caught her…would they lock her up and hold her for ransom until Byron came and vouchsafed for her incompetence?

But no one paid her the slightest attention as she entered the building—nor did they when she took a wrong turn and barely escaped being enrolled in a Komputers for Klutzes Klass at the adult learning center on the first floor. Eventually, with a beating heart, she found herself on the *Bugle* premises. Eventually, she located the clerk of the Reading Room—a young woman more interested in her book than in Natalie's motives for requesting access to back issues.

The *Bugle* did not have a VirNA, or a database—or even a computer. Back issues were stored on rolls of microfiche. Natalie asked for three sets of dates in the early 1970s. This, she thought, would remove the focus from the key dates, should anyone ever check the record to see what that woman in the pompom socks had been so interested in.

But the clerk was not interested in recording her choices. She pulled the three rolls of microfiche from the carol, handed them to Natalie, and sent her to unit seven, all without putting down her book. Natalie, after a bit of a wander, identified her machine by the large "7" scrawled in black felt pen on the side of the monitor. Cretins. Not much like the *Star*'s classy set-up. But then, who would want to delve into the history of this greasy stain on Bergen County's venerable journalistic escutcheon? Only gossip mongers and perverts….

She glanced to the left as she inserted the microfiche cartridge. No one in sight. She took off the Raybans. October was the first month on the film. She scrolled slowly forward. She glanced to the right. A spike-haired boy peered hard at No. 8, then ducked his head to make notes. Probably checking out those sleazy ads that featured mail-order sex toys….

She looked at her monitor. The words were blurred, and she had to fiddle a minute with the focus. She tried to adopt a casual attitude that would inspire a sense of normalcy in anyone who happened to pass by. She found the front page from October 6. Curious—she had expected to see the familiar blaring bugle logo, but all she saw was a sedate masthead with a little modest scrollwork. And on microfiche, the tabloid size seemed distorted.... She flipped through the pages.

There was no mention of Maury on October 6, when the *Star* had broken the story. Natalie moved to the next day, sure at least that his withdrawal from the race would be reported. Nothing on the front page.... She found it on page 7, next to a picture of a tired-looking Maury: one paragraph, no mention of boyfriend or witch hunt or scandal.

Natalie, unable to do a key-word search on the microfiche, scrutinized every inch of the 32 page paper—except for the sports section and the comics—but found no other references.

She moved on to October 8. On page 9 she found a picture of Maury's campaign manager at the press conference, and two half-page columns. She skimmed down the first column, slowing and backtracking as she neared the bottom:

...withdrawal from the race was.... Reliable sources inform the *Bugle* that Marconi's withdrawal from the race was engendered by the discovery of an extramarital affair by a reporter from our esteemed rival paper, *The Bergen Evening Star.* The reporter, Peter Kovaks, had been involved in a tense exchange at a press conference the previous week, during which Marconi accused Kovaks of harassment and yellow journalism. Other reporters present at the conference report that Marconi, known for his liberal views on social issues, felt that his fidelity to his wife of six years had been questioned....

"Crumbs...."

The viewer creaked as she cranked the microfiche backward. She had better read it from the top. Her eyes found the first paragraph, and then jiggled upward. The story was written by B. Shapiro.

Natalie blinked. "Double crumbs...."

♥   ♥   ♥

An hour later she exited the building untroubled by the fears that had kept her on tenterhooks during her entrance. Indeed, other, more reality-based concerns occupied her mind. But that fear of exposure returned with a jolt when she beheld a familiar face trudging up the stairs, headed right for her.

She swerved. But his eyes penetrated her disguise and met hers without surprise or difficulty.

"Hi, Ms. Joday!"

She managed what she hoped was a passable imitation of her usual cordiality. "Hi, Rudy." Of all the gossip-mongering, loose-lipped, tattle-tales...!

He looked behind her at the cutout of the gigantic bugle that perched above the door. A look of concern crossed his bony, unfinished face. "Say. You're not looking for a new job, are ya?"

♥   ♥   ♥

"So what are you going to do?"

Natalie, from her perch on the dining room table, sighed. "Retire from the field, defeated." She looked out the window—she had a good view of the mulberry tree that grew on the steep hillside to the east of her second-floor apartment. "I can't go snooping around the life of an ex-*Star* board member and nascent politician just because it amuses me. Besides, I found out what I wanted to know."

"I thought you wanted to identify Enigma?"

"I did identify Enigma." Trick floated up to the tabletop and sat at her side. "He or she is someone who loved Maurizio Marconi very dearly, and got upset when he or she heard that Kovaks was running for office, and decided to tell the world that he was a louse for what he did to Marconi twenty years ago, in the hope that it would cost Kovaks the race."

"That can't be right. Tell the world? He told Louise! And are we convinced that what Kovaks did was so wrong? I doubt he'd lose a single vote if the story came out. And what about those accusations of the hypocrisy...?"

"Okay, that's where I don't want to go. That's why I'm dropping it."

"But—"

"If I start checking around to see if Kovaks has been cheating on his wife, I'm doing the same thing he did to Marconi, for a much less valid reason."

"I see. Yes, of course."

Natalie stroked Trick's silky breast. "Did you contact the coroner's office?"

"Yes. My guy checked. The death certificate confirms that an autopsy was conducted, and no signs of foul play were found."

"So that's the end of the trail...."

A cardinal fluttered out of the blue sky and landed on the top branch of the mulberry tree. Natalie watched him as he sat and preened himself, and Trick watched, too.

"I guess so," said Rebecca. "I just wish we knew why Kovaks' byline wasn't on the article."

"Probably a way of supporting him—to say, 'we know this is a tough story, but the *Star* stands behind it, and our reporter.'"

"Or maybe to protect him from a lawsuit...."

"It's possible."

"But...don't you want to tell someone what you've discovered? Maybe it's important in a way you don't understand."

"It wouldn't matter. Trust me. I didn't 'discover' anything that everyone involved didn't know. It's just the passage of time that made finding it out a little difficult." The cardinal floated down to the bird feeder—a red-roofed pavilion set atop a long pole, fitted with various ingenious devises to outwit the squirrels. Trick's eyes turned black as his pupils expanded.

"I see what you mean. I guess Byron could have told you, if you'd asked...."

"I guess. That's a bizarre twist. I'll have to keep it under my hat. It would kill his reputation if people knew he wrote for the *Bugle!*" Natalie sighed. "This story turns out to be nothing but trouble."

"You stopped Enigma's letters! I think you've done good work."

"I think I was just pretending to investigate something because I felt at loose ends. I've got to buckle down and get to work. I can't waste my time like this, or risk getting management mad at me. Frankly, I can't afford it."

"Are you—? Sorry, I don't mean to pry."

"Broke? No. At least, I didn't think I was. I thought I made a good salary. But these days—with Gayanne here; with Daniel working so hard—I'm always wishing I had more money. I need a new computer, and there are so many things I want to do for them. Daniel lets me help some, and fortunately I know all the good thrift shops, but Jesus, it's hard."

"I know, believe me."

"I know you know. I know you'd do more if he'd let you, and it must kill you not to be able to."

"It's better if I stay out of it for now."

"Maybe.... Anyway, this is not the time for me to get fired—although I can't believe I'm saying that like it might be possible—and snooping around the private life of an ex-*Star* Board Member and favorite crony of Myra Vandergelden without a reason is a poor career move. So it looks like you're out of the consultancy business...." The cardinal fluttered to the near side of the feeder and Trick crouched down on all fours, trembling.

"And I was preparing such a nice profile on Enigma. I had one or two elegant theories...."

Natalie placed a restraining hand on Trick's tense shoulders. "Sorry I wasted your time."

"Don't you dare! I enjoyed it immensely. Hey, my next client is here. See you Sunday?"

"Or die," said Natalie. Trick sprang out from beneath her clutching hand, leaped to the windowsill, and the cardinal fluttered its wings and flew away.

Chapter Ten

Bereft of the Enigma mystery to amuse her, Natalie worked her way through the ensuing week as if wading knee deep in sand. Without the motivating force of her native curiosity, the work she had once been so grateful for seemed drudgery indeed. Byron, aloof and unhelpful, hacking her alligator story in half and abandoning it to the third page of Local News, and killed her railroad bridge story outright. She went to the newsroom every morning; she wanted to be seen; she wanted them to know she was working.

♥　　♥　　♥

Ginny's fingers flew across the keyboard. "For two cents I'd hack into the Server and delete all his files. That'd slow down that mealy-mouthed little viper. I could do it, too…."

Natalie craned her neck around the computer. "No wonder you get more done in less time than anyone else. How do you bitch about Tyler and type about unsolved crime at the same time?"

"It's just a knack." She kept her eyes on the monitor. "Like wiggling your ears or saying the alphabet backwards. Either you have it or you don't. Don't sweat it. It'll come to you—when you're in the Crime Bureau and Tyler is collecting his pension…."

Apparently the Tuesday morning Crime Bureau meeting had not gone well. "What's he done now?"

"Done? Done? Has he done anything? I don't think so…. Only rewritten my copy without putting in a single fact I didn't dig up, then adding his name to my byline—excuse me—putting his name first! So I'm out in the field and he's in the newsroom and he files without checking with me. It's my story! Tyler only horned in under the excuse of providing support. I told Byron if that's what support is he could…keep it. Boy oh boy I'm telling you I like to see my name on the front page as much as anybody, but I'd scorn to stoop so low as to put it there on somebody else's story!"

"Well, I don't know how low I'd stoop, since the best I've done is the lead in Local News, but I like to think I'd scorn, too."

"What I can't figure out is why the paper has put up with him all these years. If I were running things around here...."

"Joday!"

Natalie turned to the skinny little man standing in the door of the switchboard booth, next to the mailroom.

"Line eight!" he shouted.

"...I'd give you your own desk so you'd have an extension and people wouldn't yell your name at you every time you got a phone call...." The keypads clacked under her shiny red fingernails.

Natalie scowled as she looked for a phone. She spotted one, picked up the receiver, and punched line eight. "Natalie Joday...."

There was a dull silence on the line. She looked at the phone and realized there were no lights blinking—it was dead.

"Damn." She slammed the receiver down and glanced around again. There was a free desk clear on the other side of the newsroom.... She dodged around the movie critic and the political cartoonist, standing there blocking traffic....

"Joday!" shouted the switchboard man.

"Got it!" She reached across the desk and yanked the receiver out of its cradle. "Natalie Jo— Shit...." She punched line eight. "Natalie Joday...."

"Oh. So you do actually work there."

The voice was female. "Sorry...." Natalie eased herself into the chair. One of its wheels was frozen. "I couldn't find a free...." She yanked the chair forward. "Phone."

"I'd a thought a paper like the *Star* would a had enough phones to go around. Shows what I know. A course, I also thought you were being straight with me."

"I was being straight with you." Natalie did a quick check of her conscience. "Please tell me what the problem is?"

"The problem is I believed you when you said you were writing an article about how morality in politics had changed...."

Angela Marconi. "I am writing an article." It was true—she had produced about two hundred words before she had fizzled.

"Sure you are."

"I'll show you my proposal if you like."

"What's that prove? I thought you had gumption. Boy was I wrong...."

"I wish you'd tell me what's happened...."

"Like you don't know."

"I don't!"

"Go ask your cop friends."

"What cop friends? I don't have any cop friends—I hate the cops, ask anyone!" The movie critic looked at her, and Natalie lowered her voice. "Angela, what happened?"

"You came snooping into my life tryin' to dig up a juicy story, that's what happened." Her voice was bitter. "Maury was a good guy, and this just blackens his memory. It's criminal, that's what. I hope you got lawyers for friends as well as cops."

Natalie's throat tightened. "What are you talking about?"

"I'm talking about you making noises to the police about murder. What a load of hooey."

"I…." Natalie stared at the coffee stained blotter.

When Angela spoke again, the whine was gone, and only the cold and bitterness were left. "I knew it was you. What a dope I was to talk to you. I can't wait to read your story—I can see the headline: Disgraced Politician—Drunk's Fall or Sex Murder?"

"Angela, I would never do that. I—"

"I want you to know I'll go after anyone who tries to sensationalize my husband's life or his death. I'm denying any request to exhume the body. If you write any trash about my husband, I'll sue you and your sleazy paper. I'll fight you to my last breath."

There was a click in Natalie's ear. She winced, and sat still. So much for undercover reportage. The newsroom buzzed around her like a hive of bees. Ginny, still glued to her computer, had her phone tucked between ear and shoulder and was talking and typing a mile a minute. The door to Byron's office opened, and a couple of jocular sports writers burst out.

The movie critic's basso voice rose above the background noise. "Well, I heard the next step is layoffs. I think if I were a junior reporter I'd start to worry…."

♥   ♥   ♥

Wednesday afternoon found Natalie working on a piece about State funding for education. Paula had begged another favor, and Byron had given his approval. The governor, while horseback riding in Maplewood with a group of disabled school children, had held an impromptu press conference and announced the goal of having computers in every classroom by 1996. Paula signed off on the piece, but told her to get reaction quotes from the State Senate candidates and stick them in. It was her penance, Natalie reckoned, for ever pretending to have the slightest interest in politics.

She got a quote from the opposition candidate without difficulty (she was for the idea but thought 1996 was too soon). Peter Kovaks proved harder to track down. The clock ticked toward two as she alternated calls between his consulting firm and campaign headquarters. Another ten minutes and she would miss her deadline. Another twenty and she would be late getting home.

She tried the consulting firm again. "Natalie Joday calling for Mr. Kovaks again...." What she really wanted to say was, "If the *Star* is going to work Kovaks' name into every little story, the least he could do is to make himself available to say something original." The receptionist put her through to Kovaks' secretary, who put her on hold. The ever popular *Bolero*. Natalie's gaze wandered.

Louise popped through the double doors and turned left. Her face was set as if for a trip to the dentist.

The desk at which Natalie sat was awkwardly placed behind the staff bulletin board, but she could see the mailroom counter...if she craned her neck. So she had a good view of Rudy's face as he spotted Louise. He turned and disappeared into the storeroom.

"What is that child's problem?" Natalie muttered to herself.

Louise sidled up to the empty counter and waited.

Natalie, whose habit of noticing everything was congenital if not congenial, made it two and a half minutes before Rudy reappeared from the storeroom and acknowledged Louise's presence. He greeted her with a look of aloof innocence that made Natalie grind her teeth. Why did Louise subject herself to this trial? Better yet, why didn't she just smack him one?

"Natalie Joday?"

She brought the phone close to her mouth. "Yes!"

"Linda Kovaks, here. I've been hoping I'd hear from you! Are you ready to do that feature?"

"I wish I could, Mrs. Kovaks. But today I'm looking for a quote from the candidate about the governor's position on computers in the classroom. Any chance of speaking with him for a minute?"

"Unfortunately he's locked himself up at home, working on tonight's speech. But! I've got a couple of quotes we're preparing for a press release. I can give you one and strike it from the release, so you'll have an exclusive. Would that do?"

"Just fine," said Natalie. That was some exclusive....

Linda gave her the quote—he was for the computers, but thought 1996 was too late; it should be 1995. She thanked Linda, and hung up. "Whoopdeedoo...." She added the quote to the piece and filed it. No need to wait—she stood up and switched off the computer. This piece would be shoveled into whatever space needed to be filled on the political page. Of course, dutiful little soldier that she was, she would check from home to make sure they got it okay....

"Natalie?"

She looked up to find a pair of soft brown eyes peeking around the bulletin board. "Louise!"

"Could I talk to you?"

"I'm...." She looked at her watch. "I'm in a bit of a rush."

"I'm sorry." Louise took a step back. "I don't mean to interrupt your work."

"It's not that—I've got to get home. My niece comes over after school and...."

"Of course...." Louise lifted her head in humble supplication. "Perhaps I could come over? Just for half an hour or so?"

"Yeah, sure—why not?" Natalie closed her briefcase. "What's it about?"

With a guilty glance toward the mailroom, Louise reached into her book bag and pulled out a handful of letters.

♥   ♥   ♥

Natalie made it home with five minutes to spare, and parked Louise in the green chair. Trick wandered in and sat in the middle of the floor, staring at her.

She held the letters by the edges as she sat on the sofa. If Enigma had returned to trouble them, it was time to think of fingerprints. There were eight envelopes. The postmarks varied, as did the envelopes and the handwriting. Some had return addresses.... She furrowed her brow.

"Are these are from Enigma?"

"Oh, no!" Louise scooted forward in her chair. "They're from readers—wanting advice, you know."

The specter of Enigma faded, and Natalie grinned in relief. "That's great!" But her smile faded as she looked up at Louise's worried face. "Isn't it?"

Louise ducked her head. "It's good for the paper, I guess. But.... It's not because of anything I did. They're writing to you, Natalie."

Natalie's eye widened in horror. "Oh! No...." She gave a little laugh. "I don't think you can draw that conclusion...!"

87

"Two of them note that the column has improved. They like the new tough approach. You have a natural flare for advice writing."

Natalie put the letters on the coffee table. "I'm certain that's not true. I mean...I don't know what I mean, Louise, but I know I'm not any more...suited...to write this...this...kind of thing than you are. Look...." She pushed her panic away. "The only thing I have that you don't have is training. The truth is you've just got to learn to be more definite...more imaginative...not so...obvious."

"Imaginative?"

"Yeah...." Natalie clutched her hands together. "Look Louise, I don't want to be brutal but.... Your letters are...mundane."

Louise looked up with wide eyes. "They are?"

"Yeah. And also...trite."

"Trite? No one ever told me...." Louise looked at Natalie's peach tree carpet with an absorbed expression. "Mundane...."

There was a clatter on the outside staircase, and the screen door was flung upon with enough force to make its light frame smack back against the wall with a bang. Trick sprang up and disappeared.

Gayanne stumbled into the apartment as if booted from behind, caught herself with impossible agility, and then, as she spotted Louise, stood stock still. She was breathing hard, and there were tear streaks on her face.

"Hi," she said, apparently to the coat rack.

Natalie arose and muttered an apology to Louise, who, having turned to stone, did not hear.

"Bad day?" she asked as she relieved her niece of her knapsack.

Gayanne looked at the back of Louise's head. "Who's that?"

"A friend from work." Natalie led Gayanne to the dining room table. "I'll introduce you in a minute, but please save my nerves and tell me what is wrong, so we can fix it if it's broken or have a proper funeral if it's dead."

The round blue eyes were swimming with tears. Her face flushed, her chin and shoulders drooped. "Mr. DeLucca." Mr. DeLucca, as Natalie well knew, was the Art Teacher.

Natalie sat down. "Yes?"

Gayanne's eyes squeezed tight, and her chest began to heave. "He said I was gangly!"

"I'll kill him." Natalie opened her arms wide.

But Gayanne backed up a step, a look of defiance on her face. "You're a writer. Is it true? Am I...?"

Natalie contemplated her niece. "You know you are tall, and you know you are going through an awkward stage, but 'gangly' would not be a word I would choose, no. Besides, it's not nice to name call, and I'm going to fix Mr. Delucca's wagon but good."

Gayanne's expression grew wary. "You're not going to make an appointment, are you?"

"Certainly not. I'm going to put strychnine in his oatmeal. He'll die a lingering death, bitterly regretting his folly but knowing it is too late to atone." She opened her arms again.

"Good." This time Gayanne walked into Natalie's embrace. "Daddy goes in and talks to my teachers, and next day they give me this sympathetic look." She lifted her head to demonstrate the sympathetic look. "Then they treat me like I'm dyslexic or something." Her expression changed. "But don't tell Daddy I said that, okay?"

"I won't say a word. And, um, maybe you'd better not mention that I suggested poisoning Mr. DeLucca, okay?"

"Okay. Anyway, strychnine's too quick. It should be slow."

"Okay," said Natalie agreeably. "Let's dress up in black leather and beat him up."

"Yeah, that'll fix him, mean old...old sourpuss!"

"Bug eyes!"

"Knock knees!"

"Pin brain!"

"Dick head!"

"Gayanne!" Natalie lifted her niece onto her hip and returned to the living room.

"This is my niece, Gayanne. Gayanne, this is Ms. Hunt—"

"Louise...." Her brown eyes blinked rapidly. "Just Louise...."

"Okay, this is Louise." Natalie regarded her niece. "Gayanne is recovering from a run-in with an unsympathetic teacher."

"Just because I knocked over his coffee...."

Louise winced. "Was he very angry?"

"No.... He said he supposed I couldn't help it because I'm such a gangly creature. Coffee's bad for you, anyway."

"That does it!" Natalie dumped her niece onto the sofa, where she hid her giggles beneath the afghan.

The phone rang, and Gayanne bounced off the sofa, hands outstretched, like a jack-in-the-box. "It's for me! It's for me! It's for me!" The trailing afghan swept the magazines from the coffee table. She grabbed the receiver from the kitchen counter and stood still, every muscle tensed. "Hello?"

Then she relaxed, her wide smile lighting her little face. "Hi, Daddy!"

Louise turned to Natalie. "It must be hard for her. Adjusting to a new place, new people...."

Natalie retrieved the magazines and stacked them on the coffee table. "Yeah—but we're making progress. Last week it was 'crack baby.'" She threw the afghan onto the back of the sofa.

"You are very good with her. Very honest." She looked down at the notebook in her lap. "With me, too."

Natalie felt herself blushing. "Yeah, well.... Sorry about that...."

"Don't be!" Louise said earnestly. "I've always wanted to learn how to write properly. People often told me I wasn't very good...but they never told me why. But I see it now—it is boring...."

Natalie treated Louise to a calculating look. "You can fix that. You can add some variety as easy as a wink."

"I thought I was supposed to have a clear voice."

"That doesn't mean you always use the same tone, and say the same thing. You can be jokey occasionally, serious when it's called for, whimsical, matter-of-fact—as long as your own personality comes through. Be creative!"

"Creative...." Louise's eyelids fluttered. "My nephew told me to keep it predictable. To be a nice grandmotherly person and stick to traditional values. He told me not to be creative."

Natalie widened her eyes. "Well, excuse me, but he's wrong. Did Byron say that?"

"We never discussed it. I'm...not sure he was happy about my nephew getting me the job."

Natalie sipped her coffee. She didn't doubt that Louise was right. "Well, now's your chance to get some experience."

"Yes, it is, isn't it!" Louise looked into Natalie's eyes. "That was the whole point of doing the column, really—to gain experience. But it hasn't been like that at all—just struggling all alone. But now, thanks to you, I've got a chance to answer real letters—and I don't know how to do it! Oh, Natalie, could you help me?"

"Me? I don't know, Louise. What about Byron! He's your editor—it's his job."

"I know, but...how can I ask him? My nephew says staff cuts are a sure thing, and I know I'd be the first to go! You're the only one who knows my situation, and you've already proven you have a knack for advice writing."

"I...." Natalie felt her face flush, and she dropped her head. If word of this got out…. "Okay, I'll…see what I can do. But let's get one thing clear: you've got to do the writing. I'll give you some pointers, but you sink or swim on your own."

"Thank you so much." Louise's eyes were shining. "I'd love more than anything to learn how to write…."

Gayanne skipped over to the sofa and fell onto it, smacking Natalie's knee with the phone. "Daddy wants to talk to you."

"Okey-dokey. You're in charge of entertaining Louise." Natalie took the phone and went to the kitchen, rubbing her knee. "Hi."

"Hi. Are you coming for dinner?"

"I'd love to, but I've got to work. Are you okay? You sound stressed."

"I'm fine. Just a bad day. Our house manager fell off a chair and broke his leg and…never mind. Listen, if you're not coming over, wait in the driveway when you drop off Gayanne and I'll run down…. Now don't freak out—I'm all right, I'm telling you!"

"Okay, okay…. What?"

"You remember, we agreed I'd start making my monthly pay-back installments in September. It's already the 22nd."

"Oh, right." Natalie lowered her voice. "Listen, if you can't—"

"Nat, don't start! I can't take it today. I've already made out a check, and I assure you I'm budgeted to the last penny and we'll be fine as long as we all stay healthy. However, I'm willing to admit my entertainment budget is slim, so the least you can do is to let me have the pleasure of giving you something for once."

"Okay, okay." Natalie opened the refrigerator. "Wait…. Did you say check? Since when do you have a checking account?"

"Since today."

"My brother has a checking account. I think I'll frame it."

"You'll get better interest from the bank," said Daniel. "We may need it."

"Tch!" said Natalie reprovingly. "Really, Daniel, sometimes you have no sense of history!"

"That must be because I'm operating on the one-day-at-a-time principle of survival."

"Well it's getting to be about time you lightened up."

"This is as light as I get right now, thank you. Just…give me a little more time…. Speaking of which, is Gayanne okay? She sounded like she'd been crying."

"Oh…a little upset at school. Nothing official."

"What happened?" asked Daniel, bracing.

"Mr. DeLucca called her gangly."

"I'll kill him."

♥   ♥   ♥

Natalie went back to the living room carrying a tray with three glasses, a pitcher of cranapple juice, and a plate of cookies. At the corner of the room she stopped. Gayanne had unpacked her toy box and made a semi-circle of her various stuffed animals. In the middle of the semi-circle, Louise sat cross-legged on the floor, holding one of Gayanne's crayon drawings in her hand.

"And this is the much-feared dragon, Firestorm." Gayanne, one hand on Louise's knee, pointed to the drawing. "He lives in the clouds and sleeps all day. Those are the clouds. In the night, he creeps out and flies down to the Earth, looking for children who ask too many questions to eat for his supper...."

Chapter Eleven

The phone rang, invading Natalie's dream of flying. What time was it? Already 5:40, but still dark outside…the days were getting shorter. What day was it? Thursday…September 23. She slid off the bed and teetered to the kitchen. It was going to be Daniel, saying Gayanne was sick….

She picked up the phone on the fifth ring. "Hello?"

"Another dollhouse has ended up hanging from a tree. Just reported by the local patrol in Cresskill. Get a pencil. If you hurry you can get there before the County boys."

She switched on the light and fumbled for a notepad. "Tyler…?" Cresskill was a two minute drive away.

"Thirty-one Tulip Lane. Got it?"

"Yeah. Who—?"

The phone went dead in her ear.

♥   ♥   ♥

She rested her hands on the split-rail fence surrounding the yard of number 31. In the growing light, she could just make out the little figures, dangling from the bare branches of a dogwood. They looked like Christmas tree ornaments. She glanced around. There was a Cresskill patrol car in the driveway, and a patrol officer standing on the front walk, talking with a couple in bathrobes. Another man—tall, thin, and dressed in white— was hovering nervously behind the shoulder of the policeman, listening and glancing frequently at the tree. He spotted her, and alerted the policeman.

Natalie left the sidewalk and entered the yard. The name on the mailbox was Walker.

The officer blocked her way. "Can I help you, ma'am?"

She held up her ID. "Natalie Joday, *Bergen Evening Star*."

The man in the bathrobe gave her a startled look and raised a hand to his tousled hair. The woman merely frowned at her.

"I'm going to have to ask you to stay off the premises," said the officer. "We need to keep the scene intact."

"Yes, sir, I know. I've been reporting on this series of dollhouse appearances for the *Star*." She glanced at the tree. She was close enough now to make out a little boy in farm overalls suspended from the tree by a wire hook. He had no feet. Above him was a toy piano, with the keys all blacked out. "Strange happenings...."

"Hey!" The man in white wriggled around the policeman. "I read the story in the *Star*—that's how come I knew I'd better call the police when I saw the tree decked out like that."

"Okay...." The policeman stretched out his arms. "I'm going to have to insist that you stay out in the street, Ms. Joday."

"I was making my deliveries," continued the man in white. There was a picture of a cow on his shirt pocket. "I about jumped out a my skin when I saw those toys...."

"I want to hear all about it, but...." Natalie turned to the couple and pulled a disposable camera from her bag. "Is it okay if I take a picture of the tree, Mr. and Mrs. Walker?"

"No," said the policeman.

"It's okay with me," said Mr. Walker. He glanced at his wife. She nodded, saying, "As long as it's for the *Star*...."

Natalie smiled at the policeman, and saw him hesitate. She took a couple of quick shots, then retreated. The man in white went with her to the sidewalk.

She turned to him. "So people still get fresh milk delivered to their doors?" That was an anachronism if she had ever heard one. There might be a story there....

♥   ♥   ♥

It made a nice piece—two columns plus photo on the third page of Local News that evening—featuring the firsthand account of the milkman, as well as snippets from an interview the Walkers had given her. She got a nice follow-up on Friday—a re-hash of the key points plus the news that the police were stumped. Natalie tried to find some pattern in the different toys found in each tree, but got nowhere. The Walkers had neither children nor piano, nor any clue as to what it all meant. Natalie talked to Veissman, who was once again making the rounds of the toy stores with zero results. Over the weekend, she filed a "nothing new" paragraph and gave it up.

When she tried to thank Tyler, he brushed her off. He always listened to the police radio as he did his morning exercises—standard Crime Bureau strategy. That was the sort of thing she would have to do if she were to make it in this business....

♥　　♥　　♥

Louise found Natalie in the newsroom the following Monday, and gave her the first draft of her proposed column. Natalie buried it in the bottom of her briefcase lest anyone spot the brown envelope and guess what it was. She would work on it at home, she told herself. She needed to spend her newsroom time at the computer.

But that was easier said than done. Mondays, as mentioned, were always busy, but on this Monday the newsroom was like Grand Central Station. October was always a good news month—the sports writers had their baseball and football, the political writers their election, and the entertainment writers their fall releases. The best Natalie could do was a shared desk with no phone and a two year old computer with a keyboard into which someone appeared to have spilled glue. She reported the lack of available work stations to Marcia in a pained but non-accusatory note, and then sat down to slog away on a story about local paramedics she had been asked to write by a friend at the Demarest Rescue Squad. That finished, she turned her attention to a piece on the annual migration of tourists to New England to view the fall leaves. Byron had sent back her first attempt with the comment: "This is thin. Can't you spice it up with some practical tips?" What she needed was to hit up the travel editor for some solid ideas....

A sudden silence fell across the newsroom. Natalie looked up, aware that her colleagues were doing the same. The clacking of spike heels on the linoleum floor broke the silence. There was Myra Vandergelden, in a kelly-green suit, working her way around the newsroom toward the front office. Lance Wenger, looking positively leonine in a golden-brown suit, followed.

Myra paused at the glass doors and stared around the newsroom, a pouting frown on her tiny face. Natalie had a good opportunity to register her sour expression—in fact Myra was looking right at her. Then Marcia appeared and guided Myra and Lance into Byron's office.

The newsroom gave a collective sigh, and then began to buzz—not with the orchestral cacophony of the normal working day, but with the solo chatter of excited human voices. Natalie looked at the faces around her. There were anxious looks and ill-concealed glances everywhere. She realized she was not the only one who had been "wondering." In fact, if the expressions around her were any measure, she might be ill-informed by comparison.

"...Expected to announce who's getting the axe tomorrow...."

Natalie whirled around, but could not identify the speaker from amidst the group huddled around the coffee machine.

Leaving her things on her temporary desk to insure possession, she went to the cubicles at the west end of the newsroom. The travel editor, having missed the excitement of Myra's appearance by virtue of her translucent glass walls, was happy to talk travel tips with Natalie. She provided a map on which she marked several good routes for the motorist, as well as a list of bike and hiking trails. She was just beginning to expound on possible sides trips to water slides and panoramic ski lifts when her phone rang. She answered it, and then handed the receiver to Natalie.

"Natalie? Marcia. Byron would like to see you...."

Natalie's heart sank. "I'll be right there."

♥   ♥   ♥

"Sit down," said Byron.

Natalie, feeling as she imagined she would have felt if he had said, "Stick your head in the noose," sat. She had never thought of getting fired as something that would happen to her—disgraced, stigmatized as incompetent.... Peculiar feeling, fear. Humbling....

Byron folded his arms across his chest. "I got a call from...let's say, 'a friend of mine' at the DA's office...."

Odds blood, she was going to be thrown in jail. Being fired suddenly looked like a reprieve. Fear? Talk about being stigmatized!

"He wanted to talk about you—about your contacts with Angela Marconi, and your interest in Mrs. Marconi's late husband. He seemed to think—and justifiably so—that I, as your editor, would know what he was talking about." Byron's face fell into a look of pained disapproval. "It was an awkward conversation, Natalie."

Natalie mouthed a rubato "I'm sor—."

"Please! Not yet. I want us both to be clear on the scale of what's happened before you start apologizing."

Natalie lowered her head.

"Let me share the salient points with you." Byron, his arms crossed, leaned forward over his desk and consulted a pad of paper. "My friend is under the impression that I sent you out to interview Mrs. Marconi under the pretense of doing a story about the significance of changing attitudes about sexual morality as they pertain to our expectations of politicians, and that in the course of that interview you pumped Mrs. Marconi for details about her husband's life, downfall, and death. My friend then asks by what leap of the imagination we conclude that Marconi's death was not an accident, but murder, and gently asks why we are withholding evidence of a felony. He suggests that we behaved inappropriately when we approached—via an 'agent' he has yet to identify but who identified herself as working for the *Star*—the coroner's office with this conclusion instead of the police. He informs me that the coroner's office, apparently under the mistaken impression that the integrity of their work was being questioned, immediately requested an exhumation of Mr. Marconi's body—which, he adds with some distress, prompted Mrs. Marconi to file suit against the County yesterday morning for police harassment." Byron fingered his glasses and pulled them down his nose so that he could look at her above their horned rims. "Have I left anything out?"

Natalie shook her head.

"Have I got the facts right?"

Natalie cleared her throat. "Not exactly…. Some of it…the part about interviewing Mrs. Marconi, yes…."

"You didn't contact the coroner's office?"

"Well, my, uh, agent did. But only to see if an autopsy had been done. We were told that it had been, and we didn't question it."

"You didn't suggest to an assistant medical examiner that Marconi might have been drugged and pushed down the icy stairs?"

"That was, uh, the question. However, when we were assured that an autopsy had been done, we dropped it. We did not ever suggest an exhumation. Ever."

"You didn't…."

"No. I'm sor—."

"Not yet!" Byron smoothed his yellow hair over his forehead. "First tell me what you were doing interviewing someone about changing morality, when you told me you were writing about the difficulties of politicians and their families living in the limelight, and where this sudden interest in dead politicians came from."

"It's a longish story."

"Cut out the adjectives."

Natalie licked her lips. "Louise Hunt received a series of letters. They contained riddles. I wanted to know who wrote them, so I tried to solve them. This led me to Marconi. The letters indicated that he had been done an injustice. I thought they referred to the scandal twenty years ago, but it also seemed possible that they referred to his death. So I asked someone to check to see if an autopsy had been done. That's it."

"You have no evidence of any crime?"

"No."

Two lines appeared at the top of Byron's nose. "You went that far with nothing more concrete to go on than a bunch of riddles?"

Natalie closed her eyes and nodded.

"No one else in the office knew what you were doing?"

She shook her head. "It's my fault. I know it. I'll tell them you didn't know anything about it."

"Sorry, that won't help."

She opened her eyes. "Why not? It's the truth!"

He let his hands drop to the table with a sigh. "Because I assured my friend that everything you had done was with my full approval, and that you were a reporter of the highest integrity, and that if we had any evidence that a crime had been committed, we would certainly have handed it over to the police."

"You…you…you said that? You said 'we?'"

"Of course." Byron made a face at her. "What did you expect? Not that I'm not pissed as hell—excuse my French—because you didn't even give me a hint about what you were up to. I thought you knew better than that!"

"I do, but…." Natalie's head came up and her eyes flashed. "Damn it, Byron, you practically abandoned me after Ginny came back! You didn't give any direction. You told me to follow my instincts! You said you didn't care if I went on a wild goose chase!"

"I said you were too experienced for the kind of stories you had been doing before. It's time you started to think about your future. I thought you understood it was a sign of confidence to let you go out on your own!" He pursed his lips. "Really, Natalie, I don't need to know all the details, but I need to know the bottom line if I'm going to do my job. You held out on me!"

"You're right." Natalie hung her head. "I'm sorry. But I dropped the story a while ago, and I promise I won't touch it again."

"Unfortunately, that doesn't help. It's gone too far."

"I see." She lifted her head. Good old Byron; so inept when it came to any confrontation. Well, she would help him out. She owed him that for standing up for her. "Do you want my resignation?"

"What?" He put his hands flat on the table. "Of course not! Resign? And leave us in the lurch? Forget that! We need to go over these letters and riddles—and fast. And you need to tell me why you dropped the piece just when it was starting to cook. The police will be here at six, and we've got to get our stories straight."

"What? I don't—"

"Oh, unh hunh? Then button up and listen." Byron shoved his glasses up his nose. "Apparently no autopsy was ever conducted. The exhumation took place this morning. They found about a gallon of phenobarbital in Marconi's system—and practically no alcohol. Maurizio Marconi was murdered."

The look of contrition on Natalie's heart-shaped face was dissolved by this drop of hundred proof reality, and replaced by its native expression— one of insatiable curiosity, made luminous by the glow of a thousand unanswered questions seething in her head. "Oooh," she said.

Level II

Knowledge is proud that he has learn'd so much

Chapter Twelve

Doctor Elias speaking."

"Hi, me. Are you sitting down? The Bergen County Coroner conducted an autopsy on Maurizio Marconi this morning. He was packing enough phenobarb to drop a bull moose. Good call, Doc."

"Murdered...?"

"Yeah. The police are on their way over. We understand they are a little suspicious about how we knew."

"We?"

"I've been incorporated. I have also told Byron everything—Louise, Enigma, the Villain. Okay—not everything. We haven't had time to go into details, like my trip to the *Bugle*, or your name. I'm sitting in his office now—he's upstairs breaking it to Myra Vandergelden about Enigma pointing the finger at Kovaks."

"What do I do?"

"Two things. Dust off your Enigma profile. But first, can you break free this afternoon and take Gayanne? I'm stuck here, assuming I don't end up in jail, and Daniel—"

"Is in the City meeting with the lighting guy because the stage manager broke his leg and couldn't go. I'll be there."

"You can go to my house. The spare key is behind the weathervane. Ignore my cat if he bothers you; we're having a little battle about his diet...."

♥   ♥   ♥

When Byron reappeared, he brought with him Lance Wenger, who ignored Natalie and wandered over to the conference table on the far side of the room. There he sat, breathing with a faint wheeze, his broad forehead shining with perspiration, his eyes traveling aimlessly from the bookshelves to the ceiling.

"Ms. V is going to leave the police meeting to the three of us," said Byron. "The important thing is not to be bullied into telling them things that are none of their business."

Natalie raised an eyebrow. "I think I can manage that."

Byron sniffed, then rubbed his nose. "Yes. Myra's instructions are that we're to tell them everything we know that relates to solid information, but to draw the line at speculation. For example, we'll have to hand over the Enigma letters, and you'll have to answer their questions about your meeting with Angela Marconi. You'll also have to explain how you connected Enigma to Marconi, because if you don't they'll assume you're hiding something more tangible. Be nice. But...there's no need for you to share your further conclusions about...what it all means. Do you understand?"

"I understand why we don't want to talk about who the Villain is, but can we avoid it, legally? It is a fact that I stopped working on the story when I realized the letters were pointing at Peter Kovaks. Don't I have to tell them that? Particularly since they're going to find it out for themselves, eventually."

"That's exactly why we don't have to tell them—we're not holding back anything except our thought processes." Byron glanced at Lance, who nodded. "You, Natalie—and the *Star*—have a special role to play. You're part of an organization whose mandate it is to ride herd on the institutions of power in our society. It is our right to take an interest in these events, and to do so according to our own rigorous rules. The suppositions we make, the leads we chose to pursue, are our business. Our job."

"But...in this case...are we in a position to judge? The letters put the blame on the *Star* for what happened to Marconi—"

"So you have concluded." He sat at his desk, and gestured for her to sit, too. "The police are free to reach the same conclusion, and to investigate the worth of an anonymous letter writer's accusation. We will not hide those letters, or mislead the police by suggesting false alternatives. When we investigate these events, as it is our job to do, we will not hide what we find if we do not like it. Natalie...you're not dealing with the police on a personal basis anymore. You are not under suspicion of any crime—indeed, in the course of doing your job you've helped to uncover a crime. The police should thank you for that."

"But they won't," said Natalie.

"No." Byron glanced at his watch. "They won't. Just another reason to circle the wagons."

"Louise...."

"I'll talk to Louise…. Does she know you tried to identify Enigma after you wrote the letter for her?"

"No."

He pushed at his glasses. "Then the only tricky part is convincing the police that I knew about the letters and approved your visit to Mrs. Marconi without actually fibbing."

The door to the outer office opened and Marcia appeared. "They're here."

♥　　♥　　♥

Natalie followed Byron and Lance through the inner door and into the conference room. The two officers of the law rose.

Marcia stepped forward. "Lt. Camilla Perry, Sgt. Geoffrey Allan—Byron Shapiro."

"Lieutenant; Sergeant." Byron shook hands and continued the introductions. "This is Lance Wenger—Vice President in charge of Business Affairs, and the *Star*'s attorney." Lance was mopping his face with his handkerchief, and seemed startled to hear his name. "And this is Natalie Joday, one of our up-and-coming reporters…."

Natalie looked into Sgt. Allan's dark eyes. They were watchful, non-committal—like a policeman's. She inclined her head half an inch, then shifted her gaze to Lt. Perry's blue eyes. They were set in her face like cornflowers in a sunny meadow, sparkling with an inner delight.

They seated themselves around the table, and Lt. Perry spread her fingers across its shiny top. "Mr. Shapiro," she began in a voice as cheery as her face, "perhaps you will indulge our considerable curiosity by giving us your version of what the heck happened?"

♥　　♥　　♥

"Here are the original copies of the letters," said Byron half an hour later. "And a printout of our reply. And here are Ms. Hunt's notes about the letters she destroyed."

Lt. Perry took the folder Byron handed her and gave it to Sgt. Allan. "Who at the *Star* knows about the letters?"

"The three of us, Myra Vandergelden, and Louise Hunt."

"It's important to keep these letters confidential." Lt. Perry looked earnestly into Byron's pale face. "I'm asking you not to talk about them with anyone else, or publish them. For now. Agreed?"

Byron looked at Lance, who nodded sleepily. "Agreed."

The Lieutenant bobbed her head. "We appreciate your cooperation."

"No thanks necessary," said Byron. "The *Star* is committed to doing everything we can to help bring the killer to justice."

"We're delighted to hear that. Now…a few questions for Ms. Joday." She turned to Natalie. "You went straight to the Marconi story. That appears to me to be a remarkable thing." Her expression befitted someone eager to be educated. "How did you do that?"

"I looked at the letters from a different perspective," said Natalie, as nicely as possible. "It was hard to miss."

Lt. Perry rested her long forearms on the table and bobbed her head. "I don't follow you."

"The riddles made it clear that something strange was going on. Why were they there—in a letter to an advice columnist? So I ignored the obvious, and looked for another interpretation." Natalie could see that the Lieutenant was not with her. "For example—how much dirt is in a hole 6.5 feet deep and 2.25 feet wide?"

"I'm not good at math," said the Lieutenant.

"That's one way of looking at it, but—"

"None."

Lt. Perry looked at Sgt. Allan in astonishment, and then bobbed her head up and down more vigorously. "Aren't you clever. I get it!" She turned back to Natalie. "A different perspective. So…what exactly gave you this different perspective?"

Natalie kept her eyes on the Lieutenant. "That line about the boy from the sticks rang a bell…."

♥   ♥   ♥

"And so you went to talk to Mrs. Marconi…." Lt. Perry leaned her chin on her hands. "What were you hoping to discover?"

"Some clue to Enigma's identity."

"Why did you want to find Enigma? Didn't the letter you published in Ms. Hunt's column do the trick?"

Byron leaned into Lt. Perry's field of view. "She told you her curiosity had been aroused. Surely this is not surprising, given the nature of the letters, and Ms. Joday's obvious affinity for puzzles."

"I know, but there must have been something else going on." Lt. Perry's face retained its cheerful cast, but her voice revealed her doubt. "Why did she conduct the interview under false pretenses, telling Mrs. Marconi she was doing a political article?"

"There were no false pretenses," said Byron. "She was doing an article. It is not uncommon in our line of work for one story to grow out of another. I believe it is the same with law enforcement—the investigation of one crime often leads to the discovery of another."

Sgt. Allan's soft baritone floated over the table. "Since when has Ms. Joday covered the political beat?"

Byron pushed at his glasses. "Ms. Joday normally covers a wide range of topics. Recently, that range has included one or two political stories." He turned to Natalie. "Is that a fair characterization?"

"Yeah." Natalie looked at the Sergeant. He was wearing a dark brown suit and a dark red shirt. "I've done a couple of political function pieces in the last month—and I just finished one on the governor's call for computers in the classroom."

The Sergeant listened to her attentively. "What about the piece you told Mrs. Marconi you were working on?"

"It didn't pan out—not yet, anyway. I may use the material in another context." She laced her fingers together. "I still have my proposal and some copy, if you'd like to see them."

He nodded politely. "Yes, thank you."

"I'll print them out before you go…." She glanced at Byron. "Shall I?"

Byron nodded, then turned to Lt. Perry. "Anything else?"

The Lieutenant looked at her watch. "I think I've got the general picture." She turned to her partner. "Geoff?"

Sgt. Allan turned to Natalie again. "Did you discover the identity of Enigma?"

Natalie reflected a moment. "No."

"Why did you stop looking for Enigma?"

She shrugged. "Because I couldn't figure out who it was, and because the trail didn't lead to a story."

"So you just dropped it?"

"Yes."

"Like you dropped the story you told Mrs. Marconi about?"

"Yes." She met his eyes. "If a story idea doesn't work out pretty quickly, I move on. Call me fickle."

Sgt. Allan regarded his notebook. "What conclusions have you drawn about the Villain mentioned by Enigma?"

Lance stepped in more swiftly than Natalie would have thought possible. "I think we'd better leave the speculation out of it."

Lt. Perry looked up in surprise. "What's the big deal? It's a simple question."

"Whatever speculation Ms. Joday did occurred before she knew Mr. Marconi had been murdered, when she thought the events in question referred to Marconi's failed political race." Lance slumped back in his chair like a slowly melting vanilla ice-cream cone. "It would be prejudicial for her to speculate now about who she thought did what and why."

Sgt. Allan shook his head. "But that speculation is what led to the discovery of a murder. It must be relevant."

Byron gestured with his hand for Natalie to be silent. "We've explained that we didn't take the idea of murder seriously."

"Then why did Ms. Joday contact the coroner's office?"

"We've explained it was just to make sure an autopsy had been conducted," said Byron. "We noted the language in the letters about death— dirge, funeral, grave, etc., and, knowing how Enigma played games with language, we thought we'd better check it out. We were just being thorough. When we were told an autopsy had been done, we dropped it. If the coroner had not become concerned, we wouldn't be sitting here now."

"Can you tell us why your consultant specifically mentioned barbiturates to the assistant medical examiner?"

Byron smiled patiently. "Yes, but, is that really necessary?"

A ghostly smile flickered across the Sergeant's lips. "Once I start a line of questions I like to finish it. Call me single-minded."

105

Chapter Thirteen

I t was nine o'clock when Natalie arrived home and found a message from Rebecca: "Call me when you get in." After heating a cup of to-mato soup in the microwave, she did so.

"How did it go?" asked Rebecca.

"Not too bad." Natalie curled up on the sofa. "The cops were suspi-cious, but no where near as offensive as usual. We never came close to mentioning Peter Kovaks. It has a whole different feel when you're being questioned as a reporter." Where was Trick? Normally he would have joined her on the sofa for a cuddle.

"So what's the story with the autopsy?"

"Apparently your friend is nobody's fool. He checked the death certifi-cate, as he told you, which said that an autopsy had shown that Marconi had died from a head injury in the fall, and that he had been drinking exces-sively before his death. It also said the victim had symptoms of hepatic encephalopathy, whatever that is...." Natalie lifted her spoon to her lips.

"Enlarged brain caused by liver damage...."

"...Which probably led to stupor and loss of motor skills. The death certificate was signed by the Marconis' GP. But your guy thought it strange there was no blood alcohol or any other detail given. So he went looking for the autopsy report after he hung up with you. There wasn't one. It seems the doctor had used the term autopsy 'loosely,' and had done no more than a cursory examination. He gave the cause of death based on his knowledge of Marconi's history of encephalopathy, the four empty bottles of eggnog, and the fact that Marconi reeked of rum. Not very professional, but not unheard of. Your guy obviously respected you enough to keep your name out of it—in fact, he says he took it upon himself to request a proper au-topsy, not because you asked him to, but because, in the same situation, he would have recommended one, too."

"I don't mind coming forward, you know."

"Thanks, but not necessary now. Nobody seems very upset with me—since I helped uncover a murder. But who knows what tomorrow will bring."

"I bet the *Star* is hoping the case is cracked before Peter Kovaks' name gets dragged into it, right?"

"I'm sure that's a popular thought...."

"So where do we start?"

Natalie grinned into the phone. "I'm meeting with Byron first thing tomorrow. I'll find out if I'm on the story...."

"You will be. So why wait till tomorrow?"

"Okay." Natalie put down her soup and stretched out on the sofa. "Let's start with who killed Marconi, how, and why. Any suggestions?"

"Is this just between us or am I going to have to justify my opinions to the police some day?"

"If you're my consultant, it's just between us. Remind me to give you a dollar to make it official."

"Then...Angela Marconi is on my list. Maybe for insurance money, or for some personal reason. She didn't like the idea of an autopsy at all."

"And I was not convinced that she had any deep affection for Maury. She didn't hesitate to point out his many flaws. I got the impression that her attitude was 'any man is better than none.'"

"What about his first wife? Maybe she has been harboring a grudge."

"The police will question her, of course. Too bad she won't talk to me.... Okay, I'll be brave and put Peter Kovaks on the list, although I feel like I'm being disloyal."

"Steel yourself in the interests of objectivity."

"I'll try." Natalie yawned. "Fortunately, I think we're going to be hard pressed to come up with a motive for him."

"Maybe Marconi threatened to ruin his campaign. Tit for tat."

"Kovaks didn't announce that he was running for office until May. Maury was already dead."

"Good point. But.... Isn't May when Enigma's letters started showing up in Louise's mailbox?"

"Yeah.... That suggests a connection."

"Yeah." Rebecca clucked her tongue. "What if Enigma did the murder? What if this is all a convoluted plan to, um, throw the blame for the murder on someone else?"

"You forget that in a previous permutation, you convinced me that Enigma loved Maury dearly. You can't have it both ways."

"I was just checking to see if you were listening...." Rebecca cleared her throat. "Try this: What if Maury killed himself, for the purpose of bringing down Kovaks campaign? I'm suggesting this because so far the net

107

result looks likely to be just that."

"That's rather scary," said Natalie. "But I don't think we can rule it out. Okay, there's plenty here to get started on...."

"What do we do first?"

"Right now? Go to bed. At least...you go to bed. I promised Louise I'd do something for her."

"And tomorrow?"

"I want to talk to Peter Kovaks. We've got to know what really happened if we're going to stay ahead of the cops."

"It'll be interesting to compare their times with yours. As I recall, it took you one day to identify the Victim, and about two weeks to identify the Villain."

"I doubt if it will take them that long. The lead detectives on the case seem pretty smart. And by the way one of them has terrific clothes sense...."

"What diff— Oh Jeez. Your favorite homicide detective?"

"Right."

"Is that going to be a problem?"

"I don't see why it should be. We kept it very professional."

♥   ♥   ♥

Natalie curled up in bed with a glass of wine and Louise's folder. She had never done much editing since college, but she didn't think it would be too difficult. The important thing was to get it done, quickly and quietly.

Dear Louise,

I have always loved music and wanted to play the piano, but my parents said it was a waste of time as I could never make a living at it, so I never got those music lessons. When I married, I thought I would be able to get a piano at last, but my husband and I don't have a lot of money, and he can't understand why I want one, since I can't even read music. His suggestion is that I take up painting if I want to do something creative, and he even bought me a paintbox and easel for my birthday. But I feel dissatisfied. What should I do?

Mixed Media

Dear Mixed,

Why not start by picking up those paintbrushes and getting to work? You owe it to yourself to see if this brings you the same

sense of happiness you think the piano would have. This will help tide you over until you and your husband can afford that piano.
Louise

Natalie shook her head. If there was one aspect that characterized Louise's advice, it was that her correspondents were always expected to compromise, defer, and never confront. She wrote on the bottom of the page: "You are telling her to give up her dreams. This is depressing. She has every right to do exactly what she wants, and she must fight for it!"

Dear Louise,
My husband has always been my best friend, and I know there is no one in his life but me. But lately I've realized that he is not being honest with me about his work, or about how he spends his time. I've tried to talk to him, but we always end up fighting, and I don't want to upset the children. Money is getting tight, and I'm thinking of working full time again, although the kids are barely in school.
Hoping It's Just a Phase

Dear Hoping,
The important thing is the children. For their sakes you must try to talk with your husband calmly and find out what the problem is. It may be that he is feeling trapped in a low-paying job, or perhaps he is too embarrassed to admit he has a problem, and fears to lose face in your eyes. Consider a part-time job that will still allow you to care for your children. Keep a positive attitude and set a good example, perhaps he will come around in time.
Louise

Natalie's skin crawled. There it was again: Answer: bow down and repress, then wait for a miracle. It made her so angry, it really did! Why was she bothering with Louise at all, when it was clear that they didn't even speak the same language? "Phase Shmase! Stand up for yourself!" she scrawled on the side of the page. "Take those kids and get the hell out before it's too late!"

Dear Louise,
Recently I met a wonderful man, and was literally swept off

109

my feet by his charm and good looks. It all happened so fast, and was so exciting, that I never found out about him, although I am usually careful when it comes to men I date. Then, a friend told me he had been seriously involved with someone else when I met him. I confronted him immediately, and he told me I had changed his life, and that it was completely over with the other woman now, but how can I really know for sure?

Unwitting Other Woman

Natalie's eyes drifted away from the paper and toward the batik on the wall. But she did not see the yellow rangeland or the proud lions snoozing beneath the African sun. She saw a starry night, through which a warm breeze blew, and heard the strains of gypsy music. Moving slowly, as if not to waken a sleeping child, she turned the key to a tiny bejeweled memory casket in her mind, opened it, and looked inside.

"I can't decide," he had said as they stood in the park before the concert, "if it was in my office when you lectured me about police abuse of the public trust, or when we first met in the Courthouse hall at 2 AM, that I began to fall in love with you." Even in memory, she experienced the explosion of feeling, and saw every curve of his profile silhouetted against the dark blue sky. There had been only one possible reply, and she had backed him into the shadows beneath the trees and reached her lips up to his.

She closed the casket lid and waited, blinking, for reality to return. But the memories were out, surrounding her, transporting her to that night five months before when they had first met—not as policeman and sister of the accused—but as man and woman.

A group of children had streamed past them, hurrying to stake out the best spots on the lawn for their blankets and picnic baskets. They had pulled apart with self-conscious expressions. But he had held her close as they left the deep shadow of the trees.

"Geoff," she had whispered.

He had laughed. "I'm so relieved to hear you call me that. I was afraid you thought my first name was Sergeant."

She had made no attempt to phrase a reasonable reply. It was better to let him talk uninterrupted as they sauntered, arms entwined, toward the bandstand.

"I think about these things in the middle of the night. Who is this woman, I ask myself? Where on Earth did she come from? I realize this sounds rhetorical, since I did the background check on you myself, but it isn't. I found myself doubting the accuracy of my information—and you can understand how that disturbed me. Yes, I knew where you lived and what you did, and a great deal of your family history, but what was that? It could have described a thousand women I had met. But it didn't come close to describing you."

He had brought a blanket, wine, and glasses. He arranged them on the lawn, toward the back of the gathering crowd. The blanket was white. They lay down on their sides, facing each other.

He wasn't finished, but she could have listened all night. "Every time our paths crossed it was as if I had entered another world, a place where I could see more clearly, and where there was so much more to be seen than I had thought possible. And then…that day in my office…. You accused me of blind obedience to my files and reports when I should have been using my eyes and heart! It was as if you'd been reading my mind. Do you remember?"

"I remember."

"I'll never forget," he had whispered. "I've never been so confused in my life. And it's been that way ever since."

She reached out and touched his face, and he smiled—so happy—as he took her hand. It changed his face entirely, that broad smile, uninhibited, sharing.

"There's nothing to be confused about any more," she had said.

He had searched her eyes, in that way he had that made her pulse soar. "No," he had said. "I know what I want. But…I do have to tell you something about myself."

"You're not really a policeman!"

He grinned that silly grin again. "Sorry, I really am. Although for a while I wanted to be FBI, which would have been worse."

"True. All right, you can be a policeman. What else?"

"I was…involved with someone—quite involved, for a long time."

"How long?"

"We lived together for six years."

She had looked at him in astonishment. "Six years? Wow." She studied his face—there was no guilt there, only contemplation. "What happened?"

"About six months ago she told me she was having doubts. There was

111

no one else, she said, but she was restless, not sure she wasn't missing something. She wanted to leave.

"But I convinced her we had too much invested in each other to just give up without giving our future together a chance. She agreed to give it some time. We set some ground rules. She stayed at our place, and I moved back in with my Dad. We see each other sometimes—low key. I don't keep tabs on her. Is this upsetting you?"

"Not so far." It had amused her that he thought this would upset her. She would have to be careful how she talked about her old boyfriends.... "Look, I think I can help us cut to the chase. Here's my background check: are you married?"

"No."

"Are you living with anybody?"

"No."

"Are you exclusive with anybody?"

"As I explained...."

"Not good enough: yes or no—is there anyone with whom you have a commitment of fidelity, or who has such a commitment with you?"

He pulled in his lips. "No."

"Okay. You're in the clear. Your place or mine? Better make it mine, since you're living at your father's...."

"It's not that simple...."

She moved closer to him. "Oh really?"

Natalie pulled away from the memory with a shudder. It had been so intoxicating, the abandoned way he had talked about her, the intensity with which he had kissed her.... Oh well.... She turned back to Louise's letters.

Dear Unwitting Other Woman,
  It is the curse of our modern world that people think they must have everything immediately. If you had been as cautious as you claim you usually are, this situation would not have developed. Try to slow down, step back, and get to know a prospective boy-friend before you think about getting serious. Otherwise you may find yourself in a compromising situation.
  Louise

"Great!" Natalie nodded her head in a burlesque gesture of approval. "I always knew it was all my fault. Jeez, Louise!"

Dear Louise,

There's a boy at college that I just can't get out of my mind. We seem to have so much in common, not just in the things we like to do, but in the way we look at life. He is a very serious type, and not a flirt. The problem is, he doesn't know that I exist, except as a classmate in chem lab. All my other friends have boyfriends. How can I attract his attention?

Willing to Learn

Dear Willing,

It seems from your letter that you are still young, and have plenty of time ahead of you for romance. These days people are overly anxious with having a boyfriend as a status symbol. Love doesn't happen overnight, so you must be prepared to take your time while attracting his attention. You might try a new hair style or ask for his help with your homework. If he's interested, he'll let you know. In the meantime, why not just be friends?

Louise

Natalie tossed the folder onto the floor, turned out the light, and rolled over. "Tricks!" she called, but there was no response.

"Wait a minute," he had said, taking her hands in his to stop their roving. "Let me finish. My plan was to wait her out. I knew what I wanted; I knew she was worth waiting for. I was sure she would come back—that she'd take a look around and realize I was what she wanted, too. I was so sure…. And then you fell out of the sky…." He caressed the backs of her fingers with his thumbs. "And I don't recognize myself in the mirror. It's scary; this isn't me; this isn't what I'm about. I'm lying here next to you ready to abandon everything I've dreamed of and planned for, every commitment I made to Vivian and myself. It's not simple."

"Okay, I'll buy that. So you want some time to think about it?"

"No…."

His fingers had interwoven with hers, pulling their palms together, and her emotions rocked again.

"…But I have these doubts. I keep asking myself—what if I turn my back on a lifetime of happiness for a week or two of passion?"

She had felt a chill in her chest. "There's no answer to that question.

How can you ever know for sure?"

"If I knew you felt the same way I do, that'd be enough. I'm not asking for promises, but I need to know you're ready to think about a serious commitment. That this is that important to you, too."

The chill had spread. She no longer felt the heat of his hands. Unloosing her fingers from his, she raised herself on one elbow. "Isn't that…kind of fast?" She tried to joke about it. "We haven't even opened the wine."

"I don't think so. I haven't thought about much else for the past month."

"Yeah, I've thought about you, too. But…. We don't know really know each other very well…."

"I know how I feel. I'm asking you to tell me what you feel!"

She sat up. "I feel I'm…not ready to have this conversation. I'm not used to this game. You've been with somebody for six years. Six years! I've never had a boyfriend longer than six months!"

"Maybe you've never met anyone who was worth it."

"Or maybe it's not what I want." She heard the edge on her voice, but said nothing to take away its sting.

He rolled onto his back, staring at the sky.

She sat next to him, trying to think. This was all too fast, too intense. Somehow she had to convince him to ease back the throttle. "Look," she continued, without the edge, "I don't think we should be looking so far into the future. Hey! This is our first date! Let's enjoy the music, and the company, then we'll go to my place for that drink we never had. Okay?"

He had run his hands over his face. "No."

It was like a physical blow. "No?" She looked at him incredulously.

He had turned to her and raised himself on one elbow. "I guess I've made a mistake. I shouldn't have called—I should have just…. But I've been alone…. It's not your fault—I'm not even sure it's mine. Sorry. I don't know what to do…what to say."

The musicians had taken their places on the bandstand, and there was applause as the conductor appeared. Natalie had stared across the array of concert-goers, reclining on blankets and lawn chairs. Was there a way to salvage some dignity? "I believe the tried and true formula is, 'let's just be friends.' That shouldn't be too hard, since there's nothing between us…."

He had sat up, legs bent sideways, one hand on the blanket. "Nothing between us? Because we haven't slept together? You've ripped apart my life like it was made of paper!" His voice, thickened by emotion, was harsh and alien. "You think I can forget that? Sorry. Being 'just friends' is not what I had in mind."

So. He was one of those men in love with his own emotions, someone who only thought in terms of triumph and disaster because anything else was too complicated. He didn't give a damn about what she was feeling, and if she disagreed with him, he would try to overwhelm her with his anger. No wonder Vivian had dumped him.

She had forced herself to look at him, so that he would see her anger and remember it. "Let's see…you don't want to be lovers and you don't want to be friends." She had stood up. "I guess we're back were we started— Sergeant." Turning away had been the easy part; the farther away she got, the harder it became, especially when the band had started to play.

Natalie nestled her head against the pillows. The flood of memory, having run its course, faded from her consciousness, leaving her alone again in the night.

Chapter Fourteen

He's waiting for you," said Marcia in business-like tones. Marcia always knew exactly what was going on, what was important and what wasn't. Marcia didn't gossip or stare or make snide remarks. Marcia listened sympathetically when she complained about the slowness of the computers. Marcia was a gem.

"Thanks." Natalie tapped on Byron's door and let herself in.

He looked up, shoved at the bridge of his glasses, and smiled. "Do I smell Charlie's apple-cinnamon Danish in that bag?"

♥   ♥   ♥

"The important thing is not to make the same mistake twice." Byron pulled a china plate from a desk drawer and arranged the Danishes on it. "From now on you've got to work through the proper channels."

Natalie popped open the drinking spout of her coffee cup. "So I'm still on the story?"

"Of course." Holding a napkin under his chin, Byron aimed a Danish at his mouth. "This is the *Star*. We don't take a story one reporter has developed and give it to another." He took a bite.

"Which story are we talking about, by the way?" Natalie sipped her coffee. "Enigma or the murder?"

"We're going to treat it as one story with two angles. They've got to meet somewhere, presumably at Marconi. You'll work them both, with support from the Crime Bureau."

"Okay."

"But don't tell anyone—Tyler or Ginny—about the Enigma letters. We can't risk that getting out. It's our ace in the hole."

"Then how do I work with them? Won't they wonder...?"

Byron was shaking his head. "They're pros. They know there are times in this game when you can't divulge a source. They won't ask—you'll see—and it won't interfere. Besides, we promised the police." He took another bite.

Natalie gave a conspiratorial grin. "Yeah, but…."

"Did you think I didn't mean what I told them? I did. First Amendment rights are very serious. They are what will protect you—and me."

"Right," said Natalie.

"News is information—you know that." He wiped a bit of pastry from his chin. "It's our job to inform the public, but sometimes, especially when we don't know very much, we have to hold what we know close to the chest. It's tricky—trying to figure out who needs to know what, and how much to tell."

"But I tell you everything, right?"

"Everything that's relevant." He rubbed his fingers with a napkin. "However…. Just so you know…. On every story, there are levels of knowledge, Natalie, arranged in a pyramid. Everybody knows everything on their own level, and on the levels below them. But nobody knows what's on the levels above them. You've just moved up a level. Do you understand?"

Natalie looked at him warily. "Yes," she said slowly.

"Now…." He took a swig of coffee from his over-sized mug. "Let's talk a little about how we can pursue this story and still protect the *Star*'s interests. The Board met last night. We discussed the possible involvement of Peter Kovaks in the case."

"You told them about the letters?"

"No. We said only that information had been received that pointed the finger of suspicion at Kovaks, but that it was in the form of an unclear and anonymous rumor, and that we didn't buy into it. However, it is only a matter of time before the police connect Kovaks with the Villain, and we can't trust them to be as unimpressed by a nameless accusation as we are. This may come to nothing in terms of a murder charge, but it could destroy Kovaks' campaign. We need to be ready to fight. The *Star* owes him that."

"We have to tell the public that nothing has been heard except by an anonymous accuser…."

"Other people will take care of that. Your job is to investigate Marconi and Enigma. The Board directs me to tell you that while we appreciate why you stopped your initial investigation, we are now in this to the end, no matter what that end might be." He put the last of the Danish into his mouth. "The *Star* does not impede a murder investigation or shy away from the facts. Got it?"

"Yes, sir. I take it…no one…Mr. Kovaks…was able to shed any light on who might have committed the crime? Or why?"

"No. This is totally out of the blue. Kovaks says he hasn't seen or heard of Marconi for twenty years. Logically, I can't see how there could be any connection between the old scandal and Marconi's murder."

"And yet…isn't it quite a coincidence that both men were running for the same public office?"

"Yes. Maybe we're missing something in the letters. Something that explains why Enigma brought up the 1972 story, and how it relates to Marconi's murder. You've set yourself up as the expert on lateral thinking—work on it."

"Then I'd better get started. I'll want to meet with—"

"We'll talk more later." He glanced at his watch. "Myra said to send you upstairs at 8:30. Come back when she's done with you."

♥   ♥   ♥

The third floor of the *Star* Building was a sanctuary of quiet dignity. At the western end there was a chamber known as the solarium, which featured a row of bubble windows overlooking the main street thirty-five feet below, where general staff meetings and cocktail parties were held. Off the solarium, there was a small library, comprising all the standard reference books as well as a complete set of every issue of the *Star* ever printed. They were bound by month in portfolio-sized blue leather covers and suspended from an ingenious mechanism that allowed the user to swing each volume out and open it flat for easy browsing. On the south side of the building, above the newsroom, there was a network of spacious offices and meeting rooms.

Though she had been in Lance's office for the ritual signing of her first contract, Natalie had never darkened Myra's door. She entered the outer office and found herself in the presence of the CEO's private secretary, a tall, ash-blond woman renowned for her preference for padded shoulders and plaid. This person arose from her slim-line desk with a cool smile and escorted Natalie through the door of the inner sanctum.

There was a green and burgundy checkerboard carpet on the floor, with matching curtains on either side of four tall windows. A mahogany desk, of immense width but low to the ground, sat like a bulldog in front of one window, with two plush chairs, one green and one burgundy, on the near side. Four dieffenbachias with huge green-striped leaves gave the room a jungle atmosphere. The walls were covered with photographs and framed copies of spectacular *Star* headlines from the glory days.

But all this grandiosity was as nothing compared to the tiny figure in black sweats peddling madly on an exercise cycle, her skinny legs pumping up and down, her shoulders swaying back and forth, her thin cheeks puffing in and out, in and out.

"Five more minutes," she panted. "Park it."

Natalie went to the green chair and sat. She put her briefcase down and folded her hands.

Exactly five minutes later, Myra ceased peddling, groaned, and slid off of the bicycle seat. "Another day, another damned duty done." Grabbing a towel from the stack that sat on a shelf otherwise crowded with literary awards, she hobbled toward the big desk.

"So we meet at last, Ms. Natalie Joday." Her little eyes winked in and out of view as she wiped her face. "It's about damned time."

"The pleasure is mine," said Natalie meekly.

Myra wiped her neck and gave Natalie a look down the length of her beaky nose. "You're going to cause me and my newspaper all sorts of trouble with this murder investigation, aren't you?"

"I don't intend to…." Natalie stopped. She didn't like to play games without knowing the rules. "I'm not sure what you mean."

"No?" Myra went to the burgundy chair and planted her bony rear on its arm. "Aren't you the type who just has to know what's really going on? The type who never believes what she hears until she's checked it out herself?"

Natalie turned her words over carefully but could find nothing to disagree with. "That's why I went into reporting."

"Exactly. I know your type!" She laughed—a sound like a pack of turkeys fighting over a corncob. She spread the towel on her lap. "I know who you are. Oh, I don't mean the depressing family saga—your father in jail and your brother getting out by the skin of his teeth. I mean I know you! I've read your work—and nobody can hide behind their words from me. You don't follow the modern pattern—only interested in a story if it gets you something: fame, money, power. No, you think you can tell the difference between right and wrong. That makes you dangerous—did you know that?"

Natalie shook her head.

"No?" Myra removed her black headband. Her red hair stuck out in stiff wings. "In the Middle Ages people were burned at the stake for being ornery enough to \do their own thinking rather than believe what they were told to believe. You think I exaggerate? You think all those martyrs were lofty types leading saintly lives? No! They were people like you who were so determined to figure out how the fire got started they never noticed the house was burning down around them. Who the hell would want anybody like you working for them?" She looked at Natalie with faded shark eyes.

Natalie, who knew a rhetorical question when she heard one, remained silent.

Myra continued in a different tone. "But you're loyal, too—you had the guts to stick by your brother. And, more to the point, you've never done anything to blemish the *Star*'s reputation. So I'm going to trust you to keep that up. Hell, I don't have a choice! But I want to make one thing damned clear—you work for me, not for a corporate entity, not for Shapiro, not for the greater glory—for me, do you understand? And if you get around to figuring out what this is all about, you will tell me. Direct. Get me?"

"Yes, ma'am."

"Don't forget it." She slid off the arm of the chair and settled into the seat. She pulled her skinny legs up and sat cross-legged. "I've got to hand it to you—tagging Kovaks as the writer of the Marconi story. I thought we'd buried that so deep no one would ever know. Who told you?"

Natalie's heart seized up in a way that mention of being burned at the stake had not achieved. "No one."

"Don't disappoint me!" Myra looked at her sidelong with those shark eyes. "And don't start with the confidential sources bit."

"It's true! No one told me. I...I...." There was no way out. Myra had been there. Myra knew. "I checked the back issues at...another newspaper. They stated that Mr. Kovaks had broken the story."

Myra stared, then her chest began to heave. Her shoulders shook, and her turkey laugh cackled around the room.

♥   ♥   ♥

Marcia was not at her desk, so Natalie tapped on Byron's door and pushed.

Tyler and Ginny, seated at the round table at the far end of the office, turned their heads. The Tuesday morning meeting of the Crime Bureau.

"Oh, sorry." Natalie took a step back.

"Come in," said Byron. "We've been waiting for you."

Natalie entered and looked around. Byron left his desk and went to join Ginny and Tyler. Natalie sidled over to the table and sat.

"Marcia will be here in a moment with our agenda," said Byron.

"Oh, come on," chirped Ginny. "Put us out of our misery. The entire newsroom is buzzing about the Marconi murder. I'm dying for the details! Even Tyler left Charlie's ten minutes early to make sure he didn't miss anything."

Tyler smirked in Ginny's direction, but did not contradict her.

"Far be it from me to leave the Crime Bureau in suspense." Byron settled into his chair and poked at his glasses. "Some weeks ago we received information of a peculiar nature which seemed to revolve around an old political scandal...."

♥   ♥   ♥

"Natalie will be working this story full time. She'll report to me, and I'll make sure she has whatever resources she needs. But she'll need support. Where are you two this week?" He turned to Tyler. "How's the mall story?"

"About dry. The investigators hired by mall management have locked the press out but good. I have a couple of points to follow up. But I don't expect them to lead anywhere. We're at the wind-down stage, I'm afraid. I've got plenty of time for Marconi."

Byron referred to his agenda. "The Westwood burglary?"

"They caught the guy last night. I've already filed an update. In your in-box."

"Who was it, the neighbor's kid?"

Tyler gave the thumbs up. "You got it."

"What about that neighborhood reaction piece we discussed?"

"I think that should wait a day or two until the kid is arraigned."

Byron made a note. "And what has Ms. Chau been up to?" He looked up and smiled.

Ginny glanced at the silver-edged notebook resting on her knee. "Things are hopping with the Upper Saddle River robbery. Three witnesses are saying they saw a black van in the area on the night of the robbery, and one says it had Vermont plates. There is a feeling that an ex-employee may be involved. But I've got time—"

Tyler cut her off. "The Bergenfield arson trial starts tomorrow. That was your story, remember." He pointed a finger. "You didn't want me anywhere near it."

Ginny slung an arm over the back of her chair and sent him a withering look. "A stringer can cover that. It doesn't have to be—"

"And the DA is giving an update on the robbery at 11:00 AM." Tyler looked at his watch. "You're supposed to be there."

"Look." Ginny ignored Tyler and faced Byron. "Joday and I have worked together before. We make a good team. Why can't—"

"And aren't you speaking at that Girl Scout job fair about investigative journalism for women?"

Ginny's snapping eyes turned to Tyler. "Is there some reason you won't let me finish a sentence?"

"Whoa there. I get the message." Byron smiled and poked at his glasses. "You both want to be involved. Can't say I blame you."

"Maybe you can't," snapped Ginny, "but apparently someone's trying to."

"Listen, Ginny, I'm the Bureau Head." Tyler rested his elbows on the arms of his chair and crossed his fingers over his stomach. "It's my job to monitor what you're doing. And if you're going to minimize your work load, I'm going to—"

"Okay, okay." Byron pushed at the air with his hands. "Looks like I have to pull rank." He looked at his notes. "You're full up, Ginny. I know you and Natalie did a fine job together on the Dow murder, but that doesn't mean Natalie and Tyler can't do an equally fine job on this one. Also, Tyler's connections with the County Police and the DA's office will come in handy. Natalie's new at this and might not have connections with the legal institutions."

Natalie stirred. "Not the kind of connections you mean, no…."

"Who did they send, yesterday?" asked Tyler. "Gredler?"

Byron shook his head. "Camilla Perry and Geoffrey Allan."

The sulky lines on Ginny's face faded, and she slid her eyes sideways toward Natalie.

"They're good," said Tyler. "If you can stand Perry's head-bobbing. Although I don't know how focused she'll be—she has a six-month old baby at home."

Ginny smiled sweetly. "Is your point that mothers don't make good investigators?"

Tyler didn't even look at her. "I'm sure Natalie and I can work well together. Her enthusiasm and my experience should match up. I suggest we start out with a two-pronged attack. Since Natalie has her contacts in the coroners office, she might want to follow-up on the medical evidence. I can talk to the DA's office and—"

"That's kindergarten stuff," said Ginny, crossing her legs impatiently. "What about Kovaks? Is he going to allow himself to be interviewed—at least on background?"

"Of course," said Byron.

"I'll take that," said Tyler. "We're old acquaintances, and he'll probably be more comfortable talking to me. I'll head over to his shop first thing."

Ginny rolled her eyes.

Byron poked at his glasses and turned to Natalie. "What do you think, Natalie?"

Natalie's eyes stayed on Byron. "I think I should interview Kovaks. I'm the one who knows the details of the case."

Byron nodded. "Agreed. You take Kovaks. Follow up as you see fit— but keep me informed, right?"

"Yes." In the interests of her elevated position on the pyramid, she did her best not to make it sound contrite.

"Tyler—go ahead and check with your police buddies and whoever is on the case at the DA's office. Do what you do best. Natalie, I'll arrange that appointment for you with Kovaks. I'm expecting the police back at ten…. Just—everybody, keep this story under your hats as long as possible." He picked up his pen in both hands, and the three reporters moved.

♥ ♥ ♥

Natalie rang the doorbell of the Kovaks' three story house in Park Ridge. While she waited for the door to open, she noted that the leaves had started to fall from the tulip trees.

The door opened and there was Linda Kovaks, dressed in matching violet-colored top and slacks, wearing a pair of Ben Franklin glasses.

"And here's Natalie Joday," she said with a smile. "Come in."

Natalie followed her down a central hall.

"We'll talk in the study," said Linda over her shoulder. "I'm trying to catch up on the bookkeeping."

The room was small without being cramped, with two desks at right angles, and bookshelves along the walls. "I like to work here when I can— in the comfort of home. Have a seat."

Natalie lowered herself onto a small couch.

Linda sat in a black wooden chair with a wicker seat. "Peter will be down as soon as he's dressed. His schedule is a nightmare—and now this anonymous attack…." She bowed her head. "We're so grateful to everyone at the *Star* for agreeing to keep his name out of this—until we can find out who is behind it. We're grateful to you, too…. Myra was very mysterious, but she did say you've been in on it since the beginning, and understand how to be discreet. I just wish we knew what it was all about—was it an anonymous letter, a telephone call…?"

"For Mr. Kovaks' own protection, we think it's better not to talk about that."

"I see. I understand how it is at a newspaper. I won't ask any more questions." She smiled wryly, then lifted her chin. "But shall I answer some of yours, until Peter comes down?"

"I'd appreciate that." Natalie pulled out her notebook. "Can you give me some biographical info—education, when he started working for the *Star*?"

"Peter majored in economics in college. He went to SUNY Purchase because his father was a New York resident, but he has all the Boston breeding, with its tradition of public service." Linda's voice was full of pride. "He graduated in 1956. It was his dream to work in government. It was such an idealistic time. His first job was in local government—just an assistant in a public utilities office, but it shows you. However, he was great friends with Myra Vandergelden, and when she became an editor at the *Star*, she hired him as a staff writer—of course he's a brilliant communicator...."

"When was that?"

"1961. After we got married—that was in 1965—we started planning for the future. He went to night school for his MBA. We never intended to make journalism his career. But there was a period of several years when we weren't sure the *Star* would make it. The original owners couldn't face the fact that it was time to change. It was a battle, but Myra became Managing Editor and then, when the paper incorporated, CEO. She deserved it. You wouldn't believe some of the things Myra's done for the *Star*. Her goal was to change it from a family paper—baby showers and bake sales—to something that contained real news. It was a triumph, but...it also meant she needed our help more than ever. So we stayed on as a favor to an old friend. Then Peter wrote that groundbreaking series on kickbacks in the publishing industry." She gestured toward a brass plaque on the wall. "All of a sudden everybody wanted him. But Peter is intensely loyal. By that time he had moved to management. In the early Eighties, we finally opened our own consulting firm, and—well, you probably know Peter's reputation as a miracle worker in publishing. The buy-out of *Plus* magazine just when their major competitor's sponsor was looking for a new advertising package for their Precision Diet Plan? He's ideally trained for political office, I think. Practical experience, business sense...and economics is an inherently honest background—and we need honest politicians." She ducked her head. "Listen to me, I'm still giving campaign speeches when you want facts. It's a hard habit to break."

"You said Myra needed 'our help.' Did you work at the paper?"

"No. Oh, I filled in during the summers, in the mailroom or doing inventory in the printshop. But that's not why I said 'we.'" She smiled. "You're not married, are you?"

"No."

"Then it's hard to understand. Peter and I are a team. We each play a role: he's the front man, I work backstage. Only together do we make the complete package. We've built a career together, first at the *Star*, and then on a dozen other boards of successful companies. This race is the perfect example of how we work together—I'm his *de facto* campaign manager. Everything that happens goes through me."

Natalie lowered her pen. "Doesn't it bother you that all the success comes in his name?"

Linda smiled as if she'd heard it before. "No, it doesn't. I don't need to share the limelight, or take credit for his success. As long as we are coequal within our relationship, that's all the affirmation I need. As long as I know myself how important I am, and as long as he knows, I don't need the outside world's approval. The success comes in his name, but he'd be the first to tell you it's half mine." She grew serious. "My husband has an extraordinary personal charm and ability to communicate. These are rare gifts. They make him extremely effective in the business world, and will do so in public life. Me? I'm a nuts and bolts kind of gal from the projects in East Orange. I know how to work hard and fast, to plan and analyze— but I can't touch his gift for communicating his vision, or for bringing people together."

"You left out one thing, my dear: your ability to inspire the best in the people whose lives you touch."

Natalie turned and got her first close-up view of Peter Kovaks. He was tall—larger-than-life tall, but not basketball-player tall. He didn't look his sixty-odd years, and (Natalie suddenly realized) he was extremely attractive—a straight-limbed, lean body and a long, bony face, with movie-star eyes beneath straight dark eyebrows. His silver hair was soft and wavy. Natalie found herself wishing she had dressed with a bit more care that morning…maybe done something to accent her eyes…. At least she had thought to throw on the green velvet jacket over her black T-shirt.

"Thank you, dear." Linda looked at him over her shoulder. "Now come say hello to Natalie Joday."

Peter looked down at her, and she could see the interest and approval in his eyes. "Pleased to meet you."

She rose from the couch and took the hand he offered. "Thank you for taking time to see me." It was a large hand, and his grip was firm. She found herself reluctant to let go. This was something new in Natalie's experience of men.

"It has to be done." He put his left hand on top of hers. "Frankly I hope the police solve this terrible murder quickly, without digging up ancient history. But if they can't, so be it. If the old story must come out, it's important to get the true facts on the record. I'd like to think I can trust you to do that." He squeezed her hand, let it go, and sat in an upholstered chair. "So what do you want to know?"

Natalie sat down. Her face was hot, and she wondered if Linda could tell she was blushing. She studied her notebook. "The newspaper reports describe an exchange you had with Marconi at a press conference. Can you tell me what happened?"

Peter's brow wrinkled. "It was a long time ago…and I haven't thought about any of this for years." He laced his fingers and touched his thumbs beneath his chin. "My recollection is that Marconi was at odds with half the people in the room, not just me. I remember thinking he was arrogant and antagonistic toward the press. Of course, I was a little impatient in those days…. I thought it was ridiculous for him to say he was willing to talk about anything, and then get angry when the press asked him personal questions."

"Do you remember any of the questions you asked?"

Peter shook his head. "Maybe as I think about it, it'll come back. But right now? I only remember that someone asked him about his marriage, and he said he'd never looked at another woman since he'd met his wife. Then Ted Barnes from Channel 7 leaned over and said, 'Yeah, but I've heard he has no problem ogling the boys.' I remember that because I came home and told Linda about it, and we talked it over, whether it meant anything or not."

The phone rang. Linda got up and answered it.

"It's for you."

Peter stood, shook his trouser legs, and went to a side table beneath a mirror framed in black and gold. "Hello." He looked into the mirror. "Yes, she's here now. Okay…. I won't…. Okay…."

He sat again and regarded Natalie with a twinkle in his eye. "That was Myra. Warning me that you are from the bloodhound school of journalism and advising me not to try any tricks." He smiled for the first time. He had

126

nice large teeth, white and straight.

Natalie smiled too. It didn't take much effort. "So, getting back to 1972. You decided to check it out?"

Peter nodded. "Yes, although I don't remember all the factors that lead to the decision. I put the word out on the street and the next thing I knew I'd found this young man who said he'd had sex with Marconi. Then all hell broke loose."

"'Said he'd had sex?' What did you do to verify his story?"

"He had details—physical, personal, dates...."

"Why didn't you print his name? I thought that was odd—that someone who made such an accusation could remain anonymous."

"It was an editorial decision. You have to understand what was going on at the *Star* at the time. Myra and I were trying to move to harder-hitting news." He glanced at Linda. "It was a difficult decision to run the story at all—and we battled over it. Was it muckraking? Was it news? To Myra, it boiled down to a question of integrity. If Marconi was playing games with the English language to make it look like he was faithful to his wife when he wasn't, that made it relevant to the campaign. That made it news. She said it was as clear an example as she'd ever seen of exactly what the press is here to do. It would have been shirking our duty not to report it. But we didn't want to pander to the sex and scandal mongers. We would have used the man's name if it'd come to that. But it didn't—I called Marconi and asked him for a reaction statement. That was his chance to fight it, if he wanted to, but he didn't. He knew instantly he was through. So we kept the detail out of the paper. Including the name—after all, the story wasn't about him."

"But *you* remember his name...."

"I don't think that's relevant."

"Possibly not, but—"

"And frankly I don't like pursuing this angle at all. Marconi is dead. Why besmirch the man's memory by bringing this up now? It can't possibly have anything to do with the murder."

Natalie met his eyes. "When the police come, they will ask you this, and you will tell them. It's just giving them the edge if you don't tell me."

"Myra was right about you." He ran a large hand over his chin. "So be it. The name was Armand Vitek."

"How seriously was he involved with Marconi?"

"I would say not very." Peter worked his jaw thoughtfully. "To put it bluntly, their relationship was strictly business."

127

"How exactly did you find him?"

"I had some good contacts on the street. It doesn't take very long for the word to get around. He found me."

"He just appeared and volunteered to tell you something he knew would ruin Marconi? Wasn't that bad for business?"

"He seemed to think it was all a big joke. A delicious joke that a stuffy old politician had been caught with his pants down. He seemed to take it as a given that anybody who had anything to do with the government was corrupt. Not unusual at that time. Although this young man went to extremes; he told me the government was putting miniature computers in people's heads to enslave the population. He seemed to know a lot about technology."

"Can you give me a description?"

"White, male, twenty-two, little eyes, little mouth, slender, but soft rather than muscular."

"What was his manner like?"

"Foolish, naive—the kind of naiveté that is only the more pronounced in someone who thinks he knows everything because he has a lot of experience with sex and drugs."

"Where was he from? Did he give you an address?"

"No. He showed me a New Jersey driver's license to prove his ID—I insisted on that, but he said the address was an old one where his parents had lived. I assumed he was living on the street. Poor kid—I wonder what happened to him."

Natalie raised her eyes. "Doing drugs, selling sex for a living, taking pleasure in ruining someone's career—he doesn't sound like he's worth wondering about."

"At the time, I felt like you. But you're young, and so was I—oh, not in years, but in wisdom. You're young until you've done—one by one—all the things you used to despise other people for doing." He looked—a little sadly—into her eyes. "Then you look in the mirror and understand why people talk about condemning the bad things a person does, rather than the person."

Goosebumps rose on her arms, but she maintained eye contact.

He smiled. "Is that it?"

Natalie collected herself. "Just one more question. Do you remember where you were last December 23rd?"

He looked at Linda. "We checked the planner last night. I was in Chicago that weekend—doing a consultancy for a magazine. I got in late that night."

"Okay." She breathed deeply. That sounded like an air-tight alibi. "I'll just follow up on a couple of points and then let you get back to the campaign trail. Did you ever check with Ted Barnes about how he knew?"

"No. Rival news divisions…."

"Did Channel 7 pursue the story?"

"No. It was all ours. We did a good job on it, I think—considering what we were going through at the time. The pressures were incredible. We had just come through the lowest point in the history of the paper, and were struggling to set out in a new direction. We thought of ourselves as pioneers. And on the personal side, Linda's mother—a great lady—was dying of Hodgkin's Disease. We were traveling down to Essex County every other night to see her. It was hard. But we made it. And shortly thereafter we began what was the most exciting period of our lives—building the paper's readership and advertising base."

The doorbell rang, two short blasts, and Linda sprang to her feet. "Darling your driver's here, and we haven't finished your speech or called Jeannette." She rushed from the room.

Peter looked at Natalie. He compressed his lips and shook his head regretfully. When he got to his feet, she did, too.

"I'm glad to have met you, Natalie." He held out his hand again, and she took it. "I hope you know I mean that. I've seen a lot of reporters come and go, and you're the real deal."

After weeks of uneasiness concerning her job, Natalie's spirit soared under this unsought praise from on high. She felt her cheeks warming again, and was glad that Linda had left. She allowed herself to be ushered to the door, fully appreciating the simple respect with which Peter Kovaks bid her farewell.

Chapter Fifteen

Natalie enjoyed the drive back to the *Star* Building. Life had taken a turn for the better since that abysmal moment in Byron's office the day before when she had pictured herself behind bars. This was more like it! Sitting in on the Crime Bureau meeting; officially on the Enigma story; getting compliments from people who knew the business. She stopped by Charlie's to pick up a late lunch: ham on rye, with a pickle.

There were four messages waiting for her in her box, all from Tyler—call him immediately. She hurried toward his cubicle.

"There you are!" He threw up his hands. "Where've you been?"

"With Kovaks, as you perfectly well knew." She dropped into the old-fashioned wooden swivel chair he kept for guests, and unwrapped her sandwich. "Did I miss something?"

"The case could be solved for all you know! Don't you ever check in?"

Natalie's spirits were too high for his bolts to touch her. "Tyler, it's one thirty. I only left at ten."

"That's not the point, Natalie." He reached for his pipe—a strictly dramatic gesture in the non-smoking newsroom. "This is a murder investigation. There are protocols to follow. When you leave one place, you call in to say where you're heading."

"Oh."

"I suppose you think that as an independent young woman, you don't need to pay any attention to—"

"No, that's fine." She took a bite of her sandwich. "Good idea. I just didn't know it."

He twisted a pipe cleaner in his hands. "Well now you do. You can leave a message on my machine or with Marcia."

"Agreed." She took another bite. It was damned good. "And who do you call?"

He blinked at her, and stopped twisting the pipe cleaner.

She picked up her pickle. "I suppose you think that as a broad-shouldered, old-fashioned man, you don't need to pay any attention to the safety rules." She swiveled back and forth in the chair.

A corner of his mouth twitched. "I'll call Marcia, too."

"Good. Now—what'd I miss?" She took a bite of the pickle. Damned good pickle.

He applied the pipe cleaner again. "Nothing at all. The police are just getting into gear."

"What's their angle?" She noticed a photo of Marconi on his desk, obviously more recent than the others she had seen.

"They're taking a practical approach. What were Marconi's movements on the day of his death; who did he owe money to—or who owed him money; checking phone records. I'll get my notes to you as soon as I'm done writing my copy."

"What copy?"

Tyler scratched his temple with his pinkie. "What copy? Don't we work for a newspaper? Didn't the police just discover a murder? Did you think we wouldn't have anything in today's edition?"

"No…." Natalie took another bite. "I guess I'm just surprised—"

"Don't get all bent out of shape. It's a routine piece recapping the police summary and a pathetic ass-covering statement from the coroner's office. Nothing front page. No mention of busted political campaigns or that the *Star* had anything to do with breaking the case. Let me explain it to you." He made a show of conquering his irritation. "Investigative reporting isn't like covering a parade, where you just report who played what instrument and how many people fainted. You don't churn out copy every day. You wait till you've found something out."

"Okay." Natalie stood up. "I get it. You gonna use that photo of Marconi alongside the story?"

"Probably." Tyler frowned at the photo. "But I don't like the message it sends—makes him look like a loser. I'd prefer one when he was younger, before he looked so down and out."

"How would you know what he looked like? You said you never saw him."

"I don't have to know him to conclude that this photo is not complimentary! As it happens, I did see him once or twice, although not, as I told you, when he was running for office."

"There are a couple of good photos in VirNA." She crumbled the wax sandwich paper and stood. "I'll be working here for another hour—will I get those notes from you before I go?"

"I'll have them to you by 2:30 at the latest. I have an appointment at the Courthouse at three."

"I'll stop by before I go." She had one foot out the door when his summons made her turn her head.

He had put the pipe down, and was sitting very upright behind his desk, with his chin held aloft. "You, uh, really think I have broad shoulders?"

♥   ♥   ♥

She spent the afternoon and evening reading Tyler's notes, making lists of things to do, and musing over the Enigma riddles. She was still at it when the phone rang at ten.

"Yeah…."

"Hey!" came Rebecca's voice. "What happened to that suave, 'Natalie Joday….'"

Natalie laughed. "It's on strike. Tyler has called twelve times—so far. I thought you were him."

"Is he on to something?"

"No—but he sure is a terrier for negative detail."

"Such as?"

"The police interviewed the Marconi neighbors—nobody remembers anything suspicious. But they figure somebody must have been there, A) to drug him, and B) to dispose of the remaining eggnog. And maybe to give him a little shove down the stairs. Angela was out shopping from eleven to six, in the company of two girlfriends. She found Maury when she got home and called 911. Airtight. And speaking of alibis, Peter Kovaks has come up with his boarding pass for the flight back from Chicago."

"That must be a relief."

"Yeah. It alleviates the guilt of not telling the cops that, according to Enigma, he's the Villain. Although I don't know why I'm listening to Enigma. I don't like anonymous-letter writers."

"Speaking of which, I've done that analysis of Louise's notes."

"Anything?"

"Maybe. Hard to tell third hand, but I can say for sure that there were at least three references to colleges, or universities. That sounds obscure, but given Enigma's fondness for wordplay, I figure it's as good a clue as any. Also, Louise noted Enigma's increasing frustration in the last four or five letters. That tells me Enigma had some time-defined goal in mind."

"The election? No…that only works if Peter was the target."

"I also spent some time going through my reference books. You know,

132

what are riddles to you are 'logic questions' to the intelligentsia. Listen to this:

"They call me a man, but I'll never have a wife.
I was given a body, but not given life.
They made me a mouth, but didn't give me breath.
Water gives me life and sun brings me death.
Who am I?

"Do you get it?"
"No—but it sounds like Enigma's riddle about the lifeless man!"
"Exactly. Maybe Enigma based his riddles on other, well-known riddles, which maybe we can track down."
"I'm sure you're right! And I know just where to go riddle hunting."
"Then I'll let you get back to work."
"Hey. What about the answer?"
"You mean you want me to tell you?"
Natalie grinned into the phone. "It's on the tip of my tongue, but I don't have the time to spare to fish it out."
"I didn't get it either. Snowman."

♥   ♥   ♥

On Wednesday morning, Natalie sought out Glen Matsuma, the *Star*'s entertainment editor. Entertainment at the *Star* included (along with the TV listings and show biz articles picked up from the wire services) original reviews, comics, the bridge and chess columns, the crossword and acrostic, and the joke of the day. She was prohibited, given her promise not to reveal the Enigma letters, from showing him the riddles, but there was nothing stopping her from getting his general advice.

Glen was a small, slender man with shoulder-length black hair. Natalie's path had not crossed his since her early day's at the *Star* when she had written a review or two for him. He had never changed a word she had written, which in those days she had interpreted as a compliment to her powers. But now—older and wiser—she realized it was because he had been new, too, and in fact didn't know a thing about copy editing, his passion being for the comics.

Glen allowed Natalie to sit in his office and browse at will through his collection of humor and joke books. This she did for most of the morning, snickering quietly now and then, and making the occasional note.

♥   ♥   ♥

At eleven, Glen appeared to tell her she had a call on line seven from Evangelica Moony. Puzzled, Natalie picked up the receiver and said hello.

"So…they didn't fire you for muckraking…. Shucks…."

Natalie drew a blank. Then she heard the faint sound of a cigarette being used for its native purpose.

"Angela?"

"You got it, Sparks." There was a faint crackling over the phone. "Say, I was right the first time—about you bein' smart."

"That's debatable. But I assure you I am not trying to sensationalize your husband's story. I really—"

"You didn't get me. That bit about not being fired was s'posed to be my way of sayin' sorry for chewin' you out the other day."

"It was? Oh…I get it."

"Good, 'cause it's the only apology you're gonna get." Drag. "I'm ticked. The police went through the house from top to bottom, and put everything back in the wrong place. It's gonna take me months to get organized again."

Natalie made a face at the Dick Tracy poster on the wall. "Gee that's too bad."

"Yeah, well, I s'pose it'll give me somethin' to do while I'm gettin' use to the idea a Maury bein' murdered. Kind a makes me feel rotten all over again. He wasn't a bad guy, you know. He knew how to have fun. He sure got cheated."

"I'm sorry, Angela."

"Yeah, well…." Puff. "So who do you think did it?"

"I don't know."

"But you're investigatin'?"

"Yeah."

"Then how come your name wasn't on the article in the *Star* yesterday? Or do you write under a pseudo-whatsajiggy…?"

"No. Tyler Hanson is working with me."

"Okay. Just as long as you're on it."

"You don't mind…?" .

"Nah…."

"Then maybe I could ask for your help?"

"Shoot."

"Did Maury have any enemies?"

"Nah. The cops asked me that, too. And about any funny business deals.

Of which there were none, as I told them. Maury worked at the senior center for a long time before he died. Then they wanted to know about what happened in Seventy-two."

"Oh, yeah?"

"It was a instant replay of your visit. Hey, they got some cute cops these days. With flat stomachs. Or am I just getting old? Dicks, we used to call 'em. You can't say that now...."

"Sure you can." Natalie leaned back in Glen's chair. "Listen, what about his drinking? You said last time that—"

"Aww. That's what fries my butt. Here I was thinking he'd fallen off the wagon right before Christmas, and being all upset. Then it turns out he'd just had an itsy bit of eggnog, like he promised, and probably whoever did it set it up to look like he'd been on a boozer. I gotta get use to that."

"Angela, I hate to ask this, but—was Maury involved with anybody else that you know in the last few years?"

"The cops asked that, too. The answer is no—nobody. Male or female, vegetable or mineral. That I know of."

"Thanks, Angela. I'm glad you're not mad at me anymore."

"Why don't you stop by one a these days? I gotta start thinkin' about gettin' the snow blower running before it gets really cold...."

♥   ♥   ♥

Natalie, after getting permission to take a couple of joke books home for bedtime reading, retreated upstairs. She had a lunch meeting with Tyler, who reported that the police were baffled, but, in the absence of suspicious business dealings, were leaning toward an affair of the heart. They were not paying any attention at all to the old political scandal.

After lunch, she found a computer and went back to the *Star* archives. She wanted to search VirNA for the key words in the unsolved riddles. Unfortunately, most of the jokes and riddles in the *Star* Entertainment Section were graphics, rather than text, and she was unable to carry out the search. She spent an hour checking issue by issue, but soon realized it was a task beyond her scope.

At two, Louise called.

"Louise? Jeez, I owe you a call...."

"I'm sorry to interrupt. I know how busy you've been."

"Not that busy.... Hey, I'm sorry I had to tell Byron about the letters. And that I didn't advise you to go to him in the first place."

"You did what you thought was right, Natalie, and it's worked out for

135

the best. Mr. Shapiro was so nice when he phoned. He said he was used to his reporters not telling him everything. And he didn't bring up the subject of my work at all."

"Oh, man…. I forgot to give you your letters back, and my comments." She looked at the clock. "Your deadline is Friday, right? I'm on my way home in a minute. I can drop them off…."

"Thank you, that would be so kind…."

"No problem. I won't be able to stay, though."

"Yes, I know, your niece. I won't keep you. But could I ask you to see if I got any mail today?"

"I'd be happy to," said Natalie with complete honesty. It satisfied her to think that for once Louise would be saved from running the gauntlet of Rudy's buffoonery.

♥　　　♥　　　♥

"Hi, Ms. Joday!" Rudy looked up from his stacks of nickels, dimes, and quarters and treated Natalie to one of his broad grins.

"Hi there, Rudy." His ingratiating style irritated her more than usual. "Going over the petty cash?"

"That's right. Mr. Wenger says I'm the only assistant he's ever had who got the accounts right to the last penny. Gotta keep up my reputation!"

"You'll make the perfect CPA someday."

Rudy, unsuspecting of any sarcasm, looked interested. "What's that?"

"Certified Public Accountant."

He laughed to show his delight, his Adam's apple bobbing merrily up and down.

"Any mail for me?" asked Natalie.

"I'd most likely put it in your box if there was, but lemme check." Rudy loped over to his sorting table and went through a stack of envelopes. Then he searched to the very bottom of a large canvas mail bag. While he was upside down, Natalie made an idle appraisal of his math skills as visible in the open petty cash ledger.

He emerged from the bag with several bits of packing straw stuck to his hair, strengthening the image of the scarecrow that his skinny frame and too-short sleeves inspired. "Nope, sorry Ms. Joday." He looked at her anxiously. "If you're lookin' for somethin' special, I can call one of my contacts at the main post office…."

"No, that's okay."

"…Because they owe me a favor or two, and they're great guys."

"That's okay. Anything for Louise Hunt?"

As a cloud sends a shadow across a sunny plain, so did Natalie's words darken Rudy's face, leaving his eyes half-closed and his mouth sagging.

"She asked me to pick up her mail."

"Well, I don't know...."

"Well, why don't you look...."

He turned, obedient to her frosty tone and superior status, and shuffled over to the miscellaneous rack, where the mail of casual employees and those not important enough to have their own boxes in the front office was stuffed into pigeonholes marked A-D, E-K, etc. Natalie corralled her temper while he was thus occupied.

Rudy returned, holding two letters. "Yeah, she's got these."

"Thanks, Rudy." Natalie held out her hand. "She'll be pleased to have the material for her column."

"I don't know...." He kept the letters just out of her reach. "I'm not s'posed to hand people's mail to anybody else.... What if you was to read it and I'd be blamed?"

It flew in the face of nature, thought Natalie, for this boy to become so sullen because he was being cheated of the chance to torment someone senior in years but not in worldliness. "I think you'd better give me the letters, Rudy, and I'll forget you even suggested that my motive in picking up Louise's mail was to read it without authorization. Or, we can take the matter directly to Mr. Shapiro."

Rudy's face darkened even further. But he handed the letters over without further comment.

Natalie chucked them into her briefcase and snapped the lid shut. She pointed an accusatory finger at the ledger. "You've written a seven backwards in the debit column."

♥   ♥   ♥

After dropping Gayanne off at Daniel's that evening, Natalie returned to the *Star* Building. Suddenly there were not enough hours in the day for all the things she had to do, and no amount of organizing seemed to help. Her lists grew longer by the hour, and she had realized that although it only took a moment to jot down a clever question, it might take hours or days to answer it.

The 6:00 PM newsroom was empty but for a couple of financial page editors and a few stringers, hammering away at the communal computers. The night editor was sitting on a desk, flirting with one of the sportswriters.

She sat down determined to prioritize her to-do lists. "Find out if Kovaks saw Marconi before he died." Peter Kovaks had sounded sincere when he'd said he hadn't given Marconi a thought for many years. She put down "says no." "Try Dottie M. again." She placed the call for the umpteenth time. The number she had was always picked up by an answer machine, which told her: "All calls to this number will be screened," and then invited her to leave a message. No one ever returned her calls. She'd better write a letter....

The letter written, stamped, and dropped in the outgoing mail box, she turned back to her list. "Find Armand Vitek." Was it worth it? Could he possibly know anything about the murder? Could he possibly be the Villain? It seemed unlikely. And yet...if she was to trust Enigma, the answer lay in the old scandal. She wrote Tyler a memo asking him to check with his DMV contact—according to Peter, Vitek had had a driver's license twenty years ago, so he ought to have one now. She would check the phone books.

At 8:00 PM she closed the last phone book and looked around the room. The financial editors were gone. The night editor appeared to have gotten to first base.

She grabbed her briefcase and headed out the doors and down the pink stairwell. But instead of passing through the revolving doors into the outer world, she walked down the ground floor hall to the office of Davis Skemp, MLS, custodian of the Public Access Room as well as the little library on the third floor. As the *Star*'s resident archivist, he was cherished by the journalistic community—no stranger to the art of information gathering— not for his accumulation of knowledge, but for his facility in retrieving it. Originally hired to convert the *Star* into digital format, he had been begged to stay when it had been absorbed into the collective *Star* consciousness that they had all been living in abysmal darkness before his advent. Three years on, the sight of his homely face—like a pug dog with an oversized cranium—was still warranted to inspire hope in the heart of any reporter, no matter how doomed the quest.

Natalie was not surprised to find him in. She knew, having asked him out once, that he didn't have much of a social life beyond the resonance frequency of his computer.

He sat, as usual, in front of his twenty-one inch color monitor, keeping an eye on the six computers in the Public Access Room through a one-way mirror, in a room that more resembled an operating theater than an office. Everything was made of steel or glass or painted white. He refused to use paper products, and there were no books on his steel shelves. A stained-glass motto hung on the wall behind his steel desk: "Don't be afraid to express your love: Hug a tree today." It was that motto that had attracted her to him.

After a few words of greeting, Natalie stated her problem, and listened to his thoughts on how to find someone electronically.

"In another five years," he said dreamily, "you'll turn on your computer, type a name, and have fifty search engines at your fingertips. Until then, you're shooting in the dark. It's a sad truth that the computer geeks are the only ones you can find on the Internet."

"Then the Internet is worth a shot. About the only thing I know about Armand is that he knew a lot about technology."

"In that case...." Davis turned to his computer. "I'll e-mail you a list of places on the Internet to check. And there are a couple of cool bulletin boards for software developers. You may not know this, but computer games is a huge growth industry...."

Natalie let him talk, engaged by his innocent enthusiasm if not by his theme. Glancing into the Public Access Room (where one could browse back issues of the *Star* to one's heart's content from 7 to 9 PM, Monday to Friday), she caught sight of a familiar pair of shoulders and a shapely, close-cropped head. She blinked, and instinctively backed away before she remembered the one-way glass.

"What is it?" asked Davis.

"Congratulations. The cops are doing research in your archive."

Davis eased toward the window. "The one with the nice jacket?"

"Yup."

"Friend of yours?"

"Hardly."

He looked at her, his brown eyes dancing in his little pug-dog face. "You, ah, want to know what he's looking for?"

"Nope." A slow smile crept over her face. "He's on a lower level of the pyramid. So I already know." She raised a finger to her lips, and fled.

Chapter Sixteen

For the rest of the week, there was not a waking moment when Natalie was not thinking about or working on the Marconi murder. At first, she expected to hear at any moment that the police had made an arrest. Each time she saw Tyler's narrow face and round glasses approach, she thought for sure the jig was up. But he brought only his summaries of information gleaned from his contacts at the Courthouse: so many fiber samples removed from the Marconi living room; such and such a test conducted to find traces of an inert compound that might allow the forensics team to track down the purchase of the phenobarbital; bank statements showed no unusual activity; etc.

On Friday morning, Natalie glanced up from her ongoing Internet search to find Tyler standing as usual behind her.

He dropped a folder in her in-box, then leaned over her shoulder to peer at her monitor. "What are you doing?"

"Searching some public records, trying to locate Armand Vitek."

"Tch. You'll never find him that way."

Natalie didn't bother to look up. Ginny had always said that Tyler was anti-technology. "Why not?"

"Because any man who was selling sex in 1972 is probably dead by now." He straightened up. "I'd check the obits if I were you."

He left without further comment, and Natalie went back to her search. But twenty minutes later she went to suggest to Marcia that there had to be a way to keep the stringers from gumming up the mouses with peanut husks, and to inquire who was the obituaries guru at the *Star*.

♥   ♥   ♥

In the afternoon, Louise called. "I know you're busy, but I had to tell you how grateful I am for your critique."

Natalie, in the middle of answering an e-mail to a hot Internet contact who had an apparently bottomless supply of suggestions for how to find Armand Vitek, took a moment to lean back and rub her eyes. "I'm sorry I couldn't spare more time...."

"I felt like you'd been inside my head when I was writing. You've given me a lot to think about. But some things.... You said my advice wasn't specific enough...what did you mean by that?"

"Uhhh...." Natalie pulled over a nearby chair and put her feet up. "Sometimes you make a sweeping statement, like 'take a positive approach,' without giving a clue how to do it."

"Isn't a positive approach important?"

"Sure, but it's like saying to someone who doesn't know how to swim, 'Always keep your head above water.' Unless they know how to kick and stroke, they're going to sink like a stone."

"I see. Yes. And then you say it is depressing for the reader because I never recommend fighting for what the writers want. Am I writing for the reader, or for the person who wrote the letter?"

Natalie's attention wandered back to her monitor. "I promise I'll go over all this with you, Louise. But—I'm in a bind right now." She took her feet off the chair. "I've got about twenty things going on, and I need to use the computer in the newsroom while I can. I have to go at 2:30. I can come back in the evening, but...."

"Natalie? You've given me such good advice.... May I suggest...can't you find a way so you don't have to break your day—"

"No!" She spoke more forcefully than she intended, and was irritated with herself. "This is just the way it's going to be."

"Isn't there a very nice daycare center in Harrington—?"

"No daycare!" Natalie closed her eyes. She was awfully jumpy to-day.... Louise was just trying to help. "Look, I'm sure daycare is a wonderful institution. But in Gayanne's case it's not an option. She's seen too many institutions already. And frankly my brother can't afford that right now and neither can I."

"If that's the only problem, she could come to my house after school—I'd be glad to do it for nothing."

The old anger streamed out and flooded Natalie's mortal coil. She should have known better. This always happened—if people knew the real details of your life, they concluded they could run it better, because they were smarter and richer, and because you had failed and forfeited your chance. "I didn't mean to imply we're on skid row." Her tone was stiff. "We're doing fine, just fine." She winced. What an idiot she was! Now would come the embarrassed apology, the quick retreat, and the little lies to make her feel better.

"I love children." Louise's voice was very soft. "It's the biggest regret of my life that I never had any of my own. I used to have Steve and Rachel's kids over as often as I could, but they've grown up and scattered. You'd be doing me a favor if you'd let me help out a little. Or...I'm sorry, maybe you think I'm too old...."

"No, of course not. I...." Natalie stopped, puzzled.

"I've felt all my life I had a lot to give. But somehow I haven't been able to reach people to give it. My mother had Multiple Sclerosis, and it was my job to take care of her from when I was quite young. I loved her dearly, but.... She died five years ago."

"Then you've probably had it with taking care of other people."

"Oh no! Not if it's appreciated. It's the most wonderful thing in the world, then. There are many different ways to give.... Only I'm not having much success. I don't feel old, but people don't seem to take me very seriously." Her voice grew wistful. "I understand how hard it must be to let people do things for you, Natalie. You're so independent, and so smart, you're probably not used to it."

Natalie laughed. "You've got that wrong. As a kid I was plenty used to it. Social services, counselors, even daycare. I learned after a while it was better to look after myself—and my family."

"It is terrible when other people try to tell you how to live your life. But that mustn't make you close your heart to other people's generosity. Forgive me if I am intruding, but—do you have to do everything all alone? Aren't you allowed to have a back-up?"

The words entered her mind like an old friend. How many times had she begged Daniel to let her be his back-up? How much had it hurt her when he could not bring himself to accept her help?

Louise continued. "You've been helping me with my column, and I'm so grateful. I'd be so happy...."

"Gayanne has...problems. She's having a rough time at school. Half the time she's in pieces when she comes home. She flunked an arithmatic test yesterday, and.... Besides I'm afraid she'll feel like she's being pawned off."

"Don't you think she is smart enough to understand, if you present it the right way, with your intentions clear? You're covering a murder story— that's important work. She might think she was helping by freeing you up. She might even like a way to show you how grateful she is. You can find the words so she'll understand."

Again Natalie was silent.

"Ask her," said Louise. "Promise me you'll ask her."

Her anger was gone, released by the painless opening of a door that led to a part of herself she had never seen before. "Okay, I will. I promise."

♥   ♥   ♥

On Saturday, Natalie took a call at home from Linda Kovaks. "The police just left." Linda's voice was flat. "They wanted to talk to Peter about his reporting on the Marconi story in 1972. Myra told us to call you."

So. It had taken him five days. "How long were they there?"

"Two hours, maybe two and a half."

"Can you describe their attitude?"

"Business-like. Polite. Does that mean something?"

Natalie hesitated. This was a new Linda. Never before had she spoken to her without imbuing every sentence with campaign fluff. It was hard to ignore the pain in her voice. "As we told you, elements of the anonymous information point at Mr. Kovaks. The less seriously the police take that, the better for him."

"Natalie, you must know we're sitting on a knife edge."

"I know."

"If this story gets out, it won't matter that it isn't true, it will cripple my husband's campaign."

"I know."

"Can't you…. Won't you tell me what was said about him? I'm asking you as a wife who would do anything to protect her husband. You're the only one I know I can trust. Peter wouldn't like me saying this but I know Myra wouldn't hesitate to sacrifice a friend if she thought it would be best for the *Star*. Please."

Natalie's throat was tight. "I'm sorry…."

"This campaign is the culmination of everything we've ever dreamed of. Are we to lose that because of a scurrilous attack? It's only three and a half weeks to the election. What good will it do if he's cleared after the fact? The damage will have been done."

"I know. I can only tell you we're all working as hard as we can. And maybe…maybe it's good the police have recognized the possible importance of what happened in 1972. Maybe it will help them do their job better—find the killer before the damage is done."

"It's just…hard to see that right now. Peter is my whole life…. If you could just give us a hint…? Was it an anonymous letter?"

143

"Linda, isn't it better if you don't know? That way you can't be accused of manipulating the paper to protect you."

"I suppose so. That's what Peter says. But it's hard, Natalie; hard not to know the name of your accuser."

♥   ♥   ♥

Sunday afternoon found Natalie and Rebecca setting up the barbecue on the latter's patio.

Rebecca arranged the charcoal to her liking. "Your consultant has something you might be interested in...."

Natalie glanced across the backyard, where Daniel and Gayanne were putting up the croquet hoops. "Yes?"

"What comes in groups of 26?"

"Other than the alphabet?" Natalie brushed some cobwebs off the can of lighter fluid. "I have no idea."

"The alphabet will do."

"Okay. So what do I do with it?"

"Take twelve steps forward...." She gestured for the lighter fluid.

Natalie handed her the can. "Starting at...the beginning?"

"Unh hunh."

Natalie counted on her fingers. "Okay."

"Now go back three steps."

Natalie sent her gaze upward and reflected. "Yeah, okay."

"Now go forward six steps, then back one." She put down the can and picked up the matches. "What have you got?"

A smile spread across Natalie's face. "Grrr. My pride won't let me tell my name, but if you guess it I'll be tame. That is so corny."

"Isn't it?" Rebecca struck a match and tossed it onto the charcoal. "And we thought it was one of those math puzzles."

"Unfortunately it doesn't shed any immediate light...."

Rebecca watched the pale flames. "Well, add it to the pot."

There was a tapping sound from the yard: Gayanne hammering posts into the ground, wielding a mallet with unaccustomed hands.

Rebecca put the grill on the barbecue. "How is the search for Armand Vitek going?"

"Not a trace so far."

"I don't see how you can compete with the police."

Natalie returned the lighter fluid to the old blue sea chest at the side of the patio. "Ninety-nine times out of a hundred, I couldn't. They've got

144

access to income tax returns, property tax lists, driver's licenses, civil service information. But if it turns out that all the normal avenues the police use are useless, then I've got just as much of a chance as anyone to find him."

"Kovaks said Armand didn't trust the government...."

"And rent-boy is not a profession that is known for filing tax returns." Natalie wiped her hands together. "So I'm playing some long shots. It just takes an incredible amount of time...."

"It'll help, having your afternoons freed up, won't it?"

"Oh you heard about that...."

"Sure. Great idea. What?"

"Nothing...I just thought Daniel might be more forthcoming with you than with me. Do you think Louise's offer bothered him?"

"He jumped at the chance, and so did Gayanne. What's wrong? I thought you liked Louise."

"I do! Only...I wonder if she'll be a good influence on Gayanne. Sometimes I think she needs a swift kick.... You know, she let's everybody walk all over her, like, like...."

"Like your mother...."

Natalie opened her mouth to reply, then closed it again. "Come on—they're ready for us. I get the red ball and mallet!"

♥   ♥   ♥

On Monday morning, Natalie headed down to Hudson County without stopping at the *Star*, although she did leave a message on Tyler's answer machine, giving him her itinerary.

As far as she had been able to discover, there were no Viteks living in either Bergen or Hudson Counties. She had also checked Rockland County, which bordered Bergen to the north, although it had meant spending her Saturday morning scavenging through the unfamiliar environs of the New York State records system, only to discover that there were no living Viteks there, either.

Expanding on Tyler's theme, she had begun looking for dead Viteks. This strategy had led to the discovery, after another bout of crawling around windowless storerooms, of some dozen deceased Viteks—all of whom were the wrong age to be Armand. In particular, she found the death certificates of one Olena Vitek, dead of cancer at age 49 in 1973, and one Toller Vitek, also dead of cancer, at age 52 in 1969. Neither had any address other than the Hudson County Hospital. Both certificates had been issued by the

Hudson County coroner. Tyler had traced Armand's old driver's license, issued in 1970 and never renewed, to the Hudson County DMV.

She spent the morning trying to track down an obituary for either Olena or Toller Vitek in the Jersey City Hall of Records. No luck there. If she could find out what town they had lived in—if they were related and had lived in the same town—she might be able to track down someone who remembered them. No wonder fictional investigators made a bee-line for the nearest pub for information—it was too mind-numbing to contemplate checking the property tax records for twenty-five years in sixty-two towns.

At twelve, she pulled into a local diner, planning to grab a sandwich and coffee to go. She had a solid idea for her afternoon's search. She would go to the hospital where the Viteks had died, and see how well they maintained their records. Maybe there were admittance papers with an address, or a next of kin....

In the diner's anteroom there was a phone, planted on the wall between the newspaper rack and the candy machine. Figuring it wouldn't kill her to be responsible and check in, she dialed the number of the *Star* switchboard.

Given her mood of self-mortification, Tyler's greeting was particularly galling:

"Where the *hell* have you been!"

"Crawling around roach-infested cellars looking for death certificates."

"Why didn't you call in?"

"Calm yourself, Tyler." Natalie spoke without anger. She had found that not reacting to his outbursts was the quickest way to quell them. He was a fidgety soul, with an acid tongue, but she was getting a grip on how to handle him. "I left you a message, and I'm calling in now."

"Well this just isn't acceptable! I've got an interview to do in fifteen minutes! Byron's been asking where you were since nine, and I've been stalling, saying you'd be right in—"

"There was no need for you to do that." She moved closer to the wall to make room for a group of paying customers. "Stop trying to make me feel guilty. All you had to do was tell him I was in the field. I can call him now, it's no big deal—"

"Good God, woman, didn't you see the headline?"

Natalie thought back. "The Sunday edition?" Had she read it before they had used it to clean the grill?

"Not the *Star*!" His voice was strangled with his effort to restrain himself. "The *Bugle*!"

Natalie turned to the metal rack of newspapers. She searched for the festooned yellow bugle logo. There it was, overshadowing the *Star*'s solemn leader about declining enrollment in local colleges. The *Bugle* headline, blaring out in 48 point bold, was:

Candidate Linked to Christmas Murder: Old Sex Scandal
Exhumed Along with Body

above a heavily moired picture of Peter Kovaks.

"Aw…." In the interests of the toddler who passed by at that moment attached to his mummy's hand, Natalie swallowed her expletive and satisfied her need to vent by kicking the wall. "I'll be there in half an hour."

Chapter Seventeen

I t was a day notable for many firsts, not least among them the first time in her life Natalie Joday plunked down a dollar and bought a copy of the *Bugle*. She skimmed the lead story (at stoplights along the length of Route 17 and Polifly Road), braced for the worst. She found little to comfort her. It was a minor satisfaction to note that the article was full of inaccuracies and unnecessary commas, and written in a style more suited to Saturday morning TV than the coverage of a felony. The writer (one Max Bludwort) had the year wrong and spelled Marconi's given name "Mauritsio." But he spread-eagled the old scandal for all to see, sparing neither Peter Kovaks' name, the *Star*'s involvement, nor deceased's reputation. "Can it be called, mere coincidence?" he queried with great moment if little pith, "that one man, who, with the help of a once noble and respected news organ, needlessly ended the political career of another, is now, himself, running for the very same office that his nemesis once aspired to, just when this vicious murder is revealed?" Natalie's foot pressed down harder on the gas pedal.

♥   ♥   ♥

It was reassuring to find the newsroom still operating. In fact, it looked the same as ever, though the conversational counterpoint, generated from the usual ensembles of reporters and staffers lounging around watching each other work, was a little higher pitched than usual. She did not stop to gossip. Tyler had left to keep his appointment, so she went straight to Marcia.

"Tyler said Byron was asking for me."

"Earlier he was," said Marcia. "He was hoping you had some positive news. Did you see the *Bugle* headline?"

"Just now. Very unfortunate."

"That's an understatement. The police are coming at three. They sounded annoyed…. He's upstairs giving Ms. V the update now. If you've got anything, I can…?" Marcia reached for her phone.

Natalie shook her head. "Sorry. I wish I did."

"Well, don't stop looking. He's counting on you."

"Oh?" Natalie put her hands on her hips. "You know I came back from Jersey City because Tyler said Byron wanted to see me."

Marcia made a face. "What are you listening to him for? You know Tyler—he loves to worry."

"Now who's understating...."

"Why not get a cell phone? That way he can reach you if he wants to, and so can I."

Natalie was silent, visions of dollar signs flashing in her head.

"Byron said he'd make sure you had resources, right?" Marcia barely skipped a beat. Only the look in her eye told Natalie that she had seen and understood her hesitation. "Here." Marcia whirled around on her chair and opened a filing cabinet. "You file a request with Bettina in Equipment for the use of a company cell phone for the run of the story." She whipped a sheet of paper out of a folder. "Do it now, and I'll run them up and get his signature right away."

"That's...great."

"Time you moved up in the world, girl. What've you been waiting for?"

"I—"

"And while we're at it, let's get you a temporary assignment for a desk. I'm sick of you complaining about the computers."

♥   ♥   ♥

At two thirty, Natalie found herself sitting at her new desk (one of the erstwhile communal desks, henceforth reserved for her use), in the swivel chair of her choice. On the desk sat a late-model computer, with a 15 inch color monitor, Internet connection, sufficient RAM, and a brand new keyboard. In her briefcase was a cell phone, somewhat clunky in appearance, but with all the latest features. As simple as that.

It was a real satisfaction to set up her shared-files folder on her spacious hard drive. It was a real pleasure to transfer her files there and link to the Server.

"You're looking smug about something."

She glanced up to find Ginny on the far side of the desk.

"Damn right." The mouse moved smoothly under her hand. "Before I forget, let me give you my new number." She scribbled on a page of her notebook and ripped it out with a flourish.

Ginny snatched the paper out of her hand. "I don't believe it! Finally!

Why didn't they give me a cell phone?"

Natalie addressed the keyboard. She clicked on the shared-files area, typed in her password, and pulled up her Enigma folder. "Because you already had one. It's only junior reporters on base salary like me who don't have cell phones."

"Welcome to the middle class."

Natalie shot her an annoyed look.

"So how did the *Bugle* get the story? Everyone is in shock."

"I don't know. All I know is…." Natalie paused.

"Oh go on, tell me. I know how to keep my mouth shut."

"The *Bugle* must have an outside source, because if they'd checked their own archive, they would've gotten the facts straight."

"Probably they got it from the police or the DA's office." Ginny grinned. "I understand Kovaks was paid a visit on Saturday. If not the police then maybe someone here is feeding info to the *Bugle*."

"Great. That's all we need…!" Natalie stood up.

"Where are you going?"

"Hudson County. The cops are coming by for a chat with Byron—and I don't want to run into them."

"I thought you had to be home by three."

Natalie closed her briefcase and shoved a couple of pens into her jacket pocket. "Not anymore."

♥   ♥   ♥

On each of the next three days the *Bugle* ran a sensationalized report on the Marconi investigation (before the discovery of the Kovaks connection it had not even mentioned the murder). It never failed to describe (however inaccurately) Marconi's doomed political run, or to point out the "unholy coincidence" that the man who had brought him down was now running for the same office. In their op-eds, they hammered away at the *Star* for conducting a witch hunt in 1972 (with Myra cast as head of the coven) and "ruining a man's career for the sake of a cheap headline" (while on page 2 they announced the shocking news that the Governor of New Jersey preferred red teddies and kept a broad assortment of leather whips in the basement of the Governor's Mansion).

The *Star* refused to enter the fray. Myra wrote a crisply worded and highly articulate op-ed in support of Peter Kovaks, and did not stoop to justify the *Star*'s original decision to break the story in 1972. The *Bugle* responded by claiming the *Star* was responsible for Maury's plunge into alcoholism, and thus (conveniently forgetting for half a column that he had been murdered) for his death. Peter Kovaks issued a statement condemning the murder, and trusting the police to bring the perpetrators to swift justice.

♥   ♥   ♥

On Thursday afternoon, Tyler called Natalie (sitting in the parking lot of a hospice in Harrison) to tell her that the police were not interested in finding Armand Vitek. His implication seemed to be: "If they don't think it's worth it, you're wasting your time."

♥   ♥   ♥

On Friday afternoon, Natalie called Rebecca from a diner in Hudson County.

"Are you free tonight?"

"I'm free if you need me."

"Unenlightened woman. Yes, I need you. I want you to help me make a raid on Michelangelo's, a gay bar in Union City."

"Don't you believe in buying local? What can be so special about this gay bar that you must desert the perfectly adequate gay bars we have in Bergen County?"

"Haven't you heard of it? It was reviewed in the *Times* last year. 'A devastating combination of good eats and atmosphere.' It is also around the corner from where Olena and Toller Vitek once lived."

"Ah! And how did you discover that?"

"Through the local Chapter of the American Cancer Society."

"Good work. You think they were Armand's parents?"

"I have no idea. The apartment building where they lived has been torn down—it was a poor neighborhood, back then. Nor could I find any school records. But the ages are right, and the lack of detail fits the pattern."

"I know you're playing long shots, but this is a Hail Mary...."

"Yeah, I know. But.... There's an axiom in bridge—when faced with a losing hand, imagine a distribution of the cards, no matter how improbable as long as it is still possible, that will let you win, and play for that. I can't find Armand Vitek faster than the cops if he is to be found by normal means. Because they have not found him, I conclude that normal means do not apply. The Internet search hasn't panned out. So I'm taking my best shot."

"Very well. And you want me to provide support for your plunge into the unfamiliar waters of the gay subculture?"

"Hell no! I want you to be my date! I'm damned if I'll be seen in a bar that received five stars from the *Times* without a date on a Friday night. I have my pride, you know."

"Ah! An undercover assignment. Make-up.... Costumes.... Very well. I'll pick you up at eight...."

♥ ♥ ♥

"I was expecting boots and leather," said Natalie.

"We did the wild west last month." Rebecca put one foot in front of the other, showing off to best advantage her long, willowy figure, hardly disguised at all by the black tube of stretch fabric that covered her from armpits to mid-thigh.

"Yeah, but I know how much you like fringe." Natalie, in a dusty rose silk blouse, held up by spaghetti ties and air, and black pants rather tighter than good taste dictated, opened the passenger door of Rebecca's Bronco.

"Besides, I knew you'd go for the sophisticated look, and I didn't want to clash." Rebecca settled in behind the wheel.

♥ ♥ ♥

The red leather door of Michelangelo's led into a crescent-shaped room with a long, curving bar. A full battery of brass taps with glossy ebony handles glittered in the soft light. Two steps down from the bar brought customers to a parquet dance floor surrounded by a clutter of spindly tables and chairs with bowed backs.

The early crowd was thin, so they were able to choose a table that met Rebecca's preference for good light and Natalie's for having her back to the wall. A waiter went by, eyes front and moving fast—universal waiter language for "Don't bother me, I'm busy."

"So I guess Michelangelo is the owner?" Rebecca glanced around the room with a hopeful expression. "Shoot. I was looking forward to a replica Statue of David."

Natalie twisted in her chair, trying to get her hand into her back pocket to make sure she had remembered her house key. "Look up."

Rebecca craned her neck backward. "Holy Moses."

♥ ♥ ♥

At ten o'clock a little man who looked like Mr. Magoo in baggy jeans pulled back the green velvet curtain that covered a small alcove on the far side of the dance floor and flipped a light switch. He sat down at the piano and rubbed his hands briskly. Another man, who looked like an advertisement for a Mediterranean cruise, wandered across the parquet and sat next to the piano. He laid the guitar he carried on his knee and plugged it into a box on the floor.

Another ten minutes passed, then music burst from the alcove as water through a broken dam, and a dozen patrons rose and stepped onto the dance floor.

♥ ♥ ♥

Rebecca turned out to have a penchant for dancing, and was soon enfolded into a group of lithe-bodied extroverts. Natalie, after a dance or two, sat nursing a beer and scoping out the crowd. The clientele was mostly young, mostly male, and mostly organized in groups of three or four, most of whom seemed to know each other. By eleven, when the second set started (with drummer, this time), bar, dance floor, and dining area were packed.

"I think I'm gonna have to have another dance," said Rebecca as the pianist's fingers flew down the keyboard and launched into an up-tempo tune. "Join me, pumpkin?"

"Not right now. I'm getting ready to make my move."

"Do you want me to start pumping the boys?"

"Not yet. Anyway, they're all too young. Just amuse yourself."

"I obey." Rebecca slid out of her chair.

Natalie admired her easy way with the other dancers—strangers but for the common interest that had pulled them onto the parquet. She would dance alone for a while, then, communicating somehow without words, dance with anyone who moved into her sphere.

Natalie looked away from the dance floor and toward the bar.

He was back. A small, slender man who stood at the far end of the bar like a captain standing on the forecastle of his ship. He wore a black T-shirt tucked into jeans held in place by a wide belt.

She knew, because she had seen him twice before, that he would not stay long. Rising, she worked her way to the bar and sat on the last stool. The bartender was busy, so she ate a couple of peanuts.

She watched her target out of the corner of her eye. His hand tapped the dark wood of the bar, following the beat of the music. He was about sixty, barrel-chested but not fat, with a short gray beard, and long gray hair, which he wore in an unobtrusive ponytail. His wire-rimmed glasses did not conceal his quick-moving dark eyes.

The bartender swooped down on her. She ordered another beer, then added. "This is quite a place—great food, great music. How do I pass on my compliments to the management?"

The bartender jerked his head toward the standing man. "I think you just did." He took a swipe with a cloth at the bar, obliterating a couple of peanut shells and a glass ring, and sped away.

Natalie looked at the gray-haired man and found his twinkling eyes already on her. "Oh! Are you the owner?"

"The bank is the owner. But it's my name on the title certificate." He reached out a small hand. "Mike Morrisey."

"Natalie Joday." She took his hand with a smile. "Live music is getting hard to find this side of the river. I wonder why?"

"New Jersey has always been a cultural wasteland."

She glanced up. "You from around here originally?"

"Yup." Mike glanced at his watch. "I don't want to be rude, but I've got a schedule to keep. What did you want to ask me?"

Natalie looked at him curiously. "What makes you think I wanted to ask you something?"

He looked over her shoulder at the crowd. "And you're answering a question with a question.... Come on! I spotted you watching me an hour ago. Are you a cop or a private eye?"

The bartender swooped by again, slapped a coaster on the bar, placed her glass on it, and disappeared.

"I'm a reporter for the *Bergen Evening Star*."

He nodded. "My horoscope today said I'd do a favor for a lovely stranger. I don't believe everything I read, but I'm listening...."

Natalie, recovering from her dismay at being tagged so easily, took encouragement from the fact that he had not merely thrown her out. "I'm looking for Armand Vitek." The direct approach was always best when someone has admitted to being short on time. "He would be about forty-five now. I think he lived in this neighborhood about twenty-five years ago. All I know about him is he's white, gay, knowledgeable about computers, and anti-government."

"Why are you here?" His eyes moved to the other end of the bar.

"To find someone who knew him, or might be able to track him down. I think he's still living, because I haven't found any mention of his death, but he's disappeared off the planet. Do you...?"

"I know a lot of people...." Mike's eyes stopped their roving and came to rest on her face. "Why do you want to talk to him?"

"I'm working on the murder of a guy named Marconi. Armand knew him twenty years ago, and may have information that will help solve the case."

Mike scrunched up his eyes. "Let me see your hands."

With a self-conscious laugh, she held out her hands, palms down.

He turned them over, and, squinting again, lowered his face. "You've got strong fingers for somebody who doesn't do any physical work."

"I spend a lot of time at sticky keyboards."

"You should get out more. When was your last vacation?"

"I really...don't know."

He raised his grizzled face. "Oh come on."

"I don't take vacations. A day here or there for a long weekend."

He pulled her fingers back, stretching out her palms. "No boyfriend, eh?"

Natalie raised her eyes to the frescoed ceiling.

"And your love line as deep as the Grand Canyon. Afraid it'll kill you if he let's you down, eh? I don't blame you. Men are such toads." He lowered his face again, and took off his glasses. "Oh."

Natalie peered anxiously at her palms. "What?"

"You said it was a murder investigation? I'd stay out of dark alleys if I were you."

She pulled her hands away. "I never go into dark alleys...." She looked stupidly at her hands. "What makes you say that?"

Mike straightened his back. "Nothing. I'm probably wrong. Who pays any attention to palmistry? Load of crap." He rummaged for a peanut and held it in his fingers. "Come back tomorrow."

"Why?"

"Come around three."

"Can I call you?"

He shook his head. "I like to see people's faces when I talk to them about something important."

"But—"

"What, you think I don't know at my age what I mean when I say something? You got what you wanted. Now collect your bitchin' girlfriend before she causes a cat fight and blow!"

He popped the peanut in his mouth, and disappeared through swinging doors, leaving Natalie swiveling idly on the bar stool.

Chapter Eighteen

Michelangelo's in mid-afternoon looked like any other bar and restaurant five hours before opening. Sunlight fell in through unshuttered windows, fading the rich reds and blues of the furnishings to washed-out pastels. A boy in tight jeans vacuumed the carpet, while a couple of electricians worked on a row of lights in the dining room. Natalie, admitted by a young woman eating a pomegranate, found Mike sitting at the bar doing paperwork and keeping an eye on the training of a novice bartender. Natalie eased herself onto a stool at his side and waited for him to come up for air.

He took off his glasses and rubbed his eyes. "You're not gonna like this."

"Then tell me fast so I can start getting over it."

"Our friend turns out to be a bigger asshole than I remember."

"You found him?"

"More or less. I got the word to him, but I don't know where he is, or what he's doing."

"But you talked to him?"

Mike tipped his head to one side. "Not exactly."

"What do you mean?"

"You'll find out. He's gonna call." He glanced at the clock on the mirror behind the bar. "In about five minutes."

"What's the part I'm not going to like?"

"He's calling as a favor to me, to tell you to get off his ass. He says he never knew any Marconi. He thinks you're a CIA spy using me to get to him so you can arrest him for subversion."

"I get that a lot." Natalie ran a forefinger along the arc of her eyebrow. "So you did know him?"

"Honey, I've known a lot of people, especially if they're gay. I haven't seen or talked to Armand in fifteen years, and I don't think I met him more than four times, but yeah, I knew him."

"How come you didn't tell me that last night?"

His eyes twinkled. "Because I didn't know you."

Natalie raised an eyebrow. "You checked me out?"

A phone rang. Mike got up and pulled an old-fashioned black telephone onto the bar, then walked away grinning.

She reached for the receiver. "Hello?"

There was a clicking sound, followed by words spoken in a jerky monotone: "What do you want?"

Natalie thought she must have been connected to an automated operator. "I'd like to speak to Armand Vitek."

There was a pause, and then: "What do you want to say to him?"

It was a voice synthesizer. What the hell? "Is this Armand?"

Another pause. "Ask your question."

"Okay." Natalie opened her notebook. "You may have read in the paper that Maurizio Marconi was murdered last December?" It was a trick question, designed to find out if he was close by.

Pause. "I do not know anyone by that name."

In the absence of intonation, such statements were remarkably unhelpful. "Back in 1972 you told a newspaper reporter named Peter Kovaks that you had had sex with Mr. Marconi."

Pause. "I do not know anything about this. You have got the wrong name. Go away."

There was a click in her ear, and the line went dead.

Natalie stared at the phone for a moment in annoyance, then settled the receiver into the cradle.

Mike appeared and put the phone back behind the bar. "You get what you wanted?"

She closed her notebook. "Nope."

"Sorry, honey. If it helps, I don't think Vitek would ever hurt a fly. Plenty brains. No judgment. Always getting into trouble, but I don't think it was ever really his fault."

Natalie eyed him. "Maybe he hung with the wrong crowd."

"I don't think he hung with crowds. He just had a screw loose." Mike scratched his head. "A couple of screws loose...."

A buzzer rang over by the cash register. "How did you meet him?"

"He fixed my VCR."

"You're kidding."

"Would I kid a reporter from the *Star*? He was just trying to make an honest living."

"But I thought he—" Reflected in the mirror behind the bottles, Natalie saw the pomegranate-eating woman open the red door. A tall man in a white sweatshirt entered, stopped, and looked up.

"Shit…." Natalie slid off the bar stool, took Mike by the arm, and swung him in between herself and the door.

"What?" Mike's eyes slid sideways.

"You got a back way out?" she hissed.

"You kiddin'?"

He pushed her back two steps, straight through the swinging doors and into the kitchen. When she was safely inside, he turned and peeked through the diamond shaped glass.

"Damn, you hang with a hot crowd. What a doll. Who is he?"

"That's Da Man."

"No kiddin'? Hmm. I'm finally having my first psychic experience. He's gonna want to know all about Armand, right?"

"You nailed it. Although I was told the cops weren't working on this lead…."

"Too bad I haven't spoken to Armand in so many years…."

"I'm sure if you think about it *long* enough, you'll remember the last time you saw him."

"Could be, if I'm asked nicely enough." Mike sucked in his gut and squared his shoulders. "But I'm sure it's going to take me forever to remember the details. I hope he's not in a hurry. And of course then he'll have to talk to all the boys, too—they might know something about Armand. I'm sure the boys would love to talk to him." He winked at her. "You. Amscray!" He pointed toward the back of the kitchen.

Dodging around the dishwasher (a distracting sight in a purple muscle shirt), Natalie found her way through a crowded storeroom, and out into the parking lot.

♥   ♥   ♥

"He said what?" asked Rebecca.

"That he didn't know Marconi or Kovaks."

"In an electronically generated voice."

"Right. Not very helpful. I don't even know if it was him."

"Then why did he call you?"

"To get me to stop looking for him." Natalie sniffed. "It worked."

♥   ♥   ♥

On Sunday evening, she went out to dinner and the movies with a guy she had met at the American Cancer Society office. Arriving home shortly after midnight, she fired up her computer. It had become her habit, in the face of Tyler's badgering about her haphazard work ethic, to check her e-mail the last thing at night. Although she could not access the Police Ticker from home, Tyler could, and he had offered to send her any relevant news via e-mail. She took a quick shower while her computer dialed her service provider. Eventually, wrapped in a fuzzy bathrobe against the coolness of the night, she settled down in her little office off the kitchen. Trick walked by with his tail in the air, sniffed at his full food dish, then jumped onto the windowsill and disappeared through his cat door.

There was nothing from Tyler—but there was an e-mail with the subject "URGENT!" which she dutifully opened. She read the following:

meet me at the stateline diner at midnight cum alone or u won't see me tell _no one_ where u r going dont b late cause i wont wait a.v.

♥   ♥   ♥

Natalie turned left at the top of Tank Hill and burned rubber as she roared up Schralenburgh. Once on the straight, she pulled the cell phone from her bag and dialed.

No answer after 15 rings. "Damn." She dialed another number as she slowed for the stoplight at Old Hook Road.

Her brother answered. "Yeah?" His voice was thick with sleep.

"Hi, me. Sorry about the hour, but I'm on a story."

"Okay…what do I do?"

"Put Rebecca on the phone?"

The light changed and she sped off as fast as she dared.

"What's up?" Rebecca was more awake than Daniel.

"I just got an e-mail from Armand asking me to meet him at the Stateline Diner at midnight."

"It's almost one."

"I know." She went past the New Globe Theater.

"Where are you?"

"I went past you about two minutes ago, heading north. I'm just leaving Harrington Park."

"Okay, you said the Stateline? I'll meet you there…."

"No. He said come alone or I wouldn't see him."

"I don't like the sound of that!"

"It's all right. The Stateline is 24 hours and well-lit. I just hope he's still there. But I thought I'd better tell you where—"

"Nat?" It was Daniel, fully awake.

"Yeah…."

"What's with this guy?"

It would have been a vague question coming from anyone else, but she understood.

"We're talking a little hustling in his youth and an anarchistic approach to the IRS now that he's middle aged. He likes computers. He probably believes in UFOs. Nothing messy."

"Call me by two. If I don't hear from you, I'm coming up there and Rebecca's calling the cops."

"I'm not—"

"Call!"

"Okay. Jeez. That you should turn out to be such a worrier."

She switched the phone off as she crossed the town line into Northvale.

♥   ♥   ♥

Two laps of the sprawling Stateline Dinner parking lot, window rolled down and wearing her most come-hither expression, convinced her that Armand Vitek was not there. Feeling annoyed, she parked and went inside.

She sauntered up to the pink-uniformed cashier and pulled out her press ID. "Natalie Joday, *Bergen Evening Star*."

The girl's mouth opened. "Whah?"

"Can you help me? I was supposed to meet a contact here about an hour ago—but I got his message late."

She wrinkled her lip. "Whah?"

"Was there someone waiting here—white male, in his forties, small eyes, small mouth?

The girl stared as if she were a stray dog that had wandered in.

Natalie ran a hand through her hair. "I'd like to speak to your manager, please."

♥   ♥   ♥

But the manager knew nothing about any waiting stranger, and Natalie called Daniel without further ado—although she took the precaution of retiring to the ladies washroom to do so, lest Armand somehow see her and know she had disregarded his warning.

Rebecca answered the phone and heard the story. "You checked the men's room?"

"The bus boy did. I checked to see if anyone had put sugar in the salt-cellars. We both came up empty."

"What next?"

"Head home, I guess, and hope there's another e-mail message. This guy seems more and more like a jerk with everything I hear...."

"Nat, how did he get your e-mail address?"

"I don't know. From the *Star*, I guess...." Shoving the phone into her bag, she left the Stateline and returned to her car.

There was a piece of paper under the windshield wiper.

GO TO THE PHONE BOOTH ON CARLTON IN ORANGE-BURG

She turned around. The parking lot was empty. She looked in the back seat. There was nothing there but a crumpled scrap of fabric on the floor—Gayanne's bathing suit. She checked the trunk. Then she got in and locked the doors.

According to the road map, Carlton was only a short drive away. She headed up Western Ave., her eyes constantly flicking to the rearview mirror. She drove more slowly now. Was he following? Close enough to be watching? Should she risk a call? Better to cruise the phone booth, first.... She glanced at her watch. One fifty-five. Her foot eased down on the gas pedal.

♥   ♥   ♥

The booth was at an all-night self-service gas station and convenience store. Reassured by the lights and the sight of a clerk sitting behind the counter inside, she parked and got out.

Leaning against the side of the car, she waited five minutes. Nothing. Annoyed, she went over to the phone booth. It was of the hooded variety—not a booth at all, really. There was a piece of paper sticking out of the phone book.

GET ON THE THRUWAY AT EXIT 6 AND GO NORTH 1.3 MILES TO THE WEIGH STATION

♥   ♥   ♥

She got back into the car and put her hands on the steering wheel. A weigh station off the Thruway? This called for thought....

She had no reason to suspect Armand of harboring any malice toward her; it was the situation he had created—pulling her farther and farther off the beaten path—that had detonated the warning flares in her mind. She felt as if she had set out to cross a river on a sturdy footbridge—only to discover half-way across that the bridge had become a patchwork of rotten boards, and then a single wobbly plank balanced on green rocks that looked like the backs of crocodiles. If she hadn't wanted something from him, she would not even consider this. But want something from him she did.

However, she knew she had to tell someone where she was going; someone she could trust. The question was, who?

If Rebecca had been home, or in bed with someone not her brother, she would have called her. But she knew she could not call her brother again and worry him by telling him what she intended to do. In a curious twist, "protecting her family" had suddenly extended to protecting them from herself. For the first time in her life, she wondered if Daniel had been telling the truth all those years ago when he had said he had lied because he didn't want to hurt her.

A gap had opened between her work life and her family life, forcing her to look elsewhere for the kind of trust she had always assumed was found only in one's family. But where could she look?

She turned the ignition key and backed into the road. The Thruway was only a stone's throw away. As she went around the looping on-ramp, there was not a car in sight. She picked up the cell phone and dialed.

♥　　　♥　　　♥

The access road to the weigh station cut away from the Thruway across a grassy verge. Seventy-five yards in, she arrived at the weighing platform. There were no cars, no people, no lights, and no buildings. She kept the engine running and her headlights on, and checked for the third time to make sure the doors were locked. Then she waited.

Headlights swept across the verge and lit up the woods to her right—a car, making a hairpin turn off the Thruway, traveling the wrong way up the exit road from the weigh station.

Natalie ran her hands around the steering wheel.

An old Toyota Corolla slowed to a crawl and drew level with her. She was aware of a large head and shoulders in the driver's seat. The window rolled down.

He hitched an elbow over the window sill and stuck his head out. He had a round, almost cherubic face, with a recessed mouth and eyes that looked like tucks in a sofa cushion. He made a gesture with his right hand as if turning a meat grinder.

Natalie rolled down her window.

He gave a little wave. "Hi."

"Hi yourself." She noted his receding hairline and foolish grin. "You've got about two minutes to convince me I should stay."

"What?" His mouth dropped open. "Hey, you're the one who wanted to talk to me!"

"True. But my mother told me it was dangerous to meet strangers on deserted roads in the dead of night." She raised an eyebrow.

"Dangerous?" He hunched his high round shoulders closer to the window. "This is the only way I was sure we would be safe."

"If you wanted safety, all you had to do was pick up a phone."

"Oh, man, you're so innocent!" He hitched his other elbow over the sill, and she got a good view of his ancient red-checked shirt. "Don't you know? They monitor your phone calls electronically. If you use the wrong combinations of key words, you're dead meat."

Natalie rejected the first two responses that occurred to her. "I didn't know that."

"They've been after me for years, but I know how to stay one step ahead. Hey." He stuck his hand out. "Gimme my messages."

Natalie hesitated. If his fingerprints were on those messages they might be the only way of ever finding Armand again.

He rolled his eyes impatiently. "I'm not gonna say a word until you hand them over."

Natalie shrugged and gave them to him.

"Thank you, ma'am." His voice was a childish singsong. "So we don't want us to leave after all, do we!" He laughed—a rapid fire chuckle on one note. When he was done, he reached to his right and fumbled for something on the passenger's seat.

When his face reappeared, Natalie spoke. "I'm still waiting to hear why you wanted to see me. The last I heard, you didn't know anybody named Marconi."

He grinned as he unscrewed a cup from the top of a thermos. "Maybe I changed my mind."

"What made you do that?"

He shrugged as he poured a dark liquid into the cup. "I told you, they're after me, and they're getting too close for comfort."

A faint whiff of coffee reached her nose. "Look Armand, who is this 'they,' you keep talking about?"

He glanced up quickly. He had a trick of showing the tip of his tongue when he was surprised. "Them! You know. The spooks, the hedgehogs…."

"I'm not following you….

"Oh man!" He rolled his head. "Them! I know too much; if they find me I'm a goner. And it's all your fault!"

"My fault?"

"You've used my name on your phone, right?"

"Yeah…."

"And on the Internet. It's been noted." He took an enormous swig of coffee, then gave a satisfied sigh. "They're using you to get to me. You gotta lay off! I'm not easy to find, but today was too close for comfort."

Geoff on the job, thought Natalie. "Why not talk to them?"

"Oh man…. Once they find you, they never let you go! They implant a neuro-transceiver in your cerebellum and you never know it. You get cancer and die within two years. They got both my parents that way. I'm not goin' anywhere near those guys! As long as I stay on this side of the State line I'm safe."

"Why not?"

"Their center of operations is in New Jersey. You know why? The percentage of ozone in the air is higher because of discharges from the swamps. The increased electromagnetic energy in the air masks their base from surveillance equipment."

"I didn't know that either…."

"Yeah. I haven't been in Jersey for fifteen years." He took another belt of coffee, spilling a little on his shirt. "You got me into this, so you gotta get me out. That's fair, right? You gotta put it in the paper that I didn't have anything to do with old man Marconi. That'll hose down the spooks. Okay?"

"You think that's how a newspaper works? You tell us what to write, and we just write it?"

"I thought you were in business to sell papers! You'll sell lots of papers with this kind of story." He laughed again.

"Nothing sells better than sex, is that your point?"

His smile faded. Suddenly he was nervous. "Yeah, well, that might be a problem." He glanced over his shoulder at the northbound traffic on the Thruway, visible as a line of red taillights. "Because I never slept with Marconi—that's what I want you to tell everybody."

Natalie did not try to hide her surprise. "What?"

"I don't know a thing about him. See? I never met him. So lay off." He backed away from the window and into the shadows.

"Wait a minute!" If he left now she might never see him again. "I can't print that."

His head reappeared. "Why not?"

"Because we don't have any proof that it's true! Marconi is dead, so we can't ask him. And in 1972 your story was exactly the opposite of what you're saying now."

"But I'm telling you the truth now!" His tongue filled the curve of his lower lip. "That's better than proof. I was there, wasn't I?"

"Look, on this you'd better listen to me. We can't just print something somebody says without verification. You haven't proved a thing. In fact, I'm not even sure you're Armand Vitek!"

"What do you mean?" He sounded stunned. "I called you at Mike's!"

"An electronic voice called me." She gave him a stern look. "How about a driver's license?"

It was a trick question, and the guarded look that came into his eyes told her he knew it.

He pursed his tiny lips. "I don't have a driver's license."

It was the right answer, but she frowned and drew her eyebrows together, pushing him. "What do you mean you don't have a license? You're driving a car, aren't you?"

"Oh, man, you are so totally indoctrinated. Okay, yes I have a perfectly good fake driver's license, but I'm not going to show it to you, because my real name isn't on it and I don't want you to know my alternate personality." He tossed his head.

Natalie remained unmoved. "Then how am I supposed to verify who you are?"

"I don't know. Go find my high school graduation picture. Bayonne High, 1968."

Finally, thought Natalie. "How did you get my e-mail address?"

"Oh, come on, lady! Use your head! You've been e-bombing me for the past week. Did you think I didn't know it?"

"You got my e-mails?"

"Of course. Me and half the Internet. You may live to regret broadcasting your contact information like that."

Natalie leaned forward. "Is that a threat?"

Armand rolled his little eyes. "Puh-lease! I could care less about your dull little life. No offense. But other people might care."

"Oh, right, 'them.'"

"Yes, them." He looked suddenly frightened. "The Power Elite. You should start looking behind you now, before it's too late."

"Let's get back to the problem," said Natalie. "I can't print your denial that you had sex with Marconi without some proof."

He looked at her doubtfully. "Can't you just say the paper made up the story? It was a long time ago…."

It was Natalie's turn to laugh. "I don't think Peter Kovaks would go along with that!"

His mouth sagged, and his eyes lowered to the wheels of her car. "Kovaks is still around?"

"Of course. I spoke to him the other day and heard the whole story." Natalie, having started the rip, settled down to pull him wide open. "Marconi ended his political career over this—and now you want to tell me you didn't even know him? It won't wash. Besides which, you convinced Kovaks you knew Marconi intimately."

"What if I told you I lied to Kovaks?"

Natalie looked into his eyes. They were so hard to read, hidden in his concave face. "Then I'd ask you why."

"I don't think I can tell you that." He spoke in the singsong again.

"Why not?"

His brow wrinkled unhappily. "Because I don't want to cause any problems…." He chugged on the coffee cup again, emptying it. Natalie concluded that either he had an aluminum-lined throat or the coffee was cold.

"Even if it means keeping a murderer from being brought to justice?"

"Man! I thought I told you, this has nothing to do with any murder. This is…something else. You got that?"

"No."

"I thought it was pretty simple."

"Maybe it is…." She smiled suddenly. "Maybe I've misunderstood you from the start. But, jeez, Armand, you know you're not exactly the conventional man on the street."

He laughed again—a silly, childish laugh. "That's for sure. Thank Gawd!" He screwed the cup onto the thermos. "Conventional men are so boring."

"So you're protecting someone else." She made it sound obvious.

He raised his round shoulders. "Hey, I told you, I'm only interested in protecting myself. I'm just here to tell you I'm not connected to Marconi at all, so you can look elsewhere."

"Okay. I think I'm following you. But this still isn't going to wash with my editor—he's the conventional type, and he's not going to take your word for it. The first thing he's going to do is tell me to find whoever else is involved—and how. Although I can guess at that, from what you've told me."

"I didn't tell you anything!"

"Not directly. But if you lied to Kovaks, then it was a set-up, right? And since you didn't know Marconi, there had to be someone involved who did, someone who could give you the details. This someone talked you into lying to Kovaks, right? Did they tell you it was a joke?"

"I'm not saying a word." The tongue appeared again. "You go tell your editor my story. He'll print it all right."

"No, he won't. We need verification. Look, is that such a big deal? You want the spooks off your tail—maybe this person you don't want to get into trouble feels the same way…."

"I didn't say there was any other person." He tossed the thermos onto the passenger's seat.

Natalie put on her most sympathetic face. "Is it someone you care about? Someone you love?"

"That'll be the day." He rolled his eyes. "Sister, you are so naive! Love is an invention of nasty-minded men out to enslave women. Don't tell me you still buy that schmaltz. You poor thing."

"Then you go talk to them. Who knows? If they'll agree to come forward, the heat will be off you. That's the only way…."

"Why can't you just write a story and say that I didn't have anything to do with it? You don't have to print it on the front page. What harm can it do to put it in a little corner somewhere?"

"It doesn't work that way."

"If you were smart enough, you could make it work…." He settled in his seat, and put his hands on the steering wheel.

"Armand…. Think about this. If you tell me who put you up to it, I can talk to them for you. I promise I'll do everything I can to keep them out of it. I can interview them on background, which means—"

"Yeah, yeah, I saw *All the President's Men*; I know what it means."

"Well then?"

"Sorry." He put the Corolla in gear. "I've told you all I can. I gotta go."

"At least think about what I said…."

"You think about what I said." The window began to roll up. "Then print it. 'Cause it's all you're ever gonna get from me."

Natalie stuck her head out the window. "E-mail me, okay?"

The Corolla pulled away from the weigh station and bumped along the access road, directly under the "Wrong Way: Do Not Enter" sign. She noted without surprise that there was no light above the license plate. He swung right onto the Thruway, wheels squealing with the acuteness of the turn.

Natalie rolled up her window and headed down the exit. With her left hand she pulled the cell phone out of the dashboard recess.

"Are you still there?" She waited, but there was no answer. "Turn off your mute, I can't hear you."

"Sorry. Can you hear me now?"

"Yeah. Did you get anything?"

"Most of it. Is he gone?"

"Yeah." She pulled onto the Thruway and picked up speed.

"Good work. Now go home."

Natalie glanced at the dashboard. Two thirty. "Don't you think—"

"No. Go home. Go to bed. We'll talk in the morning."

"But—"

"Not now. You may be raring to go, but 'conventional' people like me need to sleep."

There was a click in Natalie's ear. She tossed the phone onto the passenger seat, and headed for Exit 7.

Chapter Nineteen

So you're saying we don't report this to the cops…?"

"That's what I'm saying."

Natalie looked unhappily at Byron. "Haven't we crossed the line between speculation and information?"

"Why?" Byron was sorting through the stack of pink message slips that had accumulated over the weekend. "Because he told you he didn't have sex with Maury? Did you believe him?"

"I'm not sure…. Does it matter?"

"What matters is that we have no evidence that he was telling the truth—as you so eloquently argued to him last night."

Natalie shook her head. "I was trying to get him to open up and tell me the story, not presenting evidence at a trial."

"But the weight of the evidence indicates he was lying to you."

"What evidence?"

"Isn't it obvious? If there was no affair, then why did Marconi end his campaign when Kovaks confronted him? Why didn't he just laugh and say 'prove it?'"

"Right…."

Byron scribbled a note on one of the messages. "Vitek was lying to you to get you off his back. Don't you see the pattern? First he said he didn't know Marconi. Then he said he knew who Marconi was, but he didn't sleep with him, never said he did. When you remind him he's on record as telling a different story, he says he lied to Kovaks. Finally, when you point out the only possible conclusion—that it was a set-up—he panics and takes off."

"But aren't we impeding the investigation by not telling the detectives we found him?"

"Tyler's contacts in the DA's office have told him they're not giving much weight to the Enigma letters, or to what happened twenty years ago. It's a minor point for them. Now, if a detective asks you if you have ever met Armand Vitek, you will of course answer 'yes.' Until that point, I don't see that you are under any obligation to come forward. Besides…could you find him again?"

"I don't know. I replied to his e-mail when I got home last night, but it bounced back. No such domain name. But Mike found him."

"That's Mike's business." He glanced up at her. "Don't worry. I'll be the first one to tell you when we enter into a situation where legally we must speak up."

"Okay." She looked at her watch. Past nine. "Then I'm off."

"Where to?"

"Another long shot. Louise recalled three references to colleges in the early letters. Two colleges have been mentioned during the investigation. Maury went to Newark College, and Peter Kovaks went to SUNY Purchase."

"Keep me posted." He turned back to his messages.

Natalie found Marcia just settling into her chair. She greeted her cheerfully and then adopted a plaintive expression. "Does having my own desk mean it's really mine, or just mine when I'm here?"

"Somebody been eating your porridge?"

"And sitting in my chair. Some cretin has changed the settings I configured just last week."

"It's your desk, your computer. But give the poor stringers some time to adjust."

"I'll have to hang a Hands Off sign on it or something."

"What about a name plate? Only twenty bucks."

Damn Trick. He could eat the Happy Cat or starve. "I'll take it."

♥   ♥   ♥

Back at her desk, Natalie called Rebecca and gave her a sketch of the second half of the night's events. "Sorry for not calling back," she said in conclusion, "I just didn't want to worry Daniel."

"I understand. And I think you're right. He doesn't need to hear the details of what his sister does in the line of duty."

"I thought you went home Sunday nights?"

"I normally do. This was just a one-off."

"Good. He's showing signs of flexibility."

"Look, this doesn't mean you're going to lock me out, does it?"

"Of course not! We need to talk about Armand. He's not what I expected. I don't think he was lying, and I don't think he was ever a rentboy."

"If he lied when he said he had slept with Maury, he might have lied to Kovaks about everything."

"Yeah, but then how did Peter Kovaks' contacts on the street find him? It doesn't add up. Frankly, I'm getting worried...."

"About?"

"About the *Star* losing it's credibility. It occurred to me last night that Enigma was trying to warn us. Because there's another, more subtle answer besides 'newspaper' and 'embarrassed zebra' to the black and white and red all over riddle."

"What?"

"An embarrassed newspaper."

♥   ♥   ♥

Natalie spent the day at the Newark College library, trying to get hold of any records at all from what appeared to the student librarian to be the dawn of time, some forty or more years ago. She had barely established that the College had existed in 1949, and that Marconi had been a student there, when the library closed.

♥   ♥   ♥

After the Tuesday morning Crime Bureau meeting, Ginny, who had filed a hot story on a breakthrough in the Upper Saddle River case, corralled Natalie and took her over to Charlie's.

"You were quiet this morning," said Ginny. "What's really going on with the Marconi case?"

"Didn't you hear Tyler? I'm being led down the primrose path by a sociopath. The police are baffled. The DA is baffled." Natalie stared at her place mat. "Bee's parents have four children. The first three are named Spring, Summer, and Fall. What is the fourth child's name? I'm baffled."

"Winter. I don't want to butt in, but...have you had a chance to talk the case over with your favorite policeman—in private?"

"I'm trying to avoid that."

"Why?"

"I don't want him to ask me a question I don't want to answer."

"I was speaking professionally," said Ginny stiffly.

"So was I!" Natalie glared at her, then snickered. "I mean it, Ginny. This story is taking me places I didn't know existed. The cops are so close behind I hear their footsteps in my dreams. Supposedly I'm under no obligation to tell what I know—unless I get asked a direct question about a factual event related to the case. Man, this isn't the way it was in the old days when the cops asked any damned question they liked and insisted you smile when you answered it. It makes me nervous to be walking around knowing things I know they'd love to know. Byron calls it 'being on a higher level of knowledge.' But now that I'm up here, I find the view disturbing. For one thing, I have to keep track of who knows what, and who I can talk to about it. You know what I mean?"

"Yes." Ginny picked up her bagel. "But…that's only half of it."

Natalie looked up quickly. "What do you mean?"

"The real issue is…how many levels are there above you? Who's looking down, wondering how long it'll take you to catch up?"

♥　　♥　　♥

Another day at Newark College, sifting through old yearbooks and enrollment lists, proved fruitless. She found no familiar names or any references to lions or snowmen or Armand Vitek.

On Thursday she went up to Purchase, New York, and introduced herself to the registrar and the reference librarian. She had an idea that she might find some mention of Armand, so she went through the student lists for 1969 to 1975. Finding nothing, she settled down in the library with the yearbooks from 1953 to 1956.

Peter, she saw, had enrolled as a freshman in 1952. He had been a member of the debating team, and had sung in the concert choir. She flipped to his studio picture, which showed the same striking good looks she had admired in the older man. She went through the rest of the yearbook. There were no references to any of Enigma's favorite words or themes. The only lion she found was in a picture from that year's production of the Wizard of Oz.

Myra's name was there, and her picture. Natalie couldn't help but observe that she had been a homely young woman—the heavy brows and beaky nose that gave her character in the Nineties must have been a burden in the Fifties. But her eyes had been just as bright, and just as intelligent.

The 1954 yearbook had a picture of Peter and Myra at a Speech and Debate event. Myra's name also appeared on the masthead of the literary magazine. Again Natalie went through the class lists, noting that Lance Wenger had arrived, although there was no photo.

By 1955, Peter and Myra were famous. Photos of them were everywhere, running the debating club; organizing a pre-election political rally; president of the junior class and managing editor of the college press. Although there was still no studio portrait, she spotted Lance in one of the Peter and Myra photos, looking in 1955 just as overgrown, although rather less weighty, as he did in 1993.

In 1956, class predictions had it that Peter would be an ambassador one day, and Myra editor-in-chief of a national newspaper. The back page photo was of Myra and Peter, in cap and gown, with Lance and an aristocratic woman with long blond hair. Their arms were linked, and they danced along a winding cobblestone sidewalk. The caption read: Four Friends Follow Fame and Fortune to Future.

Unenlightened, Natalie went home and to bed.

But she was back Friday morning, going over what few relics of the mid-1950s that still remained in the University archives. She found a couple of issues of the campus free press, and she read with professional curiosity Myra's words on such arcane issues as community bomb shelters and the offensiveness of having a bathing beauty contest at an institute of higher learning. There was a photo of Peter in that one—wearing a pair of very tight bathing trunks and high heels, striking a pose usually reserved for ladies. Sitting in a chair beside him, wearing a trench coat and fedora, and whistling with the fingers of both hands in her mouth, was the woman with the long blond hair.

Who was she? There was no caption under the photo. Almond eyes, long straight nose…. Natalie found the 1956 yearbook again. She flipped through the class lists, starting with the seniors.

She found her quite easily, staring coolly from the pages of the old yearbook. Her name was Dorothy Gayle.

♥   ♥   ♥

"Natalie Joday! Where are you, girl?"

"In the boonies, somewhere. Marcia, I need you to make a change in Louise's column."

"So Byron tells me. You've got about ten minutes, so shoot."

"Tell layout to pull the first letter and its reply. Tell them to put this in, and make it fit however they can. Put in a graphic if they need to. But don't let them change a word."

"Does Louise know?"

"Yeah, I called her."

"Okay, shoot."

Natalie stared through the windshield. "Dear Enigma, comma, paragraph. I owe you an apology. Period. I thought you were just making trouble, comma, but I am mortified to realize I misunderstood your motives. Period. I'm sure you had good reasons for wishing to operate behind the scenes, comma, and I have terminated my doubts. Period. I will do everything I can to help you, comma, and I was wrong to bring our correspondence to an untimely end. Period. But I am unclear how to proceed. Period. I hope you will forgive me for my morbid remarks, comma, and give me some clue as to what to do next. Period. Paragraph. Louise. That's it."

Marcia read it back to her. "Some cops know how to read…."

"I know. Go."

"I'm history, girl."

Chapter Twenty

Rebecca raised her eyebrows. "Who's Dorothy Gayle?"

"You know her best by her married name: Dottie Marconi. Maury's first wife." Natalie refilled her glass of water.

"She knew Peter Kovaks."

"She knew them all...." Natalie raised her glass and drank.

They were sitting in the Antlers restaurant, famous for the hundreds of wine bottles in straw baskets that hung from its whitewashed ceiling.

"I don't get it," said Rebecca. "If Peter and Myra knew Dottie, why not tell you? Why make you go through all this rigmarole?"

"Theoretically, because they don't believe there's a connection between themselves and the murder. Practically, because I didn't ask." Natalie pulled at the loaf of French bread. "They're higher up on the information pyramid, and they're keeping their mouths shut. But that doesn't mean they're doing anything to get in my way."

"I don't get that either...."

"Those are the rules of the game. Unless they decide it's relevant, they keep quiet. Unless they get asked a direct question, they don't volunteer information."

"That's fine until something happens that makes them look like they're hiding something—and makes it look like you're covering for them. Are you sure you want to play this game?"

"I'm already playing it. I've been protecting Peter Kovaks. I've been avoiding the cops because I don't want them asking me questions I don't want to answer."

"I'm not sure I like this. Won't the cops become even more suspicious when they find out Peter and Myra knew Dottie?"

Natalie scowled. "I'm sure they know it already. They must've interviewed Dottie by now. They're just not talking, at least to me. Nobody's talking. Makes you wonder who's holding back what."

"Then I suggest you start asking your own questions."

"Not yet. In fact, I'm thinking of keeping my mouth shut entirely. I've gone up a level, and I want to get my bearings." Natalie looked at the yellow candle, reflected upside down in her water glass. "Nothing fits right now. But I'm sure it's crystal clear…on some higher, more informed, level of the pyramid."

"It's all a question of perspective." Rebecca sipped her water. "Speaking of which, any luck on the riddles?"

"No. But I'm becoming an expert. I'll have to do a feature on them when this is all over. Try this one. A woman gives birth to two sons in the course of one hour on the same day in the same year. But they are not twins. How come?"

Rebecca held her fist beneath her chin. "Was it two leap years?"

"Leap years don't qualify as 'the same year.'"

"Okay, don't tell me…."

Natalie smiled. "It's so easy when you look at it from the right perspective…."

♥　　　♥　　　♥

It was twenty past nine when Natalie arrived home, looking forward to crawling into bed. She was thus annoyed, upon turning on the lights, to find the haunches and tail of a gray mouse lying in the center of the kitchen floor. Wishing her dustpan had a longer handle, she gathered it up and threw it into the trash. Then she took the trash outside. Trick himself was nowhere to be seen. Back out on the trail of Big Game, she supposed.

She took a shower and pulled on an oversized sweatshirt, then sat down to check her e-mail.

There it was. From youknowwho@whoyouknow.net.

okay i thought about it meet me at the lookout north of the tappan zee bridge on 9W at nine

"Damn him!" His e-mail had been sent at 8:30 PM. That really irritated her. What did he think, she checked her e-mail every twenty minutes? Idiot.

She ran to her bedroom, pulled on jeans and a pair of shoes, grabbed her shoulder bag, and dashed out the door. It was ten to ten.

♥　　　♥　　.　♥

Also irritating, she mused as she raced through West Nyack, was the fact that she'd been on the Tappan Zee Bridge that afternoon.

She tried to call Byron, but he was not home. She decided against leaving a message. Rebecca was not home, either, and Natalie was ready to bet that she was at Daniel's. Too bad. Armand meant her no harm, she was sure of that. Of course, she thought, as she turned off the highway, if there was going to be another game of treasure hunt she might change her mind....

But the Corolla was there, parked under a sign reading "Closed: 8 PM to 5 AM." Natalie cruised up and peered inside. Empty.

She got out of the Volvo and looked around. A set of terraced steps led from the eastern side of the car park down a short slope to the lookout. The wind had picked up, and the leaves of the oak trees rustled. Natalie slung her bag over her shoulder and moved.

He was waiting for her on a wide stone parapet, stretched out at his ease. She couldn't see his features in the moonlight, but there was no mistaking his ovoid shape.

In the absence of messages directing her to Bear Mountain or Albany, Natalie was feeling generous. "I'm late," she called from the bottom step. "But I didn't get your e-mail till almost ten."

He didn't answer. Fallen asleep waiting, no doubt. "Armand?"

He did not stir. She went to his side and peered into his—

"Oh, shit!" She spun away, doubling over.

She was aware of her hair tumbling in front of her eyes, and of the pattern of the concrete beneath her loafers—octagons divided into eight sections, like a pie. The wind gusted and leaves skittered across the ground.

Straightening up, she looked across the River. A yellow glow to the south, floating beyond the span of the Tappan Zee Bridge, marked the City, where millions of hard-working but disinterested citizens lay sleeping safe in their beds. Or not.

She turned a little. On the ground beside the parapet lay a thermos, open. She must be careful not to go near that.... Keeping her eyes away from what was left of Armand's face, she turned further. He wore a pair of ancient high-topped basketball shoes, and green pants that were stretched out of shape around the knees. The seams around the fly had given way, exposing the zipper. The layer of fat around his stomach made his belt ride low.

She wasn't feeling nauseous anymore, or panicky. What she had seen was ugly and grotesque, and she didn't particularly want to look at it again, but she must make sure that Armand was truly, really, sincerely, dead. She owed him that—she owed anybody that.

She touched the back of the hand that dangled over the edge of the parapet. It was cool. She slipped her fingers around his wrist. There was no trace of a pulse—but then, she was not trained to take pulses. She put her hand on his chest—avoiding the place where his shirt and skin had been burned away—and stood very still. She waited a minute, but felt no trace of a heartbeat. But then she was not trained to find heartbeats. She had to make sure….

Closing one eye, she looked at his head again. The skin of his throat and chin had fallen away in shreds; his mouth was open, but it was full of something—some foam—that had bubbled and run down his face before it had hardened. And his nose….

She turned away again, having seen more than enough to be convinced. "Oh, Armand," she whispered, "it wasn't 'them' after all, was it! If only you had told me who…."

She walked a few paces away and pulled out her cell phone.

There was still no answer at Byron's—not surprising on a Friday evening. She thought a moment, then dialed the *Star* switchboard and asked to speak with the night editor.

"Ruth? Natalie Joday. I need to speak with Myra Vandergelden. It's an emergency. Can you…?"

After one or two questions, Ruth put her on hold while she went to track Myra down and see if she wanted to speak to Natalie Joday. While Natalie waited, she took a quick look through Armand's pockets.

A series of clicks and beeps announced an imminent arrival.

"Hello? How do you work this damn thing? Hello?"

"Ms. Vandergelden?"

"Is that still the switchboard?"

"It's Natalie Joday."

"Finally. That switchboard person must be new, I've never…. What do you want?"

"Something pretty terrible has happened. You know the man who said he slept with Marconi? He's dead."

There was silence on the phone. Natalie headed back up the steps to the parking area. "He asked me to meet him. I think Marconi was set up, and I think he was going to tell me by whom."

"You're sure he's dead?" There was a tremble in Myra's voice.

"Yeah—his mouth is all burnt and crusted." She reached the top of the steps. "There's a thermos nearby. I think somebody must have put some highly caustic substance in his coffee. When he started to drink it…. I think a lot of it must have gone up his nose…."

There was another silence, but when Myra spoke, she sounded composed. "Where are you?"

Natalie peered into Armand's car. "Up in West Nyack. By the Tappan Zee Bridge."

"Are there signs that anyone else was there?"

"I'm taking a look around now." Protecting her hand with a fold of her sweatshirt, she tried to open the door. It was locked. "But my guess is he came alone, and brought the thermos with him."

"I see. Very well. Thank you for calling. I'll be in touch."

All the doors were locked. "Should I.... What should I do next?"

"What do you think you should do?"

"Call the cops."

"Well then, do it!" She hung up.

Natalie shoved the phone into her bag and grabbed her camera.

♥   ♥   ♥

Pictures taken, area searched, she was glad to sit down on the parapet as far away from the body as possible.

She fingered her cell phone. Should she call the New York police? Probably they would think so.... But Geoff and Lt. Perry were homicide detectives, and, as all the world knew, the *Star* was cooperating fully in the investigation of the Marconi murder, with which Armand's death was surely connected. It wasn't as if she had it in for Geoff. She respected his skills. She just didn't want him to think she had a desire for anything other than a professional relationship. In fact, the professional thing to do was to call Geoff. On the other hand, she would not enjoy seeing his face when she told him, as she knew she now must, about her communications with Armand.

Armand. She looked over at him with a stab of pain. What a horrible way to die. Next to that her own self-interest seemed insignificant. The only important thing was to find whoever had done this terrible thing.

She pulled out a little leather case and retrieved Geoff's card. As she touched it, she saw his face as she had seen it the day he had given it to her. Damn him, anyway—to look at her like that and then walk out of her life.

After eight rings a sense of anticlimax set in. Friday night...probably out working on his relationship with Vivian, or standing on the corner outside their old house. Well, she'd give him his chance if it killed her. But twenty rings was her limit.

At eighteen he answered with a peeved "Hello."

"It's Natalie Joday," she said. There was music in the background.

"There's been a development in the Marconi case."

"Yes?"

She told him, starting with, "I received a message from Armand Vitek about an hour ago...." It only took a minute. Then she waited for the quiz.

"Are you still at the scene?"

"Yeah."

"Are you alone?" The music had stopped, and his voice was no longer peeved.

"Yeah." In her ear she heard the sound of an engine starting and a door slamming.

"How sure are you that you're alone?"

This wasn't quite the line of questioning she had expected. "Pretty sure. I don't think the murderer was ever here. Armand's car is in the parking area—"

"How do you know it's his car?"

"I know."

There was a silence. "Did you call 911?"

"No. Do you want me to?"

"No. I'll call it in. Are you in your car?"

"No."

"I want you to get in your car, lock the doors, and keep the engine running. I'll be there in ten minutes."

"Where are you?"

"Half way up River Vale Road. Hit re-dial if anything happens. I'll keep this phone free."

"Okay."

♥   ♥   ♥

It was a precious moment. She sat on the stone parapet looking out over the Hudson River. The Tappan Zee Bridge—a bow of yellow lights beneath a turquoise sky and white half-moon—was a beautiful sight. It was on nights like this, under skies like this, that one remembered how good it was to be alive; how much one had.

Until that moment, she had assumed that this was a period in her life when she would ease back and enjoy a little peace and quiet. She was so lucky...the people she loved were safe and well. She no longer needed to fight the world; the victory had been won after years of warfare. But at that moment she understood that, far though she had come, only the starting line had been reached. All her accomplishments were merely foundation stones upon which she could build her life, after the design of her choice, for whatever purpose she chose.

Her life had fitted her for this—at that moment she saw it clearly—had filled her with the desire to track down whoever was going around killing people and expose them; had supplied her with the means and the strength to do it. This was a good thing to do—not for her family or her employer or her friends—this was between her and the universe. This was where she belonged. No wonder she was not afraid.

♥ ♥ ♥

She heard his car coming up Broadway, doing at least 80, though without a siren. In that moment of self-awareness, she realized there was no way of escaping the fact that she was glad he was coming, that she trusted him to do the right thing—that she had always wanted to trust him. And now she knew why—for was not his chosen path in life running parallel to her own? No wonder she was drawn to him. They were made of the same stuff; they were akin. Had he not found his way to Michelangelo's when the rest of the cops had turned their noses up at the Enigma connection? Theirs was no distant, professional relationship, and never could be.

Headlights swept the car park above, and then went out. A car door slammed. There was a pause, and then she heard footsteps. She turned her head to watch him fly down the stairs.

He slowed when he saw her, and slipped his gun into his back pocket. She realized it must have alarmed him not to find her sitting in her car as instructed.

"Sorry." She put her hands on her knees and raised her face as he approached. "I didn't want to leave him here alone." She nodded her head toward Armand and swallowed. Talking was harder than she had thought it would be.

He scanned the lookout, his expression on high alert. Then he scanned her. "Are you all right?" He was dressed in jeans and the white sweatshirt.

"Yeah, just a little…." She shook her head, then looked at the ground. How could she explain how the presence of violent death under a dark sky had transformed her?

He sat down beside her. "Are you feeling faint? I've got water in the car…."

"It's not that…." She focused on his chin, long and angular above the curve of his shoulders. She wondered what quirk of civilization or otherwise it was that kept her from throwing herself onto his shoulder and hold-

181

ing on to him until he put his arms around her and held her back. "I just feel...so sad, and...." She looked down at the tips of her loafers, jutting out beyond her knees.

"It's okay...."

He was leaning toward her, and she thought, when he touches me, I'm going to cry like a baby, and I'm glad, because it's exactly what I need, and he's exactly the right person. She held her breath.

"It's important to let your feelings out...." His voice was soft and hesitant.

She turned to the bridge, so he would not see the tears gathering in her eyes. She wondered if he could hear her heart beating.

"Well," he said. "I'd better get to work." He stood up.

She blinked. His voice had changed. The hesitation was gone, so too the softness.

"I'll notify our trauma counselors," he continued.

"What?" She turned to look at him, but he was scanning the area again, with that watchful, analytical expression.

"There are some good people in social services." He walked over to the thermos and squatted down. "They'll help."

Natalie no longer felt like crying. "That would be a switch."

He looked back at her. "You're upset...."

"I'm not upset," she snapped.

"Fine. Until I can take your statement, I want you to stay put. Not that you haven't already been over everything." He approached Armand. "I want to check out the scene myself before the Nyack boys arrive and mess it up. And there's not much time."

The moment was gone, like a dream. She felt only cold, cold and angry. What the hell had she been thinking? That he would give a damn how she felt? That he would understand? He had been right after all—he was no friend of hers and never could be. She called out to him. "Where's your partner?"

"Feeding the baby." He peered down into Armand's face. "She'll be here soon."

Level III

Wisdom is humble that he knows no more

Chapter Twenty-one

At seven AM the morning of the third day after Armand Vitek's murder, Natalie strolled into Charlie's Diner, primarily to read the morning papers over a hot breakfast, but also to cleanse her palette of the taste of courthouse instant in a Styrofoam cup—by guzzling down as much of Charlie's special Ethiopian blend as it took.

It had been a hectic three days. The first night and most of the next day she had spent at the Rockland County Courthouse, sitting or lying on whatever piece of furniture was available. She had gone walkabout only once, to steal a pencil from the desk sergeant when her own had run dry. At regular intervals, she had been questioned by everyone from the cleaning boy to the Sheriff himself, on issues ranging from why she had killed Armand Vitek to why she was not wearing any underwear. Natalie, who had cut her teeth on constabulary zwieback, was unfazed by even the most insinuating questions. She responded with a combination of exact honesty and absolute unhelpfulness guaranteed to push the long-encrusted buttons of the hardworking law enforcement officers, who, of course, recognized her ungenerous behavior for exactly what it was—

Example:

"How could you be sure it was Vitek's car?"

"I had seen him in it before."

"When?"

"Last Sunday."

"Where did you see him?"

"At a weigh station on the Thruway."

"Which weight station?"

"The one near Exit 6."

"Northbound or south?"

"North."

"Did he e-mail you and ask you to meet him there?"

"No."

"Then why were you there?"

"He e-mailed me and asked me to meet him at the Stateline."

Etc.

—Contempt.

Shortly after her arrival, Lance Wenger had unexpectedly appeared, sent, he said, by Myra, to handle her legal interests and make sure she was not emotionally eviscerated by the system. That was a first for Natalie—having a lawyer on the company tab. Unfortunately, there was nothing he could do to keep the Sheriff from exercising his public duty and questioning her until he was good and sick of her. Nevertheless, Lance dutifully sat in on her questioning. He never said a word. Natalie's respect for him grew.

In the morning, she placed calls to her brother, who took the news that she had been at the police station all night very well ("Have you caused any structural damage?"), Byron, and Rebecca. She then gave her handwritten account of her pursuit of Armand Vitek to Lance, who promised to fax it to Byron from a nearby business center.

Rockland County finished with her at three—and then gave her the cheerful news that they would escort her to the state border, where the Bergen County Sheriff's minions were salivating with impatience to get their hands on her. They impounded her car, but promised she could pick it up "when they were done." So she made the four mile trek to the New Jersey border in the back seat of a green-and-white Rockland County squad car. She was then transferred to a blue-and-white Bergen County squad car for the trip to Hackensack. Lance followed doggedly behind.

At Courthouse number two, she learned that whoever had been so eager to question her was busy doing something else. Surprise. She curled up on a bench in the little waiting room on the second floor, where the desk sergeant could keep an eye on her until somebody came to claim her. Being an old hand at conserving her energy during stressful times, she promptly fell asleep. Lance wandered down the hall reading the notices on the bulletin boards. He was especially fascinated by the FBI's Ten Most Wanted.

At four thirty, Lt. Perry arrived, looking blooming in a canary-yellow pants suit. She took Natalie to her office and fed her homemade chocolate chip cookies from a large glass fishbowl with a padlocked lid. She scolded Natalie for not having demanded a proper lunch, turned on her FM radio, and sat down to read Natalie's statement. When Lance ambled in, she fed him cookies, too. Natalie concluded that the only thing the Lieutenant had going against her was that she was a tea drinker.

After a few questions—mostly to determine why Natalie had failed to inform her that she had found and met with Armand the previous week—Lance ventured to suggest that Ms. Joday had had enough for one 24 hour period. Lt. Perry bobbed her head in agreement, but added that unfortunately the DA's office was anxious to quiz Ms. Joday face to face. They were just waiting for an ADA to finish a meeting on another case so that he could talk to Natalie "in a timely fashion."

At six they were ushered up to the DA's office for "just one or two questions." At nine, Natalie's yawns were beginning to get the better of her—more from inactivity and the heat of the room than tiredness.

The ADA looked at her with what he probably thought was sympathy. "You can take off your sweatshirt if you're hot."

Natalie sighed. "Here we go again."

Shortly thereafter, they had let her go home—to get some rest, they said, but she suspected it was so she could put some decent clothes on. Daniel was waiting for her at her apartment, nursing a bowl of tomato soup (comfort food), and full of solicitous concern for the trials she had undergone and praise for her bravery and fortitude.

She had spent the whole of Sunday at the Courthouse, alternating between Lt. Perry's office and the DA's complex upstairs. Geoff had not appeared. Lance had once again danced attendance, at least in the abstract. He seemed to listen, but said little. Late in the morning she got a copy of the *Star* from one of the janitors, only to find an update written by Tyler, and no sign of her material. She thought about calling Byron, but decided it could wait.

A trauma counselor appeared during the afternoon break. She was a sweet-faced woman eager to listen. Natalie told her, more brusquely than the situation called for, that she was not short of people who would provide all the support and affirmation she needed—as soon as she was allowed to depart this fortress of impersonal and faceless authority and go home. The woman had left her card, which Natalie had torn up and thrown away. Finding herself in the mood, she had pulled Geoff's card out of her card case and likewise torn it up.

The memory of that act of liberation caused her to stir in her vinyl seat and drink in several bushels full of air. Charlie's Diner in the early morning really was heaven on Earth.

"Welcome back, stranger."

Natalie looked up to find a pair of hazel eyes looking at her through tortoiseshell glasses. "Tyler! I was hoping to catch you. What's the latest from the crime lab?"

He slid into the seat opposite and put his papers on the table. "Should have some definitive results this morning. But I can tell you that Vitek died from trying to drink coffee laced with some type of acid. They're assuming somebody spiked the thermos earlier in the day, and that he brought it with him to the lookout. They're trying to trace his movements."

"Thank you." Natalie heaved a grateful sigh. "I've been sitting in police stations for most of three days, but nobody would tell me anything. What about the time of death?"

"No later than 9:00 PM." He signaled to the waitress, who looked surprised to see him sitting with Natalie, then grinned.

"The e-mail I got said 8:30. That means he lived within a half hour drive of the Tappan Zee Bridge."

"No. He had a laptop in his car. He probably e-mailed you from there, using a cellular line."

"Can you do that?" Natalie watched the waitress pouring coffee to the level Tyler liked. "I guess you can. If anybody could, Armand could. He was such an enigma…."

"Anyway, the police got a fingerprint match immediately. He's been living a double life under an assumed name for fifteen years. Mandy Kevit. Cute, isn't it? Vitek—Kevit. Social security number, driver's license, etc. Not that he had much of a life. Slept in the back of his computer fix-it shop in Suffern." Tyler looked down. "Poor fellow. He didn't deserve what he got."

"I can't help thinking if he'd told me the whole story when we met, he'd be alive today."

"Don't waste your time feeling guilty. I doubt if he was the trusting type—people who buy into conspiracy theories never are."

Natalie leaned her elbows on the table and raised her cup to her lips. "He sure trusted somebody."

He gave an impatient smirk. "What do you mean?"

"Isn't it obvious?" She took a sip. "After our first meeting, he must have gone to talk to whoever it was who had set up Marconi twenty-one years ago. That person, unbeknownst to Armand, and for reasons we don't yet know, murdered Marconi. Threatened with Armand's demands to tell the truth, so that he could get the cops off his back, this unknown person killed him."

"It's clear you haven't thought this through." Tyler scowled at her. "You can't make these leaps of logic! In the first place, even if Vitek's revised version of the story were true, why would your mysterious unknown commit a murder to hide it? Secondly, you forget that we agreed the revised story could not be true, because Marconi quit the race. In fact, you are missing the obvious point that there is no connection between Marconi and Vitek's death."

Natalie's lips twitched. "Except there is one obvious way to explain how Armand's revised story could be true, and why Maury closed down his campaign. Obvious if you've been paying attention. Maury could have had an affair—with someone else. Maury then assumed the man who ratted on him was the man he really had the affair with—and ended his campaign, never guessing that it was all a set-up to bring him down."

Tyler's face flushed. "You have stopped reporting and started writing fairy tales." He stood up, tucked his papers under his arm, and picked up his cup. Natalie was astounded to see that his hand was trembling. "And if you are so blind as not to see that pursuing this line will only cause further distress to the organization that employs you, God help you. You'll see me in the newsroom."

She watched him stalk away to his corner booth. Stupid of her not to see it...what had Myra said about being so interested in finding out how the fire had started...? The *Star* was Tyler's whole life. If the rumors were true, it was already facing internal difficulties. Could it absorb the humiliation that would surely follow if it got out that the paper had been an unwitting party to an ugly little fraud that had ruined a man's life? Or would it signal the end of the *Star*?

♥   ♥   ♥

Natalie received more than the usual number of grins and nods when she entered the newsroom. She sat at her desk feeling self-conscious. Marcia had been, as usual, on the ball: her name plate sat in the middle of her ink pad in burnished bronze glory. She turned on her computer with a ridiculous sense of self-importance....

Marcia herself buzzed shortly thereafter.

"Hey, girl, welcome back."

"Jeez, Marcia, I was only two blocks up the street. Although you'd think from the way my belongings get borrowed, I'd been on a world cruise."

"Somebody been at your computer again?"

"They sure have."

"You want me to write a memo?"

"No…I'll handle it. I know the culprit."

"That's best. Listen, girl, just calling to tell you not to go anywhere. Himself wants to see you. He's up with Ms. V at the moment, but he said he'd be down by 9:30. When you see him walk in, wait five minutes, then come on down."

"Okay. Thanks for the name plate. How much do I owe you?"

"I'm sorry? I didn't quite get that. These phone lines…."

"Thanks, Marcia."

"Don't thank me. Thank petty cash."

♥   ♥   ♥

Byron reappeared right on schedule—newsies were the only people in the printing industry who knew how to tell time—and shortly thereafter Natalie headed for the front office.

But she took a little detour on the way.

♥   ♥   ♥

Leaning against the mailroom counter, she addressed Rudy's angular rear end. "Have you been using my computer?"

Rudy, who had been checking the supply of number ten envelopes, stood up and whirled around. "No. I don't think so."

"It's that one over there." She pointed. "The one where you left your data files in my applications folder."

"Oh, that one. I didn't know it was yours. I thought anybody could use it if it was available. I've used it before."

"So that was you who left my computer on last week?"

"No it wasn't! I never left a computer on. What do you think I am? I don't think…." He put is hands on his hips. "I didn't do anything wrong! I didn't know it was yours!"

"It had a sign on it that said, 'Don't Use It.'"

He blinked, and his face flushed.

Natalie smiled grimly. "Look, that's great if you want to practice your typing. If you want to use my computer, just ask me. But you changed my configurations, and it's a bore to have to—"

"No I didn't!"

"Maybe not on purpose, but what you did screwed them up."

"I didn't! I just clicked on the Typer Teacher, that's all. I don't know anything about any…whatever…."

"Yeah, right…."

"I thought it said 'Not in Use.'"

"Okay, fine. Just don't do it again." She turned and resumed her route to the front office.

♥   ♥   ♥

Byron looked up as she entered. For a moment, she thought he did not recognize her. She wondered what Myra had said to make him look like that.

"You wanted to see me?"

"Yes." As he smiled, he shifted the papers on his desk into a folder. "Are you fully recovered?"

She sat down in the red leather chair. "I think so."

"Have you checked your e-mail yet?"

"Uh, not yet. Having a little trouble with my computer. Why?"

He pushed at his glasses. "We've edited your copy on the Vitek story. There was a bit of a hold-up—some of us wanted to use only the facts, and others of us wanted to eliminate the first meeting altogether. But we won out in the end—after all, there's no point in holding back what the police have on record. It's time we made our move. If we don't print, the *Bugle* will, as soon as the details leak. Which it seems they will. So we're going with it—all of it—in two parts, today and tomorrow, taking the 'an e-mail was received by a *Star* reporter' approach. I need you to go over it for accuracy—don't worry about all the passive tense. Readers love it when they know the author is talking about herself in the third person. We've changed a few minor things for legal reasons—but you need to okay it if your name's going on it."

Natalie raised her eyebrows. "Okay." Nothing she had ever written before had received so much attention. Especially considering that they hadn't thought it worth using for two days.

"I want to go with 'Murder: A Firsthand Account of the Victim's Last Days' for a headline, but Ms. Vandergelden likes 'Rendezvous with Murder.'"

"They're both good," said Natalie. "But yours is too long unless you go to three columns."

"It'll fit. It's our lead."

"What?"

"We're leading with it." His lips twitched. "Front page."

"Oh."

"First time, isn't it?"

"Yeah." She let it sink in, got a good feel for it, and then took a deep breath. "In that case…I like your headline best."

♥   ♥   ♥

It read well—clear, precise, and unemotional. It read as if all those things had happened to someone else and not her. The editors had added nothing, and taken out nothing that changed her meaning. She read it through twice, and then sent it back to Byron.

That task done, it was time to pick up the pieces of the investigation. Everything had changed since she had last updated her notes. There was Dottie Marconi—she must find a way to talk to her. Why on Earth had Peter Kovaks written and Myra approved that attack on Maury when they had both known his wife? The story had always struck her as unpleasant— now it seemed inexcusable. It was clear she needed to talk to Peter Kovaks. But these issues paled next to the problem of identifying the person who was the link between Armand and Marconi. Because that person was a murderer.

♥   ♥   ♥

It was a real test of character not to be in the *Star* Building when the first copies came off the presses at 2:45, but she spent the afternoon in Suffern, trying to turn up someone who had known Armand well enough to have heard about what had happened in 1972. That turned out to be a hopeless task. The New York State troopers were swarming over the area, and when they moved out, the plainclothes New Jersey police moved in. So she left and went down to Michelangelo's to talk with Mike. He was very quiet about what had happened, saying only, "To every thing, there is a season." He told her the nice-looking policeman had been there the day before, and had been very sweet. Mike had given him the name of the guy who had tracked down Armand. Not that it would do him any good, because all the guy knew was that if he posted a message to a certain Internet bulletin board, Armand would eventually get back to him by e-mail. Then he mixed her a drink, and himself one, too.

On the way home, she stopped off at The Food Barn and bought a five pound bag of Gourmet Gato.

♥   ♥   ♥

Tuesday found her back in the newsroom, playing phone tag with various members of Peter Kovaks campaign staffers. From her new, higher, vantage point, she had spied several pertinent questions she was itching to ask. But he was turning out to be surprisingly elusive. Nor could she locate Linda. While she waited for someone to return her calls, she cleaned up her files and answered her e-mail.

Her phone rang. Peter's secretary for sure.... "Natalie Joday...."

"So they didn't arrest you for the murder, eh?"

Angela Marconi. "Not yet. How're you doing?"

"Not so bad. But who knew raking leaves took so much effort?"

"It's good exercise."

"There you go again...putting a silver lining on everything. You never let me have any fun." There was a pause as she took a drag. "Hey, I took your advice—I'm takin' a course."

"Astronaut Training 101?"

"Nah. Day trading. I thought I might have a go at playing the market. I was always good with numbers, but in my day it wasn't considered feminine to be able to do percentages. But I'm thinkin' maybe I should stick my toes into the modern world."

"Good for you...."

"Yeah, yeah.... So, you figure out who did it, yet?"

"No. Have you?"

"Well...." Puff. "What about this guy Kovaks?"

"What about him?"

"Well, the *Bugle* says he's the one who ruined Maury's life, right? Maybe he decided to finish the job."

"He was in Ohio the day Maury was killed."

"Oh yeah?"

"Yeah."

"You figure this poor schmuck Vitek got killed because a him and Maury?"

"I think they killed him because of the story he told Kovaks, yeah."

"I was thinking somethin' like that. I thought I'd better tell you, him and Maury saw each other now and then—maybe a couple a times over the years, if that helps."

"What do you mean, 'saw each other?'"

"I mean 'saw each other.' With the eyes. Maury said he saw the guy a couple a times, at restaurants, or maybe shopping, and once he spoke to him. If that helps."

"It does. Listen...how well do you know Dottie?"

"Not very. But I don't think anybody really knows Dottie…."

"Why not?"

"She went back to nature in a big way, a few years back. She keeps to herself. Not much social life."

"Has she called you since it came out about Maury's murder?"

"No."

"Or the son—what was his name?"

"Ricky. I haven't heard from him either."

"Thanks, Angela. Thanks for calling."

"Yeah, well." There was a sound of a lighter being flicked. "If I think a anything else I'll let you know."

Natalie opened her notebook and turned to a blank page. There were some things you just needed to write using pen and paper.

♥　　　♥　　　♥

"Why Natalie Joday! You look kerflumaxed!" Ginny sat down and fished in the candy dish. "Are you making news today, or just reporting it?"

Natalie looked up from her notebook and regarded Ginny's dancing brown eyes. "I'm not sure. Can't get any perspective."

"Get out of the office for a while."

"Wherever I go, I still represent the *Star*."

"I see." Ginny held the candy in her fingers. "Are you telling me that that is a conflict of interest, suddenly?"

"No—at least I don't think so. I think I'm being told to go ahead. I think they trust my judgment."

"You're not sure?"

Natalie eyed her friend with a twist of her lips. "I don't want to ask. Because the answer might cause a conflict of interest."

If Ginny was surprised, she did not show it. "Don't worry. I know you, Joday. You're not going to let a murderer go just because catching him might upset the boss."

"No…. But it's…a problem. Right now, I'm sanctioned to pursue the story. But if I tell everybody everything I know…."

"You might find yourself off the story."

"Yeah."

"So keep your mouth shut until you're certain."

"Yeah?"

"Yeah. Any other dilemmas you want me to solve?"

"Since you're offering…." Natalie tapped her pen on the open note-book. "Tell me what's really going on with the *Star*."

Ginny blinked. "Is this idle curiosity or are you working?"

"The latter."

"Then I'll be direct. As far as I know, the *Star* as we know it is dead. The company's net worth is declining…."

"How do you know that?"

"Ever read the Financial Section? I didn't think so. Wenger says the company is viable, but the public doesn't seem to agree."

"Who stands to lose the most?"

"Financially? The stockholders. Professionally? Probably the CEO. Time she hung up her broomstick, anyway."

Into Natalie's mind came a picture of Myra, riding her bicycle for all she was worth, a tall black hat on her head. "Oh my God."

"Sorry?"

Natalie leaned over her desk. "Ginny," she whispered. "Didn't you once refer to Myra as the Wicked Witch of the West?"

"Sounds like something I would say…."

"Yes, but there was a reason why you said it, wasn't there? Think about it. It's important."

Ginny nodded, and looked at the palms of her hands. Natalie had seen her do that before; it meant she was retrieving information from her prodigious memory. "Right." She looked up. "When he interviewed me, Peter Kovaks said something like…Myra wasn't hard to work for, but don't ever give her the idea you care more for your career than for the *Star*, because if she thought you were disloyal she'd go after you like the witch went after Dorothy in—"

Natalie thought of the picture in the yearbook of the four friends dancing down the cobblestone…brick…lane…road! "Oh my God!"

Ginny pretended to rise. "Would you like to be alone?" When Natalie didn't respond, she sat back down and folded her arms across her chest. "I take it we've had an epiphany."

With all the fireworks going off in her mind, Natalie was incoherent. "This is incredible. I just realized…. Lion? But…. Electroplated detective? Tin…tin…. Man…!"

Ginny fiddled with her hair. "Shall I put out a stop press order?"

"What? No." Natalie eased back to Earth. "In fact…. This is going to be very awkward." She put a hand to her chin. "I can't tell Byron…. Or Myra…. Jesus…." She looked up. "Ginny. This looks…bad. I'm thinking…. Maybe I should just go to the cops. Let them handle it."

Ginny nodded thoughtfully. "You could do that. That way nobody will blame you for being the one to rock the boat. Of course nobody will give you credit for saving the ship, either."

Natalie was silent.

Ginny unwrapped her butterscotch candy and looked at it. "Your primary responsibility as a professional is to report fairly and accurately on the stories you cover. The coincidence that you currently work for an entity named the *Star* is secondary. Step as carefully as you like—because you don't know how it's going to end up—but don't turn back. Jobs come and go—your professional reputation you're stuck with."

"Yeah."

"Yeah." She popped the candy into her mouth. "Look, I gotta go. Orlando and I have volunteered to be cheerleaders at the Channel 24 basketball for teenage drug users at the youth center."

"Sounds like fun."

"That's what you think. Do you have any idea what basketballs do to fingernails?"

♥   ♥   ♥

Ginny was gone. Natalie turned on her computer and pulled up her Enigma folder. She reread the first riddle:

I wear a man's clothes, but I've never had a wife.
I have a job, but I've never had a life.
Many fear me, but I've never hurt a fly.
I worship the sun, but I've never seen the sky.

Beneath it she typed: SCARECROW. She reread the second riddle:

My pride won't let me tell my name,
But if you guess it I'll be tame:
Begin with twenty-six,
Take twelve steps forward,
Subtract three,
Add six,
Then take one step backward.

Beneath it she typed: LION. She reread the third riddle:

What did the Norwegian call the electroplated detective?

Beneath it, she typed: TIN MAN. Then she typed the following:

Myra: WW of the West
Dottie: Dorothy
Peter: Tin Man? Scarecrow?
Lance Wenger: Lion!?

She blinked at the screen, letting her thoughts run. Suddenly, everything looked so different. The "Gang," Enigma had called them, and wondered what evil thing they had conspired to do.

Out of the corner of her eye she saw Tyler headed toward her. He held a folder in one hand, no doubt full of the latest police news. She saved the Enigma file and switched off the computer.

Usually Tyler stood as he handed her his reports, but today he pulled up a chair and dropped into it. "Preliminary lab report." He took his glasses off. "Vitek was killed by a caustic agent called Sellacol Solution, otherwise known as potassium silver cyanide. It's used for photoreproduction in printshops—we keep it in abundance right in this building. Natalie—the *Star* is my whole professional life! What are we going to do?"

Chapter Twenty-two

The news reached the furthest corners of the building in minutes, and no one was unaware of its significance—a week of the *Bugle* hammering it home that the *Star* was somehow mysteriously culpable in Marconi's death had left even the graphic artists nowhere to hide. The newsroom held its collective breath when Byron lounged out of the front offices and up the stairs, then breathed again when he returned, apparently none the worse for wear, ten minutes later. In the absence of an official slap of the panic button, the journalistic routine continued. The weekly sports department meeting took place smack on schedule, and the fashion writers had a surprise party for a retiring colleague. But there wasn't a soul in the building whose early warning system was not on red alert.

By the time the police arrived, Natalie was long gone. But she heard the saga the next day—how the forensics team had, at 1:36 PM, ordered that the printshop be closed until they had finished their inspection—probably only till the next morning; and how Phil Spitsky, the production head, had assessed the situation in two seconds flat, closed and bolted the door to the printshop; and how Myra Vandergelden, responding to Spitzy's interoffice telephone cry for help, had gone down to the basement and single-handedly held off a brigade of policemen and women in blue coveralls and caps threatening to break the door down; and how she had proclaimed in her cackling voice, "If you give me your word of honor as policemen and women of Bergen County, I will let you in and you may conduct your investigation in a non-intrusive fashion—but the *Star* has appeared on the news stands at 3 PM five days a week for thirty-six years, and that proud tradition is not going to end today;" and how, as one who knew how to back up words with action, she had placed a call to the governor's private line.

So the *Star* went to press on schedule, and, in a sidebar to part two of its exclusive report on the events leading up to Armand Vitek's death, announced defiantly to the world that the finger of suspicion was now pointed accusingly at itself. Which would not deter the *Star* from holding itself at the ready to assist in the investigation in any way it could. In an act of divine inspiration, Myra boosted the print run, rightly predicting that the murder spread, covering three and a half pages and including a scientific discussion of what potassium silver cyanide would do to organic matter on contact, with a molecular diagram and a line drawing of Armand's face (the original photo, taken by the *Star* reporter at the scene of the crime, was deemed too horrific), would send sales skyrocketing. Which is how Natalie Joday's byline came to be attached to the lead article of the best-selling edition of the *Star* in fourteen years.

♥   ♥   ♥

Downtown Bergenfield was busy. Shoppers trooped along the broad sidewalks, ducked into the brick buildings, and cruised the shoe-store windows. Almost all made the mandatory pilgrimage to Woolworth's.

On the corner of Washington and Main, there was an old-fashioned newsagent's, wedged in between a shoe store and a children's clothing outlet. It had been there since the days when newspapers had been the best source of in-depth news, before television had come and shortened the American attention span to the time it took to make a paper airplane. The proprietor, who seemed as old as his tiny shop, was cleaning his glass counter. As usual, he kept an eye on the racks of magazines and newspapers outside. Somebody was always trying to save a buck and walk off with a paper—and usually it was the classy-lookin' ones.

Take that dame hovering around like a bee trying to decide whether or not to settle on a clover blossom. They looked like that sometimes when they were trying to get up the nerve to buy a *Playgirl*. But this one was looking at the papers. What was her problem? Sugar—there she went, picking out a copy of the *Bugle* and takin' a peek. The newsagent replaced his bottle of Windex beneath the counter and stepped to the open door.

"Can I help you, miss?"

She jumped like she'd been caught stealing candy. "No. Thanks. Just taking a look." She smiled at him—a nice smile, just guilty enough to soften his old man's heart. She put the paper back.

He glanced at her sweater and blue jeans. "Forget your pocketbook? No problem. Pay me next time." Repeat business was his mainstay. He looked upon the occasional freebie as an advertising expense—as long as it was his idea....

"No...thanks. Just...the headline caught my eye."

The newsagent looked at the news rack and read:

"Oh that." He folded his hands across his chest, striking a pose that he hoped would convey an air of wisdom. "The *Bugle* knows how to write a headline—their stock is up 17 percent so far this year to prove it. But their headlines are like rainbows—colorful from a distance, but when you look for the detail, it ain't there. If you want the truth, read the *Star*."

The young woman smiled at him again, without the guilt this time, but he still found it an invigorating experience. Her gray eyes seemed to see right through his grizzled face and harmless pose of wisdom to the genuine desire to help that lay beneath.

"I think I'll take it after all." She shoved her hand into her back pocket and pulled out a dollar bill.

♥   ♥   ♥

"Natalie Joday!" Rebecca looked up from her desk. "What are you doing here?"

"Hiding from the cops." Natalie sat in a roomy armchair. "Armand was killed with an acid used in printing—a substance that we keep at the *Star* Building in abundance. The *Bugle* is reporting…excuse me…theorizing that someone at the *Star* killed Armand to protect Peter. 'What is the deadly secret, that our noble competitor is keeping?' writes that champion of truth, Max Bludwort. 'Will the true story of Peter Kovaks, publishing consultant and State Senate candidate, ever be told in full?' Not if Peter continues to ignore my calls. Dottie Marconi won't talk to me either, but at least she has an excuse, since it was a *Star* reporter who helped destroy her husband. *Star* stock is down 12 points today. All this because Enigma had a passion for riddles that were slightly too hard to solve all at once." Natalie put her feet over one pudgy arm of the chair and leaned backward over the other. "And to top it off, I have no idea what to do next."

"Maury was murdered before Enigma started riddling, and you are not allowed to run out of ideas. Straighten up and tell me why you are in this lunatic mood."

Natalie righted herself. "Because I solved the last two riddles. Electro-plated detective: tin man, get it? And of course, who is feared but wouldn't hurt a fly? Scarecrow. Is this starting to ring a bell?" She brought Rebecca up to date, concluding, "I thought having Peter Kovaks under suspicion was bad enough, but Peter, Myra, and Lance? Oy."

Rebecca looked blank. "The Wizard of Oz?"

"Cute, isn't it. Enigma's way of telling us who the Gang members were. What am I going to do? If the cops find me and ask me the right questions I'll have to spill it all, and half the *Star's* board will be under suspicion. Or worse."

"I'm going to give you some professional advice." Rebecca leaned forward. "Although I don't buy it that you need to hide, find a quiet place and do some serious thinking. Don't make assumptions about how other people will react. They're usually wrong."

"I'll try...." Natalie sighed. "It's the first rule of journalism that just because you know one of fifty people is a liar, you can't work on the principle that everyone of them is lying. But time is against us. That's assuming Myra and Lance are innocent, of course."

"Do you think the Evil Deed Enigma mentioned was Marconi's murder?"

"I would like very much to ask Enigma that," said Natalie sweetly. "If I could get my hands around his neck...."

"The field has narrowed," said Rebecca. "Enigma identified Lance, Peter, and Myra with Oz characters. There must be a limited number of people who knew about that."

"Yeah...." Natalie rubbed her eyes. "Peter, Myra, Lance, Dottie, and the people they told. Linda...."

"Maury...."

Rebecca folded her hands. "And remember the other parameter: Enigma loved Maury. That only fits one person you've mentioned."

Natalie's eyes widened. "I wish that woman would talk to me.... I'm sure the cops haven't worked out the Oz angle yet—if they had, they'd be paying a lot more attention to Myra and Lance."

"So you and I are the only ones in the know?"

"Myra and Lance must have figured it out the minute they read the Enigma letters. From their vantage point on top of the pyramid, it would have been obvious." Natalie grimaced. "I don't like this."

"I would worry if you did." Rebecca shook her head. "This is very confusing. Is it possible the *Bugle* is right? That someone at the *Star* murdered Armand to protect Peter?"

"Protect him from what?" Natalie raised her shoulders and held out her hands. "I don't see what he did that requires protection—except being unlucky enough to land in the middle of this murder investigation! He's falling in the polls, of course. You'd think the fact that he was out of state when Maury was killed, and in Trenton the day Armand was killed—he went down Friday morning—would mitigate the situation, but no…."

"Let me ask you something." Rebecca tilted her head to one side. "You believe Armand never slept with Maury?"

"More than ever. Maury told Angela he'd seen the guy around over the years. Armand told me he'd never met Maury."

"Armand lied a lot…."

"Yeah, but for Maury to have seen him, Armand would have had to be in New Jersey, and we know how he felt about that."

"Agreed." Rebecca held her hands out. "Then don't we need to find out who Maury *did* have the affair with?"

Natalie shook her head. "I think the murderer and Armand were in on the set-up together. But there is no reason to suppose that a hypothetical real lover had anything to do with it."

"Only…but if he's out there, he must be unnerved by these murders. You know…he'd make a good candidate for Enigma…."

"In which case, we may be hearing from him." Natalie stared at Rebecca's Navaho carpet. "I thought for a while that Armand was Enigma—but I can't see how he could have known about the Oz connection. I'd better call Louise and warn her to be on the lookout for a letter from Enigma." She looked up. "You know, I couldn't do this without you. I wonder what your real bill would be?"

"I don't need to be paid, pumpkin." Rebecca rose to escort her to the door. "I do it for love."

♥　　　♥　　　♥

For the next few days Natalie avoided the *Star* building as if it had been infested with rats instead of the police. She waited to hear word of an arrest or other major break in the case. But nothing happened. So, following Rebecca's advice, she spent most of her time sitting in the gazebo at the Haworth duck pond trying to determine some useful course of action. Sometimes she mulled over her notes, juggling the names of the players and the bits of information like jigsaw pieces that didn't seem to fit. Sometimes she gazed at the orange leaves as they were pulled from the maple trees by the dancing autumn breezes under the deep blue sky.

Wednesday passed with no letter from Enigma. Natalie was disappointed enough to revisit the idea that Armand might after all have been Enigma. She went back to Purchase to see if she could turn up evidence that he had ever worked at SUNY, but came up empty. In the evening she made a list of every name she had come across during the investigation, then she sat on the steps of the gazebo and stared at it.

On Thursday she tried to locate Ted Barnes, the man who had joked to Peter about Maury liking to ogle the boys. She tracked him from Brooklyn to Long Island to Tampa, then back to Long Island: the Maple Grove Cemetery in Freeport.

In the evening, Tyler called with the police update. They had been unable to find any evidence that the potassium silver cyanide had been stolen from the *Star*. Tyler seemed tense, but when she asked if he was feeling the strain, he brushed her off, saying he was only coming down with a cold.

"I thought you'd better know," he said before he hung up, "Rudy met with Byron today. Claimed you're the one who's been leaking information to the *Bugle*. Says he saw you last month talking with an editor at the *Bugle*, or something."

Natalie pursed her lips. "How did you hear about it?"

"Rudy asked my advice. Of course I told him to forget it…. He seems to have it in for you."

"I'm quaking in my zoris."

♥   ♥   ♥

On Friday, she woke up knowing what she had to do, and wondering why she hadn't thought of it before. The only thing was, she needed to be at the *Star* Building to do it. She put in a call to Marcia, who reported that although the police brigades were still camped out on every floor during the day, their numbers dwindled in the evenings. So she bided her time, and spent the afternoon contemplating the documents in the case, and the ripples of water on the duck pond.

She was walking up Tank Hill at six when a Ford Bronco tooted at her, sped past, then turned into her driveway. She hurried up the hill, and found Rebecca and Daniel waiting for her.

"Where's Gayanne?" she asked anxiously.

Daniel put his arm around her shoulders. "With Louise. We're going to the Catskills for the weekend."

Natalie registered his hiking boots and wool jacket. "Oh." She looked up at him, a little more anxiously. "Gayanne…?"

"Is staying at Louise's. It's Reeb's birthday next Wednesday…."

"Oh." Natalie looked at Rebecca. Her hair was down, and she was wearing her faux deerskin jacket, with the fringe. "Oh! That's great!" She hauled off and belted her brother in the chest.

201

"Ouff!" He pushed her away. "Yeah, I'm going, I'm going…." He smiled grudgingly. "Gayanne says she can cope for two days."

Natalie nodded. "And how is her father coping?"

He pulled a couple of sheets of paper out of his breast pocket. "I've run up a list of phone numbers. Where we'll be, Louise, the doctor, the hospital emergency room, the—"

"Two pages of numbers?"

"No!" He glared at her. "Two copies. One for home and one for work." He looked suddenly uneasy. "Maybe I should make more."

Rebecca snickered.

Daniel glared at her, too, then turned back to Natalie. "I told her you'd call when you could, but to remember that you're very busy."

"Oh, I'll call all right. I might even stop by tonight, if I finish what I want to do in time."

"What? No Friday night date? Has the sky fallen or is the job interfering with your social life?"

"It's not that…. Frankly I just don't get the same old thrill out of flipping through the deck that I used to. To tell you the truth, Rebecca was the best date I've had in months."

Daniel put his arm around Rebecca. "She's unavailable."

Natalie watched as they turned and headed back to the car. Daniel drew Rebecca to him, and she bent her head toward his.

Chapter Twenty-three

At 6:30, Natalie called Marcia again to see if the coast was, by any definition of the word, clear.

"There's a couple of diehard women in surgical gloves going through the basement storeroom," said Marcia, "but that's it."

"Okay. I'm coming over. Who's still around?"

"Just a couple of stringers, and Phil. Byron is leaving soon. But I'll stay if you need me."

"No, thanks. I doubt if I'll even come to the newsroom."

♥　　♥　　♥

"Natalie Joday!"

"Hi, Davis. How's it going?"

"Been reading up on the rights of police to read e-mail." He puffed out his cheeks. "The world is changing, Natalie. We're going to have to rethink our concept of privacy. What a week." He looked at her curiously. "You're right in the middle of it, aren't you?"

She nodded. "And I need your help. On the QT."

"Well, sure...."

"I need to get into the upstairs library."

"Now? You have a sudden urge to read back issues? You can do that here electronically and keep me company."

"I'd love to keep company with you—any other time. But what I want doesn't come in digital format. Are there any cops up there?"

"No. Ms. V threw them off the third floor this afternoon. They were driving her nuts, I guess. But you can go up."

"Thanks. And...if anybody asks...I'd just as soon not have it known where I am."

Davis opened up a drawer and took out a key ring. It had two keys on it, one labeled LIBRARY and the other PANTRY. He handed it to her. "Happy hunting."

♥　　♥　　♥

The third floor was silent; the lights had been dimmed. Natalie turned her head as she walked past the door to Myra's office. The glass in the window was black. She heard Linda's voice in her mind: *You wouldn't believe some of the things Myra's done for the* Star…. She turned away and padded down the hall to the solarium.

Once in the library, she turned on the lights and got her bearings. She found the shelf containing the corporate records—oversized books bound in green leather, one volume for every year since 1962. She pulled out the first volume, threw her shoulder bag onto the little study table, and sat.

It was impossible to glean any emotional content from the sparse style in which the reports were written. But the financial picture was clear. Starting in 1969, each balance sheet was worse than the one before. Revenues from advertising shrank, and modest increases in circulation did not offset the effects of inflation. New equipment was needed and there was no money to buy it.

The year of change was 1972. An analysis by an outside firm summed it up: change with the times, or die. And that meant expansion, and a change in focus away from local to regional. The Mills family had fought tooth and nail to maintain control of its paper, to keep it what they called "family-oriented," but eventually they lost it to the grasping hands of the younger generation, with their ability to attract corporate dollars and their fancy marketing plans. *Myra wouldn't hesitate to sacrifice a friend if she thought it would be best for the* Star…. In the end, it had been a question of selling out to another, bigger, publishing group, or incorporating and losing control. With the turn of a page, The Mills were gone, and *The Bergen Evening Star,* Inc., was born. After that, the reports grew thicker, profits soared, but the reporting style was just as sparse.

She made a note or two, and moved on to the next book. In 1973, Myra had been elected Chief Executive Officer, with Lance Wenger as corporate attorney. Peter was not mentioned. She heard Ginny's voice in her mind: *Don't ever give her the idea you care more for your career than for the* Star…. She checked her notes. She was reaching for 1974 when she heard footsteps, then Davis's voice—usually so soft—booming down the hall.

"The library is through the solarium, Sergeant. Just a moment while I check in with Ms. Vandergelden's secretary. Ooops!" He laughed like a loon. "Nobody home. But I'm sure there's no problem. We all have instructions to help the police any way we can."

Natalie, frozen in place, heard a mumbled expression of insincere appreciation. Coming to life, she shoved the chair under the table and swept her notebook into her bag.

"Let me just find the right key...." Davis's voice was shrill.

Natalie fled to the back of the library. It was only a three story drop to the pavement below, but (fortunately) the windows were locked. She slipped behind the shadow of the encyclopedias, her heart pounding in her throat. Then she spotted a little door.

"Oops!" Again came that hooting laugh. "It's open. Silly me!"

She pulled the keys out of her pocket and tried the first one. No luck. Her fingers trembled as she slipped the second into the lock.

Davis kept up a stream of loud babbling. The key turned; somehow got the door open, slipped through, and closed it behind her. Davis's voice was transmuted to muffled, inarticulate noise.

She stood motionless, waiting for her panic to pass. When she could, she moved forward, waving her hands back and forth in the pitch-black darkness.

The room was small—the walls only a foot or two away on either side. There was a counter, and a sink. Inching forward, she found another door, and a round handle. It opened to her touch, and she slipped through, relief calming her shaking hands.

A dim light spilled through four sets of curtains. She was in Myra's office. Shoving the keys into her pocket, she took a deep, relaxing breath. Probably she was locked in, but there was no hurry. She was safe enough, for surely the Sergeant would not trespass here. She would just check the door to the hall....

She kept near the south wall, where the light from the windows illuminated the floor. She avoided the exercise cycle and circled behind the desk.

The light from the windows was surprisingly bright. There was a single file on the blotter. Beneath its plastic cover, Natalie read the words: *"Bugle Takeover: Memo to Shareholders"* in a 48 point font, with "Draft" written underneath.

She glanced at the door. The glazed window glowed faintly.

She put a hand on the cool leather of the chair, swung it around and sat. If she held the report up so that the light from the window hit it directly, she could just make out the smaller type.

The first page contained a brief paragraph about the report, explaining that pursuant to blah, blah, blah, the Board of Directors was fulfilling its obligation to inform its shareholders of all options discussed at Board Meeting blah, blah, blah. Dated 18 October.

The second page contained a list of shareholders, divided into major (more than five percent) and minor. Myra, Peter, and Lance headed the former list. She ran her eye down the latter list, and stopped at the name Dorothy Gayle.

A key scraped in the lock of the door, and there was a soft bump against the door.

Dropping the report, she slipped out of the chair and scuttled sideways along the wall and behind a dieffenbachia, then sat still as the door opened. A swath of light swept across the floor.

"Joday?"

Relief. She abandoned the dieffenbachia and hastened to the door. Davis looked out into the hall, then motioned for her to go, go, go, as quickly as she could. She slipped past him, moving quietly on the carpet, then tiptoed down the stairs. On the first landing, she remembered to look nonchalant in case she ran into anyone. She managed to keep that up till she left the building and fled to her car.

♥   ♥   ♥

The front lawn was covered with unraked leaves. Twigs, blown from the dogwood trees in the recent wind, littered the slate walkway. In the glow of the porch light, dead flowers hung from the hydrangea bushes like limp brown pompoms.

The door opened the width of the chain and Angela's left eye appeared. "Oh, it's you. Kind a late for a visit, yah?"

Nonetheless she unchained the door and let Natalie into a living room cluttered with clothing stuffed into brown paper bags. She was dressed in a red sweater and jeans that were too tight around the middle.

."You wanna sit down?"

Natalie nodded, and dropped into a sway-seated lounger.

Angie sat on the sofa and placed her cigarette case and lighter on the coffee table. "You don't look so happy. Problems?"

"Yeah."

"I just attract people with problems. It's my fate, I guess." She reached for the cigarette case. "So what's the buzz?"

"There's not a lot I can tell you. Not without maybe hurting people I don't want to hurt."

"That scumbag Kovaks...."

"Maybe—but he isn't the only person I had in mind."

"Oh?" She fiddled with the clasp of the cigarette case. "So you don't want to tell me anything. That means you want me to tell you somethin'."

"I want to know about Maury and Dottie's finances, particularly any stocks either of them might have owned. Especially *Star* stock."

"Wow. You're pretty direct when you're not under cover."

"I don't have much time."

"Afraid somebody might beat you to the story?"

"Afraid somebody might get hurt. Maybe Dottie. Maybe you."

Angela smoothed her hair back with the side of her hand. "Maury had a broker—just small potatoes—and yah, some stocks got transferred to Dottie. I don't know which ones. I had the broker sell everything and give me the cash when Maury died."

"Are there any papers? Files...?"

"One of those brown files like an accordion. We can look in Maury's office if you want."

"I want."

♥   ♥   ♥

Maury's "office" was the north corner of the TV room, an area covered by a thick layer of dust. Natalie went through the folder, and then through an old green filing cabinet. She found a worn blue three-ring binder with quarterly statements from Maury's broker, which summarized mutual funds and dividends, but there was no mention of *Star* stock. When they had exhausted the search, Natalie allowed herself to be led to the kitchen and deposited on a stool.

Angela looked at her with a critical eye as she filled the coffee maker. "Can't you find out from somebody at the *Star*?"

"Unfortunately...no."

Angela brushed a few coffee grinds from the counter into the palm of her hand. "What about Dottie? Wouldn't she know?"

Natalie rested her head on her knuckles. "I'd love to talk to Dottie. But she won't talk to me. At first I thought it was personal, because I was from the *Star*, but then I found out she has refused to talk to any reporters. She's barely talking to the cops."

Angela sat down at the table and pulled out her cigarette case. "She'd talk to you if I was to ask her for you."

Natalie lifted her head. "Would you do that?"

"Yah. If it means helping to find out who killed Maury. Besides, I was always a sucker for a hard-luck story."

"Thanks, Angela."

"Call me Angie." She held out the cigarette case. "Wanna try one? Just to say you did?"

Natalie looked at Angela's bright blue eyes, then pulled a cigarette from the pack. "Why not?"

♥   ♥   ♥

Natalie turned right instead of left at the bottom of Tank Hill and parked the Volvo on Valley Road. She locked the car and walked the hundred yards or so to the duck pond. It was after eleven, but she wasn't ready for bed.

She strolled around the back of the pond, near the eaves of the woodland that separated Valley Road from the railroad tracks. It was hard to make sense of it all. Dottie, a stockholder in the *Star*? Had Maury been, too? What if…. Natalie's head whirled. What if, upon Maury's death, his *Star* stock had gone to Dottie? What if that had increased her holdings in the *Star* just enough…just enough to what? What if Dottie had hatched a twenty-year plot to bring down the *Star*…? Or what if Myra, in an obsessive rampage, had set about slaying all the stockholders of the *Star* in order to—

A dark figure rose from the steps of the gazebo. Natalie froze. The Haworth police station, with its friendly neighborhood officers, was visible across Haworth Avenue, but her situation was vulnerable nonetheless: duck pond on one side, trees on the other, and the unknown directly in front.

He didn't move, and her initial fear waned. Probably just a local—a polite local who rose when a lady walked by—out for a late evening think. Crime in the bedroom community of Haworth was notoriously low. It was just the atmosphere of working a murder investigation that had her roiled up. She would ignore him.

As she sauntered past, he spoke. "Good evening, Ms. Joday."

She stopped, put her hands behind her back, and looked at him. Why now, she thought. Didn't she have enough on her plate? "What are you doing here?" she asked, trying to sound casual.

"Waiting for you."

So much for casual. "I only decided to come ten minutes ago."

"Then either I'm a lovelorn masochist who's been sitting in this gazebo every evening for the past two months waiting for you to walk by or—I'm a very good detective. You can choose what you'd like to believe."

She turned away from him, and looked at the reflection of the streetlights glittering on the black surface of the water. His words were like fireworks in the night sky. But his tone…his tone was self-mocking and detached—

208

impossibly detached. She understood the words, but not the tone. "Since I know you have been various other places in the evenings lately, I deduce that you are a very good detective. What are you detecting?"

"You." His voice came out of the darkness and surrounded her. "I found your pencil in the *Star* library and concluded you had been there, trying to find out the secret about Dorothy Marconi's investment in the *Star*. I'd like to know when you left so hastily, but I won't trouble you by asking, as it is only idle curiosity. At any rate, I concluded you would go somewhere to think. Ta da."

She did not turn around. "Many people use pencils, Sergeant."

"But fewer people own pencils from the Rockland County Sheriff's office."

Natalie looked up at the night sky. "That is not evidence that would stand up in court."

"But it's enough for me. These days I am highly attuned to your presence. Wherever I go, I sense you have been there just before."

She turned. "And so now you have taken your revenge." She swept the air with her arm, indicating the lawn, pond, and gazebo.

"Exactly."

It was absurd, she thought. His words floated on the meter of a sonnet, but his tone...ironic...sarcastic...ambivalent? She peered at his face, though it was invisible in the darkness.

She spoke in a mocking voice. "Well, it seems that you have caught me at last. Shall I come quietly or will you use force?"

"It's not a joke, Ms. Joday."

Disapproval she understood very well. It chilled her soul. "Why are you angry with me?"

"Why am I angry with you?" He gave a mocking laugh. "As a matter of fact, I'm not angry with you—although perhaps I ought to be, since you've been playing hide and seek with me all over the County, avoiding me—"

"I didn't avoid you—not you in particular." Still it was me, me, me! "This has nothing to do with you!"

"I wish that were true. I wish I had never taken this case." He put his hands on his hips and looked at the ground. "You know I get lied to every day. People don't answer my questions; they don't tell me everything. I know all about it—why it happens, and what it means." He lifted his head. "But I never thought you would hold back information in a murder case."

Natalie swayed as if his words were a strong wind. "I don't think that's fair." She didn't want to fight, but she wasn't going to lie down and take it, either. "Since you have been dogging my footsteps for the past two weeks, you know everything I know."

"I've seen what you've seen, yes. But you are always managed to stay one step ahead. I am forced to conclude you know something I don't. I'm asking you—will you tell me what it is?"

His unemotional pose was enough to drive her mad. But she would stay calm or die in the attempt. "We've been through this. I don't have to tell you what I'm thinking. In fact, I can't. I'm not a 'me' anymore! I'm a 'we' now. I can't always do what I might choose to do if it were only me."

He took a step forward. "Are you being pressured by someone at the *Star*? If you tell me I will do everything I can to help you...."

Her anger flared at his words. "Like you did the other night? No thanks, Sergeant." She slashed at the word as she spoke it. "I've had enough institutional help, thanks!"

He raised his empty hands. "I don't even know what you're talking about!"

"It doesn't matter." She struggled to get back in control. "I don't need your help deciding what to say and what to keep to myself."

"Then you admit it—you are holding something back."

"I don't get it." Natalie shook her head. "Why am I in the wrong? You're a cop and I'm a reporter. We have different roles to play, we represent different interests, we play by different rules."

"Don't say that." His voice dropped. "Please don't say that. I only know one set of rules when a murder is involved...."

"Because you see everything in black and white...."

"No, I don't. But in this instance—the rules we're talking about are codified law. It's my job to verify or discount information relevant to this case. You're hindering a legal investigation...."

"Not necessarily! Why can't you take it on trust that I know what I'm doing? I trust you to do your job!"

His laughter was soft and bitter. "You think you are showing that you trust me to do my job? Don't you get it? Your trust would be your cooperation!"

"I can cooperate without emptying my mind out like I'm flushing a toilet! At least I do you the courtesy of assuming you're not holding back the truth because you're afraid of getting fired. It's not like you're telling *me* everything *you* know."

"That's not part of my job."

210

"Well it isn't part of my job either! The role of the press is to be a watchdog on institutions of power. That means you! Yet you stand there and demand to know everything absolutely, and if you don't get it, you think you're being lied to. You don't get it that no one can know anything for absolute certain. You want everybody to play by your rules and you can't take it when anybody has a different idea. No wonder you never get what you want!"

He turned and walked away, a steady unhurried stride, away from the gazebo and the trees. He made it to the sidewalk, then turned and walked back, with the same stride. He did not stop until he was a foot away from her. His face was frozen, but his voice was on fire. "If you really trusted me to do my job, you wouldn't be angry because I was trying to do it, even if you disagreed with what I did. If you were capable of seeing anything from anyone else's point of view, you might have realized that people doing my job need to know things not to condemn but to prevent further crimes. You might even have realized that it is highly irregular for people in my job to give much space or opportunity to talk off the record to people such as yourself in the middle of a murder investigation. But you didn't think of any of that. Trust? You don't trust my motives, you don't trust my judgment, and you don't trust me. I thought it was because I was a policeman, but it's not. You've never trusted anyone in your life."

He turned and walked away with that same steady stride, but this time when he reached the sidewalk he did not turn back.

♥   ♥   ♥

Natalie sat on wooden stairs of the gazebo and watched the waning moon rise over Tank Hill. She was weary, but not lost. The road ahead was clearly marked. She would sleep, and in the morning see if she was any nearer to meeting with Peter or Dottie. She would stop by and see Gayanne. She rose and stretched. Looking up, she caught her breath. From the bottom step of the gazebo she had a perfect view of her yellow porch light twinkling through the trees.

Chapter Twenty-four

Gayanne was dreaming. She was in California, visiting her mother. Somehow they were back in the living room of the house in Berkeley, which was cluttered with boxes containing all her toys. But the cardboard was rotting and smelled of mold, and she knew all her favorite things were ruined. She looked around uneasily, wondering where her cat was. There was graffiti on the walls—Fuck You Bitch; Kiss My Ass; God is Dead. Her mother was telling her how they would fix the place up; that she was straight now and everything was going to be all right. Her heart was pounding. Where had she put her return plane ticket? Where was her knapsack? She heard a scratching under the floor. Rats. She couldn't take rats. The thumping in her chest grew faster....

She awoke and sat up.

Her heart really was pounding, her face and throat were wet with sweat. But where was she? This wasn't her futon in her bedroom loft! No—she was at Louise's house. That's right. Daddy and Rebecca had gone away for a romantic tryst, and she was in Louise's spare room. It was all right...it was all right....

She lay back down. The thumping in her chest was slowing, but the fear clung to her like glue—a horrible, thick glue that tightened as it dried and made her body ache. What a terrible dream! If she had been at home, she would have gone to Daddy. Even when Rebecca is sleeping over, you come get me if you have a nightmare, sweetheart. That's what he had said.

Should she go wake up Louise? Louise would understand. They had had such a good day, playing and reading *Valeria*.... Louise wrote the most wonderful stories, all about brothers and sisters that had been separated by a terrible war and what happened to them. The children in Louise's stories were very brave.... She didn't want Louise to think she was scared....

There was that scratching noise again. Rats? Her heart bounded. No...not rats...that was a key in a lock. Burglars! Burglars—out to steal Louise's jewels! She threw back the covers and slid out of bed, and crept silently across the carpet to the bedroom door.

♥　　　♥　　　♥

"Louise. Wake up Louise!" She touched Louise's plump arm.

Louise's eyes fluttered open. She looked dazed, then recognized Gayanne.

"I heard a noise, Louise. Down in the kitchen. Maybe it's burglars after your jewels."

Louise's startled eyes turned to the door. "I don't hear anything."

"It was before. I heard it. Scratching."

Louise listened again. "Maybe it was Toot."

Toot was Louise's cat. Gayanne shook her head. "I heard like a key in a lock."

Louise was studying her face. She looked very serious. "Then we'd better go take a look."

Gayanne felt relieved as Louise slipped out of bed and pulled on her black and gold dressing gown. Louise understood.

They went out the door and down the hall together, Gayanne gripping Louise's arm. At the top of the stairs they froze: a flash of light came from the kitchen. They looked at each other.

Louise leaned down and whispered in Gayanne's ear. "Go back to my room, Gayanne. There is a telephone by my bed. Dial 911. Tell the police to come to 33 Elm in Oradell. Can you do that?"

Gayanne nodded and crept noiselessly back down the hall. She was at the door of Louise's room when she heard a thump, and a cry, then more thumps.

She ran back down the hall to the top of the stairs. Louise was not there. Then she heard a moaning, and the sound of breaking glass from the kitchen.

She went down the stairs, groping with both hands until she found the light switch at the bottom. The lights came on, and she saw Louise crumpled in a heap in the middle of the floor. Out of the corner of her eye she saw a figure dressed in black crouching on the counter in the kitchen.

She screamed, a loud, piercing scream, and shut her eyes.

213

Chapter Twenty-five

Natalie looked up to see Daniel and Rebecca coming down the corridor. She met her brother's eyes, trying to reassure him before he was close enough for words. When he spotted Gayanne, curled on the orange settee beneath an overcoat with her head on Natalie's lap, his face changed, his apprehension banished by a flush of emotion that was a mixture of relief and pain.

He knelt, his eyes on his sleeping daughter. "How's Louise?"

"Doing okay," said Natalie. "She sprained her ankle and whacked her head when she fell, but she didn't break any bones."

Daniel smoothed Gayanne's tangled hair from her face. She opened her eyes, confused at first, then saw his face. She lurched at him, and he put his arms around her.

Natalie rose and joined Rebecca. "Sorry."

"Oh, Daddy!" Daniel had seated himself and Gayanne climbed into his lap.

"Are you all right, sweetheart?"

"Unh-hunh. Are you mad, Daddy?"

Daniel looked into her upturned face. "Of course not, sweetheart. I'm so glad you're all right. Why would you ask that?"

"I don't know. I don't know!" She started to cry. "Lara always got mad when anything I did went wrong!"

"Oh, Gayanne...."

Rebecca took Natalie's arm and led her to the other side of the waiting room. They sat on a pair of plastic chairs.

"What happened?" asked Rebecca.

"There was a burglar at Louise's. Gayanne woke up Louise and they went to investigate. Louise fell down the stairs, and Gayanne screamed bloody murder and scared him off. Then she called 911. Then she called me."

Rebecca looked across the room. "She's good in a crisis...."

Natalie watched as Daniel wiped the tears from Gayanne's face. Then she turned away. She was surprised to see, through the medical center window, that it was broad daylight. She glanced at the clock on the wall. Eight thirty. She went to a plastic chair and pulled out her notebook.

Twenty minutes later there were footsteps in the hall, and she looked up to see Geoff, dressed in a light gray suit, coming toward them. He nodded when he saw her, then approached the settee.

A stillness came over Daniel when he spotted the Sergeant coming toward him, and a mask came down over his face. Their last meeting had been one of vindication for Daniel, but still the Sergeant represented a world of arrest, handcuffs, jail—a part of his life he wanted to keep distant from his daughter, and from himself. He stood slowly, keeping a protective arm around Gayanne.

"Joday…." His was cordial, but still there was no "Mr." attached.

"Sergeant…."

The Sergeant looked down at Gayanne. "And this must be Gayanne. Hi. My name is Geoff Allan, and I'm a police detective. I'm pleased to meet you. I understand you were a brave girl last night."

Gayanne said nothing, but looked from one man's face to the other and edged further behind Daniel.

"It's my job to try and find who broke into Ms. Hunt's house." Geoff put his hands behind his back and leaned forward. "And I'm counting on you to help me."

Daniel's arm tightened around his daughter.

"So when you're ready, I'd like to talk with you…."

Gayanne pulled herself up Daniel's arm and stage whispered, "Do I have to?"

Daniel's face was a study. "Only when you're ready, honey." He eyed the Sergeant, and asked, as if he didn't know, "I believe I'll be allowed to stay with her?"

"Yes," said Geoff.

Gayanne looked at the faces of the two men. Again she climbed up Daniel's arm. "Does it have to be him?"

The Sergeant's back stiffened, and the silence throbbed. "Well." He cleared his throat. "I have a very nice partner. She's busy at the moment, talking to Ms. Hunt, but I know she'll want to hear your story. Would you like that better?"

Gayanne looked at Daniel's face, then dropped her eyes to the Sergeant's feet and nodded.

The Sergeant smiled. "I'll see when Lt. Perry will be free." He stepped back, and looked at each of them in turn. His eyes wavered when they fell on Natalie, but she did not move a muscle, and he retreated back down the hall.

♥   ♥   ♥

In time, Lt. Perry arrived, with her wide smile and a raspberry-red suit. She shook Daniel's hand and asked after Gayanne's nerves. She gave them a report on Louise, who, she assured them, was awake and doing fine. Louise had been very brave, but she was concerned for Gayanne and wanted to make sure she was really all right. Did Gayanne want to see her before they had their talk?

Gayanne looked into her bright eyes for a moment, then shifted her gaze to Daniel. She nodded her head, and the Lieutenant led father and daughter away.

♥   ♥   ♥

Natalie and Rebecca remained in the waiting room. Rebecca gazed at the painting of a farmhouse on the wall opposite. Natalie wrote steadily in her notebook.

She lifted her head once to ask, "What is this, Sunday?"

After fifteen minutes, Rebecca stirred. "Triplets. The woman who had two sons born on the same day had triplets. Not twins."

Natalie did not look up. "Correct."

Another ten minutes passed. Natalie closed her notebook.

"Can I ask you something?" Rebecca rested her elbow on the back of the chair. "That was your well-dressed policeman, right?"

"Yeah." She put the notebook in her bag.

"Was he one also who arrested Daniel last spring?"

"Not exactly arrested him…just brought him in. I mean—"

"I know what you mean. Daniel told me what happened. He said he was very decent to him. But I understand why you didn't want me to mention that you were seeing this particular policeman."

Natalie nodded.

Rebecca fingered the rough edge of the seat back. "I felt sorry for him—he looked so out of place. Gayanne picked up on the strain between him and Daniel." She raised her eyes to Natalie's. "And I couldn't help notice the air between you two was crackling."

Natalie tossed her head. "Oh, you know how I get about the police sometimes…."

216

Rebecca held up an apologetic hand. "I'll take that as a polite way of telling me to butt out."

"No—don't." Natalie's cheeks grew warm. She had the urge to speak, but no words came. She wanted to look at Rebecca's face, but she could not raise her eyes. Frozen again, by something she did not understand....

"What is it?" Rebecca put a hand on her shoulder.

Tears welled up in Natalie's eyes. From where? Two minutes before she had been writing furiously, thinking about the investigation, her personal life shoved back behind the needs of the moment where it belonged....

"I don't know. I really don't know...." She blinked, and the tears rode her eyelashes down to her flaming cheeks.

Rebecca reached into her bag. "I'm gonna take a wild guess and suggest this has something to do with the Sergeant with the death-ray eyes." She held out a packet of tissues.

Natalie laughed as she wiped her eyes. It was such a relief to laugh...such a relief to cry.... "Yeah. I guess it does." She blew her nose. "Aren't you gonna ask me what it's all about?"

The corner of Rebecca's mouth turned up. "I already did. The rest is your job."

"Damned psychologist." Natalie ran a hand through her hair. "With everything else that's going on? Okay. It's just...." She shook her head. "I don't know where to begin."

"Start with what's happening now, including what you feel about it, then go back to the beginning. That kills the suspense, but supposedly makes you feel better. Although I've always had a hunch that shrinks are impatient and want to hear the good stuff first."

Natalie laughed again. "I have the sense of being manipulated for my own good." She raised her eyebrows in astonishment. "I really like it."

Rebecca took an imaginary note: "The subject's trust has been gained."

Natalie's smile faded. "Funny you should mention that. Because I thought I could trust him, and it hurt a lot when I found out I couldn't. Okay." She stared at the wall. "I get angry when I see him, and when I'm angry I feel all wrong, because that's not how I feel at all, really. I feel like there's a wall between us. Not brick—something that looks like gauze but feels like ice. I feel he doesn't give me the credit I deserve, but instead of concluding he's a jerk, I conclude I've failed somehow. I feel like he hasn't treated me fairly, because he said he'd made a mistake about me, but then he looks at me the way he looks at me, and I get all roiled up." She pursed her lips. "I sound like a child, don't I."

"Yes. It's very refreshing." Rebecca grinned cheerfully. "Most adults think that having emotions is childish, and lock them in cold storage, which helps them pretend they aren't there. Since you can express your feelings so well—such a laundry list!—you're half way to recognizing them for what they are—guideposts to your version of happiness and fulfillment."

"Yeah, but you can't control outsides factors...."

"You don't need to. Not if you have the freedom of choice."

"But—"

"No. You have to accept the outside world for what it is, whether you like it or not. But fulfillment comes from within. That's lesson one."

Natalie pulled in her lips. "So you're telling me I'm wrong to want to trust people?"

"Not at all. But you might have to define trust." Rebecca pushed a strand of hair from her face. "Just because you stayed out of jail with your reputation intact, you can't think you were unaffected by what was going on around you the first 25 years of your life. On the plus side, you probably wouldn't be as independent as you are, or as impassioned as you are, if you had grown up in what you think of as a 'normal' family. On the down side, some of your basic ideas concerning relationships may be a bit skewed. There's nothing unusual with that. You just need to consider taking the time to fine tune your system—the way you would your car, so you won't crash when you try to put on the brakes or use the steering wheel. No rush— you're not dysfunctional. You explore these issues of trust when you're ready."

"Some people think I'm past ready."

"It doesn't matter a hoot what anybody thinks but you."

"Yeah. You're right. Look. I know there's supposed to be some sort of professional distance or something. You'll probably tell me to talk to some- one else But...." She wiped her eyes with her fingers. "I don't suppose you'd consider giving me a tune-up, some time?"

"I'm honored that you've asked, and I would be pleased to do so. What are friends for? Notice how I say that like I'm not dying to know what the hell is going on between you and this—"

Natalie put her hand on Rebecca's arm. Rebecca turned around and saw Geoff coming to a halt in the doorway.

"Sorry." He started to edge backward, as one taking his leave. "I was looking for Perry."

Rebecca rose with a smile that had been known to stop traffic and walked toward him (he stopped). "She took Daniel and Gayanne to see Louise.

After that she was going to interview Gayanne. Which reminds me…."
She moved toward him, and he stepped aside—into the waiting room.
"Daniel might want me to be present. If you'll excuse me?" She nodded to
the Sergeant, and turned her head to Natalie as she left. "Don't go anywhere. I'll see you later."

Natalie stared after her. She felt…she felt calm, as if life were not as
complicated as she had thought. The important thing was, once again, to
find a killer.

Geoff spoke, to no one in particular. "Well, I'll see if I can find her on
the third floor."

"Wait a minute." Natalie stood and looked at his face. She could see
the uneasiness in his eyes. "Have they caught the guy?"

"No."

"Any leads?"

"No. But…." He licked his lips, undecided.

Natalie put her hands in her pockets. "It's connected with the murders,
isn't it? And I think we know what he was after." She kept her eyes on his
face, and saw his uncertainly. "Look, it's obvious they didn't send you and
Perry here to work on a burglary…."

The corners of his lips twitched. "You'll hear about it, anyway." He ran
his thumb across the inside of his right wrist. "Somebody put what we
think are cyanide tablets in Louise's aspirin bottle."

"Jeez," whispered Natalie.

"If your niece hadn't heard the guy…." He shook his head.

"He must have…." She swallowed. "He must have read the letter to
Enigma in the *Star* last Sunday—you saw that I presume?"

His eyes narrowed warily. "Yes."

She nodded. "He must have seen it, and broken into Louise's house
hoping he could find the reply."

His voice was wary, too. "That is the conclusion I reached."

"He may have hoped he'd find the other Enigma letters, too." She
searched his impassive face for signs of interest. "Doesn't this show that
whoever the burglar was, he knew something about Enigma, but not enough
to know that the letters weren't there? And listen!" She pulled her hands
out of her pockets. "He must not have known that Louise didn't write that
letter; that Louise doesn't have the letters anymore; that she handed the
whole mess over to me…and Byron…a month ago!"

She looked at him eagerly. He was still stonewalling. She frowned.
What did it take? "This really narrows the field! Because it has to be some-

one who didn't know there was no reply from Enigma. Get it?"

His eyebrows came together and he turned his head to one side. "There was no reply?"

"Of course not. In fact, doesn't this eliminate Myra and Lance?" She peered at him anxiously. He was staring at the wall. "What, am I reaching too far?"

"There was no reply?"

"No, I—" The penny dropped. "You thought there was a reply?"

He blinked slowly, then nodded.

She made a noise in her throat. "That's what you meant Friday night about holding back infor—?"

He crossed his arms over his chest, and nodded again.

"Oh." She studied his hands—long, loose-jointed hands. "Well. We'd have shown you the reply if we'd gotten one." She looked back at his face. "Why didn't you...? Oh, never mind." Finding the murderer, that was the important thing. "So, am I reaching too far?"

"No, I don't think you're reaching too far." His face was mobile again. "Nor can I see Myra or Lance climbing in a kitchen window looking for a letter that doesn't exist."

"Good." Natalie took a deep breath. "That's something, then! Of course, that leaves everyone else at the *Star* who—"

"But wait a minute." He looked down the hall, then walked a few paces into the room. "According to Shapiro, the only people who knew about Enigma were Louise, you, him, Lance, and Myra."

"And Marcia...."

"The burglar may have been Enigma. It is possible that her plan has been to get at Louise all along...."

"You keep using the feminine pronoun for Enigma. Why?"

"No special reason," he said easily. "The name has a feminine ending. Women are traditionally...enigmatic, good at expressing themselves.... Our profiler thinks that whoever Enigma is, she loved Marconi and was out to avenge a wrong committed against him. I think of Enigma as a she, that's all."

"Very enlightened of you." Incredible. This was the conversation they should have had Friday night. She didn't care what he asked her. He was just doing his job. She could refuse to answer anything she felt under no obligation to speak. She knew where she stood. Neither of them was betraying their professional trust. Nor were they at odds. What had happened? She arched her neck and regarded him objectively. "Let me ask you something. Bee's parents have four children. Three of them are named Spring, Summer, and Fall. What is the name of the fourth?"

He looked at her for five beats, then spoke. "Bee. Let me ask you something. Haven't Enigma's letters always arrived on a Wednesday? Isn't it possible that just because Louise didn't get a letter this past week, that doesn't mean one wasn't sent?"

She had to think about it only a moment. "Unfortunately, yes."

"Is it possible that the letter could have been intercepted between the Post Office and Louise's mailbox?"

She opened her mouth, then closed it. "Maybe. Maybe.... And if so I know where to look first...." She hesitated. Would he ask her...?

He did not. "I'm hoping we'll get a lead from your niece. A partial description...height, weight...." He glanced at the clock. "Perry's good with kids."

Natalie smiled briefly. "I like your partner."

"They don't come any better." He eyed her cautiously. "Congratulations, by the way, on the front page."

"Thanks."

"Your career, at least, is heading in the right direction."

She lifted her chin. "Meaning the rest of my life isn't?"

His brow wrinkled, and he looked at her thoughtfully. "Actually, that's not what I meant at all...."

There was a ringing from Natalie's bag, lying abandoned by her chair. She went and retrieved it. As she listened, giving an occasional, "Yeah.... Okay," she kept her eye on Geoff's profile.

"I gotta go," she said as she hung up. "We'll, uh, let you know if we get a reply to that letter. Or if we find out it was waylaid."

His head moved slightly. "Thank you."

"Would you tell Rebecca, if you see her, that I'll call later?"

"If I see her."

"Thanks." As she went by him, he put a hand on her arm. She looked up uncertainly.

He looked down uncertainly. "If the killer is trying to eliminate anyone who knew about Enigma...." He removed his hand. "Keep your eyes on whoever pours the coffee."

Chapter Twenty-six

The Taconic State Parkway was an anachronism in 1990s New York State: a gray, undulating divided highway snaking along the Adirondack mountains through a hundred miles of wilderness. One rarely saw a building, let alone a town or a city. Road signs alerted drivers to deer crossings and rock slides, rather than to school crossings and merging traffic. The parkway belonged to a different era than the overcrowded eight-lane Thruway, which ran straight as a die, twenty miles to the west.

Somewhere north of Queechy Lake Natalie took a wrong turn and lost half an hour. She wasn't used to these narrow roads that wound their way through valleys and changed direction without any apparent reason. Not much like her familiar suburban stomping grounds, where missing a turn meant taking the next one a few hundred yards later and quickly getting back on track.

Eventually she found herself crawling up a black macadam road so narrow she could have touched the yellow leaves of the trees by opening her window and extending her arm. She wondered what she would do if another car came.

But none did, and after another ten minutes she saw what she had been looking for—a white mailbox hanging from the branch of a tree—and turned onto a dirt track with a strip of coarse grass in the middle that ran between open fields. Beyond those fields were other fields, some of which appeared to her untutored eye to be redolent in corn stubble and rocks. Beyond the fields were trees, and glimpses of low hills, some covered with orange, red, and copper-colored trees, some bare.

The house appeared, a massive, three-story building with a mansard roof and tall windows. Its clapboard sides were painted white, its trim black. Opposite the house was a red barn. The nose of a red tractor peeped through its open door. An ancient blue pick-up sat backed up to a pile of what Natalie took to be manure.

As she slowed, she heard the barking of dogs—big dogs. They raced around the house and toward the car, which they circled and sniffed, barking all the while—although they also wagged their bushy brown tails. Natalie, who had never had much to do with dogs, wondered if it was safe to open the door. As she had found herself being pulled farther and farther away from civilization, she had weighed the risks of being poisoned or of having acid thrown in her face, but not of being torn to shreds by gleaming white fangs inside long brown snouts.

Choosing a moment when both dogs were on the far side of the Volvo, she opened the door. They bounded around, barking madly. She closed the door.

A tall spare figure in jeans and a plaid shirt came around the corner of the barn—a woman, with short gray hair and a lined face.

Natalie waited for her to call off the hounds, but the woman picked her way around the manure pile in silence. Natalie rolled down her window and peered out over the two moist black noses.

The woman leaned on the pick-up truck and regarded her. "They won't hurt you."

The implication (however subtle) that she had shown a weakness was enough to overcome her doubts, and Natalie got out of the car. The dogs backed away a few feet, but did not stop barking.

The woman looked at them. "Enough! Shut up!"

And shut up they did, though their grins remained wide and their tails wagged with great vigor. As Natalie walked over to the pick-up, they bounded around her, bumping into her legs and eyeballing her over their furry shoulders.

"Dottie Marconi?" asked Natalie.

The woman nodded.

"I'm Natalie Joday." She held out her hand. "Thanks for agreeing to see me."

Dottie gave her a hand hardened by calluses and stained with dirt around the nails. "You said one o'clock, didn't you?"

"I got lost."

"Everyone does…." Dottie looked over Natalie's shoulder to the north. "It'll rain before the afternoon is out. Sorry, but I've got to finish my strawberry beds. I may not get another chance before the frost." She looked Natalie up and down. "You can help." She turned and headed back around the manure pile, and the dogs bounded past her, leading the way along the path.

♥   ♥   ♥

"The man from the District Attorney's office said they weren't certain who tipped off the coroner that Maury had been murdered. But Angie said it was you." Dottie rested the edge of the spade on the ground and stepped on it. The blade slid effortlessly into the dark brown earth. "How did you know?"

Watching her was an education. She didn't move the dirt anywhere, just pushed the spade in, pulled the dirt up, then twisted the spade so that the dirt went right back from whence it had come. "We followed up a tip we had received suggesting that someone had injured Maury. Since he was dead, we checked to see if the injury was a murder." She looked up at the gathering clouds. "It was."

Dottie put her boot on the spade. "May I assume that by 'we' you mean 'I?'" She turned the earth over.

"Yes. Sorry."

"And are you here today to find out if I did it?"

An earthworm twisted across the upturned earth, its reddish-brown body covered with bits of dirt. "You have no alibi, so technically you haven't been eliminated as a suspect. But that's not my purpose, no. I'd like to learn about your relationship with Peter and Myra. And I have some financial questions...."

"Ask what you want. Angie said you were okay, and that's good enough for me." She sent the spade into the earth. It made a harsh sound as it scraped against a rock.

"Thanks...." Natalie hesitated. In her albeit limited experience, first and second wives did not display this form of mutual admiration. "Will you start with how you met Myra and Peter?"

Dottie moved down the row. "I was a sophomore at SUNY Purchase. They were juniors. How did we meet?" She bent down and pulled a rock the size of an orange from the dirt. "I can't believe there are still rocks in this garden after ten years of pulling them out." She heaved it into the ditch that rimmed the garden. "They hooked up with Lance Wenger, because he was smart. He had a thing for me, so they took me into the fold for his sake. Lance was from Buffalo, originally—a real brain but too much of a coward to ask anyone to pass the salt let alone ask a girl for a date. He—"

"The Cowardly Lion...."

"That's right." She rested the blade of the spade on the ground and leaned her forearms on the wooden handle. "That's what they called him. I hadn't thought of that in years. How did you know?"

"I can't say right now."

She took the answer at face value and continued. "In retrospect, I'd say we were good college chums—thrown together rather than drawn together. Without a deep bond. We palled around as a foursome. We had good times. I made sure Lance knew I wasn't interested in anything more than being friends. He didn't seem to mind. To his credit. Most men take it as an insult."

"What about Myra and Peter?"

"They were born leaders, both of them." She resumed her work. "They were at the center of all the liberal causes before it was popular. It was exciting just being near them. If there was nothing going on, they raised hell for the fun of it. They didn't care what people thought. They taught me not to care, either."

"How did the Wizard of Oz nicknames start?"

"I don't know." The wind was picking up, and she resettled her hat more firmly. "Does it matter? The police didn't ask about that."

"It matters."

Again Dottie took her word for it. "I can't recall if it was before they met me or when they heard my name. Peter liked to tease Myra about being cold as a witches tit. After a while it got tiresome."

"So…you were Dorothy, Myra was the Wicked Witch of the West. Lance was the Cowardly Lion. Peter was…the Scarecrow?"

"No. He was the Tin Man. Myra liked to tease him about being a heartless son of a bitch. I thought it was mean—later I understood. In a way, she was paying him back for calling her a witch. But in another way, it was a compliment. My old friend Tyler said they were proud of their reputations for cruelty."

Natalie did her best to control her face. "Tyler…Hanson?"

Dottie nodded. "I haven't seen him since what happened with Maury. Is he still working for the *Star*?"

"Yes…. He's a senior reporter, now."

She turned back to her task. "He met Myra and Peter through me. That was later on, after college, when I moved back to Connecticut, where my folks had a country house. Ty was a local boy."

"How did you meet him?"

"My parents took an interest in him. Hired him to do odd jobs. He pretty much had the run of the place in summers. My Dad is a Classics scholar, and Ty was a sucker for anything he considered highbrow. He was a little pathetic. His mother was a professional teenager, the kind of woman who devotes all her attention to the boyfriend of the moment. His father showed up once every couple of years and beat her up. I guess she liked it—gave her an excuse to be miserable. Ty didn't fit in—no good at sports, no good with girls, no money backing him. He figured his way out of Fairview was to be as smart as possible and bluff the rest. He would ingratiate himself to anybody he thought would advance his social status. I didn't see it that way at first—I liked him for who he was and I admired the fact that underneath it all he was a hard worker—but it became obvious when he got Peter and Myra in his sights. They invited themselves up for weekends a couple of times a year. He followed them around like a lap dog begging the great ones for a bone. They made fun of him to his face but he just rolled over and took it." She pushed the spade into the ground with her boot. "Senior reporter, eh? I guess he got what he wanted."

"I had no idea…. Then…the Scarecrow. Was it Tyler?"

"There was no Scarecrow." A wry smile brought Dottie's face to life, and Natalie at last recognized the girl from the college yearbooks. "Tyler was Toto." She turned around at the end of the row. "They really knew where to stick the knife."

"Toto…."

"But they gave him a job when he got out of college, so…." She shrugged and rubbed her hands on her tan trousers. "Couldn't you have asked Myra these question?"

The wind blew harder. The bare branches of the trees on the hillside waved against the dark sky. Winter would come soon, here. "I guess I couldn't."

"Because you couldn't count on a full answer." She headed up the second row. "That's Myra. So sure she knows best, sure her motives are unassailable." She pushed the spade into the ground. "Me? I grew up non-judgmental. I still believe in it. I didn't mind Tyler hanging around, using me as his confidante, flattering me, trying to involve himself in my life—any more than I minded Peter and Myra dropping by at their convenience, living off my father's money. But I thought Myra was a hypocrite because she condemned Tyler for doing exactly what she was doing. That never occurred to her, of course, because when she kissed ass she did it with greater finesse. She was quite proud of her ability to bulldoze people. She and Peter considered it a legitimate business practice. Peter would lead the way with the old charm, and she'd swoop in for the kill. By the time I was thirty, we weren't really friends anymore. But it took a few years for them to get tired of me. I didn't want to hurt them. When you've outgrown someone, there's no need to make a big deal about it. You just remove yourself and they get the idea eventually. They couldn't face the truth, because it would have put them in a bad light. Eventually Peter did something I didn't like. I…said things."

"What did he do?"

Dottie paused with her foot to the top of the blade. "Went off on a three-day fling instead of staying with his father, who died that weekend. I—reacted badly." She put her weight onto the blade and it sank into the earth. "Of course they made it look like they had decided to end it with me. They invented some explanation that appeased their self-esteem and made me the villain of the piece, and that was that. I didn't care. We do what we have to." She turned the earth over and moved down the row.

"What explanation?"

She hit the spade against the ground. A chunk of dirt fell off the side, and she sliced into it. "That I had fried my brains dropping acid and lost it. That was supposedly too outrageous for their Puritan souls. And yet they had tolerated my other eccentricities for years in the interests of staying close to real money."

"What eccentricities?"

As Dottie looked up, the wind blew her gray bangs over her eyes. She pushed them away. "Nothing but what you see…. In my day it was called being a flower child, if that means anything to you. And a peace activist. That's how I met Maury."

"Forgive me, but, was Maury really your type?"

"You want to know what I saw in a shoe salesman?" Dottie smiled as she pushed the spade into the earth. "We smoked a lot of dope together for one thing. And our politics were similar. But mostly it worked because he was who he said he was, and he didn't care a hoot how much money he had as long as he could take care of his family." She stopped, and rubbed the back of her hand across her mouth. "Also he was very sensual, and very generous in bed." She kicked a clod of earth from the spade and resumed her work.

"Did Peter and Myra ever meet him?"

"No. I made sure of that."

"Then they never expressed any animosity toward him?"

"Sure they did, and just as surely Tyler kept me informed about the horrible things they said. My fault for being insane enough to think there was room enough in one county for the four of us. They thought he was loud and unsophisticated. They thought all his ideals about equality and truth in politics and the evils of money were a put-on, that he was the Wizard of Oz—the little man sweating behind the curtain, telling the little people what they wanted to hear." She turned over the earth. "Lance understood better."

"So you still saw Lance."

"Oh yes. Lance was different. Don't think anything I've said about Peter and Myra pertains to Lance."

"Did he meet Maury?"

"Once or twice over the years."

"Did Lance come along with Myra and Peter for the weekends?"

"A couple of times, right after college. But he saw that it wasn't like it used to be—that I didn't really like it—and he stopped. But he always called, and I called him. He was a good friend."

"But you never...."

"No."

"Was there ever anything between Peter and Myra?"

Dottie shoved the spade into the ground. "You mean sexual?"

"Yeah."

"I can't answer that. I don't talk about other people's sex lives—after Maury, you can probably understand why."

"Yes." Natalie followed her down the row. "May I ask...was there ever anything between you and Peter?"

She turned the spade over. "Is this question relevant? Would it make what Peter did to Maury any more or less despicable?"

Natalie looked along the row of overturned soil. She had told herself she wasn't going to try to dig up anything on Peter's sex life. But she wanted to understand these intertwining relationships. But...what right had she? "I believe it might help solve the case. It won't appear in the paper; we don't want to humiliate anyone—"

"In my day, the more people a woman slept with, as long as she was on the pill, the more she showed her independence. And I was very independent. But you're missing the point. This whole mess started because of questions like that. Because journalists think they have the right to ask anything, and if we don't answer, we're covering something up. Isn't it time you stopped?"

"Yeah." She shrugged. "I guess you're right."

Dottie stooped to pull a bit of slate out of the ground. "Brava."

The wind made the dry leaves of the nearby trees rustle. Natalie looked around the garden. There were many more plants growing than she would have thought possible in late October. Dottie stepped on the spade, which hit another rock. She stumbled.

Natalie reached out to steady her. "Can't you hire somebody to do this? Or does it cost…?"

Dottie did not try to hide her amusement. "You're a suburban girl, born and bred, aren't you?"

"More or less…."

"It shows. You're so used to looking at nice neat packages you think anything messy must be unwanted; you think those big houses in Bergen County built in the Fifties are antiques." She leaned on the spade and regarded the house, sitting on a low hill amidst tall oak trees. "This place was built in 1832. It's been renovated twice and restored once, but there are some bits of the original left. I'll show you around later. As for the garden…. You needn't worry about my health or my bank balance. Half an acre is not as big as you think it is, and I happen to love gardening."

"So did Maury."

Dottie nodded. "He preferred flowers to vegetables. Naturally our son prefers orchards. He's planting olive trees in Turkey." She scraped her boot on the spade. "Angie said you came to pump her about Maury, and she got you to fix her lawnmower."

"Uh…I guess…."

"Good, then you can help me lay the mulch before you ask any more questions."

♥   ♥   ♥

Later, Dottie gave her the promised tour of the house. Then she brought her to the kitchen, with its stone walls and raftered ceiling, and fed her on pasta stuffed with spinach. Natalie was rather subdued. Even she, inexperienced with such things, realized the house was packed with enough antiques and artwork to be a museum.

The dogs settled by the potbelly stove, in which burned sticks of apple wood. Dottie put a pot of coffee on the table and rummaged in a cabinet for cups. "Now, what else was it you wanted to know?"

"How you ended up on the *Star's* list of stockholders."

"The police asked me that." She put the cups on the table and sat. "It's no secret. In the early Seventies Lance told me the *Star* was going to become a public company, and asked me to invest. He said they were in a bind; that they needed to prove to the old owners that they could raise money. So I invested."

"This was before Maury ran for State Senate."

"A year or so before." She put her hands around her coffee cup. "Now you want to know about what happened with Maury."

"It must have been difficult for you...."

Dottie's lips twitched. "Fortunately, the need for sympathy has passed. But it was no picnic. That Peter would dig into Maury's personal life like that—in the name of truth. And Myra, too. We had gone our separate ways, but in my book, you don't screw over an old friend."

"You were more upset with them than with Maury?"

"Very perceptive. The police seemed to think I should have been beating my breast and tearing my hair out about my husband. But you see I already knew Maury wasn't a saint. So he had sex with a guy. So what? I had sex with a guy or two myself before I got tired of male egos."

"Did Maury ever tell you the name of the guy?"

"No. He only said it had been a mistake, and that he was sorry. I believed him, since we had gone to the extent of getting married and having a child. But I also believed that mistakes were there to be learned from. It happened, but it wouldn't have made any difference between us if he hadn't also imploded as a human being. Now...what Peter and Myra did...that was forever. They knowingly sucker-punched the husband of an old friend. And for what? All to sell a bunch of stinking newspapers? To up their circulation?"

Natalie remembered Peter's justification for printing the story. "Newspapers do have a responsibility to inform the public...."

Dottie raised her coffee cup. "What can I say to you? You're a reporter. That's a license to destroy."

Natalie bridled. "Reporters are human beings first."

"They are? I'm not so sure. If you'd asked me twenty years ago.... Now, I can only tell you I think the people you love are more important than your perceived duty to your job. But what do I know." She took a sip. "I haven't met anyone in your line of work who agrees with me. Even Ty put his job ahead of his old friendship with me. I—idealist that I was—thought he'd quit the paper after what Peter did. But...well, he's still there, isn't he? In fact, he cut me cold. He used to come to dinner every Sunday afternoon after he moved to Bergen County and started working for the *Star*. I thought he cared about us. But he obviously thought he could advance his career better elsewhere."

"Did you talk about it with him, afterward?"

"No. He never called. He never even wrote. The last time I talked to him was Fourth of July 1992. The last time I saw him was a year later, having coffee with Linda—dressed to the nines, with the vest and tortoiseshell glasses, talking up a storm. He'd found a new, fancier confidante, it seemed: Miss Linda never-a-hair-out-of-place, the perfect partner for the young executive on the rise."

"Linda, the Good Witch of East Orange."

Dottie's dark eyes glittered in appreciation. "Very good. But at the time it hurt like hell. Of course I was hurting a lot then...."

"Maury...."

She nodded. "I had realized our marriage was over. He'd thrown himself off a cliff and was drinking as he fell so he wouldn't feel the crash. I got phone calls every other day to come pick him up from one unpleasant dive or other. It had a bad effect on our son. Also, I didn't much like using my father's money to support him. He was stuck in a rut, and I was still growing, still changing. So I left him, although I did it as painlessly as possible. I turned my attention to saving the planet, instead of saving the people."

"Why didn't you sell your *Star* stock?"

Dottie treated Natalie to another amused smile. "If it had been Peter and Myra, I might have. But I didn't make the investment for them, so why should I take it back because of them? It was Lance. Such a funny guy. He has a terrible time. Can't carry on a conversation for beans. Doesn't know how to express an emotion; can barely express a thought. I think what might take you or me five minutes to work out, he gets in five seconds. So he tunes out while he waits for everybody else to catch up. Makes him look like he's lost, but he isn't. He called after the story on Maury came out. To say how sorry he was. That meant a lot to me."

"But he didn't quit the *Star*—any more than Tyler did."

Dorothy tightened her bony fingers around her coffee cup. "I never thought of that." She raised the cup to her lips and found it empty. "Maybe I'd have felt differently about Tyler if he'd called. Or different about Lance if he hadn't." She picked up the coffeepot and refilled her cup.

"Have you received regular stockholder reports from the *Star*?"

"No. I told Lance I didn't want to be bothered. I didn't invest to make money, but to help a friend. He's got my proxy vote. I get a note from him every year, at Christmas." She sipped her coffee. "Are you about done? I've got to feed the goats soon."

Natalie turned a page. "Just one more. Do you know about anything that Peter and Myra and Lance did that could be described as dishonest, or immoral?"

Dottie wrinkled her brow. "The police didn't ask that either. Meeting you has been interesting—not what I expected." She ran her thumbs down the sides of her cup. "Why is this relevant?"

Natalie placed her hands on her notebook. "I can't tell you that. I can't risk anybody finding out what I know and what I don't. I can only tell you I saw Armand Vitek's face after he had tried to drink a cup of potassium silver cyanide. It made an impact. I don't care about who slept with who, or who lied to who, I only want to find whoever is doing this and make them stop. And the question is relevant to that."

Dorothy pursed her lips, inhaling through her nose. "All right." Her dark eyes searched Natalie's face. "Lance told me once that Peter and Myra had done something unethical, something to do with the paper. He wanted me to forgive him, because he hadn't stopped them. I don't know why me—he's so incoherent." She paused to recollect. "He said he'd put it right if it took his last breath."

"This was before or after what happened with Maury?"

"Before. I remember talking about it with Maury, and concluding that whatever that gang of hypocrites did it was none of our business. Sorry, that's all I remember."

Natalie closed her notebook. "That's it, then."

"I don't think I've said much that will help."

"Yes you have." Natalie put the notebook in her bag. "You've told me more than you could imagine. Thank you."

When they got up, the dogs did, too, and accompanied Natalie to the Volvo to say good-bye.

Chapter Twenty-seven

Natalie was late arriving at the newsroom on Monday, having stopped off at the medical center to see Louise. She had been delighted to find her sitting up in bed, eating a bowl of lime Jell-O. Lt. Perry was there, too, serving herbal tea from a gigantic thermos. Natalie was less pleased when Louise (worried she wouldn't be up to it and fearing to disappoint her readers) asked her to cover the column that week, but she agreed without betraying her mixed feelings. "Covering" was something journalists did; it was a professional courtesy, and Natalie would just have to lump it. She had left Louise and the Lieutenant chatting about the merits of aroma therapy for the elderly.

Natalie sat at her desk, determined to reach Peter Kovaks or die in the attempt. By noon, she was becoming irritated. The situation was ridiculous. How was it possible she had managed an interview with a woman who had every reason to detest the *Star*, but could not get one word from a man who had been affiliated with the paper for almost thirty years? She stomped over to the front office and demanded to see Byron without delay.

"Letting it go to our heads, are we?" Marcia poked her tongue into her cheek as she sent Natalie through.

Natalie sat in the red leather chair and pursed her lips. "Where the hell is Peter Kovaks? I've got to talk to him!"

Byron replaced a pastrami sandwich into Charlie's waxed paper wrapper and wiped his fingers on a napkin. "He's rather busy. Did you see what that *Bugle* reporter said about him today?"

"No, and I don't care…. What did he say?"

"The lead was 'Sex Scandal Cripples Kovaks Campaign.'"

"Nice alliteration. I bet they haven't used a rhetorical device at the *Bugle* since you left. What's the point of—"

"Since I left?" Byron's eyebrows rose above the rims of his glasses.

"Yeah. What's the point of having pull if you can't use it? What about 'the *Star* is doing what it can to assist in this investigation?'"

"Kovaks is not affiliated with the *Star* anymore."

"Horsefeathers. Honestly, Byron, I'm getting the feeling he's avoiding me." Natalie placed a hand on her chest. "Does he only want the *Bugle* writing about him?"

Byron picked up his pen and made a note. "I'll do my best. Now may I eat my lunch, please?"

Natalie arose from the chair and turned to the door.

"By the way," said Byron, "I didn't ever leave the *Bugle*, because I never worked for the *Bugle*."

Natalie turned around and looked at him.

He picked up his sandwich. "I did, however, freelance for them in my youth, when they were a respectable news organ, and open to encouraging young talent." He took a bite. "Just so you know."

♥   ♥   ♥

Back at her desk, she took stock of her options. There were, she knew, a couple of crime lab workers down in the printshop, and she had overheard one of the salespersons predicting that the detectives on the case would be stopping by. But she no longer cared. The attack on Louise had changed that; put things into perspective. Rebecca had been right. She didn't need to hide after all.

She turned on her computer, and when the monitor came to life she was stunned to see her shared-files folder lying open on the desktop. The inner folders—Enigma, Marconi, Vitek—were on display for anyone to open. Heart pounding, she clicked on the Network status bar. It showed that she had last accessed her shared files at 11:35 the previous morning. At which time she had been in her car admiring the scenery on the Taconic State Parkway.

She glanced around the newsroom. It appeared as it always did—disorganized, noisy, friendly. She turned back to her monitor and settled her hand on the mouse.

♥   ♥   ♥

"Afternoon, Rudy."

He studied the envelope in his hand before putting it in the A–D pigeon hole.

"Any mail for Louise this morning?"

"Nope." He picked up another envelope.

"Have you sorted today's mail yet?"

"Nope."

Having intimate experience with this sort of mood, Natalie deemed it wise to press. "Any mail for Louise over the weekend?"

"Nope." He shot the letter into its slot.

"Anybody ask you to tell them if Louise got any mail?"

He stuck out his lower jaw and picked up the empty mail bag.

"I said—"

"I heard ya." He folded the canvas bag in half. "If anybody did—hypothetical speaking—it would a been somebody who had the right to tell me what to do." He folded the bag again. "And they probably would a told me not to mention it to anybody who didn't."

"You played with my computer yesterday, didn't you."

"No."

"Come on, Rudy…do I have to ask the security guard if you were here?"

He whirled and faced her. "Yeah, so I was here! So what! I got as much right as you to be here!"

Natalie kept her face set. "What were you doing?"

"I don't have to tell you!"

"If that's the way you want it. It's convenient that the police are already here. I'll just have them dust my keyboard and mouse for prints." She turned abruptly away, headed for the front office.

"Wait!"

She stopped and turned. He was at the window, his hands gripping the edge of the counter, the pulse in his neck throbbing.

"I said I didn't play with your computer, and I didn't! You left it on—that's all, and I turned it off. I thought that's what you wanted! You wanna call the police for that? Man! What's with you?"

"What's with me?" Natalie stepped back to the counter and stared into his angry face. "What's with you! Don't you realize we're in the middle of a murder investigation?"

He looked sideways, and his voice grew uncertain. "We are?"

"Yeah. You know…the dead man I found last week up by the Tappan Zee Bridge?"

His eyes widened. "You found a dead guy?"

"Jeez, Rudy! Don't you read the paper!"

He flushed. "I been busy! I'm takin' classes, you know!"

"Is that why you come in on Sundays to use the computers?"

"Yeah. But I didn't use yours, okay? I used the one next to yours. Okay, you'll prob'ly find my prints on the mouse. But I'm telling you—I saw it was on and I turned it off. That's all."

"What was on, the monitor or the hard drive?"

"Both. Your screensaver was on—dumb sheep all jumpin' around."

"What did you do?"

"Jeez! You want me to paint a picture? I sat down and wiggled the mouse so the screensaver would stop. Then I clicked 'shutdown.' Okay?"

"So you saw what was on the desktop."

"Big deal! So what? Just some stupid folders. You left them right there for anybody to see. As if anybody cared about Angina and Macaroni!"

"Angina? No…. Enigma." The hair rose on the back of Natalie's neck, and she stood rooted to the floor. Smitten by the beauty of it, she put her palms together and touched her fingertips to her lips.

Rudy stared at her, his look of belligerence giving way to concern with surprising quickness. "You okay?"

Natalie placed her praying hands under her chin. "Yes. I'm okay. I'm finally okay." She looked at his scrawny face and uncomprehending eyes. "You're dyslexic, aren't you?"

Rudy's eyes blinked, and his face began to flush.

Natalie—subdued, awe-filled—looked around the mailroom. "I should have known it…the backwards sevens—and you told Louise her letter was from River Vale when it was from Valley Ridge."

"River…. I always get those…." He looked away, his head wagging back and forth. "Oh, man…."

"And you read 'Don't Use It' as 'Not In Use.'" She put her hands on her hips. "Why didn't you just tell me you read it wrong?"

"I did." His shoulders had slumped.

It was her turn to blink. "So you did. I just thought…."

"You just thought I was stupid!" He threw her a reproachful look. "And you were right." He shoved his hands into his pockets.

"Oh, boy, do I owe you a big apology…." Natalie stepped through the half door and into the mailroom. She went up to him and took him by the shoulders.

He flinched backward. "What—?"

She pulled him to her and kissed him on his rubbery lips until his shoulders came up around his ears. Then she stepped back and regarded his stunned face. "Stupid? Not at all. You're brilliant! You've solved a mystery I've been working on for two months!" Putting her arms around him again, she tried to break him in half.

But he was a sturdy lad, though thin, and he did not break. He only said, "What?" and clung awkwardly to her elbows.

When she let him go, he pulled at his shirt and sat down on his stool, trying hard to look like such events were commonplace in his life. "What'd I do?"

She regarded him objectively. He was not who she had thought he was. Yes, he was inexperienced and unfinished, but he was just as anxious to do good in this world as anybody else. Only she had never noticed it before. "You've helped me unravel the identity of a certain anonymous letter writer. Unfortunately I can't tell you more—but I will as soon as I can. And look, I don't want anybody else to know what's going on, so I'd appreciate it if you'd keep quiet about this until after the killer is behind bars."

Rudy's eyes widened. "You mean—this is about the murder?"

"Yeah. Rudy, you are now a key player in the search to find the murderer." She looked at him expectantly. "And I need your help. I need an ally in the newsroom, someone I can really trust."

His shoulders narrowed and he gripped the edges of the stool. But he wasn't quite ready to believe everything was okay. "So, now you believe I didn't use your computer yesterday?"

"Yes."

"Because you figure I read so bad I couldn't a been reading much in your files?"

Her guilt reared, but her conviction held firm. "Yes."

He sniffed. "That's the first time anything good every came out a my dyslexia." He licked his lips. "Okay, whatcha want?"

"First, I need your powers of observation. Someone turned on my computer yesterday, which means they were in the newsroom."

He eyed her cautiously. "Yeah. Yeah, right."

"And you are a witness to who was here…." She took him by the arm and pulled him off the stool.

"Where are we goin'?" he asked anxiously.

She steered him into the storeroom. "Don't worry, I'm not going to attack you again." She grinned at him. "It was just the excitement of the moment."

"No problem." He was suddenly all cocky young male. "You can do it again if you like—any time."

"I'll keep that in mind…." She sat down on a corrugated box of packing peanuts and he sat opposite. "How long were you here yesterday?"

"About four hours—got here about a quarter to twelve."

"To practice on the computers?"

"Yeah. And to work on the mailroom books, too. It, y'know, takes me longer, but I don't like Mr. Wenger to know...."

"Good thinking. Now—tell me who you saw here yesterday."

He rattled off the names of a score of *Star* employees, and when he had seen them. When he rolled his eyes to the ceiling and twisted his mouth he bore a striking resemblance to Daffy Duck in a pensive mood. Natalie let him go until he was done, taking notes.

"You've got a good memory."

"Yeah, you have to when it's hard to write things down."

"Do you remember seeing Tyler leave?"

He shook his head.

"Or Byron?"

"Yeah—now that you mention it. He left in a hurry, maybe a little after twelve."

"I heard he went to the medical center to see Louise."

Rudy's eyes widened. "What?"

"You didn't know? Somebody broke into her house Saturday night. But she's okay—better than she might have been. The son of a bitch put cyanide in her aspirin bottle."

His eyes widened. "Jeez...."

"And I hate to say it, but it looks like somebody at the *Star* might know something. That's why I need an ally."

"Okay." He was having trouble staying seated. "I'll do my best, Ms. Joday."

"Call me Natalie. Now, you're absolutely sure you didn't see Ms. Vandergelden, or Mr. Wenger, or Mr. Kovaks here yesterday?"

He shook his head. "I'm sure I'd remember if they were. They hardly ever come down to the newsroom."

"Okay. Now look Rudy, I really need to know if anybody told you to pull Louise's mail. And I do have a right to know, because under federal law it's her mail, and she appointed me to pick it up."

"I don't mind tellin' ya...now. Mr. Shapiro told me to give him any mail that came for her. But none came yet. I'm sorry, Ms. Joday...Natalie...I shouldn't a been so snotty with ya."

"That's okay, Rudy. I acted wrong, too." Natalie, thinking of Rebecca's advice, pulled out her own feelings and took a look at them. "I've got to admit I was angry with you because you were always picking on Louise. I hate that, because it reminds me of...somebody I don't like. But I should have tried to find out what was at the bottom of it."

He hung his head. "Is she gonna be okay?"

"Yeah. There're gonna keep her in the medical center for a couple of days, that's all. Partly because of her age, and partly, I think, for protection. She lives alone now. Rudy…." Natalie spoke as gently as possible. "Tell me why were you so mean to her?"

"I don't know…. She just…. Aw."

"It's okay, Rudy. I won't tell anyone if you don't want me to."

"It's just…I wanted a chance, too, y'know? And at first Mr. Shapiro said okay, try. I always wanted to work for a newspaper. But then he said I wasn't good enough…didn't have the necessary skills. I'm lousy with computers. But then he turned around and hired Louise!" He looked up with plaintive eyes. "That wasn't fair. She can't type either! And she had less experience than me!"

Natalie, groping through his fumbling words for meaning, finally got the point. "You mean, you wanted to do some writing?"

The blush returned. "Yeah…dumb idea, wasn't it. But my Mom always tells me to expand my horizons and don't take no for an answer. My first job was delivering the *Star* when I was ten years old. When I got out a high school, I got this job, here. And they have the intern program every summer—so I applied. Mr. Hanson said they need people to read through the press releases and junk mail that comes in, and chop it up into fillers and stuff. I can do it…it just takes me longer. And I need to get better at the computer. Only the class I want to take is in Mahwah, and I don't have a car…."

Natalie heard herself say, "Komputers for Klutzes."

"Yeah. But I didn't go there after all—it turned out they spelled the name of the course wrong—what is that? I have enough trouble spelling. I should a known nothing in the same building as the *Bugle* was involved with would be any good. Sleaze rag."

"Does Byron know about your dyslexia?"

"A course. He said he'd try to help me out, but…." He shrugged. "He says he's gotta do what's right for the paper…. Even if it hurts."

"I agree with him, there." Natalie raised her eyebrows for emphasis. "Especially with two people dead, and another in the hospital. The question is, do you agree?"

He blinked his sleepy eyes, and nodded.

"Then this conversation never took place." Natalie glanced at the door. "I'll contact you when I make my move." She pointed a finger at him. "When the time comes, I'm counting on you."

He pulled at his shirt, gritting his teeth, and nodded.

239

She found Davis in the Public Access Room, staring thoughtfully at the green and silver innards of a dismembered computer.

"Is that all that's in there?" She peered over his shoulder. "Ew."

"Natalie!" He glanced toward the door, then signaled for her to follow him. Inside his office, he turned to her. "You know I don't normally ask too many questions—none of my business why people want to know what they want to know, I only help them find it. But…what's going on? There are police here all the time! Everyone is creeping around looking scared. Thinking they were going to be fired was bad enough, but this? And the attack on Louise Hunt? You're in the know…is it true? Are we in danger?"

"I don't think so, Davis. At least…not you."

"Oh, that's really comforting…." He slumped into his chair.

"I wish I could be more optimistic, but there's no point in denying it looks like someone at the *Star* knows something."

"Especially since the *Bugle* reminds us of that daily…."

Natalie winced. "Yeah."

"Is there anything I can do?"

"That's why I'm here. You I know I can trust."

"I'm honored. Are you, uh, still being shadowed?"

"No. It's technical help I need. What would it take for someone to hack into the Network and access my shared files?"

"Are you saying somebody…?"

Natalie nodded.

"Are your files on the Server or…?"

"On my hard drive. I turned it on this morning and my shared-files folder was open on the desktop."

Davis whistled. "If they're sitting at your computer, it would just mean knowing your password. If they're elsewhere on the Network, they would also have to know the Crime Bureau password. If they're not on the Network, well…. I could do it if I knew the Network protocols. But it would take me a while to crack both passwords and configure my computer without being noticed. Of course your computer has to be on for any of this to work."

"Who knows my password besides me and Marcia?"

"I do—not offhand, but I can access it. That's all. Unless you wrote it down and stuck it on your monitor. Or somebody might have stood at your desk watching you type it in. And then there are password cracks…it takes a while but they work."

"Can you tell where my files were accessed from?"

He shook his head. "If you show me the file, I can tell you where it came from, but not the other way around. Our Network doesn't track each access command. Maybe it should...." His hands twitched and wandered to his keyboard.

"Davis. This is important. How do we identify this guy?"

"It'll be hard...."

"He left my folders on the desktop. Why would he do that?"

"He must have moved them without knowing it. It's easy to do when folders are within folders within folders."

"He's never done that before...."

"This has happened more than once?" His face lit up. "Do you think he'll try again?"

Natalie blinked. "He might if there is sufficient bait...."

"Then all we have to do is write a little program...."

"How long will it take?"

"I can write something up in an hour or so...maybe two. Then you lay your bait...."

"I'm on babysitting duty this afternoon. Can we set it up for tomorrow morning?"

"Affirmative." Davis turned to his monitor. "I just need you for five minutes now—we'll go on the Network, and you can show me the files you want me to booby trap...."

♥   ♥   ♥

There was a silence on the telephone, and then Rebecca let out a gasp. "Of course! E N I G M A! It's so simple. Why didn't we think of anagrams? It was right under our noses the whole time."

"We didn't get it because we didn't know there was anything to get." Natalie, seated on her sofa, put her feet up on the coffee table.

"So...what do we do, now that we know who Enigma is?"

Natalie scowled at her thumbnail. "I don't know. I'm not sure I want her to know I know. Are you free tonight?"

"After eight, I am. Are you going to tell Byron?"

"I doubt it."

Chapter Twenty-eight

Natalie arrived at the office the next morning at nine. There had been no communication from either of the Kovaks, but Byron had sent her an e-mail saying he was trying to work something out. She puttered around for the better part of an hour, then threw her bag over her shoulder and left.

♥　　　♥　　　♥

"Natalie? Where are you?"

"Cruising Oradell."

"It's rigged. The file can be looked at, and moved, but not opened."

"Thanks, Davis. I hope it works."

"Now what?"

"You've set the trap; now I provide the bait."

"Don't you get eaten, now."

"Oh, no…no fear of that. Firestorm only eats curious children."

♥　　　♥　　　♥

"Tyler? Natalie. I'm headed for Suffern. I think I have a contact who may have a description of someone Armand saw the day he died. I've typed up my rough notes and some hypotheticals, but I haven't shown anything to Byron yet—too speculative. Hold down the fort. I've got to get home to babysit at three, but I'll be back in the newsroom around six."

♥　　　♥　　　♥

"Hey, Marcia? Can you give Byron a message? Tell him I've written up my notes, and think I may be on to something regarding who Maury may have had an affair with. But I've got to go check something in Suffern, first. Then I have to babysit until around five thirty. So I'll be out all day. But I'm coming in at six, if he wants to wait to see me."

"Got it."

"Thanks."

♥ ♥ ♥

The newsroom resembled an orchestra playing a neo-modern symphony of little melody and much discord: the double doors clunked as reporters rushed in and out; the photocopiers swished and clicked; the wheels of the mail trolley squeaked as Rudy made his rounds; and voices caroled on the phones and in a dozen private conversations. In those brief coincidental moments when the voices were hushed and the copiers at rest, the ticking of the old-fashioned clock above the *Star* masthead on the south wall could be heard, a relentless metronome marking time until the grand finale was reached, when all deadlines were met.

♥ ♥ ♥

Finishing his rounds, Rudy retreated to his den and busied himself counting his stamps—a daily task that provided him with a sense of accomplishment and fulfilled his love of organization. But today he kept his eyes peeled to the goings on in the newsroom, and his ears alert to the slightest sound.

So he heard the soft tap on the delivery door at the back of the mailroom. He went over and opened it a crack.

"All clear," he whispered.

Natalie slipped inside and waited as he locked the steel door. She stayed in the shadows as he went to the counter, waiting for his nod before moving forward and letting herself out into the newsroom. No one paid any attention to her as she skirted the north wall, as if headed for the photocopier.

She picked up the old wooden chair that sat, generally ignored, by the door to the women's toilet, and carried it to the back of Tyler's cubicle. She stepped onto the chair and raised her eyes over the top of the beveled glass wall.

She had a bird's eye view of a hitherto unsuspected bald spot on the top of Tyler's head, and of his computer monitor.

She could not read the words at that distance (about six feet), but she could tell what he was doing by the movement of his hands, and by what appeared on the monitor. He was on the Network, in the shared-files area. The password pop-up window appeared. His hands tapped carefully at the keyboard.

Natalie's eyes widened as the password was accepted, and the page she had dummied up the day before appeared.

Then the screen flickered—and turned upside down.

♥ ♥ ♥

Natalie leaned against the open door to Tyler's cubicle and folded her arms. She admired the fact that, when he looked up and saw her standing there, his face showed only a momentary flash of guilt before reverting to ready frustration.

"Problem?" she asked in honeyed tones.

"This computer has gone crazy, that's all." His fingers sped over the keys. "Maybe if I reboot." He hit the restart button. After a moment, the computer chimed at him. He pulled out a handkerchief and blew his nose. "I thought you were going to Suffern."

"I was thinking about it, but something else came up, which I wanted to talk to you about."

He tucked in his chin. "Is this about the murders or are you looking for more career advice?"

"Both."

"Well make it quick. I've got to finish today's update on the Vitek case—and now this computer thing…."

"I'll be as quick as I can. First, I'm hoping you can explain to me why I shouldn't tell the police what a pack of lies you've been selling. Didn't know Maury Marconi, my ass!"

He didn't show much reaction—but there was a hint of something in his eyes, maybe fear, maybe disbelief.

Natalie pushed away from the doorjamb. "And second, maybe you can tell me why I shouldn't be sitting in Byron's office right now telling him you hacked into my files."

He recovered himself quickly. "These are two serious accusations. Unfortunately, both will be hard to prove."

"Not as hard as you think. How's your computer doing?" She moved behind his desk. The screen was still upside down. "Nope. Not hard to prove at all." She sat in the wooden swivel chair.

He looked at her thoughtfully, but said nothing.

"Did I mention that I went to see Dottie Marconi last Sunday? She had lots of interesting things to say about Maury…and you. Or should I say, about you…and Maury."

Still he said nothing.

"Come on, Ty, it's not that hard a decision. If you've been murdering people lately, lie. If you haven't, tell me the truth."

He nodded, as if she had scored a point in a philosophical debate. "How is Dottie?" He wiped his nose.

"She's fine. She grows vegetables and keeps bees and goats."

"I've thought of her a lot lately—while all this business has been going on. Wondering if she knew I slept with her husband. Well. Now I know." He frowned at the wall of the cubicle.

"She doesn't know."

His brow wrinkled. "Then how did you find out?"

Natalie shrugged. "I didn't know, for certain, until you just told me. I began to suspect when I heard from Angie that Maury had seen the guy he had slept with a few times over the years. That matched up with what you had told me. But I didn't really feel confident until my talk with Dottie. But don't bother kicking yourself, because the cops are going to work it out in about two minutes. Dottie told me how you dropped her right after the campaign debacle, which was in October—but then she said she hadn't seen you since the Fourth of July. You were with Maury when she was in Connecticut in late July, 1972, weren't you. That's why you dropped her. Guilt. She wrote it off to you being a social climber who didn't give a damn about her, but that explanation didn't work for me. Of course, she didn't have the benefit of hearing you lying through your teeth about knowing Maury. Why did you do that?"

"You were pumping me about something that was none of your business."

"So I was."

"I never thought the subject would come up again." He folded his handkerchief slowly. "When it did, I was stuck with what I'd told you."

Natalie nodded. "Lucky for me. So. Are you going to talk?"

He scowled at the computer screen. "Why should I talk to you? You'll just tell the police—"

"I won't tell them…if you open up all the way. If you convince me that you didn't kill anybody and that you're not protecting whoever did. I won't tell Byron about the computer hack either. Of course, I can't prevent the cops or Byron from figuring it out themselves. But at least if you talk to me you have a chance."

"Okay. But not here." He stood, switched off the computer with vim, and reached for his jacket.

♥   ♥   ♥

Charlie's was bustling with the noontime trade of shoppers and business people. They slid into the booth by the door and ordered coffee.

"Where do you want me to start?" asked Tyler.

"Maury told Angie he talked to you once. Is that right?"

245

Tyler pulled a strip of cold tablets from his jacket pocket. "We ran into each other at an AA meeting last November. I went over to him. I don't know why—after all that time. It must have been the non-judgmental atmosphere. I knew he'd been down and out for years, and I just wanted to say a friendly word."

"How come you never did before?"

"For one thing, he avoided me—for the wrong reason, I now realize. I assumed he despised the *Star* and everyone who worked for it—including me. I couldn't blame him. For another, I was never the type who wanted to make nice and be buddies with ex-lovers—especially one who regretted getting involved. I had no idea he had carried it around for twenty years that it was *me* who gave Kovaks the story." Tyler scowled at the table.

"You never thought to tell him?"

"Tell him what? I didn't know Vitek's name—they kept that under wraps—but I had heard that Kovaks met the guy, and was convinced he was telling the truth. I had no reason to doubt the story. Hell, I had every reason to believe it! In fact, I had the gall to be put out about it. Maury had told me, when he ended it, that what happened between us was in the heat of the moment—said he'd always wondered if he'd like it—and that it was okay, but it wasn't for him. I respected that, I thought he meant it. So when I heard he'd been involved with another guy practically at the same time, I thought, well, screw you. I felt betrayed."

He shrugged. "I was young. I decided to develop amnesia. I figured I'd had a narrow escape from seeing my picture plastered all over the front page of the paper. It didn't occur to me for a moment that Maury thought it was me!"

The waitress filled their cups and left. "At the next month's meeting—December—I spoke to him again. Just a greeting. Christmas spirit. After the meeting broke up, he stopped me in the parking lot and asked me why I'd done it, why I'd ratted on him. And—I told him it wasn't me…. God."

Natalie could see the memory of that scene in his eyes, and her throat tightened. "What did he say?"

"Not much. It was the way he looked. When he realized it wasn't me. He always had the most expressive face, and he still did, even after all he'd been through. I remember the way I felt, when I realized…. I felt that way again, when you told me last week you thought he'd been set up, that it was all a hoax. My God, some hoax—to ruin a man's life…. I didn't want to believe it."

"What happened next?"

"Nothing. We were both stunned. He said he'd call me. He hugged me. A week later he was dead. He was a great guy." He looked up at Natalie. "I read about his death. I thought he'd started drinking again, and taken a drunkard's fall. Until you butted in. I'm glad it wasn't that, but...." He shook his head.

"A week passed between the AA meeting and his death?"

"Yeah."

"Did he give you any hint what he might do?"

"No. He was pretty dazed. I was, too."

"What would your guess be?"

"I've thought about it.... It seems most likely he would want to talk to Peter—I don't know if he realized Peter didn't make the whole thing up." He pulled out his handkerchief again and sneezed. "I should have told him Peter didn't know."

Natalie eyed him coolly. "What about you? Did you tell anyone you'd met Maury, and what you'd talked about?"

"No." He pulled a strip of cold tablets from his jacket pocket. "My God, woman! You think that's a story I'd want anyone to know?"

"I think you might have spoken up when it came out that Maury was murdered!"

"What for? To clear his name? Of what? I'm open to suggestions on what I might have said. All I could come up with was, 'My best friend's husband's career was ruined because somebody falsely accused him of cheating on his wife. Oh, except, the only way I can prove that it wasn't true is to point out that he actually did cheat on his wife, only with me.' It doesn't work, Joday. It would actually make it worse—because then Dottie would have known." He popped two pills into his mouth and drank a little water.

"Did you ever think that the truth might be preferable to what she's been thinking all these years? I don't know her very well, but she struck me as pretty blasé on the subject of romance. She might like to know there was a reason you walked out on her. Aside from her thinking that you sucked up to her for her money for fifteen years and then dumped her when she most needed her friends."

"She has no reason to feel that way!"

"But she does." Natalie stirred impatiently. "Look, if you're so concerned for Dottie, and for Maury's memory, why have you kept silent? Didn't you want to know who set Maury up? Didn't you want them exposed?"

"Truthfully? I've asked myself a thousand times what I would have done if I'd found out in 1972. Would I have come forward? I don't know. I was a scared kid—afraid if I said a word out of line I'd lose everything I had. But last month, when I knew he'd been murdered? No. It was too late—I didn't want anyone to know—not about the affair, but that I'd stood aside and watched him go down and then denied I even knew him. I never believed his murder had anything to do with what happened between him and me. And today? Now that it's out? It's been torture! It's poetic justice, isn't it? Now I know how Maury felt. If this gets out it'll ruin me."

Natalie frowned. "This isn't 1972, and you're not running for office. People have wised up about sex."

He eyed her skeptically. "Not all of them, my dear. Not all of them. But that's not what I meant. Lying to the police about a murder investigation; hacking into your computer to find out what was going on? That will be the end of my professional reputation."

"Damn straight!" Natalie planted her hands on the table. "What the hell did you think you were doing, anyway?"

"Primarily? Trying to keep from getting killed." He leaned forward. "Don't you get it? My God, woman! I'm living every day with the idea that I might be next! Can you blame me for trying to find out as much as I could? That whole business you and Byron laid out about secret sources scared me to death. I didn't know what was going on—I didn't know how you'd connected Maury's death with the old scandal. Not that I learned much when I did manage to hack in—I found out about the letters from Enigma, and I read the riddles, but I couldn't be sure what was going on."

"If you'd talked, Armand Vitek might be alive."

"Naturally, I've thought about that," he said sarcastically. "But I think you were right—Vitek was killed because he knew something that would expose the murderer. But perhaps I'm just saying that to comfort myself."

"To relieve yourself of responsibility for his death?"

"No. To help me sleep at night when I start to think that it might have been me out there at the Tappan Zee Bridge." He shivered, and closed his eyes.

Natalie glanced up at the clock. It was almost one. "Look. Answer me this—who at the *Star* knew? About you and Maury."

He opened his eyes and shook his head. "No one."

"How many outside people?"

He stirred in his seat. "Enough. I don't know…at the time, I probably boasted to my friends, without naming names. I don't have many of those

248

friends now."

"And you didn't tell anyone after Vitek's murder?"

"You think I'd want to broadcast it that I knew Maury hadn't slept with Vitek? Maybe you haven't noticed, but everyone who knew that is dead!"

"You think the killer found out that Maury knew he had been framed, and killed him?"

"Don't you?"

"Then either Maury must have told the killer, or someone Maury told, told the killer. You have no ideas?"

"No. I thought about Peter, but he has the perfect alibi. I was relieved to hear that! But between wondering if I was going to be murdered, and trying to avoid having my personal life spewed out across the tabloids, I haven't had much time for speculation."

Natalie shook her head. It sounded good—but could she believe him? Should she? "What were you doing at an AA meeting?"

He eyed her with ill-concealed disapproval. "My mother was a heavy drinker. She went on the wagon about a year ago. I'm trying to support her as much as I can. She's having a hard time. My younger brother died of alcoholism last year."

"I'm sorry. I didn't know…."

"We aren't friends, my dear, we're colleagues. I don't talk about my personal life—and that includes family, religion, politics, finances, and sex— with colleagues. It doesn't pay. I only tell you now because you insisted I 'open up' as you so colloquially put it. So? Have I fulfilled your requirements?"

Natalie touched her lips with her napkin.

"It's a simple decision," he said mockingly. "If you believe me, you won't talk. If you don't, you'll call the police—five minutes after you've filed your copy. I'll tell them what I've told you. So what are you going to do?"

"I don't know. I need to think about it."

"I know. It's tough to decide to ruin somebody's life." He signaled to the waitress to bring their check. "Back in Maury's day, the *Star* editors took three days."

Chapter Twenty-nine

Y ou left him sitting in the park? He told you he'd throw everything he's ever had or wanted out the window if he could have you? And, you...took off?"

"Yeah." Natalie drained the last drops out of her wineglass.

"Wow. What does a guy have to do to impress?"

"I don't want to be 'impressed.' Words are cheap."

Rebecca put her hands on her head. "He strikes you as flighty? Someone who just says what he thinks you want to hear?"

"Maybe I put that badly." Natalie reached for the bottle. "I truly don't want the sort of involvement he is obviously looking for. I like things more easy going, more fun.... If he needs to think long term that's fine, but that's not me. Y'know?"

"He won't play unless he's guaranteed a victory, and you won't play unless it's just for fun and nobody keeps score. What a pair!" Rebecca sat back in her chair. "But...could we backtrack a minute? He told you he was confused, right? Well I believe him; it's not easy to watch your dreams crumble. He seems to be having a rough time—on several fronts, from what you say, although I'm not sure you realize it. Can't you take what he said about wanting long-term commitment not as a pass-fail entrance exam, but an expression of how he felt about you when he said it?"

Natalie was silent.

Rebecca eyed her cautiously. "I think you're missing something. This man does not seem to me to be any more in control of the situation than you are—nor is he pretending to be. He has a lot going on, he needs to talk—and you haven't given him a chance."

"Why should I?" said Natalie defiantly. "He doesn't listen to me! He doesn't understand me! If he did, he'd say the right thing, and I'd throw myself at him and wouldn't care who knew what a fool I was making of myself. But he doesn't, he says something that rattles me to the core, and then I get angry and wonder what I did wrong and feel horrible." She wilted suddenly. "I don't need it."

"You get scared, not angry," said Rebecca gently. "You've got to learn to tell the difference. Try this—when you get angry, you stay and fight. When you get scared, you run or push him away. He, having no idea what it is you want to hear, reacts by pulling back, and you blame him for being untrustworthy, which is…absurd. Just as it is absurd for him to blame you for not being honest when he doesn't like or understand what you're saying."

"That's exactly what I told him! There are no absolutes. What he wants is impossible! When I point that out, he gets angry!"

"Are you sure it's anger? Strong emotions are hard to differentiate, especially if you're busy reacting to them. What if it's something else: fear, pain, or confusion. Tch. This is a textbook case of failed communication. You both need to shut up for a while."

"I gave him the chance to shut up. He didn't take it."

"By inviting him home?"

"Yeah."

"I'm not sure that's the same thing…. Natalie? Did that bother you? Really get to you, I mean?"

"Not really. Okay, yeah. Hey! I was never turned down before…. Funny…maybe that's why I've sort of been waiting for him to make a move…. Not wanting to reach out…. I didn't want to feel like that again…."

♥　　　♥　　　♥

A little before eight on Wednesday morning, Natalie locked the Volvo and strode up the walkway to the Kovaks residence. For three days her phone calls had been unanswered, and her written requests for a brief interview, faxed all over the county, ignored. Despite the unfashionable hour, she smacked the brass knocker with gusto. She glanced at the closed garage door and wondered if she ought to take a peek through its darkened windows.

The previous afternoon's *Star* was stuck in the newspaper holder beneath the mailbox. She dropped her head onto her shoulder and read: "Arrest made in Upper Saddle River Break-in." There was just no stopping some people.

The door opened and Linda Kovaks, in full campaign gear, including flag brooch and Uncle Sam earrings, appeared. "Natalie. We owe you an apology, don't we. I've told Myra…but she's not listening." Her tired face showed no regret. "There aren't enough hours in the day." She made no move to let Natalie inside.

251

"I understand." Natalie shifted her briefcase from one hand to the other. "I know it's early, but I thought I might catch Mr. Kovaks, just for a few minutes...."

Linda was shaking her head. "The driver picked him up at seven. He's having a power breakfast with some of the campaign staff." Her fingers gripped the door handle. "You have to understand. The election is only six days away, and we've got events scheduled morning, noon, and night."

"Then maybe I can talk to him on the phone...."

"I honestly doubt it. With all the negative press we're getting, there are ten things to do every minute...and talking about a murder investigation isn't one of them. Can't it wait until after Tuesday?"

"I don't know," said Natalie. "I hope so."

♥　　　♥　　　♥

Back at the office, Natalie found a note in her mailbox and headed to the front office. Marcia waved her through.

Byron held out an envelope. "This just came."

She sat down in the red chair and unfolded the letter.

Dear Louise—

Changed your mind? Hey! Guess what? So did I. I took your great advice and let my sick urges for revenge fade. Somehow, my petty desires don't seem as important as they did before. All the nightmares have gone away, and I sleep like a baby. All because of you. But...I guess I owe you. Because you've taught me the difference between petty vengeance and real problems. So I'll give you what you want. Here's the key to everything I know—

What is greater than God? More evil than the Devil?
Poor people have it, rich people want it,
But if you drink it, you'll die.

Enigma

"Do you get it?" asked Byron.

Natalie looked up at him. His eyes, which had a perpetual squint despite his glasses, seemed wholly innocent. "Yes. Do you?"

He nodded. "What do you think it means?"

"Exactly what it says. My first impression was right—Enigma had no idea Maury was murdered. The letters really were about the old scandal."

"This doesn't help us at all." He looked distressed. "I'd better call the police and let them know about this. Not that they're getting anywhere. We really don't need this right now...."

Natalie crossed her legs. "Rumor has it that there are going to be some big changes around here."

Though they had never discussed it, he did not question her assumed knowledge. "Nobody ought to be making major decisions with the paper under this cloud of suspicion. It's hard enough keeping up day to day. Well. Never mind. What's your next move?"

"Asking you when I'm going to get to talk to Peter Kovaks. I've just gotten the brush-off from Linda."

"I haven't been able to get anywhere with him. Even Myra has tried. I can't say I blame him. They've doubled their activities for the campaign, trying to keep him in the public eye. In fact...." He searched for something in the clutter on his desk and came up with a manila envelope.

"They're doing a Meet the Candidates on Thursday night. I want you to cover it. Here's your press kit." He handed her the envelope.

"Me?" Natalie put her hands on the arms of the chair. "Now?"

"Why not? You're supposed to be doing occasional political work, aren't you? That's what we told the police."

"Yeah, but.... You know I've been kind of busy...."

"Well now's your chance to get back on it."

"But...I hate politics!"

He ignored her. "There'll be musical entertainment.... Myra and Lance will be there, and so will I. And, of course, Linda and Peter. Oh. And there's a brief Q and A before the reception."

"Oh, unh hunh?" Natalie met his eyes. They looked so innocent, so non-threatening. It was a good cover. She rose slowly.

"Yes...." He rooted in his desk again. "While you're here, take the rest of Louise's mail—just a couple of letters, but I'm encouraged. Sweet lady. Glad to see her column picking up—she's been getting the hang of it...since about the time she came to you with the Enigma letters."

"What a coincidence."

"Yes, indeed. Coincidence."

♥   ♥   ♥

Natalie and Rebecca were in Daniel's flat, taking the opportunity of Daniel and Gayanne's absence (shopping for Mexican spices and other treats for Rebecca's birthday supper) to discuss the case. Notebooks and folders were spread across the dining room table, along with coffee cups and saucers that had once dressed the set of *Bus Stop*. It was five forty-five on Wednesday afternoon.

Rebecca put her elbows on the table. "I think it's Tyler. Why else would he have kept so much from the police...and from you and Byron?"

Natalie drew a triangle on a page of her notebook. "If Tyler is innocent, he had good reasons not to talk. Anyway, why single him out? Myra didn't tell me what she knew. Nor did Lance."

"But they didn't hack into your computer."

"They didn't need to. They already knew about the letters."

"Right." Rebecca sighed. "Every time someone is singled out by odd behavior, sound psychological reasons arise to show it wasn't so odd after all. You start out thinking anyone could have done it, but end up no closer to finding out who did."

"Irritating, isn't it." She drew another triangle within the first.

Rebecca slapped her hands on the table. "We need evidence!"

Natalie laughed. "That would be nice. But according to our police sources, there was nothing helpful at the Tappan Zee overlook, nothing on Armand's computers—that they could access—and nothing in his shop. None of his friends knew where he went—in fact, they all said they knew better than to ask him where he was going, because he was so secretive. And Maury died long enough ago to make the investigation of his death even harder."

Rebecca rested her chin in her palm. "Enigma must know something—after all, she started this. Why don't you just ask her?"

Natalie handed her a piece of paper. "I forgot to show you this."

"'What is greater than God, more evil than the devil....'" Rebecca fell silent, but her lips formed the words. When she was done, she looked up. "And the answer is?"

"'Nothing,'" said Natalie. "She's telling us she knew nothing about the murder. I think her intention was to use the old scandal to show that Peter Kovaks wasn't a fit candidate. I think she was as surprised to discover that Maury had been murdered as we were."

"Have you told anyone you've discovered who Enigma is?"

Natalie shook her head. "Until the killer is identified, I'm damned if I'm going to risk putting another life in danger."

"If she doesn't know anything, she's no threat to the killer."

"No, but does the killer know that? I doubt it. Louise was no threat, either, and look what almost happened. I think the killer is panicking, trying to wipe out anyone who might know anything about what really happened with Maury back in 1972."

"If that's true, then why hasn't the killer gone after Tyler?"

Natalie shrugged. "Maybe he doesn't know about Tyler."

"Or maybe 'he' is Tyler."

"We're going in circles." Natalie turned to a fresh page in her notebook. "Let's get organized. The case against Tyler. Presumably his motive for killing Maury was that he didn't want the story of their old affair coming out. Not much of a motive, if you ask me."

"I agree." Rebecca shifted her chin to the other hand. "Plus, Tyler had no motive for killing Armand—unless of course he was the one who sent Armand to Peter in the first place."

"Yes! He might have wanted to hurt Maury for dumping him, and.... Wait a minute." Natalie shook her head. "This doesn't work. Tyler helped Maury learn he had been set up last year."

"You are shaking my conviction." Rebecca laced her fingers together. "You don't suppose Tyler secretly pined for Maury all those years, and finally arranged to meet him accidentally on purpose, after which Maury rejected him and Tyler killed him out of spite?"

"Ginny informs me that Tyler has been living for nine years with a studio photographer named Rory, who is, by the way, a paraplegic. Tyler is apparently devoted to this guy, and blesses the day he met him because he changed his life by his example of independence and personal fulfillment."

Rebecca threw up her hands. "Okay, I give in. It wasn't Tyler. Unless everything he told you was a clever lie—and since your brother tells me it is impossible to lie to you and get away with it for very long, I'm going to end it there."

Natalie made a note. "Next we have Myra. It is a fact that she and Peter were very close for many years. Whatever the basis of that relationship—and no, I'm not going to argue this time that it had to be sexual for it to be intense—the question is, did Myra love Peter enough to kill someone to protect him?"

"Excuse me, but in my profession, we don't call emotions that move people to murder, 'love.'"

"No? I suppose I'm showing my inexperience again...."

"No, this is a common confusion, brought about by the massive numbers of people who cover their fear of abandonment, exposure, and poverty, in combination with a lack of self-esteem and certain life skills, with a bandage they call love."

"Yeah, but a lot of people—"

Rebecca held up a hand. "Let's stick with these people. If Myra killed Maury and Armand to protect Peter, she may say she did it for love, and your newspaper may print a headline that says she did it for love, but in fact, it would have been out of her fear of a life without Peter, or her fear of sharing his humiliation by association, and thus losing the power she has worked very hard for."

"That's good; that makes sense."

"So if we want to find the killer's true motivation, we'll have to dig deeper than 'love.' What about this Evil Deed Peter, Myra and Lance supposedly did? Maybe Myra was trying to cover that up."

"We have Dottie's story that something big did happen. I was working on that when I stumbled on that list of stockholder's in Myra's office. But I haven't been able to find any connection between any Evil Deed and Maury and Armand."

"They must have somehow known about it."

"That is too vague for me."

Rebecca grinned sheepishly. "For me, too."

"Then what about Lance?" Natalie turned a page. "Could this have something to do with whatever is happening at the *Star*? Maybe he needed to get the stockholders' approval for the merger, or take-over, or whatever is going on. Or maybe he needed them on his side to vote against it. He has Dottie's proxy vote. Is it possible that Maury, maybe without even knowing it, had received some *Star* stock in the divorce settlement? What if Lance killed Maury because he knew the stock would revert to Dottie, and then he'd have a significant block of voting power."

"That makes a lot of sense. Except…why kill Armand?"

Natalie twisted her lips. "I'll work on that."

"You know," said Rebecca reflectively, "Dottie had reasons for wanting Maury dead. It's not a good feeling to find out your husband has had an affair with a man. Maybe the first person Maury called when he found out Tyler hadn't betrayed him was Dottie. Or…get this…maybe while he was telling her he'd been set up, he let it slip that it had been Tyler, and she went bonkers."

"I love it when you use shrink jargon. But it won't fly—you haven't met Dottie. And why would she kill Armand?"

"Because he was involved in the set-up."

"But how would Dottie know who Armand was? Or find him? It doesn't fit in with our assumption that Armand went to the killer because the killer was the person who had instigated the set-up."

"Okay, I'll give it up." Rebecca scratched her forehead. "Can we at least agree that the killer used Peter to set up Maury?"

"Yes." Natalie frowned. "Although why he did it escapes me."

"What if Dottie knew about Tyler, and set Maury up to teach him a lesson...."

"Yes! Either with or without the knowledge of her old pal, Peter!" But then Natalie frowned again. "Of course, the exact opposite is also possible—that the goal was to hurt Dottie...."

"Why? Peter and Myra drifted away from her, but they didn't have any reason to hate her."

"I'm not so sure." Natalie regarded her hands. "It may not be my job to demand answers to personal questions, but I can't help having an opinion, and my opinion is that Dottie did have an affair with Peter. She said she broke off with Peter and Myra when she found out that Peter had gone carousing instead of staying at his father's deathbed. Well, I think she was the one he was with. I checked the dates. Peter's father died three months before she married Maury. Peter and Linda got married four months after that. Peter might have felt like she dumped him for a shoe salesman...."

"You keep forgetting Peter's airtight alibi."

"But what if Peter and Myra were in it together? Although I can't imagine why they would be...." Natalie sighed. "This reminds me of being fourteen and wondering why everyone was laughing at a joke I didn't get. Riddles and clues and alibis I can do, but picking apart peoples motives I'm not very good at. All these people have complex relationships, but I don't really, truly understand any of them. As you pointed out, I don't know much about being in love."

Rebecca smiled. "I didn't say that. What is it you don't think you understand?"

Natalie rubbed the corner of her eye. "Take Angie and Maury. I thought Angie didn't care much for Maury, because all she talked about were his flaws—she said he deserved what he got. I thought that was the sort of thing you didn't say about someone you loved."

"She was being honest. That doesn't mean she didn't love him. In fact, it's a sign of a strong and healthy love."

"I guess. It really touches me that she tries so hard to take care of the yard—not because she has any interest in it, but because he had cared about it."

"Sounds like they truly respected each other. Each had been through a lot in their early years, and had learned their lessons, and knew how to be happy. You've summed it up admirably, I'd say."

"I can understand that academically, but I don't identify with them; I don't feel it." Natalie pushed her chair back from the table. "I can't imagine talking about someone I loved that way. I would try to protect them from that sort of talk! I'd—" She glanced at Rebecca sheepishly. "Then take Peter and Linda. She told me they have the perfect relationship—he is the front man and she the behind-the-scenes worker. They complement one another's talents, together making a whole. His success is her success; he worships her, and she exalts in possessing his sole affection. It sounds good—but it leaves me cold. I like to see the people I love doing well, but I don't want to get all my kicks from someone else's success. I want my own. Am I too selfish to love someone properly?"

"No! You mustn't confuse selfishness with independence."

"Which brings up you and Daniel. Independence? For you two that is a duty, not a desire." Natalie's eyes were wide with astonishment. "You both want to be together, but you decide it's best to be apart. He needs time alone with Gayanne, to find his parenting legs. You give him time. You need time alone with him. He goes away for the weekend with you. What you have looks so beautiful, but it isn't me. It's like a romance in slow motion—a careful dance in which you circle around one another for the sheer love of watching each other move—as if there's all the time in the world."

"Not that much time."

Natalie heard the catch in Rebecca's voice and looked up to see her almond eyes had misted over. "What do you mean?"

"It's my thirty-sixth birthday today. I want a child."

Natalie's throat tightened. "Does Daniel know that?"

Rebecca wiped her eyes. "Of course."

Foolish to have asked…. "Of course."

Rebecca brought her feet onto the chair and hugged her knees. "I wouldn't worry about not understanding love if I were you. You may never have been 'in love,' but you know 'about love.'"

Natalie shook her head. "Maybe enough to write a feature on the subject. But not enough to understand myself. You've taught me that. There are so many different perspectives! There's Dottie: put all your love into the earth and nature, because it will always be there to sustain you, whereas people will always let you down. Then there's Tyler: devotion to someone who has so much less than you it makes you realize how much you have;

behavior so unselfish it makes me blush. And Myra: choosing non-sexual but very intense relationships with powerful or intelligent men. And finally there's Armand. He told me love was a lie invented by nasty-minded men to enslave women. I thought it was ridiculous of him to say that—but if I'm to be honest, I've got to tell you that of all the varieties of love I've seen lately, his is the closest to what I believe deep inside…. And that scares me."

"I don't think you believe that." Rebecca rested her chin on her knees. "I think that you're describing what you saw with your parents—your father, who manipulated people, and your mother, who allowed him to get away with it without fighting back and then died and left you at his mercy. I think you say that because you want very much to be assured it isn't true. I think you're afraid to be in love because you're afraid it will turn out to be true."

"Oh yeah?"

"Yeah."

Natalie stared across the room. "Sometimes I think…I don't need anything long term. I have my family. But then I think—is that fair to Daniel? To Gayanne? Am I leeching off other people's happiness instead of seeking my own?"

"No." Rebecca laced her hands around her shins. "You're just looking for it in the wrong place. It's not only knowledge that has levels like a pyramid, you know. You're ready to move up, but you can't do it if you cling too long to the way life used to be."

Natalie's eyes shifted to Rebecca's face. "Am I doing that?"

"We all do it, sometimes."

Natalie raised an eyebrow. "How do I stop?"

"You change and grow and let go with the rest of us."

"It might not be that easy. There's a lot I don't know about what 'the rest of you' do. I had the wrong kind of education. As you pointed out, I don't know what it's supposed to look like."

"You'll be fine." Rebecca uncoiled herself and stretched. "I've got your number, now—you need to understand things intellectually. If you do, you can deal with them. If you don't, you become irritable and combative. Take, for example, your Sergeant."

Natalie got up and went to the credenza. "I saw that coming."

"I should hope so—you brought up the subject."

She refilled her coffee cup. "I was talking about the murders…."

"From a personal point of view."

Natalie returned to the table. "You're not stopping there are you?" She sat. "You were saying, 'take the Sergeant.'"

"I said *your* Sergeant. Listen to you. Even a possessive pronoun is too close!"

"Just get on with it...."

"You're both doing way too much thinking—but it's what you're both good at, so there's no point in trying to change that. But you're pulling in opposite directions: your Sergeant won't let a short-term passion get in the way of the long-term commitment he wants, and you won't let long-term commitment get in the way of the short-term passion you want. This is non-productive."

Natalie pursed her lips and sniffed. "So...how do I change that, assuming I want to change that—therapy?"

Rebecca flipped her ponytail. "I doubt if that would help."

Natalie widened her eyes. "Hypnosis?"

Rebecca shook her head.

"What, then!"

"Try the low-tech approach: snap out of it!" Rebecca flipped her ponytail back where it belonged. "Use your brains. Have a conversation that isn't framed by a murder investigation!"

"We tried that...."

Rebecca leaned forward. "Try it again. Try getting to know each other before you conclude that you are both irrational, unfeeling, egotistical users. Let whatever happens, happen—and for Pete's sake find a way to respect each other's professions. Explore whatever it is that draws you together—whether in the context of the friendship he thinks he doesn't want, or the commitment you think you don't want, or somewhere in between. You're both investigators...do your stuff!"

"I'm not sure he wants to, after our last encounter but one."

"Hogwash. I saw all the unsaid thoughts crowding in his eyes—things he needs to say to *you*. He needs a chance to work through whatever he's been going through. And you need to work through your issues, to find someone you can trust."

Natalie stared at the opposite wall. "Why should I bother? The situation has stabilized. Why would I want to rock the boat?"

"That's only half of the story. The rest is that, like it or not, you think this man is important to you, even though you don't know exactly why. Part of you is scared off, but part of you is drawn to him. That's life. Sometimes you want two things at once, that seem to conflict. You have to choose."

"I know. But...I've never made a decision this important before. How do I know what's right?"

Rebecca spoke slowly. "Trust *yourself.*"

The door opened, and Daniel and Gayanne entered, laden with bags and boxes, which they proceeded to smuggle into Daniel's bedroom with great mirth. After everything was put away, Rebecca, by previous arrangement, set about showing Gayanne how to make tacos. Daniel and Natalie were sent to the dining-room table to shred lettuce and dice tomatoes.

Daniel pulled a piece of pink paper from his shirt pocket. "Before I forget," he said, and handed it to her.

Natalie unfolded the slip of paper and read it. Drawn on the bank account of Daniel Joday, dated October 27, 1993, made out to Natalie Joday, payment number two, $25.00. She smiled as she re-folded the check and put it in her own pocket. What need had she to fear what the future would bring? Had she not lived through the darkest days and emerged triumphant?

Daniel sighed, relaxing his broad shoulders. "I never could have imagined it would be so good just to sit here with you and chop vegetables."

Natalie glanced up. He was happy, happier than she had ever known him. But the worry lines etched into his forehead would never go away. "There's something I wanted to discuss with you...."

"What?" He placed a tomato on the cutting board.

"Things are bad at the *Star.* I might be looking for a job, soon. I've been thinking about what I'll go in for. It's time I specialized."

"Agreed." He chiseled the stem out of the tomato.

"I have to look seriously at crime reporting. I'm good at it, but a part of me wonders why I surround myself with cops and lawyers. Am I drawn to the things I hate by some morbid and self-destructive need? You'd think I would rather write about county fairs than this stuff."

"I don't think you have a morbid fascination with crime, if that's what you're asking. You didn't seek it out—it just happened."

"But I can't help but wonder what this means to you and—"

"Don't...!" He raised his left hand for a moment, but kept his eyes on his cutting board. "Don't even think about telling me that you'd make a career decision based on how it might affect me." He lowered his hand and raised his eyes. "You've given up enough, for me. But...if you need me to tell you that I will support whatever you choose to do—including hanging around crime scenes and courtrooms—and that you have my respect and love whatever you do, I will say it."

"But.... It hurts you. I see you wince."

261

"Yes, I wince. I can't help it. But it doesn't make any difference. You mustn't try to save me a moment's pain at the price of a botched future."

"I put Gayanne in danger…."

"Gayanne, for the first time since the day she came, and God knows how long before that, is filled with a sense of self-worth because she helped save Louise. Would you change that?"

"No."

"Then make your choice with a free conscience, and choose for yourself alone. You've been telling me for months now to relax and think about myself. Well, I think it's time you relaxed and thought about yourself, too."

♥　　　♥　　　♥

It was almost ten when Natalie arrived home. She showered, checked her e-mail and was in bed giving a repentant Trick the cuddles he required when she remembered she was supposed to be writing Louise's column. Since she would be occupied Thursday night, this was her only chance to get it done in private. Stifling a sense of martyrdom, she retrieved the letters Byron had given her and brought them to the bedroom. The first two were scatterbrained nonsense written by young women with the old familiar problems. It was the third that made her sit up and push a purring Trick aside:

Dear Louise,

Some time ago I met a woman I was powerfully attracted to. I am not someone who makes quick decisions, but I knew I would risk everything if it meant I could be with her. I was shocked when I discovered she was repulsed by my desire for commitment. I thought women wanted stability and depth of feeling. I felt insulted—what was the friendship she offered next to the abiding love I wanted to give?

For a while I was glad I had not made a rash mistake with someone I barely knew. But as time passed, I began to wonder if I had not made a more profound error. Many things in my life that I thought were permanent are changing. I have begun to doubt myself, and my values.

Recently, I saw her again. Circumstances have made it impossible to talk, but it is clear the cordial distance that is the only choice available to us is wrong. The strategies that worked for me in the past do not work anymore; each time we meet I begin by thinking

I know where I stand, and each time I end up realizing I am still lost. I feel her absence in my life like a bruise that will not heal. Worse, I see in her eyes that I have hurt her, though I do not know why or how.

Perhaps you can help me. I wrote a letter some weeks ago, but my self-doubt has been too great to allow me to send it:

"Lately, I've become aware that my steps slow and my gaze wanders whenever I think you might be near. Finding myself unable to refrain from applying my professional skills to my private life, I have deduced that I've been hoping we might meet. Not much liking the idea of remaining a bystander to my desires (however ill-defined), I've decided to write you this letter.

"I think of you often. On the surface, my life has not changed; but scratch the surface, and nothing is the same. The world I thought I knew is disappearing. I have tried to stand firm, but the change occurs beneath my feet, and I am helpless to stop it. Some invisible hand has removed a veil from my eyes. Each day I grow aware of meaning on a scale previously unnoticed—or thought insignificant—colorations of feeling and attitude that delineate distinctions I never saw before. I do not fully understand what is happening, but I date the start of the process from the day I met you.

From such permutations, one theme has emerged. I want to see you again—with consideration and without conditions—if you are willing. For it seems to me now, in the face of my own disbelief, that at the very least, we might be friends."

Should I send it?

Blue in Bergen County

Chapter Thirty

The high school auditorium was stuffed to its avocado-green rafters with political insiders, community worthies, and such assorted nondescripts as enjoyed a modestly entertaining night out at someone else's expense. A four-piece band—piano, banjo, trombone, and bass—played on the stage. Red, white, and blue bunting hung from the aforementioned rafters and around the proscenium. Tables, placed end-to-end and set with spanking white tablecloths, lined either long wall. In the center of each, champagne glasses clustered around ice sculptures of the State Capital Building.

Natalie, her press badge pinned to the shoulder of her black suit with the silver pinstripes, was absurdly pleased to discover that the glasses were plastic. Taking her champagne with her, she moved to one side and scanned the crowd.

Linda Kovaks was there…was everywhere…handing out red, white, and blue cocktail napkins and looking stunning in her tangerine silhouette. The TV crew from Channel 24 was crawling over the stage, setting up their sound equipment. She spotted Tyler talking to a party functionary and wiping at his nose. He looked terrible. There was no sign yet of either the candidates or the *Star* bigwigs. Natalie swirled the champagne and raised it to her lips.

A voice said in her ear. "I tell ya what. You drink it first, and if you're still on your feet after five minutes, I'll risk a sip."

Natalie jumped and whirled around. "Angie!" She looked around the room again. "What are you doing here?"

"It's a free country. The candidate wants to represent my district. I thought I'd better see what he's made of." She smoothed her silver dress over her hips.

"You're not registered to vote."

"Aw, you got me. Jeez you got a good memory. Don't worry, honey. I'm not gonna do anything silly. Not this time, anyway…."

"It's not that." Natalie looked around again. Myra and Lance had entered, Myra looking like a parrot in her green dress and red hair, Lance looking like a haystack in his yellow suit. "I'm just not sure it's a good idea if you're seen right now...."

"Why not? None a these jokers knows me from a hole in the wall." She touched her hair, checking to see that the blond curl over her ear was in place. "I'm just another constituent, yah?"

"Hardly. They may not know it, but...." Natalie averted her eyes as Tyler hurried past. "I'd say you were a real...enigma...."

Angie batted her lashes. She was heavily made-up, not with the modern cunning that rendered the act invisible, but with lavish swirls of violet and pink around the eyes and across the cheekbones. Her eyebrows twitched. "Most people think I'm pretty obvious."

"Their mistake." Natalie moved away from the busy drinks table and Angela followed her to the relative privacy of the bleachers.

"This dress is gettin' too tight even for me." Angela ran her hands over her hips again. "So when did you work it out?"

"Monday."

"How come you didn't blow the whistle on me?"

"No reason to. And plenty of reasons not to: until we find the killer, this is one piece of information that should not get out."

"Aw, you just wanna have all the fun." She dabbed at her lips with the side of her finger. "It sure took you long enough—although at first I thought you'd seen right through my ANGIE M anagram. Could a knocked me over with a feather when you showed up in my yard. I'd about given up hope anybody was readin' my letters."

"They were a little obscure, Angie...."

"Says who? How long did it take you to make the connection with Maury once you got started?"

"A couple of days, I guess."

"Exactly. Those letters were a work of art—goof ball enough to act like a magnet on anybody with an inquisitiveness nature, and easy as pie to figure out once you got started."

"Not that easy. I'm not sure I ever would have gotten the Oz connection if somebody else hadn't mentioned it in passing."

"Oh yah?" Angela pouted. "I thought that was plain as the nose on my face. I couldn't figure out why nothin' happened...."

"Unfortunately, Louise is not the inquisitive type."

"You're kiddin'. There really is a Louise?"

"Of course. She's about seventy and could care less about politics. You only got her attention when you mentioned spilling the beans to the editor."

"Aw! I thought 'Louise' was the same guy who'd been writin' advice columns in the *Star* for years…. Remember Sally Sayings? He was an old queen called Chuck Lamont who lived in Mahwah. I loved him…. He ran the comics page—did his own acrostics. He would a got it right away…. He was a big Judy Garland fan."

Natalie put her hands on her hips. "And what was that about the Scarecrow? There wasn't any Scarecrow!"

"Oh, yah?" Angela's ruby red lips smiled, creating deep dimples in her powder-pink cheeks. "Maury wasn't too specific about who was who. I just took a wild guess that Myra was the Scarecrow. She sure looks like one, doesn't she? Skinny old broad!"

Natalie waited for a couple of teenagers, looking uncomfortable in suits and ties, to pass by. "You never suspected Maury'd been murdered, did you."

"No. It was some shock, I'm tellin' ya. I couldn't believe it. I guess you're right about my letters bein' vague, because I never thought you'd think I meant Maury had been murdered."

Natalie advanced a step closer. "What exactly were you trying to accomplish?"

"Well, y'know, it peeved me that Peter Kovaks, after what he did to Maury, was gonna run for the same office."

"Then you knew all along that Kovaks wrote the articles."

"Sure."

"But you told me Maury'd got what he deserved!"

"I was trying my damnedest to put you off the scent. I didn't want you thinkin' I was too interested in revenge."

"I see. And I thought I was so clever, getting you to tell me so much about Maury…."

"Yah. Actually I was dying for you to ask. Maury did screw up royally. But that doesn't mean what Kovaks did was right. Now, Maury was a forgiving man…. All the years we were together, he didn't mention the story more'n two or three times, and he was never resentful. But a little while before he died, he talked about it. He was upset. I thought maybe he'd been drinkin' on the sly. He said it wasn't fair. He said Kovaks was scum. What was he talking about, I asked? He said he'd never done anything half as bad as what Kovaks had." She sighed and opened her silver handbag. "A few days later he died, and I didn't think about it any more. Until a couple a months later when I heard Kovaks was running for office. That burned me. I'm not as forgiving as Maury. And I got to thinkin', maybe it was Maury dwellin' on what had happened that had got him drinkin' again."

"So you devised a plan—to what?"

"To get you reporters poking around in Kovaks' life."

Natalie's eyes widened. "Couldn't you have done it a little more directly? Like call up the Political Bureau and remind the editor of what Kovaks had done to Maury?"

"Who'd a listened to me? I know *you* think I'm star quality…." She tossed Natalie a grin. "But most a my life nobody's paid much attention to me if anything serious was goin' on. I knew it'd work against me if people knew it was me—my reputation for accuracy back before I met Maury wasn't so hot." Angela brushed at her hair. "Now, I figured from what Maury said, old Kovaks had been messin' around with someone. I could a looked around, but I figured if I could get you reporters involved, you'd dig it up some quicker than I would. That'd fix him, I figured. So I started makin' a lot of smoke, hoping you all'd think there was a fire somewhere. Speaking of which, I about gotta go out for a cigarette break…."

"Wait a minute. Weren't you afraid the *Star* would just bury the story, even if we found out about it? Since we printed it in the first place? If I were you, I'd have sent my letters to the *Bugle*."

Angie's long eyelashes batted innocently. "I did. Only I had a be much more direct with them. They're pretty slow on the old up-take. Tch. They always were a second-rate rag."

Natalie's mouth dropped open. "That was how they kept getting inside information! You were the leak!"

Angie, lighter and cigarette case in hand, winked at her over her shoulder as she headed for the door.

♥   ♥   ♥

At the appointed hour, the band closed out its set and left the stage. A cheery voice came over the PA system and encouraged everyone to head for their seats. The TV crew from Channel 24 left the stage and retired to its bank of portable sound and lighting boards, conveniently located between the beverage tables and the door to the hall, where most of the traffic was. Natalie had seen no further sign of Angela, and was feeling nervous about it. She needed to tell her to watch herself; to warn her that whoever had killed Maury probably thought Enigma knew something about it; to tell her that if she, Natalie, could work it out, the killer could, too.

But the ushers—college girls and boys in plastic straw hats—were racing up and down the aisles at the stage-end of the auditorium, escorting ancient politicos to reserved seats, evicting groundlings who foolishly thought that if they got there first they could sit up-front. They spotted Natalie's press pass, and herded her to a roped-off area in the upper right-hand corner of the auditorium. She found herself sitting in uncomfortable proximity to a large man wearing a rumpled gray suit and the jaded expression of a veteran campaigner.

Feeling distinctly out of place, she let her eyes wander around the hall, trying to locate the major players. Linda was on the stage, testing the microphones. Natalie couldn't see the left side of the auditorium very well, so she stood up, defying the ushers. She caught a glimpse of Lance's large head poking up from the front row of the reserved seats, and assumed that the diminutive Myra was seated in the space to his left.

"Testing one, two, three...." Linda's voice floated out over the audience. "Why don't they ever say peach, pear, and pumpkin?" The crowd's laughter was swift and generous.

There was no sign of Byron, but Tyler was standing by the door, peering into the hall with the air of a secret service agent anticipating the arrival of the President. She glanced toward the back of the room. The caterers were removing the empty bottles and plastic glasses with controlled haste. There was Angie.... Standing by the bleachers, talking to a tall, elegant woman in a black floor-length evening gown. She appeared to be making an entreaty, but the tall woman was shaking her head. It was only when the unknown looked toward the stage that Natalie realized it was Dorothy Gayle.

"Lady, you're blocking my view...."

Natalie twisted as she sat, and found herself looking into Ginny's twinkling eyes. She gripped the back of her chair. "What the hell are you doing here?"

"Moonlighting." She winked. "You never heard me say that."

Natalie shook her head and turned face-front. Everyone was seated, and an expectant hush settled in. Tyler raised his hand, and the band, which had reassembled on the auditorium floor (right in front of the press corral) struck up a rousing rendition of When the Saints Come Marchin' In.

♥   ♥   ♥

The slate of candidates made its grand entrance from the side hall, bounding up the portable steps and onto the stage like schoolboys, waving with both hands to the crowd, which, buoyed by champagne and music, cheered mightily. The Master of Ceremonies, a real estate agent from Upper Saddle River and the District Party Chairman, called half-heartedly for quiet. He introduced the four candidates, ending with Peter, the man who, it appeared, had single-handedly rid New Jersey of organized crime by exposing a pornography distribution network in a series of award-winning newspaper articles.

After all that excitement, it would have taken speeches of monumental shallowness to dampen the evening, and although at times it came close, the crowd was in a generous mood. They listened with rapt attention as the candidates laid out their platforms, and (prompted by the band) cheered the slogans and empty promises with a gusto that flagged only slightly as the hour drew on.

Peter Kovaks was the star of the night. When he looked out and spoke of the need for compassion in government, the hush deepened. When he cracked an old chestnut of a campaign joke about the candidate and the waitress, the laughter was spontaneous. Even when he talked about his commitment to water purification and the need for quieter garbage collection, only one or two eyes glazed over. The TV reporter in front of Natalie whispered to her neighbor: "Damn, he's one fine looking man." That about summed it up.

♥   ♥   ♥

The party organizers had allotted a cautious half hour for Q and A. Enough, they thought, to scotch any idea they didn't welcome questions about the mystery surrounding their poster boy, but not enough to let the jackals sink in their fangs and get a good grip.

The emcee started with the reporter from the *New York Times*, New Jersey edition. She asked the candidate for Roads Commissioner a tough one about zoning laws. From the first three words of the answer, Natalie could tell he had nothing to say, and her attention turned to Peter Kovaks. He was listening with full attention to his colleague, although once he glanced toward the other side of the stage where his wife stood in the wings. Natalie turned to Linda, too, and saw her invisible nod. The questions continued.

The large man to her right had had his hand up from the first. Natalie grew accustomed to him jumping up quickly and sitting down heavily— once landing in her lap instead of his seat. After fifteen minutes the emcee called on him.

He stood up and brushed his moist hair off his forehead. "Max Bludwort, *Bugle*."

Natalie looked at him more closely. The tails of his jacket were wrinkled, and one of his cufflinks was dangling.

Max peered at his notebook. "Question for Mr. Kovaks." He waited while Peter adjusted the mike at his podium. "This concerns the murders of Maurizio Marconi and Armand Vitek. As you know, suspicion has fallen on both you and the *Star*, where you once worked and to which you are still connected through your consultancy firm. How can you expect the voting public to give you the responsibility of representing them when you yourself, are in the very center of the cloud of suspicion? And I have a follow-up."

Peter looked around the auditorium with a cool expression. "I'm glad you asked that, Max. I think it's a question that's been in the back of everyone's mind. It needs to be addressed. I won't kid you—it hasn't made my campaign any easier. I want to assist my friends at the *Star* in any way I can, and frankly I worry about their safety. But fortunately, we have a District Attorney in this county, and a police force. These good men and women are working night and day to apprehend the perpetrator of these heinous crimes. That leaves me free to devote my time to the people of Bergen County, and to their concerns. The democratic system works, Max."

Max leaped up before the emcee could call on anyone else. "If I can follow up...? You talk about your colleagues at the *Star* being in trouble. But in fact you are the only one who knew the second victim. Don't you think the voters are right to worry about that?"

Peter tilted his head. "I'm not sure I understand you, Max. Are you making an accusation? Or are you asking if I'm worried about my own safety? The answer is no. If you're suggesting that *you* are worried about my safety, I can assure you I have police protection."

Natalie looked around the room. It wasn't like her to miss the presence of plainclothes cops. She spotted one at the back of the room—a short woman standing with her hands behind her back while the waiters buzzed around her, setting the tables with coffee urns and trays of cookies.

Scanning the room for a second cop without success, she missed the next question and answer. When she turned back around the clock on the wall above the stage said 8:26. Time was running out.

As the candidate for Fire Chief finished his answer, she put her hand up.

"Last question," said the emcee, and pointed at her.

She rose and squared her shoulders. "Natalie Joday, *Bergen Evening Star*. Question for Peter Kovaks." She waited as he went through the ritual of adjusting his mike.

When he was ready, he looked at her and smiled.

She lifted her chin. "You were a reporter covering the campaign 21 years ago. Now you're on the other side of the lights. Does this new perspective make you think differently about the choices you made then? Would you have done anything differently, checked out the story more thoroughly?"

"I'm glad you asked that, Natalie." He looked down thoughtfully, and then around the room. "And I'm glad you used the word 'choices.' We at the *Star* had a tough choice to make. We chose to do what was best for the community we served. Although I had and still have great sympathy for those whose lives were affected, no, I wouldn't change a thing."

"Follow-up?" said Natalie quickly.

The emcee glanced at Peter, then nodded.

Natalie looked into Peter's dark eyes. "According to the *Star*, October 7, 1972, you informed Mr. Marconi of the article that would cause his downfall by reading it to him over the phone. Mr. Vitek's name was not mentioned in the article. My question is, why didn't you give Mr. Vitek's name to Mr. Marconi?"

Peter looked out over the hushed auditorium. "Hindsight is twenty-twenty. It is easy to fault even the most well-intentioned action after the fact. But what Natalie forgets is the facts as they played out. Mr. Marconi never asked me the name of his accuser. Why should he? He knew it. Once he realized what was happening, he didn't want to hear anymore. I didn't need to hound him with details. I was a reporter doing my job. That is all I've ever done. The people of this district can count on me to do my job, too."

"Our thanks to the reporters and to all the candidates!" The emcee stepped back from his podium and started a round of applause.

There was a hand on her shoulder. Natalie heard a whisper in her ear. "You've got guts, kid. Now we'll see if you've got credit."

She stayed face front, watching the candidates waving to the crowd. Linda had disappeared from the wings.

As the applause died down, the emcee spoke. "And now we have our Mingle with the Candidates Hour. Coffee and pastries supplied by our friends at Dough it Right. And let's welcome back to the stage that wonderful band from Clifton, The Rumbles!"

There was more applause as the band clambered back onto the stage. Then people rose, gathered their belongings, and filed out into the aisles. As she waited for her row to clear, Natalie felt another tap on her shoulder.

She turned, expecting to see Ginny. But Ginny was nowhere in sight. She turned further, and found herself looking at Max Bludwort's Rotary Club tie clip.

"You're new, right?"

"No." She looked up into his heavy face. "But this isn't my usual beat."

"That explains it."

He held out a hand. She thought he wanted to shake, until she saw the card in it.

"If you're ever looking for a job—say, tomorrow—give me a call. The *Bugle* could always use someone with your, uh, what's the female equivalent of balls?"

"Brains?" Feeling her cheeks warming, she turned away, for fear that he would think it was his hearty word choice that made her blush, rather than the suggestion that she might ever sink so low on the journalistic ladder to work for the *Bugle!*

Eventually she made it to the aisle and worked her way to the back of the room. She wanted to find Angie, fast. Why had she been so sure no one else would work it out? Why hadn't she warned Angie days ago? Byron, Myra, and Lance—they all had the same information she had, though apparently Peter did not know the current theory was that Armand had not slept with Maury. Had he known about Tyler and Maury? How could he have known…? Byron said they hadn't told Peter about Enigma—but what if they had? Had it been a mistake not to tell the police who Enigma was? Where had that cop gotten to? She couldn't see a thing in this mob.

She stepped onto the little shelf at the bottom of the fold-away bleachers. The extra eighteen inches gave her a good view of the room. People were heading toward the tables—covered with real china cups this time—in slow-moving waves. There was Linda, being solicitous again, in charge of one of the huge stainless steel coffee urns, serving the TV crew. Natalie looked around. The candidates had not yet entered. If Angie had come to make trouble, maybe Dottie had talked her out of it…. But what the hell was Dottie doing there?

A hand grabbed her wrist. Natalie jerked her head around and found herself looking down into Tyler's angry face.

"How dare you!" he hissed.

She wrenched her arm out of his grasp and continued her scan.

He moved closer. "Would you come down here so I can talk to you without shouting?"

"No." She spotted Byron. Talking to Myra near the stage apron.

Tyler clambered up beside her. "I can't believe you would behave like that!" His voice was hoarse, both from his cold and his anger. "I can't believe I tried to take you under my wing—further your career! I was a fool to think you could ever cut it!"

"Bullshit. You never thought about anything but yourself. When I first started in the Crime Bureau you avoided me and tried to keep me away from the good stories, until you decided my interests were too soft and obscure for me to be any competition."

"And is this your idea of hard news? You attack one of the kingpins of the *Star* when he is at his most vulnerable?"

"I didn't attack him, I just asked him a question. I'm investigating a murder, remember?"

"But why here? Why now?"

"Because he wouldn't answer my calls. I knew he'd be forced to talk in front of the TV cameras."

"So you did it to attract attention—to further your career?"

"Tch." She turned to face him. "Weren't you the one who told me I wasn't doing enough for my career? But no, I only wanted to get him to tell the truth."

"You used what I told you to try to corner Peter into a lie!"

"Did I?" She spotted Lance, working his way over to Myra with a coffee cup and saucer in each hand. "I thought I was trying to corner him into the truth. I'm not sure the same can be said about what he did to Maury."

"What do you mean?"

"I gave him his chance to tell me if he had any doubts about Armand's story. He didn't take it. He may regret that."

"That's blackmail."

"No it isn't. Face the facts! Peter Kovaks baited Maury and then brought him down."

"He was doing his job...!"

"No he wasn't. He never wrote another political piece in his life. He was just about the only writer *not* on the Political Bureau's roster that year! What was he doing reporting on that race?"

"He was probably just covering for someone."

"No. He went on purpose to see what kind of man Dottie had married. He was a highly paid features writer with a background in economics! Covering? If so what business did he have to pursue Maury's sex life? None! By any standard! Except one. He loved it! Come on, Tyler! You're a reporter. What would you have done if this weirdo computer geek mas-

273

querading as a rent-boy comes out of the woodwork with a sex story about a politician? To doubt him was mandatory, but nobody appears to have checked him out at all. An out-of-date driver's license? Come on! Wouldn't you have insisted on more? Wouldn't you at least have mentioned the guy's name to Maury? Peter didn't. Why not?" She moved her mouth close to his ear. "I'll tell you why. Because Peter knew about you and Maury. He baited Maury at that press conference. He must have thought it was his lucky day when Armand showed up. It didn't matter if Armand was telling the truth or not! Peter went to Maury and read him just enough of the article he'd written—especially that part about Dottie being out of town—to make him think it was you he was talking about."

Tyler turned away from her and sneezed helplessly into his handkerchief. "You'll never prove that. And it doesn't change the fact that Maury mislead the press."

"Bullshit. All he said was that Dottie was the only woman in his life. That was the literal truth. If you crucified a politician every time he fudged a point, the countryside would be covered with rotting corpses. That's just an excuse to cover Kovak's desire to hurt Dottie—to show her she'd married a schmuck."

Scattered applause from those who had not yet filled their hands with coffee and cookies marked the entrance of the candidates for their mingle. Natalie had no trouble spotting Peter's tall frame. He was quickly surrounded by a group of ladies in blue, who seemed anxious to tell him how wonderful he was.

Tyler pulled at her arm. "You have no right to accuse Peter Kovaks of this kind of behavior! That man's motivations are far above that sort of petty infighting. You are way, way off base! You've blown the whole situation out of proportion, and I'm not going to stand here and let you get away with it. Maybe you don't realize that I have known Linda and Peter Kovaks for many years, and they have been kind enough to consider me a friend. When you insult them, you insult me! Look at the record. There are not two finer people in the State of New Jersey."

Natalie exhaled with a laugh. "What are you talking about! They're horrible people! They called you Toto!"

Tyler flinched, and his flushed cheeks grew scarlet. When he continued, his voice was less forceful, but still determined. "You don't understand…they were from a higher station in life than me. I was a nobody, the child of ignorant, alcoholic parents. Myra and the Kovaks didn't have to notice that I existed, but they did—and I'm grateful for that. I never expected them to consider me a peer."

"I understand perfectly. This is me, you're talking to, Tyler, the one who used to water the marijuana plants her father grew in the basement. You think it was okay for them to treat you like shit because you were poor and uncultured? Well I don't. It was their damned obligation to treat you like an equal—and if they didn't, it's because they're heartless boors and because you encouraged them!"

Tyler took off his glasses and raised a hand to the bridge of his nose. Natalie pinched her lips together and turned back to the crowd. Where the hell was Angie!

Tyler blew his nose again. "They're my friends…."

"I'm sorry Tyler. But the truth is you have a better concept of friendship and loyalty than they ever will. I've seen Peter walk right by you without even a nod."

"He's a busy man."

"Oh, come on…!"

"That is our professional relationship. When we're socializing it's different. Besides, Linda is the one I'm closest too. We're very intimate. She's been so cut up by this. She lives and breathes everything that happens to him."

Natalie's head came up. "Intimate?"

"In the original sense of the word, meaning that we share our secrets. Must the younger generation connect everything with sex?"

Natalie blinked. "Did she know about you and Maury?"

Tyler hesitated.

Natalie gripped his arm. "Tyler! You told me you didn't tell anyone about you and Maury!"

"You asked me if I told anyone at the *Star*! Linda didn't work for the paper."

Natalie let go of him…. Linda had known about Tyler and Maury…. She turned back to the auditorium. Peter had worked his way to the center, pulling a crowd of people behind him as a magnet pulls iron filings. Beyond him, she could see Myra talking to Byron. Lance had disappeared. Over at the coffee table….

Angie was standing at the end of the table, chatting with Linda. Both women were smiling. Linda handed Angie a cup of coffee….

"Oh, Jeez!" Natalie sprang from the bleachers and sprinted to the edge of the crowd. Then the bodies closed in: gray-suited bodies of stolid businessmen; colorfully clad bodies of businesswomen and wives. They slowed

275

her progress as if she had hit a wall. She shoved and pushed her way across the room, leaving a wake of spilt coffee and gasps behind.

She caught a glimpse of Angie, moving away from the coffee urns, raising the cup to her lips.

"Angie! Stop! Don't drink it!" Her shriek rose above the buzz of the crowd and reduced it to silence.

Angela, the cup poised at her chin, looked up and saw Natalie fighting her way through the crowd. She froze, and crossed her eyes to look down at the steaming brown liquid in the cup.

Natalie stumbled to her side. "Don't drink it…don't touch it. And don't spill any!"

That last was a necessary warning, for Angie's plump hands had begun to tremble as if with palsy. The noise of cup and saucer clattering was the only sound in the hushed auditorium. Natalie took a deep breath and took them from her. She walked with careful steps, her shoulders hunched forward, back to the tables, and set the cup and saucer down. When she straightened up, she found herself looking into Linda's sere green eyes.

"What's happening here?" It was Peter, flanked by Myra and Lance. "Natalie Joday? Please explain what you are doing?"

She looked at them. The Gang. She focused on Myra, whose expression was one of wary expectation. "I should have told you sooner. But I couldn't trust anyone."

Natalie looked at the hushed semicircle that had formed around her. Angela's shoulders shook. Lance stared at her, an anxious expression on his face. Byron appeared, the plainclothes cop in tow. Linda had not moved from behind the table.

Natalie looked back at Myra. "I've got it, Ms. V. The killer had to be the person who used Armand Vitek to set up Maury; it was someone who had a critical interest in not having the truth come out; it was someone who knew enough about printing to know about the potassium silver cyanide. Maury found out he'd been set up last December. He tried to call Peter to ask him what had happened. But Peter was out of town. He reached Linda." Natalie shifted her gaze. "Anybody who tries to reach Peter reaches Linda— if I'm certain of anything I'm certain of that. Maury must have told her why he was calling—or maybe she guessed from his questions. She realized it was all going to come out—Peter would be condemned for ruining Marconi, whether or not he had known about the set-up. Maury would try to find Armand. If Armand talked, she would be fingered as the one who had sent him to Peter, the one who had given him the details that would make the story ring true. She couldn't let that happen—although they hadn't made the announcement, the preparations for the campaign were underway. She would have to stop it right there, before Maury could reach Peter; before the chain reaction started, before anyone could possibly connect her to Maury. She went to his house, armed with the phenobarbital...."

Natalie looked at Byron, and then back at Myra. "Luck was on her side. Maury's death passed as an accident. But then the murder was uncovered, and the old story was—by sheer coincidence—unearthed. By the fluke of the Enigma letters, the cops started looking for Armand. Armand went to Linda to try and get her to come forward with the story. He wanted to get the cops off his tail. He didn't recognize the danger he thought was everywhere when it was right in his face. She put the acid in his coffee, so he could never tell, so that suspicion would be thrown on the *Star*. Linda set up Maury, either because she knew how Peter felt about Dottie, and wanted to hurt her, or to further Peter's journalist career by giving him a chance at one of the big exposés he was later to become so famous for. Maybe it was a little bit of both."

Myra's brow furrowed. "And now you're saying she's tried to poison...." She looked over at Angela. "Who is this woman?"

"This is Angela Marconi," said Natalie.

Myra's eyes widened. "Why would she do that?"

"Because Angela is Enigma, and Linda mistakenly thinks Enigma knows about the set-up. You must have told Peter about Enigma, and he told Linda—"

A harsh laugh broke the silence. All eyes turned to Linda Kovaks. She was smiling bitterly, her mouth an orange scar across her white face. "This is ridiculous." She looked at Myra. "Isn't it clear this young woman is trying to sink Peter's campaign—first with her lurid questions and now this? Whether for self-promotion or out of a desire to aid this poor woman," she nodded at Angela, "I don't know. But I do know how to end this right here!"

She picked up the coffee cup Natalie had set on the table, and raised it to her lips. The crowd gasped. Linda drank, then lowered the cup to the saucer with a clink. "Did you really believe I would go around carrying acid in my purse, Natalie Joday?" She picked up a paper napkin and patted her mouth.

The shock wave that had risen within her when Linda had lifted the cup mutated into a tidal wave of embarrassment. There was a buzzing in her ears. The figures of Myra, Peter, and Byron blurred.

277

"Oh, for cripe's sake," said the emcee.

"Okay everybody…." The plainclothes officer strode forward, her arms spread wide. "Show's over."

"I'm sorry, Natalie." Myra looked at her coolly. "We never told Peter a thing about the Enigma letters. As we told you, we thought the less he knew, the better, just to avoid a situation like this."

Natalie blinked. Byron was watching her. She couldn't look at him. She would sell peanuts on Coney Island for a living before she would ever look at him again. The rest of the crowd drifted away, leaving her alone with her beating heart.

"Natalie?"

Tyler's puffy face loomed up before her. It wore a peculiar expression.

"I told Linda about the Enigma letters—not how I heard about them, and not much that was in them. But enough." He reached into his pocket and pulled out a little paper sachet. "She gave me these tonight. She said to take them at bedtime. For my cold…." They turned to Linda in unison.

There was one frozen moment that lasted forever. Then Linda acted. Grabbing the table with both hands, she tipped it away from her. The coffee urns crashed to the floor amidst the clatter of breaking coffee cups and rolling saucers. Coffee and tea spread out across the hardwood floor, causing the stunned constituents to press backward. Natalie kept her eyes on Linda. She saw her pick up a bowl of fruit punch and throw it onto the TV crew's sound board. There was a pop and a crackle, and the lights went out.

A cry of surprise arose from the crowd; a male voice boomed, "Okay, everybody keep calm." An acrid smell floated across the auditorium. A woman's voice from the hall doors yelled, "Fire!"

The crowd surged toward the doors at the back of the gym, their cries of confusion and fear increasing. Someone bumped against Natalie, urging her forward.

When you're scared, you run; when you're angry, you stand and fight. Natalie dodged sideways, and headed toward the hall. She slipped on the tea and bumped into a panicking constituent who screamed something in her ear. She groped her way through the door. It was pitch black in both directions.

She did not know the lay of the land; she would have to guess. What she would have given for a flashlight, for she knew there would be wet footprints leading one way or the other. Logic told her to turn left—that was the shortest route to the front of the building.

Don't go into any dark alleys alone. Natalie turned right and, keeping a hand on the wall, hurried into the darkness.

♥   ♥   ♥

Small clusters of constituents huddled together on the broad steps outside the auditorium. Some had run; some remained in the hope of rescuing
coats and jackets; some waited nearby in their cars. The rumor of murder
jumped from one cluster to the next, igniting shock, disbelief, and morbid
curiosity. Some, when they heard, grabbed the hands of their loved ones
and left, and coats be damned. Some moved to the fringes of the largest
cluster, at the center of which were two tall men—one of them recogniz-
able as the charismatic leader of the candidates and the other a large mound
of flesh who said nothing. Between them was a tiny woman in a green
dress. These three faced a slightly overweight woman in silver, and a muscular young woman talking into a cell phone.

"...Is somebody trying to turn the lights on...?"

"Is your wife with you, Mr. Kovaks?"

"Hey...."

"...Here! Give that flashlight to the custodians...."

"I don't know where she is...and I'm concerned about that."

"If she didn't come out the front door, she's still in there—all the other
doors are locked."

"Hey."

"...I'm sure there's been some mistake...."

"She must still be in the building, then. If somebody can give me a
flashlight I'll go look for her."

"Hey!"

"Dottie!"

"Hey!!"

"Hello, Myra."

"You'll have to wait, sir. I've called for back-up, and as soon as they
get here...."

"I've got a flashlight in my car...."

"Hey!!! Will somebody listen to me? Where's Natalie Joday?"

♥   ♥   ♥

A faint light spilled across the floor of the hall. Natalie crept to the
corner and looked around. Another hallway, streaked with gray light from
a row of windows on the left, ran fifty feet or more toward an inky black-
ness. On the right, three doors were visible—shadowy rectangular recesses

279

in the gray wall. Natalie reached down and slipped off her shoes, then moved to the first door. She rested her ear upon a sign that read Band Room. She heard nothing.

She moved silently to the second door....

♥   ♥   ♥

"Okay, Bob, that ought a do it. Close the circuit."

Lights flooded half the gym, revealing a few brave souls standing near the door, or sitting on the bottom step of the bleachers.

"What's the matter?"

"Still no lights in the south wing or backstage."

"Why not?"

"Dunno. Is there a separate box back there?"

"Dunno, Bob. Let's go look...."

♥   ♥   ♥

The noise, even through the wooden door, was unmistakable—the sound of a Venetian blind being moved. Natalie hesitated, weighing the possibilities. If Linda succeeded in getting the window open, she might get away...but how far, and for how long? Should she try and stop her? No...it was Natalie's job to stay on Linda's trail—not to apprehend or to condemn, just to stand at a distance and point; to mark her presence; to expose.

Natalie's fingers tightened around the doorknob. It turned at her touch—noiselessly and smoothly. As she swung open the door, a triangle of gray light fanned across the darkened room.

There was a scramble to the left and the sounds of blind retreat: metal chairs crashed to the ground; books fell; glass shattered.

Natalie moved to the right and crouched down. A door slammed at the far end of the room, and silence returned. She moved slowly, weaving through a jumble of metal chairs and music stands. Reaching the back wall, she found the door and fumbled for the knob. It turned.

"Linda?"

♥   ♥   ♥

"Myra, please!"

"Don't Myra please me, Lance Wenger! That young woman has ruined us! Ruined us, I say. I told her she had an obligation to report to me if she had any information! And now she has made a spectacle of herself and me!"

"But Myra...."

280

"I know what it is! She's run off to sell her story to the *Bugle*. That's where she belongs. Hey! You! Max Bratwurst! You're at the bottom of this, aren't you, you no-necked, sniveling, putrefied excuse for a reporter!"

"Myra, what are you doing...? Officer! Help! She'll kill him!"

♥　　　♥　　　♥

Moonlight fell from a high window, illuminating the shadowy theatrical flats stacked against a concrete wall. The floor was covered with wooden platforms and boxes. To the right, a scrim hung in front of heavy curtains. She must be near the back of the stage.

"Hello!" she called out. Her voice echoed through the vaulting room. "Can anybody hear me? Help!"

There was no answer, but she heard Linda, working her way over the dismantled sets toward the far side of the room.

Natalie headed after her, stepping onto a plywood platform. Suddenly the hall behind her flooded with light.

Linda, clearly visible now, had reached a door. She pulled at the handle. She pulled again, putting her shoulder into it.

Natalie sat on a plywood chest labeled *Fantastiks*.

Linda turned around. She was breathing hard. Her eyes moved left, then right, then past Natalie to the open door through which they had come. She climbed back up the stack of lumber, waving one hand in the air for balance.

Time to retreat. Natalie put her shoes back on. But Linda stopped, about fifteen feet away.

Her tangerine evening gown was hitched around her waist; her feet were bare; her face unrecognizable. For the first time Natalie understood what was meant by the expression, "turned at bay." Linda's eyes were those of someone who has already killed twice; someone who has nothing left to lose. Unnerved, Natalie rose.

Linda's head twitched. "What are you going to do?"

"Nothing. They'll be here soon." She had an idea that reminding Linda of that might discourage her from doing anything rash.

"Do you think you can keep me here?"

"No." Natalie took a step backward. "Leave if you like."

"And you will follow me." Linda twisted and reached for her handbag, slung over her shoulder by its slender white strap. She lifted the flap and pulled out a small glass bottle. "But not if you don't have any eyes to see me with." She bounded forward, straight at Natalie, removing the cap of

281

the bottle as she came.

As she jumped, Natalie saw as if in slow motion the little bottle, and Linda's moving arm, and a clear liquid shooting out at her face. She twisted in the air, but the liquid hit her face as she fell. She screamed as she landed on a pile of rough planks. There was a stinging in her eyes, cool moisture on her neck and breast, and a sharp pain in her shoulder. In a frenzy, she ripped at her clothes and wiped at her eyes with a hand protected by her sleeve.

Someone took hold of her shoulders. "Shhh, it's all right."

"My eyes!" Natalie struggled through the pain in her shoulder to get her jacket off.

"You're okay." The voice was so soothing. "It's only perfume."

Natalie's panic screeched to a halt. She was shaking all over and her head was spinning. "Are you sure?"

The hands helped her sit up on the uneven planks. "Yes."

Yes; the smell of perfume was everywhere. She touched her face. It was still there. She opened her eyes—they stung a little, but the room swam into beautiful unfocus.

She looked into the comforting face of Dorothy Gayle. "What happened?" The right side of her head felt odd.

"We came as fast as we could." She touched Natalie's hair. "You've got a lovely cut behind your ear." She looked over her shoulder. "Angie, come here. We need a piece of cloth."

"Gotcha…."

Natalie turned toward the sound of Angie's voice. There she was…stepping over something in the doorway. Something orange. She blinked. Linda—sprawled unconscious on the floor.

"What did you…?"

"We heard you call," said Dottie. "We were in the hall when she threw the perfume on you. She was fast."

Angela had her hands up under her dress, pulling at her half slip. She grinned at Natalie. "Dottie decked her with a two-by-four when she came through the door. I wish you'd a seen her go down…just like in the funnies." She gave Dottie the slip.

"I think I need to lie down." Natalie heard her words slurring.

"Of course. It's the knock on the head."

Natalie closed her stinging eyes and let the gentle hands lower her to the floor and press something against her head. She heard the wail of police sirens in the distance.

"Finally!" Angie's voice was close by. "A lot a good the cops are! I told 'em you were hot on Linda's trail, and we had a help you. But did they listen? No! They wouldn't budge till their whatdyacallit back-up came. Myra and Lance had a create a diversion so me and Dottie could sneak in when the cops weren't lookin'."

"Thanks, Angie." She was floating away from them. "Thanks, Dottie." The sirens sounded like a woman wailing in mourning.

Dottie's voice, recently so close, came as if from a great distance. "She's out. Well, Angie. I guess you were right after all. I did have some unfinished business. Not that I fully understand. In fact, I have no idea what has made all these people behave so oddly."

"Dottie, I gotta tell ya, you always were on another planet. The answer to that one is pretty obvious."

Natalie floated on a small island in the midst of an immense black sea...or was it a pebble in a goldfish bowl?

"Oh really?"

"Sure! The rich desire it but cannot buy it, the kind give it away for free, the wise cherish it as more priceless than gold, and the poorest of the poor can always afford it."

"That's easy," Natalie mumbled. "Love. It's love."

♥   ♥   ♥

Which explains how Natalie got her byline on the front page of the *Bergen Evening Star* for the third, fourth, and fifth times.

Interlude

esa nestled into a cranny in the woodpile behind the tent and looked up at the night sky. It was good to be alone for a while. She didn't mind the staring of the stars, or the whispering of the wind.

But suddenly she heard voices, and lights illuminated the tent. She heard footsteps, and voices, and saw the black shadows of soldiers cast on the tent's yellow walls. She sat still as the men inside began to talk about the war, and the coming attack on Valeria.

"Then we give the order to march at dawn," said a gruff voice. "The first column will be at the Blue Ford by sundown.

Vesa's heart leaped in her chest. No! They must not go there! It was a trap! The would all be killed, and the Valerians would overrun the Red Plains. At last she understood what Kadra had meant. The Valerians had let the citadel burn on purpose, then fallen back to draw their enemies forward to where their main force lay in wait.

She scrambled off of the woodpile and limped to the front of the tent. She hated all soldiers, but she hated the Valerians most of all.

"Hey! Who's this!" The tall guards at the door grabbed at her, but she slipped under their arms and into the tent.

The General sat at the end of a long table. Vesa dashed toward him, but strong hands caught her, and picked her up, struggling, from the ground. Tall soldiers huddled around her like vultures.

"Who is this child? How did she get into the compound?"

"She is a Valeri servant, pulled from the fire at the citadel. She has been recovering with the healers."

"Take her away! She is a Valerian spy!"

"Wait. Look at her face. She wants to say something."

"If she lived at the citadel she may know something. Speak up!"

Vesa opened her mouth, but hard as she tried, she could not make a sound. For years the Silence had protected her, and now when she wanted the words back, they would not come.

She looked at the bandages on her hands. She couldn't even write. The soldiers started to pull her away. They would lock her up, and go unknowing to their deaths. What could she do? She saw the map on the table. Green for the forest, red for the plain, and blue for the river. She saw blocks of wood, representing the troops. She pointed urgently at the map, imploring the General with her eyes.

Chapter Thirty-one

J oday!"

Natalie turned to find Ginny clattering up the stairs, her ankles splaying outward in her hurry.

"When did they let you out?" asked Ginny as she gained Natalie's side. "Let me look at your head. Gawd."

"This morning." Natalie pushed back her hair to give her friend a better view. "And it's just a little bandage, Ginny. Only nine stitches. Linda got twenty-six."

"Not enough for someone who killed two people and tried to kill two others—even if one of them was K. Tyler Hanson." Ginny peered behind Natalie's ear. "Did they have to shave so much...?"

"Looks kind of scraggly, doesn't it? I'm thinking of shaving it all off around the back to even it out, and letting my top hair kind of hang down straight to cover it. It's the latest fashion."

"Really?" Ginny raised a hand to the nape of her neck and lifted.

They headed up the stairs together.

"Are you sure you should be running around?" Ginny glanced at Natalie's sling. "You didn't drive, did you?"

"My family brought me."

"You'd think the *Star* would leave you alone on a Sunday!"

"Byron said Myra wants everyone at this meeting—she waited for me to get out of the hospital to have it." Natalie stopped on the landing. There was no one in sight. "This is D-day, isn't it?"

Ginny looked at Natalie innocently. "I guess we'll find out."

"Spill it, Chau." Natalie put her good hand on her hip. "You know you know everything."

"If only that were true." Ginny slipped her arm through Natalie's elbow. "But then—what would be the fun of investigating?"

♥   ♥   ♥

Myra's assistant pounced on them at the top of the stairs. "Ms. Joday? Ms. V wants to see you before the meeting." She opened her arm in the direction of Myra's office. Natalie turned left and followed her, while Ginny turned right and headed for the solarium.

Myra was at her desk, frowning at a piece of paper. She held up her hand palm out—the universal writer's signal to wait. Lance was standing by the window, looking down on the roof of Charlie's Diner, apparently studying the habits of the squirrels who had taken the high road into town. Natalie sat in the green chair and waited.

Eventually Myra looked up. "In my day, I thought I took reporting seriously, but it never landed me in the hospital. Usually when my writers talk about being battle scarred, it has to do with wounded egos, which don't require stitches."

"I just fell," said Natalie querulously. "It was my own fault."

Myra turned to Lance. "What's her medical deductible?"

Lance clasped his hands behind his broad back. "Two hundred."

Myra looked pleased. "You should be able to afford that. What about your mental state—are you depressed? Do you need psychiatric counseling?"

Natalie frowned. "Hardly."

"What about the family? Isn't your brother a loose canon? Is he coping all right?"

"I'm not sure that's any of your business."

"There's no need to be huffy, young lady. I am trying to express my concern for your well-being."

Natalie raised an eyebrow. "You're not doing it very well."

"Oh really!" Myra turned her head. "Is that true, Lance?"

He didn't bother to turn. "She's hit the nail, Myra."

"Oh." Myra drummed her fingers on the desk. "My apologies. Once I thought it wasn't necessary, then I thought it was too late, but now I know better, so I'm giving it a go. I'm still learning."

Natalie touched the edge of her sling with her free hand. She looked at Myra. "I'm not sure I'm following you."

"You must not be back to full strength." Myra left her desk and came to sit in the burgundy chair. "That was our mistake. My mistake. We didn't give a good God damn about Marconi, or Dottie, or their son. I mean...I didn't give a damn. I knew Dottie had invested when we most needed the money—but all I felt was pride because I didn't hesitate to nail her husband to the wall. I never stopped to consider that you can know too much. I thought I had a right to all the information I could get. I never stopped to ask, 'Myra, what the hell are you doing?' Lance did."

Myra looked at the man staring vacantly out the window. "He told me he'd quit if I printed a story like that based on an unsubstantiated accusation. Peter agreed to call Marconi and get his response before we printed. I was shocked at what happened next—I admit I'd had my doubts about Vitek. But Marconi's reaction seemed to prove the story was true, so we printed it without probing it more deeply."

Lance sighed deeply. "It was bad journalism, Myra."

"It was worse than that—it was arrogant hypocrisy. I hid behind the issue of the 'public's right to know.' I wouldn't admit how easy it was to use that argument to justify a personal desire. "

Natalie shook her head. "But it wasn't your desire—or even Peter's, really. Linda was the one who manipulated the situation. She used a piece of information, told to her in confidence, to create havoc for her own benefit—'working behind the scenes.' I doubt she cared if Peter or any of you saw through Armand's story—just as long as no one saw deep enough to find her."

Myra buried her chin in the chartreuse chiffon scarf she wore around her neck. "Linda always believed anything she did was justified, as long as she was doing it for Peter. But that doesn't explain how she found Vitek. A street boy like that."

"He was never selling sex," said Natalie. "That was just the story they concocted to tell Peter. Linda's mother died of cancer about when Armand's did, and East Orange and Belleville are right next door. They must have met at the hospital. I don't know how Linda convinced him to do it—I'm guessing she put it to him as a big joke that would appeal to his anti-government sentiments."

"Why did she kill him in such a terrible way?" asked Myra. "That to me is the hardest thing to understand. He never did anything to harm her. He kept her secret for twenty years."

"She was trying to throw suspicion on you, Myra."

"Me?" Myra's spine arched. "What reason could I have had…?"

"You live and breathe the *Star*. Who knows what you might have done to prevent an old scandal from being made public? You might well have found yourself accused of the set-up pretty soon."

"But why would I have concocted such a story?"

"To make headlines; to help the *Star* build a name for itself as a paper that covered real news."

Myra sniffed. "Linda would have had a hard time proving that."

"She had already laid enough groundwork with me to get me thinking along those lines. And you weren't exactly helpful."

Myra's mouth twisted, and she spoke stiffly. "I have to apologize for not telling you more. I thought I was right to stand back and let this play itself out. But I should have trusted you enough to tell you about the riddles."

Lance's voice floated across the room. "You've never been good at trusting people, Myra."

"Fortunately she figured everything out on her own."

"Not...everything." Natalie pulled at her lower lip with her teeth.

"Go ahead." Myra steeled herself. "Ask. I owe you."

Natalie released her lip. "Dottie told me you and Peter and Lance had been involved in something unethical once."

Myra folded her skinny arms. "That's a little vague, isn't it?"

"It had something to do with what happened with the money Dottie invested in the *Star*." Natalie glanced at Lance. "Some secret."

Myra favored Natalie with the whites of her shark eyes. "Where did you hear that?"

"I'd rather not say. The, uh, person who told doesn't exactly know that, uh, he or she was telling me something I didn't know."

Myra looked at Lance. He was watching the squirrels playing tag in the top-most branches of the oak tree. Myra's nose twitched. "Very well. I'll trust you, Natalie Joday. Do what you think best with the information. We were a handful of newsmen and women trying to get control of the paper—for its own good as well as ours. We had no money, no power, no track record. But we had gall. We got a few friends to invest in the company so that we could go public. That kept the paper alive, but it didn't change its direction. The Mills family hired a consultant to analyze the situation. We...I...bought him off. So his report would say exactly what I wanted it to. I used Dottie's money to pay him."

Natalie frowned. "But she has the stocks...."

"We replaced the funds as soon as we could. Accounting smoke and mirrors. She had given Lance a check made out to the *Star*. She never questioned him, or wanted to see the certificates. After a couple of years, we made it right."

"Peter knew."

"Yes."

"And obviously Lance knew."

"After the fact," said Myra. "Peter and I took the money, then got Lance to cover up for us. We didn't tell him what we had done until we needed him to bail us out."

"Does Linda know?"

"Peter…didn't always tell her everything."

"Then I'd say it's a good thing the murder investigation is over."

"Why?"

"Because the police knew all about it."

Myra looked at Lance. "But it had nothing to do with the case!"

"But the Evil Deed was mentioned in the Enigma letters—Angie had heard from Maury how Lance had apologized to Dottie. Angie didn't know any details, but she hoped her hints would lead to trouble for Peter. If the detectives in charge of the case hadn't been so ethical, the whole story would probably be out now."

"My God." Myra's shoulder's sagged. "I've had a narrower escape than I thought. She's a clever woman, that Angie M."

"And a loyal one. Angie wrote the Enigma letters to take revenge on Peter for what he did to Maury. I guess she succeeded."

"Peter has withdrawn from the election." Myra looked suddenly very old. "He's already distancing himself from Linda. There was a quote in the *Bugle* saying how betrayed he felt, because his own wife had 'set him up.' It made me ill…. I've protected Peter from himself for years—he didn't have a human bone in his body. He made me look altruistic by comparison. But I also used his charm and looks to seduce people as if I were his pimp."

Lance spoke up. "Be fair, Myra. You were glad when he ran for office. You wanted him away from the paper."

"Don't gloss it over, Lance. Once I thought I had it all, but lately…I've realized I've missed some things."

"You've got plenty of time left, Myra," said Lance.

"Time? Are you joking, Lance Wenger? Or just reminding me that we're late for the meeting." Myra stood, squared her shoulders, and returned to her desk. She aimed her shark eyes at Natalie. "Let me give you a word of advice, Natalie Joday. Whatever you decide to do, wherever you go, remember this: life is a front page story, but you miss a lot if you only read the headline."

Natalie nodded politely.

Myra looked at Lance. "Isn't that right, Lance?"

"Yes, Myra."

"Yes, Myra!" she mimicked. "Is that all you can say when you've just seen me groveling before this young woman who doesn't have a clue what I'm talking about?"

"Sorry, Myra. You know I feel for you. But I never was very good at expressing myself."

"Well, Lance, if I can try to be more compassionate, maybe you can do something about your reticence."

"Yes, Myra."

"People would never leave you alone if they had some clue how intelligent and soft-hearted you are."

"Yes, Myra."

"You've got to try, Lance."

"I am trying, Myra. In fact…."

"Yes?"

"Well…." He turned away from the window. "I have a date."

Natalie and Myra stared with twin expressions of disbelief.

"You're finally going out with Dottie Gayle!" said Myra.

Lance gave a shy smile—but shook his head.

Natalie's mouth wagged open. "Angela Marconi."

Lance's cheeks turned pink.

"Good God, Lancelot Wenger! How did you ever get up the courage to ask her out?"

"She asked me, Myra. It was a first for her. She says she's been trying out the idea of being a liberated woman…."

♥   ♥   ♥

One hundred and twenty-two wooden chairs had been set up, one for every member of the full-time *Star* staff. Byron met Natalie and led her to the only empty chair: in the back row between the travel editor and the movie critic (who insisted on keeping the aisle seat). When she was comfortable, Byron stuck his hands in his pockets and lounged to the front of the room.

Natalie craned her neck. A few Board members sat up front to the left, and a few Union aparatchiks sat over to the right. Davis was next to the head of the art department, and Marcia was right behind him. Tyler was there, arms folded across his breast and his head bent forward over them. So far his name had been kept out of the story, since both the police and the *Star* were disinclined to print it, and the *Bugle* was so incompetent…. Rudy was there, too, at the end of the row just in front of her…he had twisted in his chair, and was taking in her sling. When he saw that she had spotted him, he gave her a big grin and a thumbs up. Myra and Lance were on the dais at the front of the room, greeting the Union spokesperson. When Byron reached them they broke up and took their seats—all but Myra, who stepped up to the podium in the sudden silence.

"Good afternoon. I thank you for coming. I imagine that with all the gossip that's been flying around the newsroom for the past few weeks, you've probably been expecting an announcement of some sort. Probably you think it's about time." There was a ripple of hesitant laughter. Myra held her head, with its flame-colored topknot, perfectly still until it was quiet again. Then her glittering eyes darted bird-like around the room. "As you are all aware, it has been a trying time for this distinguished newspaper. To be blunt, for the past year and a half, circulation and advertising revenues have been declining. All of us have sniffed the pungent scent of change in the air, and wondered what the future would hold.

"Forgive me if I break one of the rules of good journalism and digress. In 1971 I was managing editor of the *Star*. Those were difficult times—the news industry was changing, just as it is changing now. It was the last hurrah for old-fashioned print journalism before the boom in cable television eviscerated its market share and the tabloids brought it to its knees. Back then, I was a leader in the fight to make the changes I knew were necessary. Out with old, was my battle cry, embrace the future! It was clear that a family-owned and operated paper couldn't compete. While some of our competitors survived by throwing their principles out the window and going tabloid," she glanced pointedly at Byron, "our goal was to make the *Star* a leader in hard news. To do that we needed changes from montage to management to marketing. We needed to streamline expenses and invest in new printing technology. We—well." Myra raised a hand to her scarf. "Let the record show that the *Star* became a public company, and two decades of prosperity ensued.

"What I and my friends didn't appreciate was that the Mills were good people who had done a good job—an excellent job. Oh, I paid lip service to them in public, but in my heart I thought they were incompetent, behind the times, an anchor around the neck of the *Star*. Exactly the way some of you think of me today."

Ginny's lips twisted into bow-tie shape.

"Don't worry. I'm not looking for sympathy. I just appreciate the irony—and finally understand that change is an ongoing process. The *Star* isn't 'broken' now any more than it was then. And no one of us is responsible for 'breaking' it, any more than the Mills were responsible for the paper's bad times back then. It doesn't need 'fixing.' It just needs to change—again. "The *Star* has always been a leader in the Bergen County community. It is our responsibility to make sure that that does *not* change. Once again we find the business of information gathering and dispersal transforming itself. It's not cable this time, but the Internet, it's not 'real' news that is wanted now, but 'specialized' news. Now I and my closest advisors are the old-fashioned ones—overly concerned with image, clinging to the traditions of a generation ago, afraid of modern technology. We who recognized that industry change was inevitable twenty years ago are now terrified. The fight over electronic rights is just beginning. It will be a revolution. Who knows what will come of it?

"While we fight to maintain the *status quo*, our market share drops. Our advertising brings in less and less cash. And our stock—once an unlimited source of income, has fallen to its lowest level in fifteen years. At current prices, it barely represents our real worth. At this rate, we'll be insolvent in six months.

"In the past three months, the Board has visited the possibilities of selling out, closing down, changing format, or just cutting staff and hanging on. It has been a tortuous time. We have searched our professional and private souls for answers.

"We've all done our best. But now we must do more. We have to be bold enough, confident enough in ourselves, to let go of some of the principles we once thought were unassailable. Change is at hand, whether we want it or not. We are in unfamiliar territory. We can turn back, and say 'this is not what I planned or asked for.' Or we can recognize change as a guide pointing us to the best path in our unfamiliar surroundings. We can see where it leads us. We are still the lucky ones in a tumultuous world. We have a choice.

"Thus it is my privilege to announce our plans for the future. And I do so without apology to you or sense of loss to myself." Myra swept the room with her glance, and gripped the edges of the lectern. "Following a process of full disclosure, the Board and the Union have agreed on terms. A list has been posted at the back of the room naming those employees— editors, writers, artists, printers, photographers, buyers, sales personnel, secretaries, and other support staff—who will be given the opportunity to stay. All 122 full-time staffers are included. Part-time staff will be handled case by case according to guidelines to be established. Effective immediately, there will be a twenty percent salary cut. If you do not accept this, you will be terminated as of tomorrow, November 1st."

There was a rustling in the room, and gasps.

Myra raised a hand. "These salary cuts will enable us to live within our budget during the period of adjustment, which is expected to last from one to two years. We have begun a buy-back procedure from our shareholders. The *Star* will cease to be a public company. This will stop our assets from being further devalued."

Myra looked at the startled faces. "We realize that this salary cut will cause short-term financial stress to just about everyone. But we hope, in time, to offset this unpleasant burden. We will give each employee who stays one share of the new *Star* for every twenty dollars of current monthly salary. If you make a thousand a month, you will get 50 shares, valued at twenty dollars each.

"This is the future. As of midnight tonight, the *Bergen Evening Star* is a 100 percent employee owned and operated company. The Board will dissolve in favor of a management system to be approved by the new shareholders, although we will continue in an advisory role for three months. I will step down as CEO, but will retain my post as editor-in-chief, pending approval of the new management—you. I will accept my pay cut, and I will fight to keep my job—if you want me. It is your choice whether to join me in taking this step forward. I wouldn't turn back if I were you."

♥   ♥   ♥

The official meeting was over, but no one had left. Staffers huddled in groups, talking it all over, pumping the Union reps for details. It was suicide, some said; it was the chance of a lifetime, promised others. What choice do we have, asked many? What good are our shares to us if the paper folds, remarked a few.

Natalie stood with the group gathered around the sheets of paper taped to the back wall. It was strange to see her name there. She had never seen herself as someone with assets. Welcome to the middle class, indeed. Daniel had probably felt this way about his check book. They were both in danger of moving up in the world.

"You're looking puzzled. Tell us you're not thinking of going!"

She glanced up to see Ginny and Byron at her side, with Tyler hovering behind them. "I was wondering how it works. What actual extra income do you get from having a share of the *Star*?"

"Nothing, if we don't turn a profit," said Byron. "But if we do—you get your cut over and above your salary."

"What happens to the people who don't accept today? Are they blacklisted for running scared? This is pretty short notice."

"They'll be able to return on less favorable terms and no hard feelings once we're sure we're going to make it."

Natalie raised an eyebrow. "Are we going to make it?"

Byron pushed at his glasses. "Oh yes."

"It'll be a wild year, though," said Ginny.

"They forgot your name," said Natalie. "Better tell Lance."

"No…. I'm not interested in taking a pay cut. Or in owning a newspaper. In fact…I've been meaning to tell you this…."

Natalie blinked. "You're moving to TV. Channel 24."

"Right." Ginny grinned cheerfully. "Will ya miss me?"

"I doubt it. The station is only two blocks down the street, and they don't stock butterscotch." Natalie looked at her suspiciously. "How long have you known you were leaving?"

"A while…."

Natalie turned to Byron. "And how long have you known?"

"A while…." He pushed at his glasses.

Natalie shook her head. "Nobody ever tells me anything."

"We prefer the fun of watching you figure it out," said Ginny.

"Speaking of which," said Byron. "We're going to need someone else in the Crime Bureau to keep Tyler on his toes…."

Tyler fingered the pocket of his vest. "I think I can manage to stay on my toes by myself. But an up-and-coming young colleague who can complement my experience with her energy is probably a good idea. Just remember, I'm the Bureau Head, and—"

"Oh, come on, Tyler, there's plenty of stories for two!" Ginny winked. "There's still the dollhouse dilemma to solve, you know."

"You're our unanimous first choice, Natalie," said Byron, "if you decide to stick with us and you want the job."

Natalie looked at the three of them—Ginny grinning, Tyler trying hard not to look too eager, and Byron squinting through his glasses. "Twenty percent pay cut." She fiddled with her sling, easing her arm into a more comfortable position. "And me suffering for a new computer…. I'll have to think about it."

"Oh, unh hunh?" Byron pushed at his glasses a third time. "With everything that has been—"

"Okay I've thought about it," said Natalie. "Yes."

Chapter Thirty-two

Daniel, Rebecca, and Gayanne arrived at 11:30 to take Natalie home. With them came Louise, making her first visit to the *Star* since the burglary. They found Natalie in the upstairs library, resting in the warmth of the bubble windows on a chilly morning. They talked over the news of the change in the *Star*'s ownership for a few minutes, and of Natalie's new job description.

"Where shall we go to celebrate? I'm so proud of you." Daniel kissed his sister's cheek. "I'll even let you buy."

"Hey—"

"If Nat's buying, let's go to Spiffios!" said Rebecca. "Louise, will you join us?"

Louise's eyes wandered around the room. "Oh, I...."

"Of course she will!" Natalie looked at Louise's soft face, with its lost brown eyes. "Which reminds me.... Gayanne gave me your book to read while I was stuck in bed. I thought it was wonderful."

"Oh...." Louise looked around the room. "That's sweet of you to say. But.... I know you're being kind."

"I'm being honest."

"No, no. I know…it's for children. Frivolous...."

"I was a child once. A child who watched ugliness and lies win out over truth and joy for reasons I didn't understand. I cried when I read it."

A strange look came over Louise's face.

"I told you!" said Gayanne. Daniel placed a hand on her arm.

"In fact," continued Natalie, "I feel like a fool for the writing advice I gave you. If I'd known you wrote like this, I could have said, 'Write about that, just like that,' and saved us both the time."

"But...." Louise's eyes darted around with increasing bewilderment. "Steve and Piers always said *Valeria* was nonsense—that it was too scary for children and no adult would ever read it...."

"Uh oh," said Daniel, pulling Gayanne to him as if for warmth against a cold wind. "I know what that means."

"Your brothers weren't by any chance unaware of your own true feelings when you were growing up, were they?" asked Rebecca.

Louise blinked in confusion. "True feelings?"

"Your hopes and dreams."

"I never could have told my brothers my dreams!" Louise shook her head. "They would have laughed at me."

"I hate being laughed at," said Gayanne. She disengaged herself from Daniel and went to Louise's side.

Louise put an arm around Gayanne. "They tried to encourage me to do real writing. Piers was very kind to get me the job at the *Star*. He said it would help me get my head out of the clouds."

"God forbid," said Natalie. "This is so damned polished! And you're telling me there's more?"

"Yes…. I started writing them a long time ago. For my nieces and nephews. They told me what they liked best, and I did more of that. It made me so happy…thinking out the stories. And I loved making the manuscripts pretty with the illustrations. But…."

"What?" asked Natalie.

"I couldn't type. I wanted to learn, so I could try to sell the stories—or even give them away. But these days you have to use a computer, and I don't see how I can learn. Piers said there was no point, because my stories were just fairy tales, and no one reads fairy tales any more. He sent me on a trip to Florida instead."

"Your brothers are the champions of giving bread to a person crying out for water," said Rebecca crossly.

"Well, dear. They support me, you know. I have a duty to listen to their opinions when it comes to spending their money."

"Bull…wompy!" cried Natalie. "Cut you off if you decided to take a computer course? I'd like to see them try! You cared for your mother for a zillion years, right? You said it was your job. Well, she was their mother, too. You must've saved them a fortune in nursing care. I figure it's they who owe you! What a pair of hyp—"

Daniel put his arm around Natalie's waist from one side, while Rebecca put a hand over her mouth from the other.

"What Natalie means," said Rebecca sweetly, keeping her hand in place, "is that you've been looking for advice from people who, however admirable in other respects, just aren't kindred spirits. This is a dead end in the quest for personal fulfillment. But never mind, because fortunately there are lots of people around who will give you much better advice—especially when they read your stories."

"Personal fulfillment...?"

"Hey, I have a broken collarbone, you know...."

"Sorry."

"I forgive you." Natalie raised an eyebrow at her brother, then turned to Louise. "I know someone else who wants to take a computer course.... Only he needs a ride, and he could really use some support. I think you two could get together...."

"Really...?" An eager look came to Louise's eyes.

"But what about the contest!" burst out Gayanne.

"What contest?" asked Daniel.

Louise's face grew pink. "Oh, I...sent my manuscript to a contest. I was hoping they wouldn't mind that it wasn't typed. I thought maybe they would take the artwork into consideration.... But they returned it, with a note saying it had to be typed up."

"You can't blame them." Natalie tried to be fair. "That is the industry standard...."

Gayanne was squirming at the slow pace of the conversation. "But tell them what the note said!"

Louise looked around nervously. "Shhh, dear. They said some kind words, yes. Very nice people."

Gayanne tugged at Natalie's good arm. "They said they read the first chapter 'cause the pictures were so unusual, and thought it was 'worthy of consideration,' and she should type it and send it again before the deadline. They said they urged her! They said 'urged!'"

"Well then we'll do it!" cried Natalie. "You can pay someone to type up a manuscript, you know."

"You can? Oh, but I'm afraid...."

"There's nothing to fear! We can find someone—half the staff will be looking for outside work now that we're all paupers. Or I'll do it, if you're so damned worried about your brothers. Except—I have this broken collarbone—which everyone seems to forget—and won't be able to type for a week or so. When's the deadline?"

"It's October 31st—today."

A sigh of disappointment went around the room. Gayanne flopped down in a chair and sat like a rag doll.

"I'm sorry." Louise smiled sadly. "I should have told you last week. But with all that's been going on.... It doesn't matter. It's more important that you've all been so kind. There's no hurry...."

"No hurry?" The voice came from behind the encyclopedias. They turned as one and beheld Myra Vandergelden.

"No hurry?" repeated Myra. "Louise! You're seventy-two! What are you waiting for? Let's get going, girl!"

Louise's mouth opened and closed.

"Writers...." Myra rolled her eyes. "Never mind. Natalie? Isn't the Central Post Office in Fort Lee open until three on Sundays?"

"I think.... Yeah...."

Myra turned to Rebecca. "What time is it?"

Rebecca's hand flew up. "Uh, quarter to twelve."

"Then we have three hours...."

Natalie spoke very hesitantly. "It's a nice thought, Ms. V, truly. But...it can't be done. The fastest typist in the world can only crank out ten pages an hour...."

"Can't? Did you say...can't? You underestimate me, young woman! Do you think I got to be CEO because of my looks? Ha!" Myra headed for the door, calling over her shoulder, "Follow me! We have no time to lose!"

♥   ♥   ♥

Myra Vandergelden stalked across the newsroom, her chartreuse scarf trailing behind her like a tell-tale. Natalie, Louise, Rebecca, Daniel, and Gayanne hurried after her. At the front of the room, she whirled, and looked at the faces turned expectantly toward her.

"Lance?"

"Here, Myra!"

"Get out your calculator and take notes."

"I'm too damned short," said Myra. She looked at Daniel and eyed his lithe frame. "Young man? Help me up onto a chair!"

"Yes, ma'am!" Daniel helped Myra scramble up onto a wooden chair, and steadied her as she faced the astounded newsroom.

"All right, people. Now listen up! I'm CEO of this paper for another twelve hours, and I have one final task to accomplish. It's a damned good thing you all stuck around—even if it was to gossip. We'll show everybody how much we can accomplish if we all work together!" She motioned for Natalie to come stand beside her. "Show of hands, please. How many of you can type fifty words a minute?"

♥   ♥   ♥

"All right, then. That's eighteen chapters and eighteen typists. The longest chapter is fifteen typewritten pages. Lance?"

299

"We're short, Myra. We need another hour or four more typists."

"Then we'll just have to—"

"Ms. Vandergelden?"

Her red head whipped around. "Who spoke there?"

A creaking sound came from the north side of the newsroom. Rudy appeared from behind the half door of the mailroom. "I...I...I did, Ms. Vandergelden."

Natalie felt Myra's hand tighten on her shoulder as she turned to face the mailroom clerk.

"Do you want to volunteer to type, young man?"

Rudy's face was as red as Myra's hair, and glistening with sweat. "N...n...no.... But...the...the...mail truck doesn't leave Fort Lee till...till five. I...I...I know some of the staff, and, and I c...c...c...could ask if they would t...t...take a late delivery—"

"Good man!" cried Myra. "Now here's someone who knows how to use his head. Lance!"

Lance waddled to Myra's side and looked up at her anxiously. "Yes, Myra?"

"Lance. You're on this man's team! The Buick is out front. Take him wherever he needs to go. You have your cell phone?"

Lance raised his briefcase. "Yes, Myra."

"Good. Young man, find out how late they can accept delivery and still use today's postmark! Report to Mr. Shapiro." She cocked her head at Rudy, standing wide-eyed and open-mouthed on the side of the room. "I want to see you when this is all over. I like to reward initiative. A boy like you could go far—couldn't he?"

"Y...y...yes, Miss Vandergelden."

"Of course he could. Make an appointment with my secretary." She thrust out her arm and pointed to the door. "Now step on it."

Lance waddled past her, stared a moment at Rudy, and then the two of them made for the door as fast as they could.

Natalie felt Myra squeeze her shoulder again.

"There's our extra time. Typists! Assemble in Marcia's office to await assignments. Laticia! Have you disassembled the book yet?"

The secretary stepped forward. "Yes, Ms. V."

"Excellent. You and Byron get started on that photocopying. Work as fast as you can, but keep it accurate! You never know. We may get one of those damned editors who can't see the content for the typos. Davis? Let's get started on the computers. You'll have to set it up so that after you re-

300

ceive and collate the chapters, Francesca can format the text from her own machine. Can you do that?"

"Yes, Ms. V."

"Francesca—can you do the job in half an hour?"

"Well, if I double space everything, and use a 12 point text throughout, either a Times New Roman—"

"I don't want to know the details, young woman—if Byron Shapiro says you're the best damned typesetter he's ever seen, you are. I asked can you do it!"

"Yes, ma'am."

"All right then, people! Any questions?"

The room was silent.

"All right then. Now let's go win this contest!" She thrust her right hand into the air, and the newsroom broke into cheers.

Natalie and Daniel helped Myra down from the chair. She brushed them off and rearranged her scarf, then checked to see that her blouse was tucked in.

Natalie leaned close to her ear. "Good work, Ms. V."

Myra's eyes darted around the room. "You don't think it was too manipulative, playing up the teamwork angle like that?" she asked out of the side of her mouth.

"Not a bit."

♥   ♥   ♥

An hour later, Natalie sat at her desk, looking out across a newsroom over which an unaccustomed quiet had fallen. Marcia, Tyler, and Ginny were typing furiously, along with fifteen other staffers. Byron was going from desk to desk, making sure there were no duplications, and checking progress to see if they needed to bring in a back-up typist. Davis and Louise were visible in the front office, sitting at Marcia's computer, preparing to receive the completed chapters. Daniel and Gayanne, just returned from Charlie's laden with hot coffee and sandwiches, were moving quietly up and down the aisles fortifying the workers. Natalie alone was unoccupied.

It felt wonderful.

She sighed as she put her feet up on a nearby chair and reached for her coffee. "There's no place like home."

Epilogue

Bergen Evening Star, 31 October, 1993, Life Styles, page 7

D ear Blue,
Sometimes the modern woman may seem a little hard to fathom, even contradictory. Try to understand that you are not the only one with something at risk; she may be reluctant to open herself up emotionally, or she may never have been in love before.

The two of you seem to have been engaged in a fight for the moral high ground. Each has burdened the other with the need to fulfill idealized expectations. Instead of worrying about labels, why not try to help her come to terms with her dilemma—just as you want her to help you come to terms with yours. Whatever name you put on your relationship is not as important as its quality.

Your situation reminds me of a story. Once upon a time, a Girl and a Boy had a very tumultuous relationship. It seemed that every time they met, they argued. But still they could not seem to avoid each other. Eventually, the Boy sent a message to the Girl, asking her to meet him. The Girl wrote three answers to the Boy, but she couldn't make up her mind which to send. By chance, the Boy found the messages:

1) Come to my house Tuesday morning at nine. I'll meet you there.
2) Don't come to my house Tuesday morning. I won't be there.
3) Don't go to the gazebo Monday evening at seven. I won't meet you there.

The Boy didn't know what to do. But an old wise woman said, "Only one of the three messages is true. Find out which one that is, and you will know exactly what to do." The Boy pondered this dilemma for a moment, then smiled. The solution was simple, really.

Good luck!
Louise

finis

Ordering Info

Title	Quanity
The Hatch and Brood of Time by Ellen Larson *Book 1 in the NJ Mystery Series*	☐
Unfold the Evil by Ellen Larson *Book 2 in the NJ Mystery series*	☐

Price: $14.95 per book, plus $2.50 S/H for the first book, $1.00 for each additional book (subject to change without notice).

Fax questions to –

1 603-308-5993

Secure Internet orders, go to –

http://www.savvypress.com/orders

Postal orders, send check or money order and a copy of this form to –

Savvy Press
PO Box 84
West Rupert, VT 05776

Your name: _

Ship to: _

_ _ _ _ _ _ _ _ _ _ _ _ _ _ _ _ _ _ _ _

_ _ _ _ _ _ _ _ _ _ _ _ _ _ _ _ _ _ _ _